W9-CTL-439

WITHDRAWN

WHEN I CLOSE MY EYES

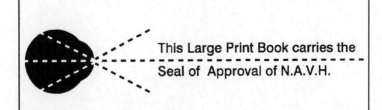

This Large Print Book carries the
Seal of Approval of N.A.V.H.

WHEN I CLOSE MY EYES

ELIZABETH MUSSER

THORNDIKE PRESS
A part of Gale, a Cengage Company

Thorndike Press® Large Print Christian Mystery.

The text of this Large Print edition is unabridged.

Other aspects of the book may vary from the original edition.

Set in 16 pt. Plantin.

LIBRARY OF CONGRESS CIP DATA ON FILE.
CATALOGUING IN PUBLICATION FOR THIS BOOK
IS AVAILABLE FROM THE LIBRARY OF CONGRESS

ISBN-13: 978-1-4328-7517-6 (hardcover alk. paper)

Published in 2020 by arrangement with Bethany House Publishers, a division of Baker Publishing Group

Printed in Mexico
Print Number: 01   Print Year: 2020

This story is dedicated to my
firstborn grandson,
Jesse Andrew Musser.
You made me a grandmother,
and it has changed my life,
filling it up with more love
than I thought possible.
What a joy to watch you grow up!
I love you and I like you,
Your Mamie

The clouds hang low, a mist caught between the carpet of mountains. I stand at the top of the lookout and gaze into a never-ending motion of undulating valleys and peaks. On and on, seemingly forever, they rise and fall in lush green hues and deep blue ridges that span past history. The mountains hold my imagination, and I feel a call to their beauty. Then they fade out of view as the mist floats above and around them, like puffs of smoke. I hover in the mist; I feel the calling of the dawn. I see the first ray of light piercing through the mist and I know. I am forgiven.

These Mountains around Us,
Josephine Bourdillon

■ ■ ■ ■

PART ONE:
THE BEGINNING
OF THE END

■ ■ ■ ■

Chapter 1

October 2015
Friday

HENRY

The lady came out of the bookstore — it was all decorated for Halloween, all sizes and colors of pumpkins making faces at me from where I watched across Haywood Street in downtown Asheville. She walked along the sidewalk, with that big church with the fancy domes in the background, then turned down Walnut Street. I crossed the street and followed her at a distance. Not many folks around for a Friday afternoon, and nobody else in the private lot where she'd parked her car, a real nice Mercedes. Seeing her close up made me hesitate — she didn't look like a criminal to me, just a nice-looking middle-aged little lady carrying a black computer bag in one hand, walking along at a clip, like she knew exactly where she was headed and needed to get there quick.

I slipped into the narrow alleyway beside the parking lot, steadied my Glock, and took aim. As she clicked her key and went to open the Mercedes door, I pulled the trigger.

In the same moment I heard a voice at the end of the alley call out, "Ms. Bourdillon! You forgot —" and the lady turned as my bullet raced its way silently through the air, so that it hit her on the right side of the head instead of full force in the back, as was my intent. But I saw her fall to the ground, lying in a puddle of blood, as the voice turned into a piercing scream. I disappeared around the corner and through another narrow alley to where I'd parked my pickup, out of sight. Nobody saw me — they were all hurrying to that poor lady, I imagine. And I would've congratulated myself if I hadn't been trying my best not to retch all over my truck.

Saturday
I walked into the store like Pa told me, bought a soda and some chips like any lazy teenager, and then Pa came in with a stocking over his face and pointed his gun at the terrified cashier. Who musta been calm enough to

punch an alarm button, because the cops came in a second later and blew Pa's brains out right in front of me.

I woke myself screaming. If only it were just a dream, and not a memory.

On my way to the john in the motel room, I flipped on the TV, only half-awake after last night's binge. I had drunk myself into oblivion after the kill. I called it that in my head, a "kill," like Pa did when I downed a deer or even one time a bear. Except this time it was a once-living-and-breathing human being. My head felt like *it* had received the bullet, and I threw cold water on my face. I looked into the chipped mirror at my red eyes and stubble, ran my hand over my chin, and said out loud, "Well, that's over, and the money'll be in the account soon."

I tried to crack a smile but instead watched my eyes get all teary. I swore. Threw more water on my face. My doc kit lay by the toilet, its contents scattered on the stained linoleum floor. I reached down and fumbled for a couple aspirin, swallowed them down, and then got out my razor and shaving cream, letting the spigot run the water warm. From the bedroom I heard the jingle of the morning news.

"Today's top story: Beloved author Josephine Bourdillon still lies in critical condition in the Neuro Trauma ICU at the Memorial Campus of Mission Hospital in downtown Asheville. . . ."

I dropped the razor, heard it hit the sink. Then I grabbed the thin white towel and rushed back to the TV, wiping shaving cream off my face as I listened to the reporter — a blond girl who hardly looked old enough to be out of high school — standing outside of some hospital.

"Police are calling it an assassination attempt. Ms. Bourdillon had just left Malaprop's Bookstore, where she was doing a reading and book signing, when she was shot. Police have released no other details. . . ."

I felt my stomach twisting, felt last night's alcohol and pizza churning up inside, and hurried to the john to throw up. Then I yelled, way too loud for the thin motel walls, but stopped myself before putting a fist through one.

Now what?

You'll receive the second half when the job is done, cash, four days after.

I turned back to the screen where the reporter was listing this lady's accomplishments, but I couldn't pay attention to what she was saying. All I could think was: *You gotta die, lady. You gotta. Or I won't get the money for my son. I'm sorry, lady. But you've just gotta die.*

Then I put my head in my hands, unable to process the horrible mess I was in now. *What were you thinking when you agreed to murder, Hughes? What in the world were you thinking?* And the tears just came while I remembered. . . .

It was two weeks ago, right after Libby called me at work with the bad news. At the end of the day I left the printing plant and stopped off at the bar with a buddy. No way could I go straight home to Libby. Not till I'd thought of a solution.

The third beer got me to feeling better, loosened up a bit so I felt like telling Birch my problems. "It's my boy, Birch. They say he needs another operation on his heart."

Birch still wore a crew cut, his hair almost as blond as mine. We shared the same tattoo on our right forearm. Got it done in a parlor when we were on leave in Fort Bragg. Used to shake hands every day when we were serving in Afghanistan together, just to show off the tattoos. It made us feel real close. Connected.

Now I stared at the image of the sun on Birch's forearm. "Sun ain't risin' in the Hughes family today, Birch. In fact, feels like it might be settin' for good. Jase needs

15

surgery and boss's acting like he might let me go if I miss work again."

I took another gulp, finished the beer, ordered another.

"Tough break, Hughes."

"We've not got money enough for rent and groceries, much less another surgery. Being already so far in debt makes all the nightmares come back in full color. Screaming sound effects too."

Birch knew all about my childhood, and we'd witnessed the Afghanistan horrors together.

"Libby still working?"

"Yeah."

"You'll find something else to bring in more cash — you always do."

I shook my head. "Don't you sometimes just want to give it all up?"

"You know it."

"I've screwed everything up for Libs and Jase."

We sat there, just drinking and not talking.

"Just need to win the lottery or something," I threw out after a while.

"You still got your guns, Hughes?"

"Of course."

"You were the best shot in the platoon. Best shot of anyone I ever knew."

16

"That ain't gonna get me a job, Birch."

He hesitated, ordered another beer, then said, "I might have something for you. Not the lottery, but pay's dang good." He lowered his voice so as I could barely hear him over the noise around us.

The more he talked, the more I told myself *No way!* Wouldn't ever have agreed without the help of four beers and the desperate feeling way down in my gut.

"I know the guy — he's good for the money. He's the middleman. You never even have to know who hired you."

"You already done a job like that?"

Birch gave a shrug. Looked up at me. "Doesn't have to be a career, Hughes. But it'll give you some fast cash. You could try it, this once."

He reached over to shake my hand, nodded down to the tattoo. "You're real good with the gun. Might as well use what you're good at. Might let you see the sun a little too."

It sounded like a good idea at the time. . . .

PAIGE

She lay on her back, her mouth half-opened, the tube inserted, a string of drool escaping beside it, which was, excuse me, just gross. Her head was shaved on the right side, where the bullet had penetrated, and now she resembled a corpse beginning to be mummified, her head swathed in white gauze that ended right at her eyebrows. The rest of her face was very pale. The labored breathing, done by machines, reminded me of the even drone of the ceiling fan in my parents' bedroom. Pretty spooky.

I sat beside the hospital bed and stared, blurry-eyed, at the apparition of my mother. My soft and kind fifty-something mother, petite, with dark brown eyes that either filled with compassion or fantasy, now closed. I wondered if they'd ever open again.

Coma. The word struck terror in my soul. The thing that most people did not emerge from or, if they did, emerged as vegetables. That my mother lay in this state, so still, so unalive, so lost from me, I could not grasp.

Yesterday we'd watched the sunrise from the porch of our home on Bearmeadow Mountain, both of us speechless as always before the vista of mountains spread out like a rippling carpet on every side.

"We live in a paradise," Momma had said. "We get to watch God painting the mountains day after day after day."

In the spring the mountains looked green and soft as velvet, but when October came around, the velvet blanket turned into an intricate tapestry of reds and oranges and deep yellows.

I blinked back tears at the memory, a sharp contrast to my surroundings. The hospital room, white and sterile, was filled with sights and sounds that came not from nature but from technology, and were indispensable in keeping my mother alive.

Yesterday, before I rushed off to school, I gave her a high five after reading her the latest letter from an adoring fan, an elderly woman who had found hope in one of Momma's stories.

When I turned sixteen last year, I took over the job my older sister had been doing, answering the fan messages that came through her website or Facebook or email, doing the social media stuff. Momma paid me for it, of course. She was embarrassingly hopeless with technology. Her job was to write. And write. And write.

It was beyond fathoming that someone had deliberately tried to kill her. An assassination attempt, the police were calling it. As if Momma were the president of the United States. Who assassinated a middle-aged novelist? I suppose if she wrote horror stories or trashy novels or something defaming a religion, someone might wish her dead. But my mother wrote historical fiction. Sure, some of her stories made white people feel uncomfortable, even guilty, but the issues she raised had been decided by a president who got himself assassinated a long time ago.

Well, it wasn't quite beyond fathoming. We'd enjoyed reading that letter yesterday, but I thought about a couple of other letters that had arrived about three weeks ago, handwritten in big bold print. Just some wacko, I'd thought. But I never should have shown them to Momma.

Wackos are exactly the type of people who kill their heroes, right?

My line of reasoning was interrupted by my father coming into the hospital room.

"Daddy!"

"Hey, Paige," he greeted me, and we hugged tightly. For a long time.

Then he tiptoed over to the bed, as if he might wake Momma — oh, if only he could — with his footfall. Daddy was tall and lean, with black, black hair, even in his fifties. He had only an edging of gray around his temples, which Momma liked to say gave him a debonair look. They were both aging well, my parents. Or had been.

Now the word *gaunt* flashed through my mind — Daddy's ashen face, always clean-shaven, was now covered with a salt-and-pepper beard, and his eyes looked hollow. He hadn't slept at all, had only left me alone with Momma long enough to get a cup of coffee in the ICU waiting room down the hall. Now he stood over the bed looking displaced, as if he had somehow ended up in the wrong room, staring at someone else's wife.

"Any more news?" I asked.

In truth, I didn't think I could stomach any more. Last night, barely three hours after the shooting, the doctor had called Daddy and me into a room.

"There are two scales we use for measuring the severity of the coma and tracking the patient's progress," he'd explained, "the Glasgow Scale and the Rancho Los Amigos Scale. A three means very little hope of recovery. A fifteen means normal."

He'd lowered his voice. "Mrs. Bourdillon's combined score upon arriving at the ER was a four. That is normal with a traumatic head injury. The first job was to stabilize her. We've put her on a ventilator, and we're draining the fluid — the swelling is putting too much pressure on the brain. Hyperventilation may also be performed to help relieve the pressure. She's also on antiseizure medication. . . ."

Now Daddy shook his head. "I don't think

the police have any new leads, although they found the bullet" — the bullet that had passed straight through Momma's brain and onto the parking lot pavement — "so they'll be able to identify the type of gun."

But Daddy's mind was not on finding the shooter, I knew. His mind was on how to get Momma back.

He sat down beside her bed, reached under swaths of white sheets, and took her hand. "Feeny," he whispered to her. "Can you hear me, Feeny? Squeeze my fingers if you can hear me."

His voice sounded so desperate, so broken, so different, that I sucked in air. I rubbed my head, feeling the throbbing beginnings of a glorified headache, and said, "I'll leave you two alone for a while," the knot in my throat causing my voice to sound as strange and foreign as his. I pecked him on the cheek and stepped into the hall.

Just like that, our lives had turned upside down and inside out.

I went down to the cafeteria on the second floor — Café 509 — and was standing in front of the hot entrées when the sound of my own voice shocked me. It blared from the TV across the room.

"We can't imagine why anyone would possibly want to hurt my mother," I was saying

22

to the reporters, who had accosted us early this morning outside the hospital. "We just don't know." I ducked my head, but a woman stuck her mic right in front of my mouth.

"Your mother's latest novel, *These Mountains around Us,* describes lynchings. Do you think this could be the case of a deranged reader taking out his frustrations and disagreements on your mother?"

"Her last novel? Um, it takes place a hundred and fifty years ago. . . ." My voice sounded so far away, and I looked really horrible — I hadn't had time to wash my hair or put on makeup or anything — and Daddy had reached out his hand to shield the cameras from my face as we walked inside the sliding glass doors. But in my mind I was thinking, *Well, we can't imagine anyone except for some crazy person who wrote a couple of awful letters a few weeks ago.*

I kept my head down as I plucked from the shelf the one thing that had caught my eye — a chocolate-chip cupcake. I ordered a cup of chai and slid the off-white tray along the steel bars, barely lifting my eyes to inspect the other entrées — which nonetheless looked a lot more appealing than the food at my school cafeteria. I couldn't stomach anything else.

"Investigators are asking anyone who has any clues about the case to call . . ."

JOSEPHINE

1966 . . . The house was brimming with people, important people, laughing and talking, their tall, skinny glasses bubbling with the golden liquid that made them happy. They were so noisy! Terence, dressed in a black tux, came over to Josephine.

"Hello, there Miss Josephine. My, ain't you looking pretty tonight. Can I get you something to drink? A Co-Cola, maybe?"

"Hi, Terence. I'm glad you're here." She reached out and took his hand and followed him back to the makeshift bar, where Daddy had all the drinks. "Could I have a ginger ale?"

"Sure 'nuf, angel."

"Terence, do you like to dress up like this and go to the parties?"

"Can't say that I mind, Miss Josy. I like to change from my overalls into this tux." Terence worked for her parents during the week, making the yard look as if he'd gone over it with a comb and brush and emery board. Every blade of grass in place, every shrub trimmed and even. And twice a year he acted as the bartender at her parents' parties.

"Do you like to watch the people get drunk?"

24

"Miss Josy, you ask such interesting questions for a six-year-old. You know as well as I do that not all these fine people are getting drunk. Most of them are just enjoying themselves and having a little alcohol." He handed her a tall clear glass with a gold rim, filled with ice and ginger ale. "Here ya go, angel."

Terence always called her *angel,* and he always looked out for her at the parties. She didn't know why the parties frightened her. Why so many fancy-looking people in fancy-looking clothes and drinking fancy-looking drinks made her stomach cramp.

Yes, she did.

She shut her eyes, and in her mind she heard the screech of the tires and Mommy's scream, remembered how she and Kit had been flung against the front seat.

Daddy had cursed, rubbed his temples, looked around, his eyes red and wide and terrified. "Everyone okay?" he mumbled.

Kit had grabbed her hand and said, "We're okay, Daddy," but Josephine tasted blood in her mouth where she'd bit her lip. She'd started to cry, but her big sister frowned and shook her head. "We're fine."

1968 . . . Josephine didn't want to go to camp. Not that spend-the-night-away-from-home camp, not any camp. She didn't want to take riding lessons. All she wanted to do was stay in her room and read Nancy Drew mysteries and write her own stories. She loved to close the door and lose herself in another world where her pencil scribbled the words that were so jumbled in her head. So many stories! How would she ever get them all down?

"Josephine, it's dinnertime."

"But I'm not finished —"

"Josephine! Now!"

"Yes, ma'am."

She traipsed downstairs, talking to herself, repeating the scene in her mind so that maybe she'd still remember it after dinner and the news. . . .

But later, Josephine wound herself into a protective little ball on her bed and tried to hide from the world. Such a dark, scary world! Why did Mommy and Daddy have to watch all that news on TV? People were blowing each other up in some country far away, but it could happen here. It could happen in her neighborhood. Why last month, two hooded men had burst into Francie Lewis's house and held a gun to her mother's head.

Every time they watched the news, more stories filled her mind — scary, sad stories that she didn't want to write. But it could happen. It could. She crawled under the covers and shut her eyes tight, but she could still see the black-and-white images of soldiers and hear the missiles exploding and the screams. She could imagine the little boy back home whose father just got blown to smithereens. She could practically feel him inside her head, and it made her want to run. Or hide. She'd hide.

HENRY

The TV was still blasting out the news in the motel room. I hadn't known anything about the person I was hired to kill. Just enough details to get the job done. And now, turned out this lady was a dang-blame-it bestselling author. I didn't know what she wrote, but it didn't sound like something that should get her killed. She wasn't any Stephen King or some crazy terrorist either.

That's not your problem, Henry.

No. My problem was that if Miz Josephine Bourdillon didn't die, I wouldn't be receiving another envelope in three days with all that cash inside. Jase's surgery was scheduled for two weeks away. It made me feel weak to think about all the money we already owed. We were so far in debt we weren't ever gonna get out.

Jase was born with a hole in his heart. Three major surgeries had kept him alive

27

for almost seven years, but after each one he'd have a complication. The doc said this surgery might fix his problem permanently, but it couldn't wait any longer. I closed my eyes and could see Jase's skinny, freckled face, his green eyes — pretty like Libby's — all lit up with World Series hype. Then he was doubled over and wheezing, and I was rushing him out to the pickup.

I squeezed my eyes shut, squeezed that crushing pain away.

I knew I needed to get home quick, before Libby started on one of her worry fits. She got anxious when I was away for too long. But before driving home, I stopped off at a Books-A-Million. Nobody would have guessed from looking at me that I liked to read. Once my boss, Mr. Dan, saw me with a book while I ate my sandwich at lunch and said, "You a reader, Hughes?" He looked surprised.

My last year in school, eighth grade, I was soaking up the books in my English class, to my own surprise. But then Ma got sick and died, and Pa took me out of school. If he'd ever seen me sitting in a chair, reading a book, well, I reckon he'd have taken the Remington and shot right through the book into my chest.

I didn't have the time or money to do

much reading now. But the thing about books was once I got started on one, if it was really good, well, I couldn't put it down. I liked going into the big bookstores and zigzagging in between all the shelves, touching the covers of the books out on the table, wondering what kind of stories the authors had hidden inside.

I found Josephine Bourdillon's novels back in the historical fiction section. Bunch of them. *Maybe I should read her stuff,* I thought, and I almost pulled one off the shelf. But then I thought, *Are you crazy?*

Yes, crazy, but not stupid. I always got a bit reckless when I stopped taking my meds cold turkey. I ducked my head and pulled my baseball cap down low, hands deep in my pockets, and went back to the pickup.

I scrolled through the messages on my phone. Libby's message read, *Jase is at the ER. They have to move the surgery up.* I cursed. But no message from my contact. No. Of course not. My job was to finish my job.

But how was I gonna do that, with half of America's attention focused on a middle-aged lady lying in a coma in a hospital room somewhere in the mountains of North Carolina?

CHAPTER 2

Saturday

PAIGE

"Can you get Hannah at the airport? Her plane gets in at seven. Delta 424 from Paris. You can take your mother's car."

"Sure, Daddy," I said, but even in the Mercedes I hated driving along all those hairpin turns, and the airport was almost two hours away. Momma would never have let me drive from the mountains near Asheville to the Charlotte airport — the only one where Hannah could get a flight from France on such short notice — in the dark. I'd gotten my license the year before and had only done the trip twice and never at night. But when Daddy looked at me with his deep, dark, and now vacant eyes from where he sat, glued to the chair by Momma's hospital bed, I could only agree.

"I think I'll stop by home first and get a

30

shower," I said. I needed a warm blast of water and another cup of chai to wake me up enough for the drive. Daddy simply nodded as I kissed him on the forehead. I glanced at Momma, lying motionless, attached to life by a tangle of wires. Daddy didn't look up as I slipped out the door.

Our neighborhood was perched on a vast green plateau on Bearmeadow Mountain, the huge log-cabin-like homes separated by sprawling yards with lush green grass and towering trees. The colorful city of Asheville was about thirty minutes away, in a valley surrounded by the Blue Ridge Mountains on every side. Once a boring small town, Asheville had recreated itself into a cool, artsy village. That was in the eighties before I was born, but I'd heard Momma tell the story of how the downtown area was dying but not quite dead. With the battle cry *Love Asheville, Don't Level It!,* a local businessman had led the fight against bulldozing eleven acres of the downtown to build a mall. That campaign preserved Asheville's historic buildings, which provided a launch space for new small businesses into the 1990s. It also brought an influx of artists. But I think Momma was creating her stories before Asheville became the hip place for the arts community.

Milton, our golden retriever, greeted me at the front door. I bent down and buried my face in his fur. "Hey, buddy." He wagged his tail, anticipating a walk. "I'm in a rush right now, but Mrs. Swanson promised to take you out in a little while."

I showered quickly, threw on a pair of jeans and a sweat shirt, filled a travel mug with chai, and left Milton pouting by the front door.

The surgeon's words haunted me during the long drive to the airport. I tried to distract myself first by watching the palette of colors surrounding me — pale yellow and burnt orange, with an occasional burst of scarlet — as I zigzagged down the mountain road. Then I pictured my big sister in France doing her junior year abroad, lucky thing. Except that now Momma had gotten shot, and Hannah was flying home on a bright autumn day in October when she was supposed to be touring Cézanne's art studio in the outskirts of this really cool town called Aix-en-Provence.

Our father was French. The first time he stepped on American soil was in 1978 when he came to the States for college — on a soccer scholarship. Even after we were born, he still spoke English with the slightest trace of an accent, which to us sounded very romantic. For all of our growing up years, Momma and Hannah and I spent a month each summer in France at my grandparents' beach apartment in a tourist town called La Grande Motte — literally "the big mole hill." There was nothing old and charming about La Grande Motte. The town was developed in the late 1960s by an architect — he transformed a long stretch of beach on the Languedoc coastline of France into a tourist destination. Once, according to my French grandmother, the sun-drenched beaches were nothing but a desert of sand dunes and lagoons. After the architect finished, La Grande Motte was a fancy holiday resort. The architecture was supposedly inspired by the Inca pyramids in Mexico and the nearby Pic Saint-Loup — the highest peak in that region of France. But Hannah and I thought that from far away it looked like a bunch of gigantic Lego buildings, geometrically stacked beside the Mediterranean.

The French either loved or hated the unique town, but for my family, there was no debate. This was a little taste of paradise — ten kilometers of the best beach in France, much better than the rocks of Nice. And if we got tired of the Legos, there was lots of old, old France just around the corner in Montpellier and Aigues-Mortes and the Pont du Gard. The architect had planned the town in such a way that every apartment had a beach view. Ours was magnificent.

We always spent the month of June there. French children didn't get out of school until late June or even early July, so we had a much more private experience before the mad rush of tourists in July and August. Most French got five weeks of vacation a year, and many chose to spend four of those weeks at some beach — the whole month of July or August. The French even had a name for these tourists: *Juillettistes* (who vacationed in July) and *Aoûtiens* (those who vacationed in August).

Well, I guess we were *Juinistes* — at least Momma and Hannah and me — taking our vacation in June. At first Daddy could only take a week off from work, but as he climbed the insurance ladder, he eventually spent two and even three weeks with us — idyllic weeks where we rode bikes and Camargue ponies and sailed and built amazing sand castles that mirrored the Lego buildings around us.

My best friend, Drake, came a couple of times too.

And we spoke in broken French with our grandparents.

So when Hannah had the possibility of studying in France she leapt at it, choosing Aix-en-Provence, about two hours from La Grande Motte, and enrolling in an art class in Cezanne's territory outside of Aix. Momma had planned to head to La Grande Motte in November to do a little touring with her, and then Daddy and I were going to join them for Christmas.

I wanted to go to France for my studies, too, and then I wanted to be a writer like Momma. Except I wanted to write crime fiction set in late nineteenth-century or early twentieth-century England, like Sir Arthur Conan Doyle or Agatha Christie or Dorothy Sayers. Maybe even with a little history about Louis Pasteur included — we'd just seen a pretty interesting documentary about how he'd invented the vaccine against rabies. I wanted to write novels and live in a cobblestoned village like Aix-en-Provence and buy baguettes from the *boulangerie* every day like Hannah did.

I turned on the radio, and it was of course on Momma's favorite station. Christian music. Well, that was okay, but I flipped the dial.

■ ■ ■ ■

Hannah, in the words of one friend "the world's sexiest co-ed," looked anything but when she finally stepped through the sliding doors at the international baggage claim. She was completely undone, a total mess — and I'd never describe anything about Hannah as messy. Her thick blond hair was pulled off her neck in a clip, but strands dangled every which way, and she had no makeup, nothing on her face except dark rings under her eyes. She wore a bright blue T-shirt with Van Gogh's *Starry Night* printed on it and skinny jeans and her bulky green backpack.

We grabbed each other and stood there while other passengers whisked past us, pulling their shiny carry-ons. I held on to Hannah tightly, feeling desperate and relieved at the same time.

"Let me take the backpack," I said, and without waiting for her answer I hoisted it off her shoulders and onto mine, and we headed for the parking garage.

"How is she?" Hannah asked, and I could tell she dreaded my answer.

"Still in the coma. No change — at least that we can see." I said it matter-of-factly and then burst into tears.

We stepped to one side of the concourse to let the stream of travelers going to and from their gates pass us by, both of us wiping our faces with the backs of our hands.

Finally Hannah asked, "Do they think she'll come out of the coma? Do they know if . . . well, you know, if her brain function is normal?"

I looked sideways at my big sister, still swiping a stubborn tear. "Has Momma's brain function ever been normal?"

Hannah just stared at me for a second, and then she burst out laughing, and so did I.

"Sorry. I know that was awful, but if I didn't say it, I'd say something else a lot more awful."

"Like what?"

"Like they keep calling it an *assassination* attempt — which is, you've got to admit, too weird." I gnawed on my upper lip.

"It's unthinkable."

"And Daddy almost acts like he's in a coma himself — he can't make a decision and just sits by Momma's bed, begging her to wake up. It's pitiful." I glanced at my sister and almost added, *You know . . . like before.*

We stepped through the sliding doors and

into the muggy Charlotte Indian summer where the sky had turned black. Hannah raised her face up to the clouds and took a deep breath. "Good ole North Carolina!"

When we reached the car, I mashed the button to unlock the door.

"Thanks for coming, Paige. I can't believe Daddy let you drive all this way alone. Especially at night."

"It's like I said. He's not himself."

"Of course not."

"He just sits there, staring into space. Like he's in shock."

"He is. We all are."

"So I'm the one answering the phone and letting all the ladies in the church know about it, and the police said to put it on Facebook, and we're inundated with messages, and I don't know when the last time I closed my eyes was. . . ." Even as I said it, I suppressed a yawn.

Hannah grabbed me again. "It's horrible, and you've been amazing, but you need sleep." She brushed the back of her hand across my face, the way Momma would do, then tucked a wisp of hair out of my eyes and yawned.

"So do you."

"I'll doze in the car, and then you can drop me off at the hospital, and Daddy and

I will take the night watch."

I put her pack in the backseat and said, "Thanks."

She nodded off within ten minutes of leaving the airport, while I clutched the steering wheel and stared into the black night and wished this were just a larger-than-life nightmare.

"And Momma received two handwritten letters — I'm pretty sure they were from the same person — and they were, you know, threatening. Really creepy, kind of." I was crawling along the interstate at fifty miles per hour in the rain, grateful that Hannah had woken up.

"When was this?"

"Oh, at least two or three weeks ago."

"Did you show them to her?"

"Yeah. Unfortunately."

"And?"

"Just what you'd expect. She got a bit scared, and then she felt all guilty and kept second-guessing her story. And I kept telling her that the letters were probably from a white supremacist freak who had a grandfather in the KKK, and she should chill."

"And?"

"Well, you know how those things affect her. I wish I hadn't shown her."

"Yeah. I remember once when I had your job" — she flashed a smile — "Mom got a really nasty letter from this person who was barely literate. Mad about Momma using a degrading epithet in her dialogue. But it was totally justifiable; I mean, Momma was showing that the character who said it was a first-class jerk. But I'll bet she spent a week fretting over how to respond. I shouldn't have ever shown it to her. One out of hundreds of fan letters is mean, and she can't get it out of her head."

"Exactly. That's what happened with these letters. She got totally obsessed. I finally convinced her just to ignore the weirdo."

"Do you still have the letters?"

"Of course."

"Then you need to show them to the police."

"Hey, I'm the detective. Who says they get to snoop around?" But I gave Hannah's shoulder a squeeze. "Boy, I'm glad you're here. I know it sucks to leave France, but it's all so unreal. And so scary. Hannie, I'm afraid she's going to die."

JOSEPHINE

1968, April . . . How could all the grown-ups be laughing and joking and wearing their fancy clothes as if nothing had happened? As

40

if the world hadn't gotten a whole lot darker in just a week.

"I'm sorry about Mr. King, Terence," Josephine said, sipping her ginger ale and staring out at the crowd of happy people.

"Thank you for sayin' it, angel." He wore his tux as usual, and served up the wine and champagne and mixed drinks with a "Here you go, ma'am" and a smile. But Josephine saw sadness behind his eyes. "It's an awful thing — to be motivated by hate."

The dark brown whiskey bottles and the elegant bottles filled with Daddy's favorite wines from France stared back at her, but in her head Josephine still saw the images from TV — a mass of people walking behind a mule-drawn wagon singing a song about freedom.

"These people are sorry, too, Terence," she said. "They don't show it right now, but they care."

Terence bent down to her height and rested his big hands on her shoulders, hands that trimmed hedges and filled glasses with sparkling wine. "Miss Josy, you listen to me, and you listen good. There's a whole lot of evil in this world. And you got a heart that feels it more than others. But don't you go tryin' to carry it — you give it to the good Lord, you hear me? Can't be carryin' it on your mighty thin shoulders. The Lord, now He's got big shoulders. You tell Him about it, and then you go on out and drink your ginger ale. Ain't up to you to fix the world's problems."

Josephine nodded, head down, and blinked back a few tears. "But how can I help, Terence? What can I do?"

1968, December . . . The party lasted way past her bedtime, but Mommy and Daddy didn't come to get her. Josephine didn't mind much, with the house all lit up with candles and the Christmas tree sparkling with the perfect silver balls and the twinkling white lights and the music playing Mr. Bing Crosby. Everybody liked hearing Mr. Bing Crosby at Christmastime. She liked Mr. Andy Williams even better, and when his voice came from the record player, she smiled.

She yawned and found her way to the den where Terence — dressed in his black tux but with a bright green vest — was serving drink after drink after drink. She crawled under the little gate and sat in a folding chair beside him.

"They're all going to be drunk, Terence. They're all going to have wrecks on the way home. I just know it."

"Now, Miss Josy, don't you be worrying none about them folks. Ain't it about time for you to go on up to bed?"

"Kit hasn't come to get me yet, and I can't find Mommy."

"Well, I'm sure she's here somewhere. You want me to take you to your momma, Miss Josy?"

She followed Terence through the big den into the living room and through the dining room to the little den. Across the room crowded with fancy people, Josephine could see Kit standing beside her mother. Kit was two years older than Josephine. She wore a bright blue satin dress, and her thick golden hair was pulled back in a bow. Josephine looked down at her yellow dress — she'd picked out the wrong one, she could tell by Mommy's expression when she first came downstairs.

"There you go, Miss Josy," Terence whispered, letting go of her hand and turning back through the house.

Josephine eased her way in between the adults, who smiled down at her. She'd almost reached her mother when the lady standing next to Kit said, "Your Kit is the most stunningly beautiful child I have ever seen." She drew Kit close. "You are just gorgeous, sweetheart."

Mommy caught sight of Josephine. She gave a pasted-on smile and motioned to her to come over. "Thank you, Janie. And you've met Josephine before, haven't you?"

The woman nodded. "Oh yes, of course." But she didn't say anything about Josephine being pretty. No one ever did except for Terence.

Mommy came to the rescue. "Our precious JoJo is so talented. She writes poems and stories and is just the sweetest, most thoughtful little girl in the world."

Josephine squished herself up against Mommy's silky dress.

"I don't think mischief ever crosses her mind. Now Kit, she's another story. . . ."

The women laughed.

HENRY

The first part of the drive sure was pretty, along I-40, that big ole highway that curved around just about as much as a mountain road, with the leaves all starting to show their fall colors. But then, just like that, when I left the highway for the little back roads to home, the sky turned dark and rain started pelting the windshield.

I had the radio on, and the announcer said the hit man had been an expert, which meant training, probably military. They'd even pinpointed the type of weapon.

Yeah, I'd been in the military all right, but

44

that's not where I learned to shoot. No, that was all Pa.

I never had the guts to say "no, thank you" to my pa, and especially not when he had a gun on him. That meant target practice, every day after school, in the back woods.

"You got the eye. Got the control. When you git a little older you'll be a fine sharp-shooter, son. I guarantee."

What he meant, but didn't say, was when I reached my fifteenth birthday I'd be old enough to go out with him on his "private missions." I didn't like thinking about it, but I didn't argue with Pa. And by then my ma wasn't around anymore to stand up for me. When she took sick and died, that was it. Pa pulled me out of school after eighth grade.

I switched the radio to country and tried to think of something else, but my head kept throbbing to the beat of the windshield wipers, my mind all foggy, seeing Miz Bourdillon walking and then turning and the bullet hitting her at just the wrong angle. And I kept thinking about her books that I'd seen in the store, and I got a notion to get one of those books and read it.

One thing about being off the meds, I'd get an idea in my mind and it wouldn't go away, no matter what. I made it to our little public library right before closing time. I pulled a newspaper over my head like a makeshift umbrella to keep the rain from drenching me. Libby wouldn't like me coming home all wet.

"Hello, Henry. How are you doing?" The librarian, Mabel Garrison, looked up from the computer and over her reading glasses just like she'd been doing ever since I was a kid. She hadn't changed one bit in almost twenty years, tall, thin, dressed in a dark suit, hair streaked with gray, eyes bright and looking plenty smart.

"Not bad. Doin' all right. Forgot my umbrella."

"And your boy?"

"He's managing. We're hoping for a surgery soon."

"Well, we're praying for you at church. Every Wednesday night."

"I sure do appreciate that, Miz Garrison." That's what I said out loud, but inside I hated it that everybody at that church had to know my family's business.

I made my way to the stacks, winding through the nonfiction to the fiction, alphabetical by author. A big gap opened between Borderly and Bowers. Guess I wasn't the only person with a sudden interest in Miz Bourdillon's books. But there was one left, and I plucked it off the shelf like I'd found gold and took it back to the checkout.

"I'm surprised you still found one," Miz Garrison said. "Everybody's come in wanting the latest." She lowered her voice. "They're saying because it raised issues about white supremacy it might have, well . . . you know. Might have caused the assassination attempt."

I kept my face blank.

"But I've read it, and it's good. Her books are all good. Clean. Inspiring. A little mystery, a little religion, a little history. Not fluffy at all, but there's usually a love story. This one's about reconstruction after the Civil War, and I tell you I didn't know half of the truth. Pretty complicated and shady." She shook her head. "But nothing to get yourself killed over, mind you!"

Then she got a funny look on her face. "Nothing unless you were a black man living in the Deep South in the late nineteenth century and involved in politics." She let out a sigh, took my library card, and flashed it under the lighted screen.

I nodded as if I understood, wanting to hurry her along but not wanting it to show.

"But the one you've chosen is her first novel, I believe. One of my favorites. I'm sure you'll like it." She handed my card back to me along with the book.

"Well, I don't exactly aim to read it. It's for my wife — ya know, she saw it on the news and all. . . . She's never read one, so I said I'd go on down to the library and pick one up."

"Well, there you go, Henry. You tell Libby hello from us — and we're praying about Jase."

"Yes'm."

"Thank goodness you're home." Libby greeted me with a frown. "I've been pacing the floor like a maniac." She felt in my pocket for my cell phone. "Don't you know how to use this thing? You could have called."

"Sorry, honey. Battery died."

"Same as always. You're not in junior high, you know. It's called being responsible."

"I got your text yesterday. How is he?"

"Stable. They let me take him back home. He's in bed."

"Lemme go see him."

She caught my arm. "Don't. You'll worry him looking like you do. Go get yourself a shower and shave."

No man in his right mind wanted his boy to be afraid of him. That was what I told myself over and over again. But in truth I handled my boy just like Pa handled me. I didn't know any other way.

"Hey, Papa," Jase said, and my heart softened. If only I could force my face to soften too.

"Hey, Jase."

He looked wrung out — pale as the moon, rasping to breathe, bony arms reaching toward me. Pretzel arms, twig arms. One snap and they'd break.

"You hangin' in there, buddy?"

He wheezed and nodded.

"Your momma taking good care of you?"

"Like always, Papa."

"Well then." I reached over and mussed his chestnut mop of hair.

"Glad you're back, Papa."

"Yeah. Me too."

I turned to leave, and he added, "Did Momma tell you what the doctor said?" I tried not to hear the hint of dread in his voice, the expectation of bad news.

"Yes, she did, son. We'll be getting you into surgery in no time at all."

In our bedroom Libby wrapped her arms around me and nuzzled into my bare chest. "You look like you've had a bad day."

I knew what was coming next.

"You been taking your meds, babe?"

I grunted yes, but truth was I'd stopped ten days earlier when the prescription ran out. Had to — I wasn't any good with a gun when on the meds.

"I'm just worried about you is all."

I pushed her away, and I caught the fear in her eyes. Why'd the two people I loved most on the planet get that crazy, scared look so often?

"You got enough worries with Jase. Don't spend your time frettin' over me, girl."

"Henry, I *am* worried about you. You know what the doctor said. Going cold turkey had bad side effects the last time."

"You don't believe me, do you, Libby? Just like always."

I didn't mean to shove her as hard as I did. She stumbled backward and fell against the bed. Now she looked at me like a panicked doe before the kill.

"Libs, I'm sorry. Don't be nagging me about the meds. About anything. I told you I'd earn some extra money, and I aim to do it."

She wrapped her arms around herself like she was cold, and I almost went to hold her, to show her everything was fine. But I didn't.

The first time I roughed Libby up a little, she made me go see a doctor. Psychiatrist. I got a diagnosis all right. A fancy title: post-traumatic stress disorder. Well, yeah. Any fool could tell you that, after the way I was raised and watching my pa get shot and then with everything that happened when I was in the war. The doc and the meds helped me calm down, took away a bit of the anger and, thankfully, the nightmares. Horrible nightmares where I relived all those really traumatic things again and again and again.

Now the nightmares were back, and I knew I needed to start up the meds again. But I couldn't, not until I'd finished my job.

PAIGE

As she'd promised, Hannah stayed with Daddy at the hospital. They sent me home to sleep. Which I did not do. Milton practically attacked me at the door, his oversized paws on my sweat shirt and his wet tongue on my face.

"Chill," I reprimanded and let him out to pee. Poor dog — he knew something was wrong. He'd sat by Momma's office all yesterday afternoon and started doing this weird howling in the night. Fat chance I'd get any sleep at all.

The reporter on the late news, her name was Lucy Brant, after assuring the world that Momma was stabilized, started reciting all the stats of how many people come out of comas after a day, a week, a month, or even years. Then she told this confounding story of a man who'd been in a coma for over twenty years and everyone thought he was just a vegetable and then they figured out he'd been able to understand everything all along and now he communicated with a computer.

Great. Just great. And so comforting.

Milton pawed the door to get back in; then he lapped up his bowl of water and settled beside me on the floor. Now Lucy was informing me, with the stupidest smile on her face, that some people were put into an induced coma after a bad head injury, to give the brain a rest.

Momma's brain sure needed a rest, I thought. *Even before some wacko blasted a chunk out of it.* Momma just had way too much imagination.

Evidently, once those patients woke up, they told stories of crazy nightmarish hallucinations. The drug-induced comas literally took them on a bad trip.

But Momma's coma came from the injury itself, and people who woke up from that kind of coma, according to Lucy, said things like, "I knew everything that people were saying. I wanted to respond, but I couldn't. I had dreams but I also was lucid at times, and I felt great comfort, knowing my loved ones were there."

So I spent half the night researching comas on the internet and texting with Hannah, and I vowed that one of us would be sitting beside Momma for just as long as she decided to stay asleep.

HENRY

I couldn't sleep. At two in the morning, I crawled out of bed, grabbed a can of beer from the fridge, and settled into the La-Z-Boy in the den. I popped the can open and started reading.

"What are you doing out there at this hour, babe?" Libby called from our bedroom. She came to me and perched herself in my lap. She hadn't bothered to put a robe over her see-through nightie.

"Just reading a novel by that lady who got shot."

"Why do you want to read a book by her?" She rubbed her eyes, ran her hands through her hair — I liked it when she did that, the way she combed it back with her fingers and then gathered it into a thick ponytail. The lamplight gleamed on it, showing the red highlights. Libby gave a yawn, then smiled.

At least the fear was gone from her eyes.

She took the book from me and turned it over, looking at the lady's photo on the back cover. Same photo they'd been flashing on the news for the past day and a half. Miz Bourdillon wearing a light green sweater. She wasn't looking at the camera, but staring at something in the distance, a half smile on her face.

"She looks nice," Libby said. "Honest, you know? She looks real." She handed the book back to me. "Poor lady. They say if she does wake up, she'll be a vegetable. She won't be writing any more books."

"Uh-huh."

"Well, don't stay up too long."

"I won't."

But I needed to do something to keep my mind from racing. That happened when I went off the meds, and then I made mistakes. Was that why I'd missed my shot? No, it wasn't my fault. The lady moved — no way I could've predicted it. But I could predict one thing — we had to have the rest of that money soon. Before the surgery. Didn't we?

And what if my contact decided that I'd screwed up too bad, and he leaked my name to the press? Would he do that? He said I'd get the rest of the cash four days after the job was completed, just to make sure I didn't "leave any loose ends," as he put it. But now, a very long loose end named Josephine Bourdillon had unraveled my plans.

Just die, lady. Just die.

It wasn't like I offed people every day. This was supposed to be my first and last time. Pa always said, "You gotta do what you gotta do, son, to keep bread on the table." I was doing my best.

Libby went on back to bed, and I sank deeper into the chair and kept reading. Got swept up in it pretty fast, like I used to in school. The main character in the story was a down-and-outer. Ha! I could relate.

I didn't go back to bed until almost dawn. By then the voices had calmed, and I'd figured out the next step. Either the lady would pass away or, if not, I'd keep watch from afar. At some point when all the commotion died down, I'd hear from my contact what to do. Or maybe I'd just have one of my own brilliant ideas. Those came a lot more often when I was off my meds.

JOSEPHINE

1969 . . . She put up the bridle and saddle and hurried to feed the horses, thrusting her hands into the thick, sticky molasses and oats. It smelled so sweet that more than once she'd been tempted to try it. The horses nickered as she filled their troughs. But she wanted to hurry, hurry! Before the stories collided and she could not separate them again. Three stories, four, all cantering through her head, galloping, the hoofbeats, a thousand hoof-beats resounding on the dusty path.

She tossed the hay into Scallywag's stall, then Velvet's and Freddy's. She hurried to fill their water buckets. A rat scurried across the barn floor, and she stifled a scream. Josephine didn't mind the mice, the cute pale gray creatures that skittered across the hayloft. But the rats, big, bloated, deep gray with their shining eyes and their fleshy tails. . . . She shivered whenever she even thought of them.

But even a rat couldn't scare away the stories. Josephine rushed up the stairs to her room and dug out the spiral notebook and found her pencil. Oh, where was the sharpener? She opened the drawer and rummaged through it. There! The stories, the stories, the stories.

Her nine-year-old scrawl was illegible to anyone but herself. Tomorrow she'd correct it. Tomorrow she'd add the illustrations and the adjectives. But right now she just needed to scratch out the stories quickly, quickly, while they bumped and crowded in her imagination.

She loved riding the horses, she loved talking to Kit as they lay sprawled on their beds at night. But her happiest moments were these, with the spiral notebook sitting on her desk and her imagination spilling out onto the blank page until it filled up with life.

She woke up in the dark to loud, awful curse words coming up from below, and it was her father's voice yelling them! But in such a strange, deep way. And Mommy was shrieking. She had never heard her mother's voice so high and loud. She tiptoed out of bed to the stairway and stared down through the bannister.

"I know all about her, Dick! How dare you come home in the middle of the night drunk and smelling of her."

More cursing. Then, "Let go of me! Right now, Dick!" Her father was shaking her mother hard.

Josephine didn't mean to cry out.

Both of her parents turned startled eyes up to her. She ran back to her room, threw the covers over her head, and sobbed into her pillow. "Please, God, don't let Daddy hurt Mommy. Please, God. Please." She waited in the dark for Mommy to come and explain it all. She waited and waited and waited, but no one came.

The next morning at breakfast, her mother still had curlers in her hair, and all around her left eye was dark and bruised. But no one said one word about what Josephine had seen the night before.

CHAPTER 3

Sunday

PAIGE

Daddy came home in the middle of the night and found me asleep on the couch in the family room with Milton curled up beside me. I stumbled up to my room, didn't even undress, just fell into bed.

I slept till nine o'clock, and when I came downstairs Daddy was finishing up his scrambled eggs and toast and coffee. Daddy always made us breakfast. At least that hadn't changed.

"There's more eggs and bacon in the skillet. Butter and jelly on the table." He was wiping his mouth with a cloth napkin, and he was dressed in a dark blue suit with a yellow tie.

"Are you going to *church*?" I didn't mean to sound accusatory, but Momma was lying in a coma. Surely church could wait.

"I'm just stopping by to update everyone," Daddy said, glancing down at his watch. "Then I'm heading back to the ICU so Hannah can come home and get some sleep."

He didn't say it, but I knew Daddy needed those people at church, needed their prayers and support. The fridge overflowing with casseroles and soups and the stacks of baked goods on the kitchen counter testified to their love. But he needed to see them in person.

"Okay. Tell everybody thanks. I'll come to the hospital after lunch, okay?"

He nodded, folded his napkin and placed it on the table. Then he got up and took me in his arms. He still smelled like Daddy, starched shirts and aftershave, but he held on to me a little more tightly than usual, a little longer too, and when I looked up, his eyes were still vacant and red.

Mamie and Papy Bourdillon, my French grandparents, called after Daddy left for church. They lived in Lyon, and it was late afternoon for them. "Paige!" they said in unison.

I loved the way they pronounced my name in French, soft and romantic, rhyming with *mirage* instead of *age*.

Just hearing their voices, I got tears in my

eyes again. "Mamie! Papy!"

"*Comment ça va, ma biche?* And Hannah? How is she?"

I assured them that Hannah had arrived safely, and we were both doing as well as could be expected.

"*Et comment va notre chère Josephine?*"

"Nothing has changed with Maman. *Je suis désolée.*"

They loved Momma, and as the story went, Mamie's mother taught my mother how to cook. They enjoyed telling stories of Momma's floundering French and pitiful attempts in the kitchen, but they told it so lovingly that rather than feeling condemned, Momma laughed right along with them.

And they loved our visits. They didn't fly. Cars, trains, boats, and public transportation worked just fine for them. They'd only taken a plane twice in their lives — first for Daddy's graduation and then for Momma and Daddy's wedding. I wished they would come now.

"And our dear Patrick?" Mamie asked. They both pronounced it as *Patreek.* "How is he?"

To that, I answered with a bold-faced lie. "He's being strong for all of us."

Late that morning, after Hannah had slept

61

a little and then pulled herself out of bed, we sat on the floor in Momma's office, cradling our mugs — hers of coffee, mine of tea. Momma called her office The Chalet, giving it her writerly flair. The Chalet was a wood-paneled room on the third story off the back of the house with rafters that rose in an *A* — like a Swiss chalet, Momma said — and with a magnificent view of the Blue Ridge Mountains beyond. Momma romanticized most things.

"She's in her own little world," Daddy would whisper, and that meant *Stay away. Let her create.*

Imagination Momma, we sometimes called her, and she'd laugh. We always paid special attention to her laughter — it didn't come that often.

At that moment, out the window, two bright orange butterflies — or maybe they were particularly colorful moths — were doing a mad jig around each other, twirling and twirling and twirling beside the window box that hung over the wooden porch railing and was filled with yellow and orange marigolds. The butterflies flittered and spiraled down and off toward the woods where the leaves on the hickories had just begun their gradual change from avocado green to sunshine yellow. The view from her window inspired Momma, and when she let me sit at her desk — the one Daddy had made for her from an oak he'd had to cut down — I felt inspired too.

I used to sneak into her office when I was a little girl and lose myself among the smell of old books and Momma's endless cups of tea — all kinds of exotic brands — and a candle burning with the scent of the season. Autumn pumpkin in the fall and holiday spice in winter, rose bouquet in spring and lavender afternoon in summer. She usually let me stay, curled up in a corner, once I had crossed the threshold.

Momma's office enchanted me. One bookcase — the one we'd found at a neighborhood garage sale when I was about nine or ten — held all of the novels she'd written, eight to date, published not only in English, but also in several other languages. It intrigued me to compare the covers of the different editions — for instance, a woman's face and a misty background with a swastika on the English cover, whereas the Dutch cover had a woman seen from the back and the swastika much more prominent.

"I used to love to come in here." Hannah interrupted my reverie. "It is so much like Momma, so cozy with its disordered order."

Yes, Momma was cozy in a disordered way.

"And we're everywhere." On the wooden walls of The Chalet hung photo after photo of the family: Momma, Daddy, Hannah, and me at varying ages, plus photos of our grandparents on both sides of the family. Also extended family members, and every one of our pets, past and present, as well as many friends, especially Ginnie and Bert and Drake Ellinger. Momma had more friends than anyone I knew.

Photos and every craft we'd made for her since kindergarten also sat on shelves, on top of her filing cabinet, and on the chest of drawers where she stored her office supplies. Momma had no use for fancy — she wanted symbolism. Everything meant something to Momma.

"Yeah. You feel loved in here, don't you?" I said.

Hannah reached for my hand and grabbed it, holding on with the same intensity with which Daddy had wrapped me in his arms earlier. "It's unbelievable. Surreal. She's so pale. She looks dead, the way her skin is all translucent and yellow and her eyes are closed, and that breathing tube in her mouth and her lips sagging, and ten tubes attached to her and all those machines lighting up in red and green numbers. It freaked me out to see her like that."

We both started crying, really sobbing, at last, which felt like relief, clutching each other in our shock and anguish and dark questionings. After a while Hannah whispered, "I can't imagine that she'll ever be normal again — if she lives."

I got us a box of Kleenex from the bathroom and while we blew our noses, still crying and then smiling at each other through our tears, I went to Momma's desk and opened her laptop. I waited for the screen to come to life, and the screen saver flashed a photo she'd received only a week ago of Hannah at the flower market in Aix, her face bent over a perfect sunflower.

"Look how content she is, Paige," Momma had said. *"She's in her element."*

I blinked back the image, blinked back more tears, and could still hear the little squeal of delight Momma had given when Hannah's photo had zipped through cyberspace and landed in her inbox.

I clicked on her fan mail account and groaned as 2,367 new messages frantically loaded, bringing the total number of messages she'd received since the shooting to just under 7,000.

Hannah peered over my shoulder. "Dear

65

Imagination Momma sure is loved. Have you read any of them?"

"Are you kidding? This is only the second time I've even turned the computer on since the shooting. It's been so overwhelming. Mrs. Swanson, bless her neighborly heart, is the one who has been taking in all the food people bring by. And letting Milton in and out of the house."

At present Milton lay sprawled beside Momma's desk, right under my feet. He had a knack for getting in the way, and I respected him for it. I reached down and fluffed his golden coat.

"You know Mrs. Swanson's loving every minute of it, Paige. She doesn't have a whole lot else to do. We should ask her to check the mailbox tomorrow if no one is here. I'll bet Momma will be getting hand-written notes too."

"Good idea." I stretched, yawned, and then glanced over at the four clear plastic bins stacked in the back left corner of the office, each filled with fan mail — "from before the internet made sweet letters on beautiful stationery obsolete," as Momma would say. I lifted the lid off the top bin — in which I stored her most recent snail-mail letters once I answered them — set the lid on the floor, and squatted down.

Hannah plopped down beside me. "Wow. This brings back memories." She motioned to the other three bins, all the same size. "She still keeps every letter, doesn't she?"

"Yep. Every email too."

"Good job organizing them by month and year. Impressive."

I stuck out my tongue. It was Hannah who had organized Momma's office before she left for college two years ago, and I, with much more of Momma's creativity than Daddy's organization in my blood, had simply tried to keep up.

I found the two letters near the top. Both were handwritten on pink stationery, with big, bold block printing in bright pink Sharpie.

Hannah pored over the first one. "Why, this isn't threatening. It's . . . it's rather harmless."

I looked over her shoulder. "If you say so. Personally, I think 'Be careful what you write in the future because there are still plenty of people in this nation who agree with white supremacy and they can be dangerous' sounds rather menacing."

"Maybe it's a kid just mimicking something he heard his parents say. It's like the letter writer knows someone who's mad as a hornet about what Momma wrote, but the writer himself isn't. Let me see the other one."

She perused it. "Okay, this one's worse. 'I'm not kidding. Your book is going to get someone killed if you don't watch out. Watch out!' Weird. Well, for sure you need to show these to the police. They'll be interested." Holding the two letters as if they were laced with poison, Hannah said, "But who would do this? It's evil. It's as if . . ."

"What?"

"Nothing."

But I prodded. "Just say it."

Hannah turned her cinnamon eyes to me, and in them I read something almost holy and profound. "Momma writes truth in a way that gets into people's hearts. It's as if something bigger than just a person doesn't want her writing truth anymore."

In our family we had a line — the line of faith. Some had crossed it. Others hadn't. Those who believed looked at everything in life through that lens. Like Hannah — beautiful and pure and faith filled. Daddy played life like a game with Jesus as the captain of his team. Momma made everything a lot more symbolic and complicated. And me? I just couldn't see it. I'd tried. But I couldn't see it at all.

68

"Sorry for getting all spiritual on you, Paige."

"No, it's fine. I asked. So you think these letters and the assassination attempt have some kind of spiritual implications?"

She tilted her head, narrowed her eyes. "I think we need a whole army of people to keep praying for Momma."

"Well, you've got that." For emphasis, I pointed to the laptop with its endless emails and Facebook messages.

"Yeah, but I think I need to set up a CaringBridge site so they can really know how to pray."

And I knew she didn't mean it that way, but I felt scolded. So I changed the subject. "Do you have a return flight booked?"

"Daddy insisted I stay only a week. I don't see how I can help much in that amount of time. Momma'll probably still be in the exact same shape in a week."

"But you're here now, and that's what counts. And Drake is coming tomorrow, and then it'll be the three of us again."

"Just like old times," she said, with a little catch in her voice, sitting cross-legged on the floor in a sweat shirt and jeans, her hair spilling over her shoulders like moonlight.

I chewed on my lip for a minute and then broached a subject that had kept me awake after I'd finished researching comas in the night. "Hannie, do you think the police will question Daddy?"

"What do you mean? I thought you were both questioned that first night."

"Yeah, we were, but not in detail. Like, how much money is Momma worth? Does she have a big insurance policy — will they think Daddy had something to do with it?"

Hannah rolled her eyes. "You read way too many crime novels, girl. Put that out of your mind. For right now, let's get this stuff to the police."

"But . . . I mean . . . won't they find out about The Awful Year?"

She dropped the letter and froze, her hand in midair, then lowered it and turned. Her face had blanched. With a barely perceptible shake of her head she said, "Don't go there, Paige. . . ."

I retrieved the piece of stationery without meeting my sister's eyes and pretended those last seconds had not occurred. Sometimes bad memories, the worst ones, couldn't be dealt with in the middle of a fresh crisis. So we placed both letters with their envelopes in a clear ziplock bag (not that they weren't already completely covered with my fingerprints), and we drove to the hospital.

HENRY

Of course Libby took Jase to church on Sunday morning, like always. Wanting people to feel sorry for us, was what I told her. We didn't need pity, like I saw on Miz Garrison's face when she looked over her glasses at me. I didn't want pity for my son; I wanted an operation that would fix him. Why didn't they hand me some money for *that* instead of a scrunched-up forehead and a whispered *"We're prayin' for Jase."*

I stayed home and read more of Miz Bourdillon's book. I figured maybe reading would calm my mind a bit.

The book said interesting things that I hadn't thought about in a long time. The main character was a boy about fifteen or sixteen, I reckoned, who had gotten into trouble. Then he met up with an old woman who half the time seemed crazy and half the time seemed really wise. She said things like *"You don't have to accomplish everything at once. Life isn't a fifty-yard dash, boy. Life's a cross-country adventure. Don't rush it."*

Sounded like my ma. Before she passed away, she said things like that. *"Henry, you got all your life to figure that out. Don't you be in such a hurry."*

Thing was, Pa didn't agree. If he ever said, *"Take your time, boy, take your time,"* it was when I was looking through a site finder on a rifle, and he meant that I'd better concentrate real hard on pulling that trigger and I'd better not miss or else. I never doubted Pa's "or else." To him, showing love to his family came with a lot of slapping around and beatings and other things I've tried my best to forget.

But on that Sunday morning, reading Miz Bourdillon's book, I started feeling all satisfied and warm, like when Libby fixes her barbecue pork and it makes the whole trailer smell welcoming. Something was seeping into my spirit — that's how the pastor at Libby's church would have said it — something was seeping in that made me think. On just about every page something was happening that meant more than you thought was happening, if I could put it that way. Reading it, I felt like I had stepped right into that young boy's shoes, and I was walking around in them so fine and comfortable I didn't even hear Libby and Jase come home from church.

At lunch there was a prescription bottle sitting by my plate. "When you get this?" I asked.

"After church at Walmart."

"Well, I was gonna get it."

"I know. But you've been busy, and I

thought if I could help. . . ." She was watching me now, and I knew the look — fear. Always fear.

"Okay." I managed a glance her way. "I'll start back up on the meds. I will."

Libby's face, her beautiful face, melted into a smile. Man, I liked to see that smile. I reached for the bottle, opened it, slid out a light blue pill and threw it in my mouth. Made like I was swallowing it down, but I didn't.

Libby put her hand on my shoulder. I almost thought she was gonna start bawling. But she just said, "Thank you, babe. You keep taking them, every day. No more starting and stopping."

After lunch Jase went to his room for a rest, and Libby came over to where I was sitting. She got that funny little tinge in her voice, the one that comes when she has to bring up something unpleasant. "Do you think you can come with me to talk with the surgeon tomorrow? He moved the appointment."

I shut the book. "What time is it?"

"Four."

"I should go back to work. Boss won't like it if I'm gone much longer."

"So go on back, and just get off a little early. I'll meet you at the hospital."

"How you aim to get there if I have the pickup?"

"We'll be okay on the bus."

Jase didn't like riding the bus if it was crowded. Sometimes it got him all panicked. "Naw. I'll take the bus in to work. You come by and pick me up before the appointment."

"All right." Libby leaned over and kissed me softly on the mouth. She smelled like that lavender oil she sometimes used. "Thanks, babe."

PAIGE

The Mission Hospital took up several city blocks and comprised St. Joseph Campus, Memorial Campus, the Rathbun House, and the Cancer Center. In short, it was a maze of buildings near the downtown area. Momma was on the fourth floor of the Memorial Campus, in the Neuro Trauma ICU.

"No reporters at the visitors entrance," Hannah said.

"Thank goodness. Yesterday morning they followed me all the way into the parking garage. I guess Momma is old news now."

Up on the fourth floor, at the entrance to the ICU, we were greeted by two policemen. I had met one of them, Detective Blaylock, the day before. Stocky, midthirties, balding, with a black beard and what I'd call a cynical smile. The other officer was a crisp-looking woman, short, big chested, dyed-red hair, maybe forty. Officer Hanley. They nodded at us as we headed to Momma's room. Daddy was sitting in his chair by her bed. Same tubes, same machines.

"Mamie and Papy called. They send their love. I told them you would call them back later." He gave a half nod, and I kissed him on the cheek. "Any change?"

He shook his head. "None that I can tell, but the surgeon is coming by in a few minutes to talk with us."

"We're going to show the detective those disturbing letters Momma received recently. Is that okay?" I tried to sound casual.

Daddy didn't respond.

I asked again. "Would that be okay, Daddy, to show him the letters?"

He gave a little jerk, as if awaking from a dream, and nodded. "Good idea. Good idea, girls. Thank you."

"And if he wants to see anything else?"

Daddy barely looked up. "Yes, of course," he mumbled. "He can look through anything he wants. I've already given the detective permission."

I leaned over the bed rail and kissed Momma on the bridge of her nose. "I love you, Momma. Everyone is praying for you. And Drake will be coming tomorrow."

When I explained my story to Detective Blaylock and showed him the two letters, he asked, "Mind if keep these?"

"Not at all."

"And can I take a look at the rest of your mother's fan mail?"

"Sure. That's fine."

"Good. I'll be coming by your house this afternoon. Can you read over all the emails before I come and flag any that might be suspicious?"

"That'll be a cinch," I said under my breath, but he heard me.

"Excuse me, Miss Bourdillon?"

"My mother has received almost seven thousand emails since she was shot — seven *thousand* — and hundreds of Facebook messages. And," I added, "I haven't looked at any of it."

Detective Blaylock lifted one bushy black eyebrow, poked out his lower lip, and said, "All right, then. I'll put Officer Hanley on it full-time. She'll come over to your house later. Anything the slightest bit suspicious, we need to see it. Anything at all."

At one thirty the surgeon, Dr. Moore, a wiry little man with thick-rimmed glasses, escorted us into his office. "Think of a brain injury like real estate," he said, almost enthusiastically, as if we were actually considering purchasing a house. "What matters is location, location, location," and he smiled.

Daddy's face darkened, and I thought he might punch the little man. Dr. Moore must have caught on because he added, "And your wife's extremely lucky that the bullet hit at the least dangerous location — the right frontal lobe."

He took his hands out of his lab coat pockets and moved to a poster containing a detailed diagram of the brain. With his pen he began pointing out regions in the brain. "The bullet entered and exited the brain — first positive sign — nothing still stuck in there. And as I said, it penetrated only the right region, not both regions — second positive sign. Much less damage. And lastly, the bullet was narrow and fast. Think of it like a football pass."

Again Daddy growled at the surgeon's unsympathetic analogy.

"A tight spiral pass gives a lot less resistance going through the air than one that wobbles from side to side. It's the same with a bullet. The shooter used a handgun from fairly close range. The smaller and faster bullet created less damage as it passed through the brain than if it had been slower and wobbly. The combination of velocity and bullet dynamics and the location that the bullet entered the head determine the extent of the injuries. As I said, we are hopeful. Each day brings a little brighter outlook."

Then he frowned. "But I won't kid you. Ninety percent of victims of headshot wounds do not survive. Many who do are permanently disabled. We don't speculate because we've seen the gamut. One patient has severe trauma and survives, another has a less serious brain injury and dies. Only time, and great patience and perseverance, will tell."

He reached out a hand, which Daddy shook reluctantly, and then added, after glancing down at a chart in his other hand, "But her score is up."

We looked at him blankly. I wondered if he was still talking about football.

"The combined Glasgow and Rancho score has moved from a four to a six in only twenty-four hours. That's progress, really important progress."

"But what does that mean, Doctor? What has changed?" I'd studied both of those charts on the internet the night before. "When she first arrived at the hospital she had no eye opening, no verbal or motor response, right?"

He nodded. "Correct."

"Well, she's still got her eyes closed and hasn't moved or said a thing."

"Good observations and good questions. The attending nurse in the night noticed a slight twitch in her eyelids, and one of her hands jerked." As we left his office Dr. Moore repeated, "That's progress."

"You hear that, Daddy? He said it's progress."

Daddy simply nodded. With Hannah and me on either side of him, we made our way back to Momma's room, where he slumped into the chair by her bed and buried his head in his hands.

"Daddy, go on home and get some rest. Hannah and I will stay here with Momma."

He finally lifted his head, gave a weary smile, and said, "All right, girls. I'll come back by five so you can meet Officer Hanley at home and go over the fan mail."

Well, at least some things had registered with him. I stepped out of the room and watched him leave. From the back he looked composed, a lanky middle-aged man in a tailored blue suit, pushing open that heavy steel door marked ICU and disappearing in the distance.

While Hannah set up the CaringBridge account on her phone, I sank into the other chair by Momma's bed and thought about a wobbling football and a house sitting in the perfect location on the beach. Once, as I rambled on and on to Momma about who knows what, I thought I saw a flicker of her eyelids. But when Hannah called the nurse over, nothing.

Nothing for the next three hours that we sat by her bed.

JOSEPHINE

1970 . . . The choir was singing that song again, "Just as I Am," and the church was so crowded — every pew and in the balcony too. The ladies wore the most beautiful hats. Josephine especially liked Mrs. McBurney's hats, a different one each week, bold and bright with a long feather, or small and lacy and pastel. She liked even more to sit in Mrs. McBurney's Sunday school class and hear her talk about Jesus.

Ever since Josephine was really young, no more than three or four, she'd liked to talk to God, especially out in the woods behind the house with the stars shining down. That was easy, like talking to a friend who listened and helped when the dark thoughts crowded in.

As the choir sang she stood and made her

way to the aisle. The sapphire blue carpet ran smooth under her patent leather shoes, but her knees trembled. She wanted to "go forward" — she wanted everyone to know she loved Jesus. But she was scared. What if she didn't do it right? What if it didn't work?

1971 . . . The first time Josephine found Kit with Daddy's whiskey bottle she was eleven, and Kit was thirteen. Kit was on the floor, leaning against her bed, sound asleep. Josephine carefully lifted the bottle from her sister's hands and hurried downstairs, where she set it back on the shelf. Maybe Daddy wouldn't notice it was only half-full.

The next time Kit was awake, sitting in their walk-in closet. "What are you doing, Kit? Are you drinking Daddy's whiskey?"

"None of your business," Kit snapped, then cursed. Then she frowned and said, "Sorry, Sis. Sorry."

"I don't think that's a very good idea."

"Yeah, well, I don't care. He drinks himself to oblivion. I thought I might like to see how it feels."

"Oh, Kit."

1972 . . . Mrs. Schaeffer, the eighth-grade English teacher, stood in front of the class, beaming. "Students, you have all done a fine

81

job with your short stories. A very fine job. However, there is one story that is exceptional. I believe we have the makings of a novelist in our midst."

Josephine looked around at the other students. A novelist! She hadn't known that another of her classmates loved writing the way she did. Who could it be?

"Josephine? Josephine, would you be willing to read us your story?"

Josephine jerked her head around. "Mine? You want me to read my story?"

Mrs. Schaeffer was smiling and holding out the manuscript. All fifty pages, written in Josephine's loopy cursive on loose-leaf paper, skipping every other line. She swallowed hard and stood beside Mrs. Schaeffer, who handed her the stack of papers. She felt her face go red. A voice in her head chanted, *But what if they don't like it? What if they don't like it?*

I had to write this story, she answered it. *I had to.*

But what if they don't like it?

CHAPTER 4

Sunday

PAIGE

Daddy came back to the hospital at five as he'd said, and I spent Sunday evening in Momma's office with Officer Hanley, going through all 7,603 emails and the thousands of likes and messages on Facebook. So far not one had seemed threatening. All encouraging, all expressing shock and concern. By nine I was seeing cross-eyed. Hannah had literally fallen asleep as soon as we got home, and I'd sent her to bed for a nap.

I had just let Milton out — for the fourth time in three hours — and woken Hannah up and come back into The Chalet when Officer Hanley called me over to Momma's laptop. "Have you seen this one before?"

The email had a bright floral background and the font was a pretty cursive. It read, *I just knew something like this would happen.*

Anytime someone is courageous enough to challenge the status quo, well, what do we do? We murder him or her! Old as history. That's what they did to Jesus. . . .

The diatribe went on and on and on, venting about gun laws and the downfall of the US and the call for Christians to stand up and fight.

"She sounds a bit extremist, doesn't she?" I noted.

Hannah walked into the office at that moment and stood looking over my shoulder, reading the email. "Extremist maybe, but she makes some good points."

Officer Hanley simply starred the email and asked, "Do either of you recall ever seeing this background or font on an email before?"

"No," Hannah said. "But I haven't been looking at my mother's fan mail for several years now."

"Not at all," I said. "I think I'd remember something like this. It's a bit unusual. And the content — it doesn't sound like she's written to Momma before, does it?"

"Precisely. And it doesn't sound like she is actually writing to your mother now. I say *she,* but I suppose it could be a man." Officer Hanley scrunched up her face and brushed a wisp of red hair off her forehead.

"She is sending out a battle cry."

I pondered that, then shrugged. "Maybe, but she wasn't trying to remain anonymous. She signed the email with her first name, and her email address is her first and last name. She even has her street address under her signature with a fancy little pumpkin emoticon beside it."

Officer Hanley was staring at me.

"What? Did I say something wrong?"

Her face actually relaxed into a half smile. "Not at all. You're observant, Paige. It's a good trait. Helpful. Keep observing."

Hannah and I returned to the hospital late that night. Hannah was sitting by Momma's bed in the ICU, holding her hand, whispering to her, trying unsuccessfully to make her voice sound soothing, when she said, "I think she just moved! Her hand twitched!"

Daddy and I rushed over to the bed, along with the nurse.

Momma's fingers jerked again, and we stared at them, watching the faint movement as if it were as big a miracle as Jesus raising Lazarus from the dead.

"Maybe she's in pain," Daddy said.

Momma didn't move again all that evening, but the nurse upped her morphine. Hannah sat there holding Momma's hand, and I opened her email account on my phone and began reading aloud to her the messages that had come since the shooting. Nearly every single one ended with something like *I'm praying for you, Mrs. Bourdillon.*

JOSEPHINE

1973 . . . . She was not going to cry! She would not. But all those red marks on the paper? She had worked for hours and hours and hours, in the middle of the night. What had she done wrong?

"Josephine, this is an excellent story," Mrs. Nixon said. "You are a gifted writer. But you didn't follow the instructions! No matter how creative and well-written the story, I cannot give you a high mark when you didn't do the assignment. I believe a C+ is actually quite generous."

Generous! She had never received a grade lower than an A− in English! How had she missed the instructions? Right now they seemed perfectly clear. But she'd had the idea and then she had been up so late working on the play for the Thespians, and then Kit had come home drunk again and needed to talk. So Josephine had to write it in only a few hours, and she hadn't really read the directions again.

And now she had failed. A C+ was failure. Her parents would certainly see it that way.

"If you would prefer, I will let you do a rewrite. You can get it to me by the end of the week. Would you like that?"

She could barely meet Mrs. Nixon's eyes. She felt like a child of six! What was the matter with her?

"Yes, yes, of course. I would like that very much. Thank you, Mrs. Nixon." She stood and left the classroom with a smile pasted on her lips, but what she heard in her mind was Failure!

Mr. Butler handed the essays back to the class. When he got to Josephine's desk, he was smiling broadly. He handed her the essay and across the top in his characteristic red felt-tip pen scrawl was marked: A+ Excellent work, Josephine!

She felt her cheeks grow hot and could barely make eye contact with her young history teacher.

"I love how you incorporated history into your story. A courier for President Lincoln." Then he winked and added, "I guess you aren't going to be a Confederate dame, are you?"

Josephine tried to smile and stammered, "Maybe not. . . ."

He patted her shoulder. "I'm just kidding. But seriously, you have a gift."

That's what they all said. A gift. A gift. A gift.

For Josephine, the attention of her teachers scared her and excited her. She wrote what she was given. Perhaps it was a gift. All she knew was simply this: She could not *not* write. But once in a while she wondered if being "gifted" was a curse. Sometimes she didn't want to have a gift; she'd rather have a date. She wanted a boy to call her on the phone, take her to see a movie. She didn't want to be different; she wanted to be like everyone else. Like Kit.

Monday

HENRY

I shut off the alarm twice, and finally Libby had to shake me awake. "It's those meds," I grumbled, stumbling out of bed, playing the part so she wouldn't start guessing. "My eyelids are so heavy I might have to pry 'em open with a toothpick."

I got dressed and went into the kitchen and had myself the omelet Libby had made, with some cut-up fruit and a bagel. She made sure that Jase and me ate a hearty, healthy breakfast — that's how she described it. Real good cook. She also had a fine mind, and she'd finished high school. I dreamed of sending her on to college one

88

day. For now she had a pretty decent office job as an assistant to a bigwig businessman.

I got to work early — seven thirty — and my boss, Mr. Dan, gave me the once-over and said, "Glad to have you back, Hughes. Got a lot of work today."

"Yessir. I'm in. Have to leave at three thirty, but I'll work through lunch and put in extra hours tomorrow."

"It's your boy again?" He knew about Jase, because I'd had to miss work a couple times when Libby couldn't get off and Jase needed to be hauled to the ER.

"Seeing the surgeon today," I said.

"All right then." He made like he was leaving, then turned around. "But I have to be able to depend on you, Hughes. You do good work, but I can't have you in three days and out two. You understand what I'm saying? I've got the big man breathing down my neck."

"Yessir." I understood. Understood loud and clear.

They'd pricked and poked Jase for over an hour, and now he sat bare chested, with a nurse in some sterile, chilly room while the surgeon told us the news from the leather chair in his office.

"I don't like what I see." He made his

hands into a tower, bringing his fingers together. "His heart rate is getting more erratic. I'm sorry. We've got to move the surgery up." He pulled up a schedule on his computer. "We need to get him in this Friday."

He must've seen how hard Libby was clutching my hand, because he added, "Don't worry, Mrs. Hughes. This surgery has an excellent chance for success. But we can't wait. He's got to be strong enough for the operation."

He talked on for a while. Libby kept grasping my hand real tight and sniffing and jotting down notes in that little spiral notebook where she recorded every single thing any doctor had ever said about Jase. I tried to listen, tried to concentrate, but all I kept hearing were the words *Four days before the second payment. No loose ends, no loose ends. . . .*

As we walked out to the pickup I knew I was clenching my jaw, grinding my teeth, all the things Libby noticed I did when life started caving in.

"You were a rock star, sweetie," Libby said to Jase, making her voice all light and airy, like she did every time she tried to pretend things was going fine.

"I like that doctor, Mommy," Jase said,

big green eyes staring up from under his chestnut mane. He glanced my way and gave his sheepish smile. "Do you like him, Papa?"

"I like him fine," I said, but my voice sounded gruff, and just as Jase was reaching for my hand he dropped it down to his side and looked away.

I tried again. "He's a real fine doctor, Jase, and we're mighty grateful to have him. He said he's gonna make your heart just right. This time it'll be put back together so well you won't ever have to go to no hospital again."

Libby looked over Jase's head and shook hers, flashed me a frown.

"Leastways not for a long time," I added. I held the door open as Jase climbed into the pickup, then Libby.

"That'll be great, Papa. That'll be corn-puddin' great." And he grinned, then snuggled onto my shoulder and closed his eyes while I drove us on toward home.

Libby just stared ahead, turning that little spiral notebook over in her hands while I was turning the rest of my life over and over in my mind. *No hurry, no hurry! Hurry!*

"I've gotta be gone again. Leavin' soon as I get you both home. Twenty-four hours is all. I promise."

She nodded, twisting the spiral, wiping a few tears, biting her lip.

We stopped by Jase's favorite fast food place on the way home and bought dinner. Once I got them inside the trailer, I flipped on the TV and sure enough, the scrolling headline under the main story said Miz Bourdillon was still in a coma. Then they went on to something about a college football game.

I stood in front of the TV, eating my hamburger, letting the ketchup and mayonnaise leak down onto my chin and forgetting to wipe my mouth. I kept hoping that Miz Bourdillon would just die. But she wasn't dead yet, and so I had to go and see what I could do.

"Be careful," Libby called after me.

Jase came to the screen door and said, "See you tomorrow, Papa?"

"Tomorrow, son."

PAIGE

Daddy spent the night sitting next to Momma, and then Hannah and I sat with her all Monday morning while Daddy drove back to the house to get a little rest. I guess if you had to be at a hospital, this was a pretty good one, because every room had an amazing mountain view. Not that

Momma could see it, but Hannah and Daddy and I could. Somehow the endless chain of mountains that kept changing its clothes from variegated green to bold primary colors, well, it felt like hope.

Momma's sister arrived at the hospital on Monday afternoon, having driven up from Atlanta. She grabbed me in her exuberant way, wrapping her tanned and wrinkled arms around me. "Oh, Paige. It's the worst. I tried to get here over the weekend but . . ."

I loved Aunt Kit, in spite of her excuses and missed appointments, in spite of the way Momma always seemed a little disappointed with their visits, in spite of the way Aunt Kit always seemed a little too enthusiastic. She smelled of expensive perfume, and she had on designer jeans and a matching silk blouse and jacket in autumn golds and gingers that set off her perfectly highlighted blond hair. She'd been a model for some of the biggest agencies, and she still looked pretty hot, even at almost sixty — when she was sober.

"So glad you're here, Aunt Kit. Perfect timing. I'll take you in to see her now. Remember, she may be able to hear and understand what is said around her, so talk *to* her, never *about* her. Sit with her and talk to her. And be sure to note even the

93

faintest movement. Hannah and I will be back in about two hours."

I led Aunt Kit into Momma's room, and as soon as she saw Momma, she gave a sob, covered her mouth, and whispered, "JoJo, JoJo. It can't be." Then she collapsed in the chair by Momma's bed, took her sister's hand, and started to talk.

JOSEPHINE

1973 . . . "You're only fifteen, Kitty!" Mother was screaming, her high-pitched voice rising over the sound of the washing machine. "You will not go out with a boy who is nineteen. I absolutely forbid it!"

"I'll do what I want!" Kit cursed her mother, threw her velvety blond hair over her shoulder, and stormed out of the room.

Josephine followed her sister down the stairway and out into the thick summer air. Kit wrapped her arms around her little sister and cried. "They don't understand anything at all. He's a cool guy."

"They just care about you, Kit. They're afraid."

Kit made a disgusted, mocking face. "All they care about is keeping up appearances. They don't want me to spoil their perfect reputation. As if the whole town doesn't whisper about Daddy behind our backs."

Josephine felt her stomach cramping. "Kit, please."

"You're the perfect child. Keep being perfect, Sis."

"I don't want to be perfect. I want to be like you. I want to be popular and beautiful like you."

Kit put her hands on her hips, her tied-dyed shirt pulled tight across her chest. "JoJo, you just be yourself. Don't be like me. I'm not such a great example to follow these days."

But she was smiling.

1974 . . . "I'm sorry you're leaving," Josephine said, looking Chet Conrad straight in his clear gray eyes.

The boy shrugged, his skinny shoulders slumped forward. "Just wanted to let you know."

She tried to swallow the lump in her throat. What could she say, anyway? Everyone in her class talked about Chet in whispers and gossip. *He's a little off in the head.* They either felt sorry for him or teased him unmercifully.

Josephine didn't exactly feel sorry for him. Sometimes she wanted to say, "Chet, I know. I know it gets confusing inside your mind. Me too." She never told him that, but they used to sit together at recess, and he had the most interesting things to say. Maybe part of his brain didn't work so well, but he made her laugh, and he had another part of his brain that worked darn-near perfectly.

The next day the gossip increased. *He's not coming back to school. His parents sent him someplace else — to rest, they said. But we know where he's going. Straight to the crazy farm.*

Josephine blinked hard to keep the tears from leaking out of her eyes.

That night she took out the journal she kept tucked in the back of her desk, hidden from Kit and her parents. Not that they cared, not that they ever would look. Still, what she wrote there might disturb them, and she didn't want that. Now she pulled out the little bright green spiral book and flipped to a clean page.

God, something is wrong with me. I can't tell you what it is, but I just wish someone would come along and plug up this empty space in my brain. If I could plug it up, then I'm sure I wouldn't fall through that hole into the scary, dark parts of my mind. I'm positive I'd be like my other friends.

And even though I pray every night for you to plug it up, you never do. And that makes me afraid.

She got out her Bible then, opened it to the Psalms — her favorite part — and searched for the verse that her teacher had read in

Sunday school a few weeks ago. "When I am afraid, I will put my trust in You. In God, whose word I praise, In God I have put my trust; I shall not be afraid. What can mere man do to me?" She blinked back tears and wrote down that beautiful verse in her journal. But then she added:

What if I can never plug the hole up? What if it gets bigger? I know what would happen. Then I'd be just like Chet.

1975 . . . "Terence, if I interviewed you for the school paper, would you answer my questions? I'd change your name and everything."

"What kind of questions?"

"Like how it feels to be the only black person at a fancy party and to have to treat everyone as better than yourself and hear all their derogatory comments about race and stuff."

Terence laughed. "Miss Josy, if you ever wrote something like that and put it in the paper, half the black folks in town would be fired, I guarantee it. We don't need no trouble like that."

"I know. But it just isn't fair."

"You listen to me, Miss Josy. I've known you for all your fifteen years of life. You've got a real good heart. You let the good Lord keep your heart pure and don't you worry none about me. One day He'll show you what to

97

write. But for now, you just leave that alone. And Miss Josy, I like my job just fine. I'm mighty happy to have it."

Kit had gotten herself into trouble again — drugs, boys. Her parents no longer thought it a great advantage for Kit to be gorgeous. The same day they got Kit out of jail, Josephine received word that her short story had won first prize in the county competition and would be sent on to the regionals and then perhaps to the nationals.

"We're so proud of you, JoJo," her mother said.

But Josephine heard the unspoken words. *Keep performing. Be perfect. We need you to be perfect. Please.*

Fred O., the youth pastor at her church, encouraged all of the kids in the youth group to memorize a Scripture verse. Josephine chose the one she had written in her journal after Chet left school. She liked that verse.

One day she got up her courage to talk to Fred O. about the hole in her head. Only she didn't call it a hole. She just said that sometimes she felt sad. He listened as if he really cared.

"Josephine, I'm no expert on much, but I know one thing. When I start feeling overwhelmed or angry or discouraged, I try to read what God has to say about it in the Bible. And I keep a list of Bible verses that talk about whatever is bothering me. Sometimes I even memorize those verses."

He showed her how to use a concordance to look up key words in her Bible. She found lots of verses about fear and worry and sadness. From that day on, she kept a list of Bible verses in her journal. When the voices got loud, when the hole seemed to grow wider, she would turn to those verses and say them out loud like a prayer.

"Be anxious for nothing, but in everything by prayer and supplication with thanksgiving let your requests be made known to God."

"When I am afraid, I will put my trust in You. In God, whose word I praise, In God I have put my trust; I shall not be afraid."

"The Lord lifts the fallen and those bent beneath their loads."

And to her great relief, the noise in her mind lessened and eventually stopped altogether.

PAIGE

After leaving Aunt Kit with Momma on Monday afternoon, Daddy, Hannah, and I rode the elevator down to the ground floor of the hospital. Detective Blaylock wanted to ask us a few more questions and had arranged to talk to us in a little office off the back of the hospital gift shop.

"Thought that would be more convenient than meeting at the police station," he said, but I didn't want to answer any more questions at all, no matter where they were asked.

On the way to the gift shop I asked Daddy, "Is Momma worth a lot of money? I mean, does she have a big life insurance policy on her? Are the police going to come after you and ask all kinds of overly personal questions? Will you be a suspect?"

"You've got almost as big an imagination as your mother." He almost smiled. "I suppose they could dream up about any scenario they wanted, sugar. But don't worry about it. Your mother is going to wake up and be fine."

Did Daddy really believe that? As we arrived at the gift shop, and he followed the detective into the back, I realized that he hadn't answered my question at all.

Hannah and I absent-mindedly browsed through what was a very upscale shop, with designer handbags, a bunch of kids' toys, and a section in honor of National Breast Cancer Awareness Month. There were jewelry displays and flower arrangements and many faith-based presents. Halloween candies sat in a bright orange bowl by the cash register. When I saw a bright pink balloon with *It's a Girl!* written on it I got a pinching in my chest. How I wished I were at the hospital for the happy occasion of a baby's birth instead of watching my mother barely holding on to life.

When Daddy came out of the office with the detective, he acted even stranger than he'd seemed the past two days. Uneasy, rubbing his eyes again and again — that habit only manifested itself when he knew he had a good chance of losing a client.

He stood beside me and the balloons while Hannah went into the office. "How'd it go?" I asked him.

Daddy shrugged. "Went fine, Paige."

"Well, I want a lawyer before they question me. You never know what kind of crazy things they'll invent about our family."

Daddy looked at me, exasperated. "Paige, just answer his questions, honey. Please don't be belligerent. I can't imagine you have a whole lot to hide." He tried to force a smile but it didn't work, and so we stood there in silence.

Finally Hannah came back. "No big deal," she said.

I went into the office, as neat and organized as the gift shop, and Detective Blaylock closed the door behind us. He had apparently moved a ceramic pumpkin filled with bite-sized candy from the desk to the floor, and now his notebook and a few files sat on the desktop. He sat down in the chair behind the desk and motioned for me to have a seat in the only other chair in the room. A few beautifully wrapped gifts sat by the door, no doubt waiting to be delivered to patients.

"Coffee?"

I shook my head.

Detective Blaylock had a restless type of personality, sitting, standing, sitting again, fiddling with a pen and a little notebook, running his hands across his balding head.

After asking a few polite questions about how I was doing, he went into police-business mode. "How was your parents' marriage?"

I squinted at him, grimaced, then gave a dry laugh. "Why are you putting that in the past tense?"

"Excuse me?"

"Momma's not dead. Their marriage isn't over. So you should say, 'How *is* your parents' marriage,' right?"

He gave a grunt. "Right."

I sat up as straight as I could. "You know as well as I do that if I say they have a great marriage, no problems, love each other deeply and devotedly, you won't believe me. You'll think I'm covering something up. So I'll just say, their marriage *is* solid. Stable. Good. They do love each other."

He sat back down, gave a little shake of the head, scribbled something, and almost smiled. "How was it growing up with a writer?"

"What do you mean?"

"I mean, your mother got a bit of notoriety for her novels. How was that for you?"

"She still gets a lot of notoriety," I corrected him again.

Now he was frowning at me.

I crossed my arms over my chest and probably sounded a little defensive. "Look, what do you know about my mother?"

"I know what I've read about her. Came from a wealthy family in Atlanta, brilliant in high school, all kinds of honors, full scholarship to college, met your dad" — he looked down at some notes — "in 1980 when they were both in college. Married in 1984. Your dad is in insurance. Your mother sold her first novel at thirty-three. Her second novel did well, and she started seeing some success."

"You can read all that on her website. Or on the dust jacket of her books. That's not my mother." I reached into the ceramic pumpkin and plucked out a piece of candy, never taking my eyes off the detective.

"I beg your pardon?" He stood up, braced on his arms and leaned over the desk, glaring at me.

"You know that writers write their own bios, don't you? They have to tell you the good parts. Momma's not afraid to tell the bad parts, but we convinced her to leave it off the website and the dust jackets."

Once again Detective Blaylock sat back down, leaning over, elbows on knees. I guessed he was trying to figure out how to read me, and frankly he looked a little pissed off. "Would you mind telling me the truth about your mother then, Paige?"

"Have you ever read any of her books?"

"No."

"Well, read them. She tells the truth in her books. That's why her readers write her those emails — you should read some of them too. Or ask Officer Hanley about them. My mother's readers thank her; they tell her she offers hope even in the midst of situations that seem impossible. If you read the letters, you'll see what I mean. And if you read her novels, well, you'll understand more about Momma."

For a moment he didn't budge, then he

sat up straight and frowned at me.

I pretended not to notice. "Her books mean something to her readers. They touch a place inside. They're not just entertaining; there's always something more. That's all she ever wanted, anyway. To make people think, to give them hope even while they wrestle with the hard things in life." My voice was getting scratchy and off pitch. "Momma is complicated, that's what she is. She's got a huge imagination coupled with a really deep, dark dose of reality, and she mixes it in her stories."

I turned away, fished a Kleenex out of my jeans pocket, and blew my nose. "And she's generous. She believes in people, even when there is absolutely no reason to. She's kind." Blew my nose again. "And I tell you, I cannot really imagine one single person on the planet who would want her dead. Not even the wacko who wrote those letters. No one would want Momma dead. Everybody likes her."

He was scribbling away again on a notepad.

I let him finish, then said, "Can I ask you a question, Detective Blaylock?"

That caused him to smile. "Isn't that what you've been doing? Interrogations are usu-

105

ally performed by the officer, not the civilian."

I blushed. "Sorry. I have a big mouth. But this is what I want to know. Even though I can't imagine anyone wanting to kill my mother, someone obviously did. So will he or she come back? Like on TV, the killer always somehow mysteriously gets a white lab coat and sneaks into the victim's room and puts cyanide or quinine or something in the IV, and the patient dies. Will our crazed reader be sneaking around this hospital, waiting for someone to be careless, and then go in and smother my mother?"

He actually laughed.

"I didn't mean it to rhyme."

"You're very entertaining, Miss Bourdillon. I believe you said yesterday that you inherited your mother's big imagination."

I did not return a smile. "I'm perfectly serious. Could you please answer my question?"

"I guess it *could* happen. That's why we've got police everywhere. No one will sneak into her room, Miss Bourdillon. Don't worry."

He stood, and I guessed the interview was over.

"But you still don't have any clue who tried to kill her, right?"

"We've got those two letters, we've got the bullet, and we're working on other leads." He opened the door, and I walked back into the gift shop.

"I hope so," I said. "I sure hope so."

As I walked away, I felt satisfied. I hadn't revealed anything at all. Certainly not about The Awful Year.

CHAPTER 5

Monday

JOSEPHINE

1975 . . . She and Kit were curled up together in bed, giggling. Josephine wished this night would never end. Kit's eyes were bright with mischief and good, clean fun, and they weren't talking about Vietnam or LSD or the boys Kit was sleeping with. They were talking about ballet!

Kit pulled her out of bed and announced, "Now I present to you my stunning little sister, JoJo."

She lifted Josephine's hands and whispered, giggling, "Like this." They stood in ballerina form. "Now a pirouette." One by one, Kit led her through the basic steps of ballet. "See, silly Sis! You could be a ballerina, too, if you wanted to." She twirled Josephine around and around and around. "But you're not meant to be a ballerina, JoJo. Everyone knows you're

108

meant to write."

She was twirling and twirling with Kit, dizzy, dizzy, and then they tumbled on the bed together, laughing again. "So just write."

Out of breath, Josephine felt her cheeks flush. "Kit, should I write even if it hurts?"

Her big sister didn't hesitate. "It will hurt, JoJo. But you're brave. I'm not so brave, but you, you could dance to the moon and back with that heartfelt faith you have." Kit started to cry. Then she hugged Josephine to her fiercely. "So dance your stories onto paper, JoJo. No matter what."

PAIGE

When Daddy, Hannah, and I got back upstairs after our interviews with Detective Blaylock and stepped into Momma's room, Aunt Kit looked completely wrung out — her airbrushed former-model allure had faded, and her face was pinched and drawn, her deep blue eyes red from crying. She was holding on to Momma's hand almost fiercely, and when she glanced up there was a wild expression in those eyes.

"It's terrible." Aunt Kit swiped a bright orange fingernail where her mascara had smudged and said, way too loudly, "She hasn't moved at all. No response to all my wild stories. Nothing."

109

Daddy put his finger to his lips to indicate Aunt Kit needed to lower her voice. "Thanks for staying with her, Kit."

Aunt Kit, oblivious, continued talking too loudly. "I made her life so hard." It came out as a sob. "I made her be the good girl, the perfect, intelligent, talented girl. I was the drop-dead gorgeous girl." She gave a thin smile. "That's what they called me. Can you imagine what that did to me? And to your mother? She did everything right because I did everything wrong. She had to drag that weight around. The little sister to the goddess Kit." Now Aunt Kit sounded drunk, although I was almost positive she was stone sober. "She picked up after me and kept writing her stories. And I ridiculed her for it. I laughed when she begged to go to parties with me. . . ."

"Shhh, Kit," Daddy said. "This is old news. You and Josephine worked all that out years ago." Daddy's face was pure annoyance as he took her by the elbow and escorted her out of the room.

I followed and said, "Daddy, you go on and stay with Momma." He nodded, looking relieved, and left us in the hall.

Indeed, we'd all heard the stories. Momma had even written one of her novels with a

Kit-figure in it — with my aunt's permission.

"I know it's old news," Aunt Kit said. "But just because we said the truth out loud, that doesn't take away the scars. And now look at her, so still. I've been trying to tell her again that I'm sorry."

Her remarks irritated me. Somehow my aunt's dramatics always came back to spotlight herself. "Aunt Kit, please, don't be talking to Momma about hard things. She needs to hear lots of love and hope. Don't ease your conscience by unloading on Momma when she can't defend herself."

Aunt Kit swiveled around and glared at me for a long moment, and then her face softened. "Yes, you're right." She flashed a plastic smile. "I'll behave. I promise."

"Daddy's staying with Momma right now. Why don't I take you back to the house? There's tons of food. And you can get set up in the guest room. I'll come back later and spend the night here."

Aunt Kit merely nodded, making a racket with her high heels on the shiny hospital floor as she followed me down the hall.

We were greeted at the front door of our home by three small postal bags overflowing with letters. Our neighbor, Mrs. Swanson, had left a Post-it on one bag that read

Saw the postman bringing these in. He said they were all addressed simply to Josephine Bourdillon, Asheville, North Carolina. I told him he could leave them on the porch. I'm keeping watch.

"Wow, this is what I'd call fan mail," I said, unlocking the door. I picked up one of the bags and carried it into the kitchen, where I set it beside Milton's water bowl. Aunt Kit followed me into the house, empty-handed. "Would you mind bringing the other mail bags inside?" I snapped. "I'm going to take Milton for a walk."

I'm pretty sure Aunt Kit rolled her eyes at me. Then she kicked off her high heels, went onto the porch, and picked up the two other bags. I grabbed Milton's leash and hurried him out the door before she could say anything. When we returned twenty minutes later, the bags sat right where she'd left them inside the door, and Aunt Kit was nowhere in sight.

I got myself a plate full of baked goods, sat down beside the bags, emptied the letters onto the kitchen floor, and counted them. There were almost three hundred. I ate cookies and cake and opened them, one by one.

HENRY

Took me three hours to get back to that mountain town in North Carolina. I got to see a real colorful sunset — all oranges and reds — the sky almost the same colors as the trees on those mountains. I drove nice and respectful — no use getting picked up by the police — and got to the hospital around ten. Dang big place, all spread out and not just one building. But that Lucy on TV had said Miz Bourdillon was on the "Memorial Campus in the Neuro Trauma ICU." Felt real thankful to Lucy for that information.

I finally got parked and found my way inside. Had my Glock strapped under my shirt. The map in the lobby of the hospital said that trauma place was up on the fourth floor, but I knew there was no way I'd get near that lady. Cops were everywhere. Wondered if I could get a little information from someone — maybe a reporter. I went up to the cafeteria on the second floor — nice place, all clean and decorated for Halloween — and got a burger.

There weren't any reporters around that I could tell, but other people straggled in, all of them looking sad and lost and confused, like they didn't have any idea of what was coming next. But I couldn't tell if any of

113

them was kin to Miz Bourdillon. I tried to sit still, act calm, but I kept drumming my hands on the table. A lady with a little kid looked over at me, kinda annoyed like. I felt sorry for the boy — he was younger than Jase, and I could tell he'd had just about enough of this big ole hospital.

Picked up Miz Bourdillon's book, but I couldn't concentrate. What *could* I do? The map had shown several waiting rooms on each floor, so I finally decided to go on up to the fourth floor and sit up there. I rode the elevator up and followed the signs. Walked right past a policeman who was pacing the hall, and I broke into a cold sweat. I knew he couldn't see the Glock, but what if they were frisking people on this floor, trying to protect Miz Bourdillon?

I hurried on down the hall, my heart hammering in my chest. I needed to hide from that policeman and was glad to open the door to the waiting room and disappear inside. It was more private than the cafeteria, but still plenty of space, and the chairs were cushioned and looked comfortable. The room had two vending machines and a little kitchen area with a microwave and a little fridge and a spot where you could serve yourself a hot drink for free. Several ladies were sitting in chairs, all huddled together, and looked like one was crying.

Got myself a cup of coffee, but my hands were shaking a little, and I spilled a bit on my jeans. The ladies didn't seem to notice. I sat down on the other side of the room and took out my book again. Pretended to read, but I was really listening to see if they were talking about Miz Bourdillon. Didn't seem like it, and after about fifteen or twenty minutes they got up and left.

I was sitting there all alone still wondering what to do next when a young woman came in. I recognized her right away as Miz Bourdillon's daughter who'd been talking on TV.

Wasn't that some luck! Smiled to myself, then kept repeating in my mind, *Slow, Henry, slow.*

She had on a baggy gray sweat shirt and jeans and a baseball cap, and I figured she didn't want to be recognized any more than I did. But there wasn't any hiding her pretty little face with the turned-up nose and her hair — chestnut, the same color as Jase's, except hers was thick and long. She got herself a little Styrofoam cup of something hot and sat down on the other side of the room.

"Hey," I said, nodding across at her.

She jumped a little and glanced up at me. "Hey."

"Fine time for a cup of coffee, right?"

She shrugged. "Hot chocolate."

I pretended to go back to reading, then looked up and said, "Hey, you're that writer lady's kid, aren't you?"

She looked at me suspiciously and nodded.

"Sure am sorry about your mother. Right awful thing."

Another nod.

"Is she doing any better?"

She was holding the cup in front of her face, staring down at her hot chocolate. "If you don't mind, I'm not very interested in talking. You can find everything you want to know on the internet."

"Sorry. Sorry. Yeah, it's pretty awful to have your private life on display. But at least it lets people know. I bet they pray. I mean, it sounds like people really loved your mother." I held up the novel. "In fact, I decided to read one of her books."

The girl didn't smile. She flipped her hair over her shoulder. "Yeah. You and everyone else on the planet. Great way to up your sales. Get yourself almost killed."

I chuckled, then wished I hadn't. "I guess you're right about that. Went to get this at the library, and it was the only one of her books left on the shelf. Anyway, I hope she'll get out of that coma soon. I bet she will. My boy — he's had a bunch of operations. His heart. We thought he wouldn't live, but now they're sayin' one more surgery and he'll be okay. So see — I bet it'll work out okay for your mother."

She shrugged again but didn't reply. I tried to think of something else to say but couldn't come up with anything. Then I thought about the policeman I'd seen in the hallway and got shaky all over again. Better be going before he caught me here. I got up to leave, and she called after me, "Good luck with your son."

You said too much, you fool. Too much, too much. Maybe I should have started back on the meds.

PAIGE

I watched as the burly man lumbered out of the waiting room. He was big. Huge, but all muscle. Probably midthirties. His hair was whitish blond, long, and scraggly, and his pale blue eyes twitched a little when he looked at me, like he was nervous, or worse, maybe not quite all there. He was the kind of man that made people afraid at first glance, with eyes that couldn't focus very well and tattoos all over his neck. There was one that looked like a medieval sun peeking out from under his sleeve. He talked like a redneck and didn't seem like the kind of person who would be reading one of Momma's books. But as he left the room, all I felt was pity. My mother was in intensive care, but his *son* had heart problems. I thought that must be even harder.

When I returned to Momma's room around midnight, I found Detective Blaylock sitting outside her room, intently reading something on my father's laptop.

I flinched.

Officer Hanley had taken over reading all of Momma's incoming emails — she had, in fact, taken Momma's computer completely. *"Confiscated it,"* I'd said under my breath earlier in the day, which had not escaped Officer Hanley's hearing. She'd also taken Momma's cell phone.

"We've granted them access to our devices and signed a consent to search form, Paige, so it's perfectly normal," Hannah had chided me.

Normal, yes, but Momma kept her journal on her laptop and didn't allow anyone to read it. Occasionally she'd read us something she'd written there. Her journal was a prayer and a petition and a record of her life — of our lives. What if she'd written something about The Awful Year?

Now, seeing Detective Blaylock with Daddy's computer, I felt my stomach tense into a hard knot. What were the police going to discover about my family's life?

Detective Blaylock looked up at me, his face about as washed-out as Daddy's. "Up mighty late, aren't you, Paige?" He still seemed a little pissed at me, but at least he was calling me Paige instead of his infuriatingly condescending *Miss Bourdillon.*

"I'm taking the night shift. My dad and sister went back home, and I just got something to drink." I suppressed a yawn. "I'll go in and sit with Momma for a little while."

"Okay, but I'll be here till six if you want to try to get a little sleep in the waiting room."

"Thanks." This time I gave a full-fledged yawn.

HENRY

I left that waiting room, hurried to the elevator, and rode down to the lobby. I wandered around the bottom floor of the hospital, trying to get a feel for the ginormous place. I made my way to the main entrance and studied the map again for just a second and then hurried outside. What was I thinking? Wasn't too smart to be traipsing around the hospital in the middle

119

of the night. Might look suspicious.

I went out to the pickup and drove to that same motel where I'd spent the night Friday, over on the west side of town, then knew that wasn't a good idea either. So I ended up sitting in a Waffle House for a few hours reading the book, trying to figure out what to do next.

I almost stopped reading that novel because it was making me mad. I was afraid the boy — the teenager who had gotten himself into all kinds of trouble — was gonna turn out to be a pushover. He'd had an awful life and been mistreated, and I understood that. And he was afraid — not of his father but of someone else close to him. And I knew just how that felt.

Then he went and listened to the old lady — the one who was batty and wise at the same time. And that was when I got mad. The lady in the book said, *"You can't change what happened. But you can let it go."*

"How?" the boy asked, and she'd answered, *"You make peace with him."* So he went and made peace with the scumbag. I threw the book across the room. Thank heavens the place was empty, and the waitress had gone back into the kitchen.

But Miz Bourdillon wrote it in a way that you still wanted to know the truth, even if you were mad. So I got up and picked the book up off the floor, sat back down in my little booth, and finished it. And turns out he made peace with that man and with himself.

Well, I couldn't make peace with my pa because he was dead. And even if I could, I wouldn't. No way.

But the boy did, and the old lady said it was so the boy could live with himself and go forward and get better.

"Ain't gonna be doing that on your own, boy. You know that, don't you? You have to look at the part of you that fills up with thanksgiving on a crisp fall day with the sky a deep blue. You have to think about smelling the fire tickling the twigs in the fireplace and how comfortable you are under that thick handmade quilt. You think about those little things. Because they're big. Real big, I tell you. And that's the soul. You dig in deep to yourself and let that higher good grab you."

Miz Bourdillon didn't say *forgiveness* like a preacher would, but that was what she was talking about. And she didn't say *sacrifice,* and she didn't say *faith* — words they used all the time at Libby's church. And she didn't say *higher power* like in AA or *God* like in the Bible. But she showed it all right there on the page. The old lady just gave up her life, if you could say it that way, and the way she did it, in one of those twisting endings, well, it floored me all right. I was blinking back tears.

But then it got me thinking. Could that really happen? Could somebody really give up her life like that? Nobody at a church or self-help group had ever explained it to me the way it was written in that book. Leastways I didn't remember such a thing. And I wondered, even though I knew it was impossible, what if I went up to that Miz Bourdillon and asked her to forgive me? Maybe if I told her I was sorry, maybe that would make the awful pinching inside — and the way I wanted to hit at something — maybe it would make those feelings go away. And when I smiled at Jase and Libby, they'd really see a smile, and there wouldn't be any more fear in their eyes.

Tuesday

PAIGE

Someone shook me awake where I had curled up on a few of the chairs in the ICU waiting room. I forced my eyes opened and looked up, and as soon as I saw him, some of the burden slipped off my back. "Hey," I said and stretched.

"Hey yourself. You okay? I've sent you about a hundred texts."

I held up my cell phone. "I haven't even gotten to my texts. I've been reading Momma's emails and letters and talking to the police and getting Hannah and going through the past letters — you know, the ones I told you about, and —" But I broke down before I could finish.

Drake Ellinger was the one person besides my sister who I'd let see me cry.

We'd grown up together, lived in the same neighborhood and went to the same church. Our two families had gone on vacations together every year until his parents' divorce, and he and Hannah and I had seen each other through a couple of things I couldn't even mention. He was the big brother I'd never had, one year older than Hannah. He protected us from bullies when we lived in the same neighborhood, and he nodded understandingly when I swore I'd never go to church again, and we kept on being friends through one awkward early teenage crush (mine on him) so that we were practically inseparable. Except, of course, he now attended a college a few hours from home and was in his last year of engineering school.

I found another Kleenex in my pocket and dabbed at my eyes. "What time is it anyway?"

"Five thirty."

"You drove straight through the night?"

"Yeah. I had a big project to turn in and then headed out. Wish I could have gotten here sooner."

"Being here now is great. You're awesome, Drake. Thanks." I started crying again. "Sorry. It's just that it's been awful, the shooting and all the news coverage and now the police are questioning Daddy and Hannah and me — you know, more 'thoroughly.'" I emphasized the last word with air quotes. "Like they think it might be about Momma and Daddy and money. Money! The detective asked if they had a good marriage. And a few other things I didn't want to answer."

"Shhh." Drake wrapped his arms around me, and I felt protected. Safe. "You need to get those tears out, Bourdy. And you just answer what you can. Your father is the gentlest man on earth. I don't think they'll pull up much dirt on him."

"But they could. You know they could."

"I know. But I don't think they'll link that

to what's happened to your mother."

"Unless I tell them."

Drake cocked his head and gave a small smile. "Which you won't."

Drake knew me almost as well as Hannah did, so when he assured me that I wouldn't do what I feared the most — slipping up and saying way too much to the police — it felt lots better than the hot chocolate I had downed in the middle of the night. "Thanks for being here. I have so much to tell you."

He glanced at his cell and said, "Well, it's almost six. Is it too early to see your mom?"

"Family can visit anytime day or night — and you're considered family — but it'll be pretty rough on you to see her. Maybe you should get something to eat first."

He got a pained expression on his face. "You're probably right — it won't help Momma Jo for me to break down in front of her." He gave a heartfelt sigh. "And I haven't eaten anything in a long time. So maybe I should buy you some pancakes at the Waffle House first."

This he said with a hint of playfulness in his voice, so I responded in like manner. "I'd prefer something decadent at the French Broad Chocolate Lounge."

"Of course you would, you little snob. But

125

as you well know, it doesn't open until eleven."

We were teasing each other as usual. Maybe a little bit of normal life was possible. I stretched again and yawned. "Fine. Take me to the Waffle House."

As we made our way in the predawn to Drake's car, I thought about all the nights he had spent on our couch while his parents' marriage was falling apart. I remember asking, "Who are we going to be friends with now, Daddy, Ginnie or Bert? Will you have both of them over to the house?" I couldn't recall if Daddy ever answered my question, but none of us ever minded Drake coming around at all hours. He'd talk till early in the morning with Momma, getting out all the anger and angst that kept building up as he went through the devastation of his parents' divorce.

Drake wasn't the only one who came to talk to Momma. I had images of dozens of others — teens, young women, older ladies — sitting on the couch in the den, the fire blazing in the hearth, and Momma bent forward, totally concentrated on whoever needed her attention. She was so approachable, and her books so truthful and poignant, that people just naturally felt like they'd gained a new best friend when they

126

finished her stories. And Momma, who had a very hard time separating the urgent from the important, looked on every soul who wrote to her or asked to come for a visit as someone worth listening to, as if he or she were a true friend. She just soaked in the stories, just sat there listening and praying and caring.

A thought flashed across my mind. Could it be that a reader had confided something dark and dangerous to Momma and then later, realizing she'd revealed way too much, decided she had to kill her? I shook the thought away. Surely not.

What I *did* know was that Drake had got out a lot of anger and moved forward, and so had many others. But what we had not understood, for the longest time, was the toll it took on Momma.

HENRY

Wasn't any use staying at the Waffle House or anywhere else in that town. I had to be at work at eight or else, and I didn't need no more *or elses* in my life. Hadn't gotten one better idea about what to do next, but boy, did I keep thinking about that book. I wished I could just go see Miz Bourdillon, ask her a few questions, but that wasn't gonna happen. I had a job to do, and it wasn't talking.

I hated to think about that, though. It sounds crazy, but I had started feeling real close to Miz Bourdillon. Maybe I could get another one of her books from the library. They say writers put a lot of themselves in their stories, so maybe another book would tell me more about her. Not the same as talking to her, but it was the best I could do.

I liked her daughter too. She reminded me of Jase, and not just because her hair was the same color. Libby and me, we always said we were glad our Jase had a lot of spunk. He was a fighter. And Miz Bourdillon's daughter, I could just tell she had a lot of spunk too.

Driving along I kept reciting to myself: *Four days since the shooting. Three days till Jase's operation.*

Then I started trying to come up with a way to have Miz Bourdillon die, because it didn't look like she was gonna do it on her own. There wasn't any way my contact could *make* me kill — legally, of course. But there were plenty of ways he could convince me that the job had to get done. I dreaded those things.

All those thoughts were swimming round and round in my head, like to make me dizzy and sick. I thought about the meds again. I could hear Libby saying, *Henry, you know cold turkey is bad. You get so confused. And every time, it takes you longer to see the effect of the meds when you start back.*

But I couldn't start back till I knew if I'd have to pull the trigger again. One thing I knew for sure. If I did, I sure as heck wasn't gonna miss.

My eyes were blurring on that dark, curvy I-40, so I pulled off at a rest area and parked way far away from the lights and the little bathroom. Set my phone to wake me in three hours, and I slept.

CHAPTER 6

Tuesday

PAIGE

I ordered a stack of blueberry pancakes at Waffle House and smothered them in butter and blueberry syrup.

"Still got your sweet tooth, haven't you?" When Drake smiled, his dimples showed. He had somehow turned out to be rather handsome. But to me, Drake was just Drake. Curly, sandy blond hair, blue-green eyes, thin, the body of a long-distance runner, intense and intensely loyal.

"Yes, and don't say anything else about it."

"Bourdy, you could eat pancakes nonstop and still be thin as a rail."

I nodded. "And thankful for it. I don't plan to quit eating anytime soon."

He laughed, and I peppered him with questions about school, thankful to forget the horror of Momma for a few minutes. "Are you dating anyone?" I always got around to that question.

And his answer was always the same. "Bourdy, you know I'm not looking."

My response was too. "Ha, that's impossible." And I could have quoted verbatim what he said next.

"The way I see it, I don't need to spend a lot of time hunting for the perfect girl. As long as I'm doing what I'm supposed to be doing, I'm pretty sure she'll cross my path, and then I'll know."

One thing that had rubbed off on Drake during his late-night talk sessions with Momma was faith. Like I said, many people came to see Momma, and somehow as they were pouring out their hearts, Momma just naturally directed the conversation to faith. In God and the Bible. I'd overheard enough of those conversations to know that she never tried to force anyone to believe a certain way. But as she listened and shared her own story, with all its bumps and bruises, and how faith had played such an important role in helping her through the journey, well, it seemed a lot of those people started wanting what Momma had.

That I had not embraced this faith that she and my father held so dear must have torn her heart out, but it never showed. All I saw was Momma doing her best, with God's help, to hold her life together — along with the lives of about half the world.

Drake and I dozed in the Neuro Trauma ICU waiting room till eight, full from our breakfast at Waffle House. The ICU staff — professional and yet humane — said he could go in for a visit after the nurses finished their rounds. When I asked the attending nurse about Momma's score, she gave a tight smile and said, "She's still at six today, Paige."

It didn't get any easier, taking the people who loved Momma in to see her. Drake's expression mimicked Hannah's and Aunt Kit's, mashing his lips together, hand drawn over his mouth, clearing his throat, wiping at something in the corner of his eye. Finally he sat down in the chair by Momma's bed.

"Momma Jo? Hey, it's me. It's Drake. So good to see you, Momma Jo. Looks like you've got the best bed in the whole place. I'll bet you're comfortable."

He glanced at me, and I rolled my eyes and whispered, "Act normal, you moron!"

He frowned a little, wrinkled his brow, and then started talking like the Drake we all knew. "So the last year in engineering school is pretty rough. I told you when we talked

132

in the summer that I was dreading it. My grades are okay so far — I've only had a few — but everyone is feeling the pressure to get noticed. I've got my first interview scheduled in a week. A big plant down in south Georgia. They're going to fly me to Columbus and drive me to the plant. It's in the middle of nowhere, but the pay is awesome."

I nodded my approval and slipped out into the hall.

Daddy and Hannah had come back to the hospital — Aunt Kit was still sleeping at the house. I told them that Drake was with Momma, so we all went into the waiting room.

Hannah's eyes glistened with tears as she told me, "The CaringBridge site is getting so many comments — people from all over the world are praying for Momma. I believe God is going to heal her, Paige! I really do."

I admired my sister's faith. I just didn't share it.

Daddy acknowledged her comment with a slight nod and said, "I had a good talk with Mamie and Papy this morning." Now his eyes filled with tears. "zey sure are worried about your momma."

Whenever Daddy talked on the phone with his parents, or when he was overly tired, his French accent grew a little more pronounced. I loved him all the more for it.

He sat down in one of the cushioned chairs. "Get any sleep?" I asked him.

"A leetle."

Daddy was completely worn out. He hadn't shaved, maybe hadn't even showered. He must have fallen asleep in his clothes, because he was still wearing the same thing from the night before.

"Long night with Aunt Kit?"

He winced. "Don't even get me started."

I knew what he was thinking about as he sat there all hunched up, looking disheveled and lost, and I wanted to tell him that I would never, ever say a word to the police about it, would never hint at anything that they couldn't find out themselves — and they could find most of it, anyway. But the truth was, I didn't know everything either, and that sent a little shiver through me.

Normally Daddy had a very welcoming and unintimidating personality; he was someone who attracted other people easily, gained their confidence. That worked very well in his line of work — people just naturally trusted him. And he was trustworthy. Thoughtful, hardworking, kind, attentive, observant. And fun. With that trace of a French accent.

But I'd seen nothing welcoming about him since the shooting. He'd withdrawn, and he barely addressed Hannah and me. I imagined he was torturing himself about The Awful Year. Or maybe about Aunt Kit.

I trusted my dad, but what I really wanted to ask him was something I had never quite dared to bring up, in spite of my big mouth: *What actually happened back then, Daddy? Can you please just tell me what really happened?*

Drake stayed with Momma until noon, when I shooed him off to our house to get some lunch. Then Hannah and I alternated sitting with Momma, talking and hoping desperately for some tiny movement, but none came. Hannah pulled me away, saying, "Daddy's turn again," trying to sound lighthearted. Momma had not made any progress in the past twenty-four hours. Reluctantly I followed Hannah to the elevator and rode down to the all-too-familiar Café 509.

The cafeteria felt almost cozy. Facts about pumpkins were written in fancy lettering on a wooden-framed chalkboard with a reminder: *Try our delicious pumpkin bread or mouthwatering pumpkin muffins. Gluten free!* All different sizes and colors of pumpkins tumbled artistically around a display table.

We each ordered a pumpkin muffin, and Hannah got a cup of coffee while I ordered my chai. We sat at one of those little square tables as far away from the big TV screen as we could get.

I didn't want to talk about Momma so I said, "Drake will be back in a little while. With Aunt Kit."

We caught each other's eyes and grinned. *Poor Drake.*

Then I teased, "Hannah, you haven't told me if you've met any hot guys in France."

She rolled her eyes. "Can't you think of anything better to ask about than that? I've been there all of three weeks."

"Well, then before. When you traveled around Europe with Sophie and Tess?"

"I met the most wonderful and interesting people in the world, but no young man swept me off my feet. No worries."

I did worry about her a little. When you looked like Hannah, guys flocked around. I think I feared she might subconsciously slip into a lifestyle like Aunt Kit's. Fortunately Hannah had a good dose of common sense and was not impressed an iota by her own looks. *"As if I had anything to do with it,"* she always said.

"What about you, Paige?"

"No one. Except the men in my stories, and they're always really messed up."

She rolled her eyes again. "Someday you're going to wake up and see the truth."

"What are you talking about?"

"About Drake."

"What? I got over my awful crush on him about five years ago, in case you don't remember. I never want to be crazy love-sick like that again."

"No. You've made that point many times. But I'm talking about Drake. The way he looks at you. The way he cares."

I did not want to hear that. "Drake is like my big brother! You don't fall in love with your big brother. There's a name for that!"

"Hey, calm down. You don't need to tell the whole cafeteria." She was smiling, like she'd discovered a secret. "I'm just pointing out the obvious. Of course, if you don't have any feelings for him, I would never want you to lead him on."

"You're dead wrong, Hannie." But I thought about the way Drake looked at me, the way he'd held me. "He's not interested in me."

But he wasn't interested in anyone else either; he'd told me that a hundred times.

"I'm just sayin'."

I felt a slow blush creep up my face. "Can

we talk about something else?"

"Sure. What have you been writing lately?"

"Oh, little mysteries à la Dorothy Sayers — remember Lord Peter Wimsey?"

"You're writing mysteries that take place in 1930s England?"

"Yes! It's a blast. I did so much research for Momma about that period in England — you know — the Duke of Windsor and Wallis Simpson. So much drama and romance. And murder too. And you don't have to worry about DNA! I love figuring out a whodunit." I jumped up, almost spilling my tea. "That's it! We've got to write it all down. I'll bet we know more than we think."

"Whoa. What?"

I sat back down, meeting Hannah's eyes. "Maybe we can come up with possible suspects. Help the police out a little."

Hannah reached for my hand. "Paige, you don't need to protect Daddy. No one's going to find out about The Awful Year."

She'd read my mind, just as Drake had. Tears pooled in my eyes, and I gripped her hand forcefully. "Just humor me please, Hannie. Please."

She frowned and nodded, and in those small gestures I read the full extent of her love for me, for Momma. For Daddy.

"Well, I guess suspect number one is the wacko who wrote the new snail-mail letters."

"Right! Yes!" I stopped, took a bite of my muffin, fished in my backpack for my phone, scrolled down, and started typing in names. For number one, I simply wrote *Wacko;* for number two, I wrote *Diatribe fan with fancy font and flowery background.*

Hannah sipped her coffee while I typed.

"Remember that time the guy wrote to Momma because he said she had written about his life in her novel? And he wanted to sue her until finally Daddy proved that she had no inkling who he was?"

Hannah nodded. "And remember when that lady showed up at the house carrying a three-pound box of saltwater taffy because one of Momma's protags loved saltwater taffy? And Momma hates the stuff."

"But we didn't." We giggled. "Charity Mordant. That was her name." I typed it into my phone. "Although sending saltwater taffy doesn't exactly qualify her as a suspect."

"No, but remember" — Hannah's eyes were glimmering with mischief — "Mrs. Mordant came to three different book signings in three different states, and even got Momma's phone number, and we thought she might be a stalker!"

"True. But she wasn't."

"No, she was a really devoted fan. But let's see if we can think of any possible stalkers from Facebook." Hannah actually looked excited.

So we escaped reality for a little while, pretending we were trying to solve a murder mystery in a novel. Somehow it felt less oppressive.

"Remember when the lady said her daughter killed herself after reading Momma's book?"

Hannah turned away. "I don't like to think about that one. We were just little kids, so all I know is what Momma told us. It took her weeks to recover. She even tried to see the bereaved mother, but didn't have her name."

"She's had a lot of weird things happen to her, hasn't she? A lot of readers could have been a little off."

"Yeah."

I put my phone down. "I've been thinking that maybe one of her readers poured out her heart, you know, with all kinds of confidential stuff, and then realized she'd told Momma too much. And maybe decided it was too dangerous for Momma to have that information and so she had to kill her."

"That's sick, Paige."

"I know. I know. But *if* that was the case, well, either you or I would have read the letter that shared the confidential stuff too."

"So are you suggesting we go through all those years of snail mail and email? We can't even get through the stuff that came yesterday! And anyway, Officer Hanley still has Momma's computer."

"I know, but maybe we'll remember something."

Hannah started to say something else, thought better of it, and shrugged. "If there really was something confidential that someone would kill for, don't you think we'd have remembered it already? Unless it was something less obvious. I'm going to pray that the Lord shows us if there's something we've forgotten. And in the meantime, do you think we should show this list to the police?"

"Well, actually, they've probably had enough of my ideas for a while. Detective Blaylock isn't exactly thrilled with my ruminations, if you know what I mean."

We sat there in the comfortable chairs of Café 509, nibbling on our muffins, sipping coffee and tea, and reliving memories of Momma's potential enemies — or overly devoted fans, I should say. And, of course,

Hannah noticed how relieved I felt when we had seven names on our suspect list and not one of them was Daddy's.

HENRY

Made it through work okay, and Big Dan seemed pretty pleased with the project we finished ahead of time. Before driving home, I stopped off at the library and was relieved to see that Miz Garrison wasn't at the circulation desk. I didn't recognize the younger woman who was there instead. I made my way back to the fiction section and sure enough, the shelf of Miz Bourdillon's novels was still almost empty, just like before. But one book was there, a different one, and I grabbed it and probably had a ridiculous smile on my face when I set it down for the librarian to scan.

"You and half of America are reading her books," she commented, not really looking at me. "Did you enjoy this one?" She patted the cover of the one I was returning.

"Mighty good. Yeah. First one of hers I've read." Then I remembered that I'd told Miz Garrison I was getting the book for Libby. "Read it after my wife. Now she wants another one."

"Well, this one is actually my favorite, I think," she said, as she checked it out and handed it to me. "It takes place during the Depression, but it's very relevant for today." She cocked her head. "Strange, isn't it, how historical fiction can foreshadow the very future *future,* if you understand what I mean."

"Strange, yep. That's the word." I had thought the very same thing about the novel I just finished. Took place in the 1950s, but spoke to me as if she'd set the whole thing in my little town in present day.

I left the library feeling real smug and comfortable to have another one of Miz Bourdillon's books with me, but I didn't know exactly why. When I got home I had barely cut the engine and stepped outside the cab when Libby flew out of the house and into my arms and hugged me real tight.

"You're my big cuddly bear!" She sounded happy. "I'm sorry I was hard on you. I know you're worried about Jase, and you're doing your best. You'll take care of us. You always do. And I love you, Henry. You remember that."

I put my hand on her cheek real soft-like. "Thank you, Libs. I don't deserve you one bit, but I sure love you too."

"We got some positive news, finally. The surgeon's assistant called, and they've scheduled the surgery for Friday, so we have to take Jase in the night before. But it's a different hospital this time. Dr. Martin said it's one of the best in the country for heart surgery. He prefers it, since this time it's open-heart surgery —" She stopped and sniffed. "But Jase will have the best treatment possible, and I told my boss, and he let me off for Friday and Monday. It sounds like the hospital is really nice, and it has a place for families to stay. Isn't that great? And now that you and Birch got another job that pays so well —" She stopped again. "Henry, are you okay? You look like you're going to be sick."

"It's good news, Libs, about the doctor and all. But I'm beat. Lemme take a little nap, and then you and me and Jase'll go out to a restaurant and celebrate."

She wrapped her arms around me and said, "That will be perfect. Perfect."

I lay there in bed trying to figure it out. I shouldn't have mentioned Birch's name to Libby. Didn't want him dragged into this mess. Poor Libby thought we were doing some great service for the country to earn a bunch of extra cash. I couldn't even remember what kind of lie I'd made up.

I wondered if I should call him, though. I figured somebody was still expecting the job to be done, the "loose end" to be tied up. Should I ask Birch what to do? Or just wait to see what happened?

I'd wait. Well, heck, I knew how to do that. Been waiting most all my life.

JOSEPHINE

1976 . . . Kit stormed into the bedroom and tossed the school newspaper on the rug. "You sneaky, backstabbing excuse for a sister. . . ." And there followed a string of curse words that Josephine had never heard her sister use. "You wrote this about me, didn't you? You thought you'd get some attention by ratting on your big sister."

Josephine had never seen her so furious. "Kit, I didn't say one thing about you in the article."

"You might as well have just said I was an alcoholic."

"I wrote that paper for science class, and they asked me to shorten it and put it in the school paper. It had nothing to do with you."

"Right, Miss Goody-Two-shoes. As if everyone isn't going to read it and know you were talking about me. You're just jealous because you can't get a date."

"Kit, stop it! You've been drinking. You don't mean what you're saying."

Kit gave a bitter laugh.

"Everything is always about you," Josephine

pronounced in a tiny voice. Her hands were shaking, and she felt like a child. "I think you need to get help, Kit. And that has nothing to do with the article. I'm worried about you."

"Help? Ha! Where am I going to get 'help'?"

"There are loads of places, Kit."

"And you think our darling, sophisticated parents would put their daughter in a rehab center, and ruin their pristine reputation?"

"Of course they would. They aren't exactly thrilled to have a daughter who's an alcoholic. You're breaking their hearts."

Kit slapped Josephine with such force that she stumbled backward and fell against the wall. Then Kit ran to Josephine, crying, "I'm sorry! I'm so sorry. Oh, JoJo. What is happening to me?"

Josephine pretended her head wasn't pounding ferociously from where she'd collided with the wall. She sank to the ground with Kit beside her and held her sister in her arms. "I write what touches my heart, Kit. What I care about. Injustice, cruelty, prejudice, addiction, depression. I know they're upsetting things in our society, but I can't stop writing about them. I swear I never meant to hurt you. Can't you see? In my stories, there is always hope."

"I lost hope in hope a long time ago," Kit said, chuckling a little at her play on words.

"Then let me believe for you, Kit. I'll help you find a place to go. I'll explain it to Mother and Father. Please, Kit. I love you, Kit. Please."

Kit's face was streaked with tears. "Do you really love me, JoJo? In spite of all the mess I've made of my life?"

She hugged her big sister close. "I love you just as you are, a beautiful mess. You're going to get through this, get stronger. . . ."

She did love her sister, so much it caused her stomach to cramp every time Kit lay drunk on the bed. She would help her. But sometimes Josephine wondered if she carried the yoke of her sister's defiance, if it weighed her down more than it weighed down Kit herself. Sometimes, Josephine felt she was responsible for her parents' reputation and Kit's sanity and a whole lot of other problems from friends who constantly confided in her. And it all felt way too heavy on her own skinny shoulders.

Lord, I don't know how to put down all these things I'm carrying. It seems like the wedge is growing bigger and bigger and that deep, dark hole is beckoning. But you say that your yoke is easy and your burden is light. I'm afraid I don't understand what you mean at all.

1978 . . . The yard smelled like spring, every tree boasting flamboyant blooms, the roses hanging heavy and pungent as they twisted up the latticework. The backyard overflowed with young graduates, the girls in bright floral sundresses and the boys in their khakis and polos. Her parents' friends stood in tight groups interspersed among the high school students.

A band played in the gazebo.

"Your parents must be so proud, Josephine. You stole the show with your valedictory speech! And a scholarship for your writing — congratulations!"

Josephine smiled politely at Mrs. Lincoln. She wished the movement would travel down to her heart and her gut, but they were fluttering with fear. Kit had called last night to report on her latest modeling excursions in Venice. Her parents had begged her weeks ago to come home for Josephine's graduation, but if Kit even remembered the date, she made no reference to it on the phone. "Venice is a dream world, JoJo. You should come on over."

Kit's modeling career had started after high school and took her first to New York and then to Paris. And though Kit only confided the truth of this pseudo glamourous career to Josephine, her parents weren't fooled. Josephine watched them shrink more and more into their isolated lives, a smile pasted on her mother's face as she described Kit's life in the best possible light. In truth, as Kit's letters to Josephine revealed, Kit was in self-destruct mode. Drugs, boys, fashion, self-absorption.

"Doing okay, Miss Josy?"

Josephine turned to see Terence, impeccably dressed in his tux, sweat beading on his forehead, his snow-white hair a mass of tiny curls. He held a tray filled with cheese straws and little cucumber sandwiches cut in triangles.

She reached out and took his free hand. "Oh, Terence. You know I'm not. Kit is killing herself, and that is killing Mother and Father. And they fight all the time." She felt her eyes brim with tears.

Terence squeezed her hand and looked her in the eyes, his so dark and full of love. "Miss Josy. This is your party. All these folks are here to celebrate you. So for this night, I'm asking the good Lord to help you forget about Kit and enjoy what is here. You deserve that, young lady. Ain't nothing you can do about Kit tonight, angel."

1979 . . . The ski camp with her college church group during spring break was supposed to be fun, but she'd had such dark thoughts pursuing her for the last weeks. Bad news from home, from Kit, and not a date in sight. While her hall mates primped in their beautiful gowns, preparing for the spring formal, Josephine locked herself away in the library.

Here in the mountains of Colorado, she felt surrounded by hyperbole — the brightest white snow, the boldest cobalt blue skies, the deepest green firs, their branches peeking out under the heavy sleeves of snow. Josephine fell to her knees and cried out to God. "Help me, Lord! Help me leave the guilt and helplessness behind!"

That evening, as the students gathered around a bonfire, she watched Marcia, the beautiful thirtysomething chaperone, smiling with warmth and joy into the night. The next day Josephine rode on the ski lift with her and found her to be a fascinating, wise, and godly woman, an artist who exuded compassion. Josephine felt it so strongly, a tug in her spirit. God had put Marcia in her path to help her.

Heart hammering forcefully, Josephine made her lips pronounce the words. "Marcia, could I talk to you sometime . . . about some things . . . things about faith? I mean, could we maybe meet for lunch or coffee once in a while when I get back to school?"

She felt her face turn scarlet, but Marcia, eyes soft and deep, said, "I'd like that, Josephine. I'd like that very much."

Their weekly meetings were a gift, a great gift, and gradually Marcia helped her understand how to let go of the burdens, helped her redirect her spiraling thoughts, pointed her more fully to Christ, encouraged her to meditate on Scripture, to let God's Word tape over the cruel voices that played like a cassette in her mind. The voices didn't go away completely, but she learned to recognize them sooner, to prepare herself for the mental fight. And she learned that she could not fix her family.

"You can't carry them, Josephine," Marcia repeated often.

But letting go of that voice, the one that told her to be perfect and that saving her family was her responsibility, was easier said than done.

HENRY

Talk about coincidence, well, this sure was one. My boy was gonna have his surgery at the same hospital where Miz Bourdillon laid in her coma. Libby said they told her it was one of the fifty best hospitals for heart stuff in the country, so I figured that was pretty good.

The first time Jase had surgery he'd been way down in Georgia — emergency when we were visiting Libby's folks. The other two times he was operated on in a hospital in a nearby town. But this time the surgeon said we'd go to Mission Hospital, and when Libby said that name I got to feeling queasy. I knew that hospital. I'd just been there.

That was a good coincidence, right? Maybe I could keep an eye on Miz Bourdillon.

Or maybe it was a bad coincidence. Maybe the cops would be keeping an eye on me.

I had way too many thoughts in my head.

Jase ordered the biggest steak on the menu at Bourbon's Steak House, and that made Libby glow. Sometimes she did that — had this glow about her, like maybe an angel had just taken up residence inside her and the goodness was shining out. Or maybe it was her own goodness. And Jase had a little color in his face too.

"Papa, Momma said we're going to a big hospital and it has a pretty view from the windows of all the trees changing color. Won't that be something, Papa? My kindergarten teacher last year told us all about the different leaves, and I'm gonna lay there in the bed after they fix my heart and look at the leaves and try to figure out which ones is oak and maple and pine and hickory."

He coughed, choking a little — that happened if he got to talking too much while he was eating, and Libby stopped glowing and said, "Take your time chewing, Jase."

I tried to distract her while Jase caught his breath, but no luck. Jase started wheezing, and then all the sudden we were rushing him out of that restaurant and by the time we got to the little ER in town, well, he was just about green.

When they got him stabilized, the young doc on call met us out in the crowded waiting room where a baby was crying and a little boy with a broken arm was moaning and an old man was doubled over in some kind of excruciating pain. He said, "I've called your surgeon, Dr. Martin. He wants the ambulance to take your son on to Asheville. Now. He'll meet you there and decide if surgery can wait until Friday."

Libby got in that ambulance, looking all rigid and terrified as she sat beside our boy. Then the doors closed and the driver pulled out into the road, the lights flashing red emergency and the siren screaming its warning.

So there I was again, driving on that winding I-40 in the night, and all I could think was how Miz Bourdillon didn't die and how Jase might be the one who died instead.

And what kind of coincidence would that be?

CHAPTER 7

Tuesday

PAIGE

Aunt Kit insisted on staying with Momma that night, along with Daddy, of course, so Drake and Hannah and I went back to the house. Mrs. Swanson had turned on all the lights and set the mail in the kitchen — another three bags filled with letters — and placed on the counter four boxes of cakes and cookies from our favorite bakery, the French Broad Chocolate Lounge. She'd also left a note: *Milton howling his head off so I'm taking him to sit with me. I'll be up till nine. If you get in after that, just let him sleep over here.*

I headed to Mrs. Swanson's at six thirty, passing the other houses spread out along the ridge, each with a wraparound porch that gave a stunning view of the mountains. I stopped in front of Drake's former home, three houses down the street from ours, on the same side. It was lit up and a dozen pumpkins adorned the stone steps out front. Drake's parents had not liked Halloween, so seeing the eerily smiling pumpkins, carved and candlelit, made me do a double take. Drake's mother kept the house until Drake finished high school and then put it up for sale back in 2011. They'd had to beg, borrow, and steal to get a buyer, after the housing crisis of '08. But now somebody had made it their cozy Halloween home.

I came to Mrs. Swanson's house and climbed the long stone stairway. The Swansons had been the first to move into the elite subdivision nestled on Bearmeadow Mountain when it was developed in the late eighties. They had moved their brood — four children and goodness knows how many cats and dogs — to this mountain paradise, which nonetheless was accessible to Asheville's best schools. Her husband passed away a few years back, and all the kids were grown, married, and had kids of their own, so Mrs. Swanson managed her mountain home alone. She turned seventy last year, but according to her youngest daughter had more energy than all four of her children and their spouses and kids combined. I believed it. Though small in size, her strength of character matched the mountains around us. When I was a kid, if she ever glared at me, shaking her head, her permed white hair looking like a starched cloud, blue eyes blazing holy wrath, well, I paid attention.

I knocked on the door, and when Mrs. Swanson opened it our Milton greeted me with a woof and planted his paws on my sweat shirt. I grabbed his collar before he could take off down the street for home.

"Come on in, dearie." Mrs. Swanson ushered me into the hallway as I practically lifted Milton up to keep him inside. "Now calm down! For heaven's sake!" she addressed the dog crossly, and he gave a little groan and sank to the ground. "How is she doing, Paige dear? Any change?"

"Not much. Her score has only gone up a little." At her blank stare, I clarified. "They rate her reactions, brain function, and other stuff. She's twitched her fingers and flickered her eyes, which means she is no longer considered to be in a completely vegetative state."

"Whatever that means. She's only half a vegetable? Good grief! Well, I suppose that's good to hear. I left the cakes on the counter and put a few more casseroles in the fridge, and made a list of everyone who came by or called."

"You're a saint."

She scrunched up her brow so that her white eyebrows almost touched in the center and said, "We're all saints, Paige, every single believer." Mrs. Swanson attended my parents' church and had a very literal way of interpreting the Bible.

"Yes, of course. But you're getting extra jewels in your crown this week." I thought she'd like my biblical reference. I winked at her, and she lifted her eyebrows and gave a fake-pious smile.

"I hope you've kept some food for yourself," I added. "We'll never be able to eat it all."

"I wouldn't dream of it. You've got guests coming and going all the time." She lowered her voice. "Saw Josy's sister came. Finally."

I did not want to go near that remark. Mrs. Swanson detested Aunt Kit — how was that for Christian charity? Mainly because she thought Aunt Kit was a renegade who "didn't deserve to have poor Josy for a sister" — and our neighbor almost worshipped Momma. Of course she wouldn't call it that.

She took a breath and continued, "That red-haired policewoman's been poking through all the mail, yesterday and today. Always flashes her badge at me and never smiles. Just sticks her big chest out and makes her way into your house. Very irritating."

"She's just doing her job."

"Well, I'll bet you anything that woman considers it part of her job to go through the fridge and eat whatever she darn well pleases!"

I laughed. "Well, if that's the case, she doesn't leave any evidence."

Mrs. Swanson wasn't impressed with my joke.

"Thanks for everything, Mrs. Swanson. And the nurses said that soon Momma can have visitors besides family. So I hope you can come by in a day or two."

Her face lit up. She reached down and rubbed her wrinkled hand into Milton's sandy coat and said, "Well, I would appreciate that very much."

"And I know she is hearing what we say. I just know it. So you be sure and tell her happy things when you come."

Hannah fixed the three of us a feast from all the food the friends from church and school and Daddy's work had left, and Drake started a fire, and we sat in the den with Milton eyeing us pitifully. Occasionally I'd toss him a piece of meat, completely against the house rules, but it seemed to me like almost all the rules had already been broken. The den — we called it the family room — had a cathedral ceiling and a stone fireplace that took your breath away. On either side was a huge picture window with an amazing view of the mountains in the distance. We used to have the youth group from church over in the fall and winter when Hannah was in high school. We'd roast marshmallows and snuggle under fleece blankets, the girls giggling about their latest crush and the boys talking about some video game until the youth pastor made a joke and got us back to talking about boys and video games *and* God. Somehow Bull — that's what we called him — always tied in real life with religion. I used to love those youth weekends at our house.

In the winter Momma and Daddy and Hannah and Drake and I would all cuddle on the oversized couch and watch it snow outside — which quite honestly was better than going to the movies. Momma would say we were "experiencing joy in the exquisite simplicity of beholding creation." That's how she put it. Momma believed that God was always preaching sermons to us through nature and that anybody with an ounce of sense could see it, all planned out and everything.

So Hannah and Drake and I sat on the leather couch — we'd pulled it smack-dab in front of the fireplace as we'd done on a hundred other occasions — and it felt just right and at the same time not right at all, because how in the world could we keep enjoying this room without Momma lighting all the candles on the mantle and then slipping around the corner into the kitchen, where she'd be humming an old Baptist hymn and baking us something sugary and chocolate?

Milton rested his head on Drake's knees, then wiggled over to Hannah, who knew just how to rub his tummy until he almost moaned with pleasure. We laughed a little at that, but the conversation lagged.

"When are you going back to school, Bourdy?"

"The teachers are chill — they know I need to be with Momma. No big deal."

"Really?" Drake looked unconvinced.

"I'm serious. You think I can concentrate on AP French and physics and precalc with Momma lying in a coma? And I'm not going to spend my day in school when I can be hanging out with you and Hannie."

160

Drake shrugged, then said, "What about your soccer games?"

"I've only missed one so far. Coach has been great. She said she knows I'll make it up in effort."

Drake grinned. "No doubt about that. And Hannah, when do you go back?"

"My return ticket is for this weekend." She looked over at me. "And Daddy insists that Paige go back to school when I go back to France."

I honestly could not remember a time when the three of us were at a loss for words, but probably a whole minute passed in silence, the only sounds the crackling of the logs in the fireplace and Milton's deep breathing as he slept at Hannah's feet.

Finally Drake broke the silence. "Can we talk about it? I really need to talk about it all, but I won't if it's too upsetting."

"No, I mean, yes." Hannah pulled her hair back into a ponytail, then let it fall again to her shoulders. "Yes. Me too. Paige, tell us every single thing that has happened in the past weeks and months. Not just those fan letters. But anything else, anything. . . ." She sighed. "Anything else about Momma."

Finally, I thought. I started out cautiously. "Well, nothing that made me suspicious. No one was prowling about. The new novel

161

got pretty good reviews — not stellar, but pretty good. And from what I could tell, it was selling okay —"

"I'm not asking about the book, Paige!" Hannah sounded annoyed. "I want to know how Momma and Daddy were doing. Had there been any problems?"

When Hannah pronounced the word *problems,* the three of us knew what she meant. I shrugged. "No, they were fine." But my voice sounded off, even to me. Momma and Daddy were never just *fine.* Their relationship could never be defined by a one-syllable word of mediocrity. "Momma got upset about those letters, but otherwise she kept to the routine and wrote all day and took Milton for two walks same as always, morning and evening. And sometimes she and Daddy would sit out on the porch before dinner, and after dinner if the night was clear they'd go out and look at the stars." Far from the city lights, we could see thousands of stars on clear, dark nights.

"She was doing some kind of research for the next novel, and occasionally she'd ask me to look up something. She knew I was busy, reading about different colleges and with soccer and debate club. And she had the youth group over once last month — you know how she likes that — and I even

162

went. Things seemed normal." Another word that did not in any way apply to Momma.

"But what about Daddy? How was he?"

"Worried," I blurted out without thinking. "No, not worried. Preoccupied." There, I'd admitted it.

"About what?" This from Drake.

"No idea. It didn't seem like a big deal, but you know he's never missed one of my soccer games before, and he forgot, he *forgot*, twice, in September."

"Your dad forgot about a *soccer* game?" Drake sounded incredulous.

"That's what he claimed, but when he said it, Momma looked like she might cry."

"Did Momma attend your games?"

"Oh, sure, she and Milton were there. But Daddy not being there freaked me out a little. I mean, seems like he could have come up with a better excuse than that he forgot. He never forgets anything."

Drake got up and put another log on the fire, and Hannah took our empty plates back to the kitchen — Milton had licked them clean — and when she came back, I could tell she was fighting back tears.

"Sorry, Hannie."

"No, we asked. We needed to hear." She

sat back down on the couch with me in the middle.

"It's just . . ." I cleared my throat. Why was I sweating to pronounce the next words in front of my two most favorite people in the world? "It's just that somehow, the way he was acting reminded me of The Awful Year."

Hannah and Drake glanced at each other with something like dread in their eyes. I shouldn't have pronounced those words. Not yet. Then they each put an arm around me, so that we were sandwiched close together, just like all those other times, and I got up my nerve and asked, "Hannah, what do you remember most about The Awful Year?"

"I remember that you cried every night for a month when Drake's parents split up, and I remember Daddy taking us out on the porch and telling us about Grandmom dying, and I remember how devastated Momma was at the funeral. And then Granddad died a few months later. And Aunt Kit was drunk at Granddad's funeral, and I think that just was the final straw to break Momma's heart. And Daddy sent her away to La Grande Motte for a few months, just to rest."

I nodded. Occasionally Momma went to

our grandparents' place alone. To write. But after her parents' deaths, she went simply to recover.

Then I reached for Hannah's hand and held on tight and whispered, "And what do you remember about Daddy during that time?"

But Hannah pulled her hand away, stood up, and started pacing in front of the fireplace. Drake took my hand in both of his. I begged Hannah with my eyes, but she shook her head and kept pacing. "I can't remember anything about Daddy. I can't let myself remember anything."

JOSEPHINE

1980 . . . Mount St. Helens had just erupted the week before, and if her classmates weren't talking about that, or stressing about end-of-the-year exams, they were raving over the new Star Wars film. But Josephine could not engage in any small talk. She'd never been good at it, but now her mind was completely preoccupied with him.

The first thing she had noticed were his eyes. His kind eyes. Josephine read eyes easily, quickly, almost immediately. Then she always asked herself: Do the eyes show hope and goodness? Do they show faith and love? How she longed for the eyes of those she

165

cared about to shine with these qualities. But in Father's eyes she read aloof disapproval and underneath that, a level of pure fear that someday soon his persona would crumble. Mother's eyes held disappointment and a fierce pride. And Kit's — oh, dear, defiant Kit. Not even rehab had changed her eyes.

But Patrick's eyes were a warm brown shade of kindness. The only other eyes she'd known that held such kindness were Terence's. It still broke her heart to think of her old friend. He had passed away the year before, and how she missed him.

She'd met Patrick for the first time at the end of a long Saturday with a bunch of rowdy kids. Every week she tutored a few junior high girls with the Christian parachurch group she belonged to on campus. And once a month all the tutors from several different colleges got together to play sports and feed about a hundred of these children.

She had her hands thrust in red, sudsy water, washing a big metal pan, scrubbing the stubborn bits of burnt lasagna that were still clinging to the sides. Dozens of other pots and pans were stacked all around her.

"Need some help?" he'd asked.

"No, I'm fine," she'd said without even looking up.

"You sure are," he had replied in a teasing

way, and that's when she spun around expecting to see another flirtatious jock, but instead, all she saw were his eyes. Then his face — which was not bad to look at either. She'd softened.

"You haven't slowed down all day."

She shrugged. "This is one of my favorite days of the month."

"Really?"

"I enjoy getting off campus, forcing myself to stop studying for a while."

"That's why you come, to stop studying?"

She laughed. "I come because I love the kids — they're so real. Sometimes my life at school seems so small." She blushed. Why was she admitting deep thoughts — well, deeper than Star Wars and exams — to a stranger? "Do you go to Belleview? I haven't seen you before."

"I play on the soccer team — for your rival."

"Ah. And why do you come here?"

"Well, it's definitely not because I have to force myself to stop studying." He'd given a warmhearted, full-bodied laugh. He had the trace of an accent . . . French, she thought. "I come to teach the kids a little about soccer, watch them have fun, and talk about faith."

She'd fallen for him hard and attended almost every one of his soccer games, cheering unabashedly for the rival team when they played her school. He was tall and sturdy, broad shouldered, athletic. But so unimpressed with himself or anyone else. At ease with himself. Patrick Bourdillon, despite being French and having an aristocratic and romantic sounding name, was utterly true to what he believed in — simplicity and fun. To Patrick, life was a game and he loved playing it. There was always a chance for a comeback or a last-second save.

He lived his Christian faith in much the same way — exuberantly, naturally, contagiously. Josephine never really understood what attracted Patrick to her — the brooding, melancholic, perfectionistic girl — but she was thankful for it, whatever it was.

Every star was out behind her parents' house. Patrick had agreed to be her date for their summer party. Josephine wished she could have introduced him to Terence.

"You look very handsome in that suit," she said. "Almost as good as in your soccer uniform."

"Wouldn't want to disappoint your parents the first time they meet me." He took her hand, and she felt light and carefree. "So tell me a story, Feeny." She liked that he'd found a nickname for her that no one else used. And she liked that he wanted to hear her stories.

"How about a poem?"

"Poem will do."

She stared up at the dotted sky, then closed her eyes and listened to the blending of peoples' voices.

"A million stars chattered on about earth
Like who was poor, and what the rich were worth.
Enough to feed the Milky Way one night?
Enough to follow Saturn's nocturnal flight?
God said, 'Not paradise or sky or cloud
Holds wealth of which humanity is proud
'Tis paper and coins of which the heav'ns know not
That bring man wealth until his mind's forgot
The beauty of night, the strength of sun and moon;
Nor doth he know his wealth will vanish soon."

Patrick clapped his hands, lifted an eyebrow and asked, "Did you just make that up?"

"Of course. It's a silly habit. Making up poems, the first thing that comes to my mind. They never mean anything."

"That one kind of means something, doesn't it? And in iambic pentameter to boot."

"Well, well. My soccer player knows about iambic pentameter!" She laughed. Oh, how he made her laugh, even when that wasn't his intention. "Don't be impressed, Patrick. It's the only thing I know how to do — make up poems and stories. I can't cook or dance or . . ."

But he grabbed her around the waist and said, "I'll teach you to dance. And as for cooking, my French grandmother has taught me a thing or two over the years."

And she laughed again, a trill, a delight.

That first time Josephine introduced Patrick to her family, Mother and Father raised their eyebrows. He'd grown up in France, his family was part of the bourgeoisie. He even had a lovely accent. But soccer? Soccer wasn't a career. Soccer was just a game.

Kit, home on a rare visit, raised her eyebrows too, but Josephine recognized, with a sick little twitter in her stomach, what those raised eyebrows meant. "I think soccer players have the sexiest legs," Kit purred.

Patrick chuckled. "If you say so, Kit," and he'd winked at Josephine.

"Well, go on. Say what everyone else says." They were walking to his car after the visit.

"Which is? You have an interesting family?"

"No. That I have the most beautiful sister anyone has ever seen."

He actually looked pained at her statement. "I wasn't paying a lot of attention." He pulled Josephine close, holding her around the waist.

"But I do know something. She has an absolutely beautiful sister. And she's the one I want."

Josephine couldn't find her voice for a few moments. "Thank you for saying it, Patrick."

"I said it because I meant it. I don't give fake compliments, Feeny. What you see is what you get."

He drove her back to school, parked his car in a spot reserved for staff, and laughed when Josephine chided him.

"It's two in the morning. I can leave it here for thirty minutes."

They strolled across the campus, and he left her at the entrance to her dorm. "I know that probably was no fun, growing up in your sister's shadow. But that's over. Let it be over."

When he kissed her, every thought left her head and she melted into him, right there on the dorm steps where anyone could see.

1981 . . . He made everything seem possible. All the stuff that overwhelmed her, to Patrick was a game. But she had to tell him. "Sometimes I get very down. I go to really dark places in my mind, Patrick, and it scares me. I start wondering if maybe all the stuff I say I believe doesn't really work for me. I'm afraid to tell you the truth, afraid you'll freak out and go away. . . ."

"Shhh. I'm not going anywhere, Feeny." His big rough hand covered hers. "I'll be right here, no matter how dark it gets."

"Do you think it's true, Patrick, what the psalmist says? 'If I say, "Surely the darkness will overwhelm me, and the light around me will be night, even the darkness is not dark to You. And the night is as bright as the day. Darkness and light are alike to You."' Is it true?"

"Feeny, what makes you ask me that question?"

"I believe Jesus is with me, all the time. But if He is and yet I still feel such darkness, such shame, well, maybe I'm just making the whole thing up. Maybe the idea of redemption, of forgiveness, is too big." She watched to see if he backed away as her mother had the one time she'd tried to explain the darkness to her.

"Oh, sugar," Mother had said, "you are sweetness incarnate. Don't you let anything worry your little head."

The only person who had ever really understood was Kit. But Kit had descended into a much darker pit than Josephine could even imagine, and she couldn't reach her anymore.

"I have my faith in Christ, I have material comfort, I have work that blesses me and others and mostly, mostly, I have you. So how can there still be darkness?"

"You're an artist, Feeny. You have a mind that thinks deeply about things. And I've never met another person who is as sensitive as you are — you feel everything, and it becomes a lot to carry."

Yes, for so long it had been a crushing load that weighed her down, that bent her to the ground.

He cupped her chin in his hand. "Hey, Feeny. Feeny, look at me. I'll help you carry it. We'll figure it out together, okay?"

1984 . . . It was just like Kit to make a grand entrance on Josephine's wedding day. Her bridesmaids were fiddling with her hair and her mother was fastening the last of the beautifully covered silk buttons on the wedding dress when Kit stumbled into the church parlor. She mumbled a feeble excuse for her tardiness. Then, "Will someone pull-eese help me fix this dress?" she demanded, mixing in plenty of four-letter epithets.

Embarrassed, Josephine said, "Mother, you go on and help her. I'm fine."

But as her mother whisked Kit to the ladies' room, Josephine missed those last whispered moments between mother and daughter, and she felt a pinching in her soul.

Thank goodness Kit didn't make a fool of herself during the ceremony. Josephine looped her arm through her father's and pecked his cheek. "My little girl. My little angel." At least Father was sober for the occasion.

All through the reception Josephine smiled and nodded and watched Kit out of the corner of her eye. Kit insisting on a dance with Patrick, Kit talking way too loudly, her words slurred, Kit sobbing when Josephine tossed the bouquet, Kit wearing the bridesmaid's gown so low off the shoulder that it showed way too much cleavage.

Josephine pretended not to notice, pretended that her dear friends who surrounded her and hugged her and whispered silliness in her ear could truly shield her from Kit's antics. In reality, she was counting the minutes until Patrick would spirit her off with no way for Kit to follow.

They spent two weeks on their honeymoon in France, tucked away at the chic apartment in La Grande Motte. Alone! There in La Grande Motte, lying next to her lover, her husband, with the fiery sun setting over the Mediterranean just outside the window, the demons were far, far away, and she felt at peace.

The second week they ventured three hours north to Lyon to visit Patrick's parents who, in turn, drove them around France so she could meet all the relatives who hadn't been able to attend the wedding. Then they came back south to see Patrick's beloved grandmother who lived in Montpellier, and all the while Josephine blushed and babbled in baby French. A fairy tale — she was living a fairy tale. No screaming parents, no inebriated Kit, no taunting whispers in her mind. Just Patrick and France.

PAIGE

We ended the evening by praying for Momma — well, Drake and Hannah prayed really sincere, heartfelt prayers, and I just listened. Then Drake pulled out the sofa bed in the den, which he'd slept on for months after his parents' divorce, and Hannah went up to her old room on the second floor. I had planned to go to sleep too, and climbed to the third floor. But instead of turning to go into my room, I went into Momma's office. The moon, a dazzling white, made the tree outside her window cast dancing shadows across the spines of those old, old books. I watched them for a moment, then flipped on the lights.

Every book in The Chalet held a memory. I reached to a shelf and fingered the brittle cover jacket of *Gone with the Wind*. 1936, first edition. Signed by Mrs. Mitchell herself. Beside it, early editions of *The Wonderful Wizard of Oz* and *Alice's Adventures in Wonderland.* I could smell my past in those books, could feel the delight of sneaking into The Chalet and finding a stool and standing up high to get to this shelf. I'd pick one — maybe *The Black Stallion Returns* or *Misty of Chincoteague* or *A Little Princess* — and I'd cuddle up with my book, snuggled in my bed across the hall under a hundred-year-old quilt, with my ceiling falling away on either side of my bed, just as it did in this room. During The Awful Year, when I was nine, I read a children's illustrated version of *A Tale of Two Cities* three times, finding in that tale of woe the only way I knew of escaping our own tale of woe with the whispers, the clawing grief, the hollow sound of an empty house.

"Momma! What's the matter, Momma?"

I escaped The Awful Year. That was the title we gave it, Hannah and I. We titled everything in our lives, as if Momma were writing our stories — which in a sense she was. Most of the titles held a little hint of playfulness: The Year of the Crazy Crushes, The Month of Mono and Murder Mysteries, The Tequila Time, The Magnificent Month at the Motte, The Days of Drake, and on and on and on. . . .

But we found nothing the least bit humorous about The Awful Year, so the name stayed simply awful: the year both of Momma's parents died, the year of the financial decline, the year when Drake's parents divorced. The year that Daddy . . .

But I couldn't go there. Could not revisit that pain.

I ran my fingers over the novels' spines, then put the stool back by the wall, as if I were afraid Detective Blaylock would notice that I'd moved it and question me.

I sat down at Momma's desk and opened her laptop, which Officer Hanley had returned. The computer lit up with Hannah's lovely face bent over that sunflower. I went to Momma's fan mail account and read through the latest emails.

Please get well, Mrs. Bourdillon. You are my favorite author, and your books have changed my life.

You've given me healing and offered me hope.

I'm sorry I never wrote you before. I hope and pray that you can read this, or someone will read it to you.

I'm praying for you, Mrs. Bourdillon.

Email after email, from the thirteen-year-old girl who dreamed of being a writer to the eighty-three-year-old great-grandmother who read all of Momma's books and then passed them on to her daughters and granddaughters, they all had a similar thread. *Thank you for writing your books. They've been important in my life.*

Momma always said that the painful things in life got redeemed in her stories. "It's like what C. S. Lewis talks about, Paige. He says that even though pain hurts, that doesn't discredit what the Bible says about people being made perfect through suffering."

I didn't want to think about C. S. Lewis and pain. I clicked back on the last email and read it again. The next time I sat with Momma, I'd read her more of these messages, as well as the snail mail. Maybe in her semivegetative state the words would travel into her brain. And lying there, as her brain rested, she'd actually believe what these people had written, and then the other things that swirled and tumbled around in her beautiful, sometimes-tormented mind would be quieted for just a little while.

HENRY

I couldn't quite believe I was here again, same as last night but with everything completely different. Dr. Martin met us at the Mission Hospital at ten that evening, and by that time Jase was in a room and pretty stable — at least he was sleeping.

"Surgery tomorrow morning — I'm bumping my other patient — he's got to have it now."

Libby was trembling. "But you said he needed to be strong enough for surgery. Is he strong enough now?"

And there was that big, important doctor towering over my little Libby, putting his big, skilled hand on her thin shoulder and saying, "I'm sorry, Mrs. Hughes, but we don't have a choice."

Libby grabbed me tight around the waist and buried her head in my chest and cried.

The surgeon's voice didn't sound soothing, but his words were okay. "Remember, Mr. and Mrs. Hughes, there's a good chance we can repair his heart so that he won't need any more surgeries."

But I didn't hear the words *repair his heart* after Dr. Martin had left. All I heard again and again and again was that maybe my boy wouldn't need any more surgeries. Maybe not, because he'd be dead.

Libs and I decided she'd go on and drive back home and get to her work on Wednesday morning while I stayed during the operation. She couldn't risk losing her job — that'd mean we'd lose our health insurance too. It didn't pay for a lot, but it was something. I knew Mr. Dan wasn't gonna like my call, but at least we'd finished the project that had been stressing him out for the past month. And Libby's boss, well, he counted on her to keep his schedule — said she was the most organized assistant he'd ever had — but he didn't have a real tender side.

"He's got several important meetings tomorrow, and if I'm not there, he'll throw a fit." Poor Libby; she had a boss with a temper almost as bad as mine.

The doctor had already told us we couldn't stay in Jase's room that night, but a nurse explained to Libby about the place where families of patients from out of town could stay.

"It's free, babe," she reported to me, "and there's a room open tonight. I'll drop you off there, and they'll get you back in the morning so you can see Jase before surgery."

The hope that sang out of Libby warmed me a bit, helped calm all the crazy thoughts that kept rumbling around in my mind.

About midnight Libs and I went into Jase's room. All the machines were lighted up and helping him breathe, and Libs went over and bent down and brushed away all that hair and kissed him on the forehead.

"I love you, Jase," she whispered. "I love you so much it hurts. A good hurt, you know. A corn-puddin' kind of good." He didn't wake up, and I didn't say anything to him at all, because my voice wasn't always as calming on him.

Libby followed the directions to the hospitality house, a big ole sprawling place, far as I could tell in the dark, and soon as we drove in that circle driveway, an older couple came out to greet us, real friendly like, even though it was after midnight.

I left my overnight bag in the lobby, and I walked Libby out to the pickup. The moon was full and so bright. I held her and said, "It's gonna work out — it's all gonna work out. Now you drive real safe back home and try to sleep a little. I'll call you at work soon as he gets out of surgery."

"If I see my boss and explain it, I know he'll let me come back. I just have to see him in person. Then he'll understand."

I watched her drive away, my pretty little wife. I knew she'd put on the radio to some religious station that played hopeful music or maybe some kind of sermon all night long. She'd drive and cry and pray.

The old couple showed me to my room, and I thanked them. For the past few hours I hadn't thought one second about Miz

Bourdillon, but now, in that real nice big room with her book as my only companion, I started reading again. And I couldn't help thinking about the kindness of the staff at the hospital and that couple here at the hospitality house waiting up for us, and being so kind and thoughtful, and how they wouldn't be welcoming us like this if they knew who I was.

But they didn't. Thank God, they didn't.

CHAPTER 8

Wednesday

PAIGE

Aunt Kit met Drake and Hannah and me at the door of Momma's room, looking a little crumpled, but her eyes were bright. "She squeezed my hand! Twice! In response to a question. I think she is hearing us."

I felt two things at once: a leap of joy and a stab of jealousy. Momma had squeezed Aunt Kit's hand? *Aunt Kit?* We'd had no sign of movement from her for over forty-eight hours, and she'd chosen to respond to Aunt Kit?

Immediately I berated myself. Momma had shown signs of understanding something, and it certainly didn't matter who had asked the question.

"That's awesome, Aunt Kit! Awesome," Hannah said.

"Sweet," Drake added.

183

She glowed with pleasure. Then frowned. "I'm going to need to get back to Atlanta, but I'll be here over the weekend."

I actually felt relieved at this news. Daddy and Aunt Kit had never been close, and I felt he'd rest better with her far away. "That sounds good. Thank you for coming." I gave her an awkward hug.

Hannah looped her arm through Aunt Kit's and said, "I know it's meant the world to Momma. We'll keep in touch as she progresses." Then my sister winked at me, and I watched my aunt click her way down the hall and out of the ICU as Drake and Hannah ushered her to her car.

I found Daddy sitting by Momma's bed. When I entered the room he glanced over at me and said, "She squeezed Kit's hand."

I read the expression on his face as easily as I had felt my flare of jealousy — extreme gratitude, and yet a longing for Momma to respond to him, to his voice. So far her eyes had fluttered twice — once when a nurse was administering meds and once with me — and then Hannah had felt her fingers twitch, and now she'd squeezed Aunt Kit's hand. She hadn't responded at all to Daddy.

I leaned over, resting my head on my father's curved back, circling my arms around his chest. "She's going to wake up

184

soon. I just know it. But until she does, Daddy, you have got to go home and sleep. You're going to be sick. Have you eaten anything in the last twenty-four hours?" He couldn't see me, couldn't see the fear, the tingling suspicion. Carefully I added, "And you aren't talking to us. I know you meet with Detective Blaylock several times a day, but you never tell us what you two talk about. I know everything is horrible, but please don't shut us out. Talk to me!"

He let go of Momma's hand and pivoted around. Then he turned his hollow eyes on me and reached for my hands, and his were shaking slightly. Those large hands trembled with exhaustion and emotion. "You're right, Paige. I'm so sorry."

I thought he'd stop with that admission, but his grip tightened, and he stood up and walked with me out of Momma's room, practically pulling me along. "It's just that I keep thinking this is all my fault."

"What is your fault?"

"The shooting."

I froze.

"If I'd sent her to the beach as we'd planned, it never would have happened."

I breathed again.

"I wanted her to head to La Grande Motte at the end of September for a month, as she did after every other book release. But she insisted that she should wait a little longer. She didn't want Hannah to think she was spying on her."

"They weren't even going to be in the same town!"

"No, but you know your mother. So we bought the tickets for early November, after the leaves had reached their peak over here." His voice caught a little. Shaking his head back and forth, he whispered, "I should have insisted."

Relief flooded through me. Daddy had not been brooding about The Awful Year and hidden secrets. He had simply been blaming himself for poor timing. A feeling of protection for my father surged through me, almost like the shock I'd gotten the week before when I'd accidently touched the knife to the side of the toaster as I was trying to fish out the toast. A zap — strong, warm, electrifying. Almost too enthusiastically I said, "But Daddy, think about it. If someone wanted to shoot Momma that bad — they'd figure out another time and another way, don't you think?"

He cocked his head. "Maybe. Maybe."

"Well, one thing I know is it's not your fault." I threw my arms around his neck and

186

felt gratified with the powerful hug he returned.

"Thank you, Paige. We're going to get through this."

"Go home and rest. Aunt Kit is leaving, so you should be able to get some sleep."

He gave a little chuckle and nodded.

"Drake and Hannah and I are here. Go home. The fridge is crammed with food."

"Okay."

"And I took Milton to Mrs. Swanson's. I think she's having the time of her life keeping watch over the house, collecting the casseroles and mail, and taking care of the dog. But she'll probably let you have him back, if you beg."

Daddy actually grinned at that remark, which felt like progress and hope.

Our father played at life. Hannah and I had always loved his perspective, especially since Momma was often brooding, temperamental, and overly sensitive. And with Daddy, we got to be athletes, and we loved it. He'd kicked a soccer ball with us from the time we were tiny. As women's soccer kept growing in the States, I hoped to follow in my father's footsteps with a soccer scholarship to college. And then follow Hannah's example and spend a year abroad in France.

But Daddy had not shown the mischievous, playful side of himself — his real self — since before the shooting, and I longed to have him back.

Aunt Kit's presence had only seemed to make it worse.

During one of her visits a month or two earlier, she must have gotten into an argument with Momma. I was at the window in my room, staring out at the stars when I heard Aunt Kit storm out of the house, slamming the door. Daddy came out seconds later, running after her. Looking down from my window I saw him grab her arm. Daddy was never one to raise his voice, and I'd never seen him grab anyone but me, and that was during The Awful Year. But he twirled her around and yelled, "Kit, you have got to leave Jo alone! Take your craziness somewhere else! You're going to be the death of her, I swear it!"

Daddy never swore or cursed, but after he pronounced that, he did swear, using words that made me blush and sent Aunt Kit away in a fury.

JOSEPHINE

1985 . . . For Josephine, marriage was bliss. Patrick played for a minor league soccer team, and she worked for a small neighborhood newspaper. Neither made much money, but they had their dreams. Someday Patrick would join a professional team, and she would write a novel. For now, they lived in a tiny apartment where they laughed and loved, far away from her mother's frantic social schedule and her father's philandering and drinking and outbursts of anger. And far from Kit, who jet-setted between Europe and America, doing what she did best — ruining her own life.

One thing Kit said, Josephine agreed with. Soccer players did have the sexiest legs. At least her soccer player did.

1986 . . . *Generous,* Josephine said to herself, looking out at the sandy dunes and the sparkling sea beyond. She felt great gratitude for Patrick's family's generosity, paying for their plane tickets to France. Every moment at La Grande Motte felt like a coming home in Josephine's spirit. While Patrick volunteered his time to travel with the Christian soccer team, she stayed in the apartment where she could watch the sun set over the Mediterranean.

And she wrote.

But she often spent the weekends in nearby Montpellier, learning to cook French style with Patrick's grandmother, Mamie Bourdillon, and practicing her fledgling French. Surprisingly enough, Mamie reminded Josephine of Terence. On the outside they had nothing in common, from their skin color and gender and language to their culture and social status. But Mamie displayed a type of no-nonsense kindness that Terence had shown too.

Josephine found herself falling in love with France when they visited that first June. She wished she never had to return to the States. She wanted to stay in this old world with its simple rhythms, like shopping at the *marché* on Saturday mornings with Mamie, whose first thought on waking was, *What shall I fix for lunch?* Mamie could have hired a full-time cook to prepare the meals, but she preferred to do it herself.

Josephine tried to imagine a life where she didn't wrestle with twenty demons before getting out of bed. Where the simple pleasure and necessity of lunch was the most important item on the day's agenda.

1987 . . . Patrick was traveling with a Christian soccer team somewhere in Africa for two long months. For the first time, the tiny apartment felt lonely. How she missed him! She snuggled in bed, reading Pat Conroy's latest disturbingly brilliant release, *The Prince of Tides.* She had stayed up way too late, caught up in the tragic tale, and had just turned out the light at one o'clock when the phone rang. She climbed out of bed and rushed to get it, expecting to hear Patrick's voice in a patch of static.

Instead she heard her mother's shrill, panicked cry. "Kit's in a coma." Then she whispered, "Drug overdose. We're so afraid, Jo."

With no way to reach Patrick, Josephine threw on a pair of jeans and drove straight to Atlanta. She sat by her sister's bed at Piedmont Hospital for three interminable days until she came out of it.

"I promise I'll sober up, JoJo. I promise," Kit mumbled.

When Josephine returned to work, her boss said, "Don't do that to me again, Jo. I know it's family, but the stories have to get out. On time."

Josephine sifted through the thick stack of multicolored index cards. Some were so worn they felt limp in her hands. Her Bible verses. Ever since the youth pastor, Fred O., had encouraged her to use Scripture to calm herself, she had begun writing the verses on index cards and carrying them with her on her daily walks. Some days she merely repeated the words to herself, but on the darkest days, she prayed them out loud, a desperate crying out to God. Today she picked two bright yellow cards, both worn thin. She prayed the verses for Kit and for herself. Verses about anger and forgiving someone time and time and time again.

After her three months in the treatment center, Kit asked to move in with Patrick and Josephine. "Just for a few weeks, JoJo. Promise. I cannot return to our parents' house of lies."

Josephine felt something inside her die.

"Feeny, I don't think it's a good idea," Patrick said when she told him of Kit's request.

"But she's my sister. I have to help her."

Two weeks turned into two months, and the cozy apartment so filled with love now felt cramped and tense. There was no room for intimacy with Kit's larger-than-life drama imposed on them.

Josephine felt the darkness creeping in on her, closer and closer, but Kit's darkness superseded her own. It was as if Kit were hijacking her life, grabbing for any attention she could get. And the way she looked at Patrick made Josephine's stomach churn.

One night Kit stepped out of the bathroom barely wrapped in a towel and stumbled into their bedroom, completely inebriated. Josephine grabbed a blanket and threw it around her. Patrick, eyes ablaze, yelled, "Get out! Get out now!"

"You can't turn me away, Pat!" slurred Kit. "You know you don't want to turn me away!"

Josephine pulled her into the kitchen. "You have to leave, Kit," she whispered. "I'm sorry, but that's it. You have to leave."

Kit gave a pitiful laugh. "You're just afraid I'll take Pat away from you! Well, I guarantee if I wanted him bad enough, you couldn't do anything about it."

Josephine felt her knees go weak. Heart hammering and in a small voice she said, "I'm not afraid, Kit. But you can't stay. I think you're jealous of my life. I want you to find the life you're meant to live. Not mine. Not Mother and Father's. Yours. And you can't find it here. I'm sure of that."

She found the courage to say the words, but it felt as though it cost Josephine her last shred of sanity.

1989 . . . The first miscarriage happened at eleven weeks. Josephine had never seen so much blood. Patrick lifted her off the kitchen floor and carried her to the car, his face pasty white amid all that red.

The second time she made it to fourteen weeks, and this time Patrick was in Africa with the soccer team. Her elderly neighbor drove her to the ER, and Patrick didn't even know anything about it for two long weeks.

Josephine tried to pull herself back from the edge of that dark hole, but she felt nothing but a withering of her soul, as if her physical and spiritual strength had dried up completely. When she read the Bible verses on the index cards, the words seemed to be in a different language, one she didn't understand at all.

When Patrick finally got back home, he knelt before her in tears. "I'm so sorry I wasn't here, Feeny. I'll quit traveling with the team. I won't leave you again."

"I don't want you to give up your dream, Patrick."

"You're more important than my dream. I love you so much, Feeny. I'll do anything for you."

She knew he spoke the truth. He cared for her, loved her so much. But sometimes she feared he loved her too much. What would he do for her? Give up his job, his calling, his dreams? Would God ask that of him?

PAIGE

When Hannah and I returned to Momma's room, Drake was bent so close to Momma that for a second I caught my breath. Was she talking to him? I watched in silence. *No, no, of course not.* But he was talking to her, low and soft.

"Momma Jo, I'm leaving now, and the

194

next time I come, we'll continue this conversation. Please don't worry. I love you, Momma Jo." He kissed her softly on the cheek, then stood up and gave a nod our way.

Any movement? I mouthed.

He shook his head.

"It almost looked like you were having a real conversation," I added when we were out of Momma's room.

"How I wish. But I believe you're right. I think she hears us. And I think she was delighted with my news."

"What news was that?"

He took my hand. "Just reminding her how much I love her and how she really saved my life. How she's family to me."

But I could tell he'd said something else too. "And?"

"And now I've got to be getting back to school. Walk me to my car?"

Hannah gave me a wink — the nerve — and went into Momma's room.

"Sure." But I didn't want him to go. I had more questions, more things I wanted to hash out with him.

The sun was bright, enhancing the colors on the trees, making them sparkle as they softly twirled in the breeze. Momma loved fall, and I had a lot of memories of hiking in the hills with her at this time of year.

"You going to hang in there, Bourdy?" The way Drake pronounced my nickname made my stomach do a little flip-flop.

"Yeah, sure. We'll figure this thing out." It came out as a squeak.

We'll figure this thing out? That's a worse line than *You've got the best bed in the whole place.*

"Agreed. So here's what I really want to say." I cocked my head to the side. "Do you remember other things about The Awful Year?"

He gave a halfhearted shrug, his posture deflating the slightest bit.

"You do remember something!" I accused.

Drake stopped, took both of my arms in his hands, and got the sweetest, saddest look on his face. Then he took his left hand and rubbed my cheek softly with the back of his hand, as he had done a hundred times before when he wanted to calm me down. Only this time it sent chills through me, and then I blushed, and all I could think of for a few seconds was how Hannah said that Drake cared deeply for me.

The gesture was kind and compassionate, but perhaps, the thought zipped through me, perhaps not like a brother stroking his sister's cheek. It unnerved me so much that

I actually jumped when Drake started talking.

"Oh, Paige. I spent half of that year on the couch in your den, pouring out my heart to your mother. Of course, I have a hundred memories."

A thought struck me, something I had never considered before. "But did Momma pour out her heart to you too? Did she tell you anything that would make what happened later make sense?"

"So many hard things happened that year. I'm sure she talked about some of them," he said vaguely.

"You won't tell me, will you? Is it to protect Daddy? Is that why?"

This time he pulled me into his arms and held me against his chest where I could hear one of our hearts — or perhaps both — thump, thump, thumping. "Paige, I promise I would tell you in a second if I remembered something from those difficult weeks and months that could shed light on what's going on right now. I promise."

Then he bent over and kissed me oh, so softly, on the cheek. He squeezed my shoulder and was gone.

I walked back into the hospital and went down to Café 509 feeling light-headed, heart and mind racing, not paying attention to anything but Drake's last comment. I actually bumped into someone who was carrying a tray, and when I looked up and muttered, "Excuse me. I'm so sorry!" I saw that it was the tattooed blond man I'd seen in the middle of the night on Monday.

He looked startled for a second, his pale eyes unfocused, then he recovered, recognized me, and said, "Hey."

"Hi. Gosh, I wasn't looking where I was going. Did anything spill?"

"Nah, just a little of my Coke. Got plenty left."

I watched him lumber over to one of the tables and sit down. He fidgeted with the paper on a candy bar, peeled it down, and took a bite of the chocolate and then a sip of his Coke. His hands were trembling, and he seemed pretty strung out.

I walked over to the table and asked, "Is your son okay?"

When he looked at me with his scary eyes, I couldn't help it, I felt sorry for him again.

"He's in surgery right now. Pretty hard on me and my wife. She's gotta be at work — she'll be heading over here in a little while. Surgery lasts a long time." He wrung his hands together. Then looked up at me again. "Got another of your mother's books. Trying to keep my mind busy." He patted the paperback that was lying beside his tray.

I stood a little way off, my hands in my jeans pockets. "I know what you mean. It's horrible to keep waiting."

"Your mom any better? Not saying too much on the news these days." Before I could answer, he added, "Never mind. I remember you don't like to talk about it. Sorry to ask."

"She's still in the coma."

"Well, I'm sorry to hear it."

"Thanks. I hope your son pulls through the surgery okay."

He nodded and turned his head down and started reading the novel, his mind seemingly a million miles away.

HENRY

He'd been in surgery for a long time. Five hours at least. Every once in a while a nurse would find me in the Pediatric ICU waiting room on the third floor and say, "He's doing fine, Mr. Hughes. Still in surgery. Don't you worry."

I didn't know what else to do with myself but read and walk and drink some more Coke.

About one or two in the afternoon, having texted Libby three times, I went back down to the cafeteria to get some lunch. I was just sitting down when I looked up and in walked Miz Bourdillon's daughter. Again.

She sat down across from me and asked, "Is he still in surgery?" She had this expression on her face, like she really cared about my boy.

"Yep. They been letting me know every hour or so how it's going. Last time the nurse said maybe only another hour. Thought I'd get a quick bite before they're done."

She was running her hands through her thick hair and staring at the novel by her mother, trying to read the title, it looked like to me.

"It's the one about the alcoholic and the way she's tryin' to make up with her family."

"Oh yeah. That one is a bit sad."

That surprised me. "Doesn't it have a happy ending?"

"No, it ends all right, but there are a lot of sad parts."

I got up my nerve and said, "Can I ask you something, Mia Bourdillon?"

"You can call me Paige."

"Okay. I'm Henry. My boy, his name is Jase." I was fiddling with the novel, turning it over in my hands. "Have you read every one of your mother's books?"

"Sure. I've read them all."

"Do you think she believes all that stuff she writes about?"

She frowned at me. "What do you mean?"

Slow down, Henry. Slow down. Don't go scaring this girl. Take it nice and easy.

"About forgiving people. Did she mean what she wrote in that first one — about the teenager forgiving the man who abused him so bad? Do you really believe people can forgive?"

She sat silent for a moment, then said, "Well, I know my mother believes in forgiveness — on an eternal scale and a very small human scale too. And I have to admit, I've seen it happen lots of times in my family's life — people forgiving each other."

I couldn't help it — I blurted out, "What does it look like?"

That made her nervous, and she started twirling a strand of her hair around her finger, staring out the window. "It's a little complicated to explain."

I didn't think she was gonna say anything else, and I was kicking myself for asking too many questions. But after a while she said, "But when it happens, you feel it, a relief, a long sip of water on the hottest day of the year."

I think she was surprised at herself, too,

because she paused again and her pretty face got all red. Then she started blinking back tears, and I was gonna say, "Never mind," but she kept talking.

"It's like Momma says — the forgiveness isn't for the one who hurt you; it's to keep all the bitterness out of your own heart. And it's spiritual. That's the only way to say it. It changes something in your heart." She smiled a little, and her face was so pretty when she did, her big brown eyes sparkling a little with tears.

"Yeah, it sounds spiritual, or something, in her books."

"I can tell you for sure that Momma believes what she writes. I don't always buy it, but she does. She's very spiritual."

"I like the things she says, but I don't think they can be true."

The girl — Paige — shrugged. "Yeah. Well, sometimes I feel that way too. But she's been through a lot and forgiven some pretty awful things." She flashed me her cute smile. "I haven't forgiven a lot of people, but somehow Momma has."

I had nothing to say to that, but fortunately my phone beeped with a text from Libs, and Paige said bye and left.

JOSEPHINE

1990 . . . It always came back to the blood. So ironic. Seeing the blood every month was a vivid reminder that she was not pregnant, but also a scarlet memory of the miscarriages. She wrote for the paper, collected rejection slips from magazines, and watched Patrick's passion ebb as he left his dream of playing on a top-level soccer team for a job in insurance.

And then the monthly blood.

Again the darkness encroached. "You've given up so much for me, Patrick, and I can't give you the one thing we both long for."

"We're okay, just you and me, Feeny."

But every phone call with her mother suggested a new treatment or asked if she had contacted a different infertility specialist.

"Yes, we've tried, Mother," she'd confide. "But I've gotten pregnant before. The doctors say it will just take time."

Josephine thought about loss and how it drew so many closer to God. She reached out for her Bible and whispered, "Just make everything I go through worth it, Lord. I don't know how you'll do it. But please just somehow make it worth it to you."

1992 . . . When Patrick found her in tears that

night, he drew her into his arms. "Your period?"

She shook her head and whispered, "No."

"Then is it something with Kit?" Her sister had never asked to live with them again, but that didn't mean she didn't ask for other things.

"No, no. Not at all. Just a rejection letter from a magazine." She swiped her tears and tried to smile through them. "My third this month."

"Let me see that thing," he said. Before she could protest, he had pinned the rejection letter to the rubber dart board in their little study and began throwing darts at it. "Didn't some famous writer say that rejection slips are badges of courage?"

She laughed. "I haven't heard that."

"Well, I say it's just a matter of time until they'll be calling you the next Victor Hugo, and Jean Valjean will rise from the grave and christen you a genius."

"That sounds heretical, soccer boy," she teased back, then took a dart and threw it with all her might. She hit the letter right in the center.

"I know what we need, Feeny," Patrick said after pinning two more rejection letters to the dart board. "We need a vacation. La Grande Motte is calling. Maman and Papa are dying to see us. Mamie too. Please, let me suggest it?"

"Another handout from your parents. And you don't even have vacation time."

"I have ten days." His eyes, those beautiful soft brown eyes, were twinkling. "I'll go for ten days, and you'll stay for a month."

"A month!" The thought of it made her heart race with excitement. "I have a job, too, remember."

"But didn't your boss say that you can now send him your articles through fax?"

"Only if your parents will let me use their fax machine."

He raised his eyebrows and gave a wink. "I imagine I'll have to twist their arms, but it's worth a try."

As she walked on the beach with her feet in the icy water, the darkness began to dissipate. And when Patrick returned to the States, she sat down at the little table that gave a view of the Mediterranean and started writing her first novel.

Josephine watched her bulging stomach with wonder. Twenty-eight weeks. Every time she caught her reflection in the mirror, she blushed and smiled and thought of the gift it was that this baby had been conceived at La Motte. "A French baby," she teased Patrick.

The early contractions kept her bedridden. The dry heaves never ended. She lost weight. But the baby grew. When Kit called, high and needy, Josephine simply said, "Kitty, I can't come. Not this time. I want this baby to make it."

The jealousy and anger in Kit's voice felt like just one more stab, an agonizing and never-ending contraction.

1994 . . . She cradled her daughter in her arms and stared into those dark gray eyes that stared back at her. Hannah Isabelle. Named after her American and French great-grandmothers. Life and lightness returned to their apartment. And hope.

PAIGE

I tiptoed into Momma's room; the sun was setting outside the window, and it made the leaves shimmer like multicolored pennies. I took hold of my mother's hand. She still lay there, eyes closed. Her head bandaged, with a tuft of hair, dark and matted, escaping beneath the gauze, tubes all around, the beeping sounds, the calm.

"We had the best time last night, Drake and Hannah and I," I told her. "Just like old times, sitting in front of the fireplace. Drake was actually able to build a roaring fire. Remember how he never did a very good job, and we called him a failed Boy Scout? Well, anyway, we sat there eating all this absolutely yummy food. So many people have brought food . . . the neighbors, people from church and from Daddy's work, from the library. And to date you've received over ten thousand emails and Facebook posts from your readers. You sure are keeping me busy, Momma.

"Can't wait till you're back in the kitchen baking your delicious blond brownies. The desserts that people are bringing from the Chocolate Fetish and the French Broad Chocolate Lounge are awesome, but nothing can beat your blond brownies."

I wasn't sure, but I almost thought I felt a very slight movement in Momma's hand.

"We talked about how much fun we'd had on those weekends when the youth group came with all of us scattered around the house in our sleeping bags. And how the first year you made that huge pan of lasagna. You bought this enormous lasagna dish and then once you got everything ready to bake, you discovered it wouldn't fit in the oven! You had to get Drake and Dad to carry it over to Mrs. Swanson's and use her brand-new, state-of-the-art oven. Mrs. Swanson, bless her heart, was thrilled of course.

"Can't wait till we have the youth group over again. I'll help you with the lasagna. Or spaghetti. Remember, I know how to fix that too." I chuckled. I had never been interested in cooking, but Momma insisted I know how to make one meal, and so she taught me how to make spaghetti sauce — Bolognese — which could also be used for lasagna.

"And Drake acts all worried about his last year in school, but you and I know he will do great. I'll bet he gets a job offer after his very first interview." I knew I sounded a bit desperate, wanting to keep talking, to keep giving her a chance to connect. But then not wanting to wear her out.

"And Hannah will tell you herself, but she agreed to go back to Aix on Saturday."

Momma definitely squeezed my hand with that. I jumped a little and got chills — of excitement — and tried to continue talking normally.

"Yes, that's great, isn't it? She's going to be touring five or six art museums in November. The Musée d'Orsay and the Louvre, of course, and several others when they go up to Paris, but she's also going to see the Bayeux Tapestry in Caen. And take the course on painting *en plein air* from the wonderful lady who teaches in Aix.

"And Daddy said we'll keep the plans just like we had them. We all know you'll be excited to go back to La Grande Motte — we've still reserved it from Mamie and Papy for those two weeks at Christmas, and of course Hannah will be with us. And if you want to go in early November, that can still work too, and you'll just stay and write until we get there. Think of it, Momma, two months at the beach!"

I had made up such a string of lies that I felt like I was in the middle of inventing one of my own stories.

"And Drake is interested in coming to La Motte, too, and Ginnie even said she might enjoy a break at the beach. She calls at least three times a day. Daddy isn't letting anyone but family come yet — well, and Drake. But Drake is just like family. . . . But in a few days, when you're feeling a little stronger, we're going to let others come, little by little. Mrs. Swanson first. She's been an angel with all the mail and the food and Milton. Oh, Milton! He misses you something crazy, and you know how Mrs. Swanson bosses him around, poor devil. But he's getting walked twice a day, and I promise I won't let Mrs. Swanson stay with you too long. . . ."

On and on and on I talked, but Momma

didn't move again. I read her more emails and letters from fans and friends, and then the sun set and I sat in the dusk, feeling the coolness descend on the room and the little flutters of hope float off with the last rays of sun. In the silence I heard again the beep of the machines, breathing in and out, in and out, for little Momma.

HENRY

Libby hadn't made it to the hospital yet, but they finally let me in to see Jase after the surgeon came and said that everything went just fine. The doctor had a confident look about him, but I figured he had to look that way. I went into Jase's room and sat down by his bed and couldn't keep the tears from falling. They'd broken open his chest — didn't say it like that, but that was the truth — and put in a pig's aorta instead of whatever was in there first. And Jase seemed more fragile and frail and white than ever.

Everything in me was shaking, my hands, my head, my mind, especially my mind. I felt woozy, weak-like, even scared. Yeah, terrified for my boy. You'd think I'd be all relieved when that surgeon said things had gone well, but I didn't trust anyone too much, and there wasn't nothing good in the whole wide world about watching your boy lying there so still and pale and looking just about dead.

I got up and then sat back down, up and down, with every beep of those machines. Up and down, watching to make sure his little chest was going up and down too. Like to drive me crazy, all that noise, not too loud, just constant, and then some other machine chiming in, as if they were trying to make music for some horror film. I'd seen plenty of those. Too quiet, too loud, too much.

I was clutching Miz Bourdillon's novel real tight when I finally decided to sit back down and read it. The story had upset me a bit, and then with her daughter saying it got even sadder, well, I wasn't so sure I wanted to read it anymore. But I hadn't brought anything else with me, and I didn't want the TV to be blaring while Jase was trying to rest.

So I read that book, and nurses would come in and look at Jase, and once or twice I stepped out to the waiting room while they did stuff. And I got to be kind of thankful for the story, because I was getting right caught up in it and forgetting how worried I was for my boy. The words just kept on carrying me along, and I got to the sad part and had a few tears, but right after, this real sweet scene came out of the blue, surprising me. Like the bad stuff hadn't been able to snuff out the good stuff, or maybe it even happened *because* of the bad stuff. Yeah, that was it. Got a bit confusing in my mind. And I kept thinking about this line: *"You don't need a candle unless it's really dark in the house."*

I got to the end, and Libby still hadn't shown up at the hospital, and it was getting dark outside. And suddenly I couldn't keep it in anymore. Just right there started weeping, sobbing, and the poor nurses kept looking at me funny, with sympathy but a little something else in their eyes, like people did lots of times around me. I guess they were scared. Or just felt sorry for me.

But Miz Bourdillon had written my story again. It was about good coming out of bad and about new beginnings, and about light shining in darkness. And though she didn't put it exactly like that, it sounded just like something Jesus or maybe someone else in the Bible might say.

I had to see Miz Bourdillon. I just *had* to. Had to ask her the questions that was percolating in the back of my mind and then dripping down into my heart. Libby always said I asked the craziest questions and I should leave people alone, and lots of times

212

people got scared when I talked too much.

Couldn't talk to Miz Bourdillon yet, but maybe when she came out of her coma, maybe Paige would let me talk to her about her stories. And here's what I wanted to say to her: *Miz Bourdillon, you think good can come out of bad, I know, and I'm glad you didn't die, and I hope you get well, and I bet your next book will be even better . . . but here's my question: Maybe good can come out of bad for you, but what about for that person who tried to kill you? Can anything good come out of it for him?*

That's the question I wanted to ask her while machines kept breathing for Jase, and Libby called me on my cell and said she was driving real slow along those curvy roads and she wasn't gonna get here before midnight.

"But you go back to the Rathbun House and get some sleep, hon. You've got to get some sleep."

So I watched the machines proclaiming my boy's life on that screen in neon reds and greens, and I went beside his bed and leaned over and said, "Live, sweet boy. Please live. You'll see. Things is gonna be different. Better. You just keep on breathing and getting well." I surprised myself with how soft and soothing my voice sounded,

and then I shocked myself good by saying
something else. "These hard times are
gonna be used for good. Make you stronger,
son. Make you better inside and out.
They're changin' your heart."

In and out, the machines breathed for my
boy as the sun set over those fiery mountains, and I sat by his bed and did something
I hadn't done in a real long time. I prayed
the only prayer that came to mind. "Let him
live, God. Please let him live."

■ ■ ■ ■

PART TWO:
BACK FROM
THE DEAD

■ ■ ■ ■

CHAPTER 9

PAIGE

Six days after the bullet sped through Momma's brain, she opened her eyes.

Hannah and I had gone back home, and Daddy had sat with her through the night. I woke to my cell phone ringing at 6:00 a.m. Dread zipped through me as I saw Daddy's number on the screen. But when I put the phone to my ear, all I could make out was his voice, all happy, almost laughing.

"Her eyes are open, and she squeezed my hand and her score just rocketed up! From a six to an eleven! Imagine that, Paige, she's at an eleven."

I listened to his jubilant voice explain how he'd fallen asleep in the chair by her bed, and then when he lifted his head off the sheet where he was resting it and looked at Momma, there she was, eyes wide open, staring straight ahead.

"Feeny! Feeny!" he'd fairly screamed. She didn't turn her head, but when he grabbed her hand she squeezed it long and hard.

"How amazing is that!" I said. "Let me wake Hannah, and we'll come down right now."

"I've already called Hannah," Daddy said with a chuckle, "and told her the great news. I also suggested she go back to sleep for a little while. You should too. If you come down a little before ten, you'll get here in time to see the doctor when he makes his rounds, and we can all ask our questions."

I lay in bed, replaying the conversation, feeling something light and hopeful settle in my spirit. I had followed the Glasgow Scale every day, charting Momma's progress or lack of it. I knew that the score of an eleven, after six days in the single digits, meant hope of possible partial recovery.

But go back to sleep? Totally impossible. So I crept across the hall into Momma's chalet and sat on the floor, surrounded by all the snail mail from yesterday that I hadn't had time to look through. As I opened each envelope and perused each letter, I thought of Henry, his pale blue glassy eyes and his straggly blond hair and his baseball cap and how he was reading Momma's novel. I thought of all his questions, asked so sincerely, almost with a childlike desperation. So many of the letters Momma received from her readers asked those kinds of questions. But other letters were more like confessions, I thought with a quiver of fear, where readers literally poured out their hearts to her, told her their deepest secrets.

And one of them realized she'd revealed way too much.

There it was again, that thought that had infiltrated my mind the other morning. One of us would know too, if someone from the past few years had told Momma something super confidential. I had not remembered any such letter, despite Hannah's prayers. Neither had she. But she was still praying that God would speak into the dark corners of our memories.

But Momma had opened her eyes! I wanted to think about that. Light! Not darkness. Not right now.

So I went over to a bookshelf where paperbacks were stacked vertically and horizontally, with photos of family and friends arranged on top. I picked up a photo of the four of us, taken by a professional five or six years earlier when we were at La Grande Motte. We were sitting in front of a sand dune, and the Lego structures were blurred out behind us. The sun hit the dunes in a way that cast halos over our heads, as if we were jeans-clad, barefoot angels, waiting to welcome Jesus, walking on the sea.

The photo next to that was of Momma and Milton. She had on jeans and a light blue fleece and her hair was blowing in her face, her head snuggled against Milton's thick coat. That triggered a memory, and I tiptoed down to the ground floor and through the back of the house to Daddy's study. He said he didn't need breathtaking views of the Blue Ridge Mountains to distract him; he preferred a windowless room where he pushed his numbers. His study had a special aura to it — a mixture of business and sport, organization and plain fun. I stood in front of his desk, a French antique from his mother's family, which he kept neat and organized. At the moment, a thin folder with a photo of a beautiful rainbow on the front sat in the middle of the desk. Some of my father's clients delivered their financial information to him in strange ways. I fingered the folder, smiling, then looked around the room.

The shelves held hardback copies of financial tomes, but also biographies of Pelé and other soccer greats and a bunch of

Daddy's soccer trophies. On one shelf were perched six soccer balls, old and torn and filled with Daddy's favorite memories of the sport. Another shelf was stacked high with all kinds of board games and brainteasers. When the youth group came for weekends, Daddy loved to engage them with his ever-growing collection of wooden puzzles. And of course, he had his favorite French novels and photo books of the Midi, where he'd grown up.

Interspersed on the shelves were photos; I was looking for one in particular. I found it on the shelf beside *Liar's Poker* and several other stock-related books. I reached for the photo in a sterling silver five-by-seven frame. In it, Momma sat with Milton. The shot had been taken at the same time as the one in Momma's office, but in this one Momma was looking directly at the camera, and the black-and-white photo made her dark brown eyes almost bewitching. She had her arms looped around Milton's neck and a cross hung around hers, sparkling and catching the sun.

Momma always wore that cross. A Huguenot cross. Daddy's ancestors had been Huguenots — the first French Protestants who were eventually forced to flee the country when Louis XIV revoked the Edict of Nantes in 1685, taking away religious liberty in France. I knew the gory history of the Huguenots and how some had fled to the shores of South Carolina.

Daddy had given the Huguenot cross, made of eighteen-karat gold, to Momma for her birthday one year, and she rarely took it off. Like so many things in Momma's life, it symbolized something — Daddy's love for her, I think, and their love of France, and the strength of faith in the midst of persecution. But I knew for sure Momma was not wearing the cross when she was shot. The nursing staff had given Daddy Momma's personal items on the second day — her wedding ring and earrings and watch, but no necklace.

I decided that to celebrate her progress, I'd take her the Huguenot cross. That would doubtless make her happy.

But though I searched through her jewelry box and drawers for the next hour, I couldn't find the cross anywhere. I hoped that wasn't some kind of foreshadowing of doom. Not right after Momma had decided to open up her eyes after six long days.

JOSEPHINE

Patrick was talking to me again in that soft, soothing way, assuring me that all would be

222

well, as he had done from the very first time we'd met. "I can hear you, Patrick," I tried to say. Maybe the words were only in my mind. But his hand, so large and comforting in mine, I felt that. I tried to squeeze it. Did he feel it? Could he hear me describe to him the depth of my love? Would he understand? I tried to open my eyes again, but I couldn't. I wanted to come back to him, to the girls. I was trying, trying, trying. . . .

1995 . . . She didn't know she could feel so much love, with Patrick holding her so tenderly, loving her so thoroughly, while little Hannah napped in the next room. "Shhh. Don't wake her," she giggled, out of breath from lovemaking. He kissed her lips, her cheeks, her belly.

"And now I have a surprise for you," Josephine said, her eyes twinkling. She reached over to the bedside table and picked up an envelope. She carefully retrieved the thick stack of folded papers, straightened them in her hands, and began to read. "Dear Mrs. Bourdillon, it is with great pleasure that we send to you a contract for your novel *The Lonely Truth. . . .*"

She handed the papers to Patrick, and squealed, "Can you believe it!" and then burst into tears. Happy, happy tears.

"Félicitations, mon amour!" Patrick cooed in his French as he perused the papers. "My sweet, sweet Feeny. Do you have any idea how proud I am of you?"

She wiped her tears, finding the depths of his love in those dark, expressive eyes. Love, kindness, trust. She gave a playful smile then and said, "Hmm? Now how should we celebrate this? Seeing as we're both naked and in bed . . ."

His eyes lit with desire, and he kissed her again.

1996 . . . Patrick found Josephine lying on their bed in tears. He rubbed her back softly and whispered, "Bad news from the family?"

She sat up and hugged her knees to her chest. "No. Not that. Just a rotten review."

He frowned. "Feeny, don't pay attention to reviews."

She flashed anger. "Wrong answer, Mr. Sexy Legs! This is my first novel, Patrick. You know what that represents for me. So when my first review is bad, well, at least let me wallow a little."

"Can I see it?"

She shook her head and sniffed. "He called it 'sentimental drivel.' "

Patrick's face broke into a smile. "Why,

that's a compliment, Feeny. That's just that snobby reviewer's way of saving face instead of admitting that he cried through the whole book."

Patrick took the letter and speared it next to the many rejections she'd garnered throughout the years.

1998 . . . "Another girl, Feeny. A beautiful little girl with a shock of reddish-gold hair." Patrick kissed her lightly on the forehead as he placed the newborn in her arms. Josephine stared into her daughter's little face, slipped her finger in the tiny fist. "Well, *bonjour,* my precious little Paige Mariette."

She looked up at Patrick. Tears streamed down his face just as they did hers.

"Another miracle," Josephine whispered. "The Lord's seen fit to grant us another miracle."

When I opened my eyes, I had no idea where I was, but I saw Patrick leaning his face so close to mine. I couldn't read minds, but I could read eyes. And in his eyes I read a mixture of relief and foreboding.

"Can you hear me, Feeny?" he was saying, excitedly, loudly. Then he said to someone else, "She's got her eyes open again!"

I opened my mouth, but no sound came out. Perhaps I hadn't opened my mouth after all.

"Can you hear me, Feeny?" he repeated.

Why were my hands not moving? My mouth?

Patrick read eyes well too. "Don't be afraid, Feeny. You're okay. You're in a hospital. There was an accident."

I must have blinked because he hurried on. "Yes, blink if you can hear me. Can you understand what I'm saying?"

I had never thought before about the weight of a blink. Spontaneous, uncontrolled, split-second. Now I tried, and I could not tell if I succeeded until he cried, "Thank God, Feeny!" Then, "Can you feel my hand in yours? Can you squeeze my hand?"

My head wouldn't move, although I was nodding as hard as my brain would let me. I was still concentrating on the blink, still asking my brain if I could feel Patrick's hand, when he let go, and I heard, as in a fog, "Nurse, nurse! She's opening her eyes and responding to me again!"

Then I went back to the darkness, somewhere in another place in time.

HENRY

They chased me out of the ICU at midnight while the nurses kept scurrying around, assuring me, "He's doing just fine, Mr. Hughes. You go on and get a little sleep."

So I got a ride back to the Rathbun House, feeling all fidgety and alert. At some point I must've finally fallen asleep, because next thing I knew, Libby was sitting on the side of the bed, all wrung out, her face so pale and her hair all tangled. Didn't look like she'd gotten any sleep at all.

Jase!

"You seen him, Libs? How's he doing?"

She shrugged, not looking at me, which wasn't ever a good sign. "I got in at two. Sweet nurse let me sit with him for a few hours." She was wiping her eyes, and I felt my chest tighten. "He's stable."

"Thank God," I whispered.

Then she started talking in her professional secretary voice, all business. "My boss said I can have today and tomorrow off. You go on and take the truck to work today, Henry. Then head on back here tomorrow after work and we'll be together over the weekend."

"All right," I said, going into the bathroom. I came back out, pulled on my jeans, and gave Libby a kiss on the forehead.

As I pulled away, I saw Libby's face, all streaked with tears, and she was turning her hands over and over in her lap, like she did when she was real worried. She managed to look up at me, sniffed a couple of times. Her thin body trembled, and when she ran her hands through her hair, they were trembling too.

"Henry," she said, and she motioned for me to sit down. "Henry, I found your guns in the truck." She was shaking all over. "The pistol and the rifle. You promised you wouldn't carry them in there anymore."

"Sorry, Libs. I must've forgot or something."

"When did you forget, Henry? Those guns weren't in the truck on Sunday when I drove to church. Why'd you put them back in there?"

"I don't remember, Libs. Sorry."

"You're sorry! That's all you can say? You're driving around with guns in the truck, and you haven't taken your meds. You've been off your meds for over two weeks! Why'd you pretend you were taking them?" She produced the brown pharmacy bottle, filled with the pills.

"You're asking me too many questions, Libs. Leave me alone now. You go on to sleep. Lemme get on the road."

I went into the bathroom and cursed under my breath. Hadn't even thought about the Glock and the Remington. Hadn't thought about the pills either. We'd gone to the restaurant and then Jase started choking, and there wasn't time to think about the guns or the meds. I splashed water on my face and brushed my teeth and came back out.

Libby was holding Miz Bourdillon's book. "And why in the world are you reading another one of that lady's novels? You never read novels."

"Just getting my mind off of Jase is all."

Libby was crying real hard now. She threw the book on the bed and pulled her arms around her the way she did when she was afraid of me, like she might curl into herself and be safe. And she was looking at me like she didn't believe me.

"I went to the library yesterday after work, Henry, to get some books to read to Jase here in the hospital. And Miss Garrison asked me if I liked the book. . . . I said, 'Which book is that?' and she said, 'Why, the one Henry got you, the one by Mrs. Bourdillon!' Why'd you tell Miss Garrison that *I* wanted that book? What's going on, Henry?" She shivered, her eyes just as deep and sad as a doe's, and then she went into the bathroom and shut the door.

I felt the anger building, the rage, and couldn't do nothing about it. While Libs cowered in the bathroom, I put the pillow over my face and yelled, then punched my hands hard back and forth on the mattress, but I left her alone.

Once I'd calmed down she came out of the bathroom, her face all screwed up. "What have you done, Henry? For God's sake, what have you done?"

My mind went racing real fast and everything went blurry, and then I got all panicky and blurted out, "I've done something really terrible, Libs. Gonna be the end of me." I went over to her, and she backed away, a horrified look on her pretty face. "No, Libs, I won't hurt you. I won't." And I grabbed her tight and held her so close where I felt her heart just ramming into my chest, and she cried for a while and then I said, "I gotta be going. You tell Jase I love him, and I'll be back tomorrow night."

I picked up the book and the brown bottle of my meds and tossed them both in my bag and left the room with Libby just standing there, eyes wide and trembling, like a deer before the kill.

I went out the front door of that fancy guest building, and I sure was glad that old couple wasn't there to greet me. Kept telling myself to chill, because the surgery went okay and wasn't nothing to worry about, even if Libby had found the guns. No one else knew. But when I got shaken, well, it took awhile to get my presence of mind back.

Thought maybe I should go ahead and start taking the pills again. Maybe. Drove right past a few police cars and for a while I thought one of them might be following me, but every time I glanced in the rearview mirror, all I saw was a long curvy highway.

I didn't know what Libby was thinking, the way I left her there with bad news, not explaining anything. But I felt like one of those leaves outside my window at the guest house, quivering back and forth and then just floating to the ground. Could almost hear the crunch of it getting crushed under my boot.

I flipped on the radio and sure enough, it was one of Libby's religious stations, playing a real melancholy-sounding song. But something in the tune pleased me enough that I didn't flip the dial, just listened. And the more I listened, the more I got this tingling sensation, like when my hand or foot goes to sleep, except this time it was inside me, in my heart, the tingling. Because the words that man was singing were the very same words I had read in Miz Bourdillon's book. Except I knew they weren't completely her words; they came from somewhere in the Bible.

"I'm leaving you well and whole. That's my parting gift to you. Peace . . ."

He was singing almost exactly those words, and then he kept repeating, "I leave you peace, peace, peace."

And there I was careening along that curvy highway, glancing in the rearview, afraid of some cop following me, and then I was bawling my eyes out, listening to that music about peace. Face it, I'd never really had a moment of peace in my life. Don't even know what that would look like, but I wanted it. Right then, I did. And it made me think about Miz Bourdillon's first book and how that's what that poor down-and-out kid was longing for, but also that real rich society lady in the other book whose life was crumbling around her. They both were wanting peace.

And strange as it sounds, I just ended up saying out loud, "Okay, I'd like to have some of that peace too. Don't know how, so please, whoever you are, could you show me how to get it?"

And my heart just kept quivering and the

music kept on playing, and soon it was some other song, lots more upbeat and all. But I just kept hearing those words over and over in my mind. *I give you peace.*

PAIGE

On the way to the hospital I asked Hannah, "Have you seen Momma's cross?"

"No. But she rarely takes it off."

"Yeah, I know. But she wasn't wearing it the day she was shot. The nurse gave Daddy her wedding ring and watch and earrings, but no cross."

"Well, I'm sure it's at the house some-where," Hannah said.

My cell phone beeped with a text, but I didn't reach for it. "No, it's not. I just spent an hour looking. You know how much that cross means to her. It's so symbolic."

"Hey, just about any gift she ever received became symbolic. It's no big deal. The big deal is that she opened her eyes."

"True."

"You don't sound very convinced."

I shrugged. "It's just, I don't know . . ."

"Ah, I get it! You think it's a clue to the assassin."

"Maybe."

"Like he shot her and then ran and took

the cross off her neck before anyone showed up."

I stuck out my tongue. "Don't be ridiculous. Of course not."

"Look, Paige, I'll be back in France in a few days. I'll go buy her another Huguenot cross. I'll buy ten of them if it'll make you feel better."

I could tell Hannah was getting a little annoyed. "Okay, forget it. I'm nuts."

"You're not nuts, but it's just not important." Without warning, she burst out laughing. "But hey, I know why you're so concerned. That cross is your inheritance! We were all at La Grande Motte, and Daddy said we were going to Montpellier for Momma's birthday to get her a special gift and then eat at a restaurant." Hannah's eyes were shining. "You were what, four or five?"

"That's what they tell me."

"And we went into the fancy jewelers, and Daddy bought that eighteen-karat-gold cross, and Momma was so proud and began explaining the symbolism." Hannah imitated Momma's deep Southern accent. "Now girls, just look at this beautiful cross. It's very symbolic — do you know what that means? See here, the crown of thorns is twisting around the cross and those little knobs on the end of the cross symbolize the eight beatitudes, and here, if you count the points, it's the twelve apostles. And the beautiful little dove that hangs from the bottom of the cross is symbolizing the coming of the Holy Spirit, how He came down from heaven when Jesus was baptized. . . ."

Hannah took her eyes off the road for a second and glanced at me. "But you weren't paying one bit of attention. And when Momma tucked you in to bed that night, you reached up and touched the cross, which was now hanging around her neck, and asked, 'Momma, why is there a dead bird hanging from your cross?' "

We both cracked up, as we did every single time we told that story. I didn't really remember the incident the way Hannah did, but I remembered what Momma said to me so often in the years following. "My little stinker. I tell you what — I'll give you this cross when you're old enough to understand the significance of that little dove. It'll be yours."

I laughed along with Hannah, but inside I was frowning. That cross still belonged to Momma, and suddenly I wished I had already inherited it, and she could see it hanging around my neck now that she'd awoken from her coma.

As Hannah parked the car, and we got out

and walked to the entrance to the hospital, I clicked on my phone and scrolled down to read the text I'd received. It was from Drake. *I remember something else about The Awful Year. I'm coming home tomorrow night. Save the evening, and I'll explain it all.*

Okay, I texted back. *Momma has opened her eyes. She may be coming out of her coma.*

I sent my text into cyberspace and felt the tension in my cheeks, the tension between a smile and a frown.

Hannah and I arrived at the hospital at nine thirty. Daddy was sitting beside Momma. To us, she looked exactly the same, intubated, eyes closed, unmoving.

"She's just resting a bit now," Daddy said, his voice still carrying enthusiasm.

Soon Dr. Moore, the wiry little surgeon with the thick-rimmed glasses, came into her room with a host of medical students surrounding him. He introduced us to his team. As they talked amongst themselves, the nurse practitioner pulled me aside.

"I know you don't have a lot of warm fuzzies for Dr. Moore. He has a pretty pitiful bedside manner, but his brain works great. I just want you to know that your mother's brain, and the rest of her, couldn't be in better hands." The nurse's eyes met mine, twinkling, and I nodded.

"Thanks," I whispered. In the six days we'd been keeping vigil at the hospital, I had come to respect the nurse practitioners as the ones who would tell me the truth. I took a deep breath and moved closer to where Dr. Moore and his cluster of students stood.

"So I hear our patient has opened her eyes," he said, directing his gaze toward Daddy. Then Dr. Moore went up to Momma, very close, and shook her on the shoulder. "Mrs. Bourdillon. Josephine. Can you hear me?"

Nothing. But when he reached over and pinched her forcefully on her neck, she squirmed enough for me to detect movement. Her eyes flew open.

"Well, what do you know! What about that! She's come out of that coma! Good for you, Josephine."

The doctor was laughing. He turned to his students and said, "Mrs. Bourdillon was at a four on the Glasgow Scale when she came in. Fortunately, the bullet entered and exited the right lobe; it missed the high-value real estate such as the brain stem and the thalamus and the ventricles. . . ."

There he went again, talking about real estate! But this time, I smiled with him.

"She had barely progressed to a six in the

past five days, but now, well, now . . ." He glanced down at his chart. "This is the beginning of the sixth day and look at her! Eyes open, responding to pain. She's moving from the VS" — Dr. Moore looked over at Daddy — "the vegetative state, into the minimally conscious state, what we call the MCS. All things considered, this is remarkable."

JOSEPHINE

I knew those voices, voices of absolute joy! Hannah! Paige!

"Momma, oh Momma! We love you. We're here with you."

I heard my girls, but a thought kept swirling somewhere in my subconscious. Hannah? Hannah shouldn't be here. Hannah was in France.

Both girls were leaning over me, so close that I could see their beautiful faces! Hannah brushed her fingers across my cheek, and I tried to smile. Then Paige kissed my hand.

"She looks afraid, or in pain," Paige was saying.

No, I wasn't in pain, but I was thirsty! So thirsty.

"I don't think she understands what has happened," Patrick said.

Had he told me before? I had no idea where I was. Something was very, very wrong, but everyone was whispering and assuring me that everything was very, very good.

Patrick's face came into focus. I could understand the words he was saying. *Hospital. An accident.* I wanted to ask him what kind of accident, because I didn't remember anything about that at all.

"But she knows us. That's a miracle! People are praying, and God is answering, and she knows us." That, of course, was Hannah.

I tried to tell them again that I was thirsty. I needed a drink. But no sound came out of my mouth at all.

PAIGE

Hannah and Daddy were still in the room with Momma when I slipped out and rode the elevator down to the lobby to order a chai latte from The Bean Shop. I texted several of my girlfriends at school about Momma's amazing progress. I also wanted to check to see if I had another text from Drake.

I did. *Marvelous!* it read. *Give her my love.*

The Bean Shop had specialty coffees and teas, other beverages, and hot and cold

239

lunch entrées, and one hundred percent of their profits went to funding special projects for the hospital. That sounded pretty good to me. At the moment, the shop — which was actually just a long counter with tables and chairs to the right of the hospital entrance — was empty except for a young woman who stood vacant-eyed in front of the shelf displaying sandwiches. I could hear her sniffling and saw out of the corner of my eye that she kept wiping tears. I walked to the counter and placed my order. She glanced up at me, and I nodded her way and said, "Waiting is always hard."

"Yes." Her voice was a shallow hiccup.

"Is someone from your family here?"

"My boy. My six-year-old boy. He had open-heart surgery."

I had two thoughts at once — she didn't look any older than Hannah, and maybe she was that blond man's wife.

"Is your husband Henry?"

She eyed me warily and wrinkled her brow. Then she gave the barest nod.

Seeing her anxiety, I explained. "I'm Paige. My mom's in the ICU up on the fourth floor. I met your husband on Monday night and then saw him again yesterday."

"Monday night?" Now she looked terrified and drew her arms around herself. She cleared her throat as if she were going to say something, but didn't. Finally she managed, "You're Mrs. Bourdillon's daughter, aren't you?"

"Yes. That's right. Your husband told me about your son. How's he doing?"

She swallowed several times, coughed, and whispered, "Henry told you about Jase?"

"Yeah. I guess we just started talking in the middle of the night to help us forget how worried we both were."

She was thin, really *too* thin, and her strawberry-blond hair was twisted up in a loose knot, and she wore on her face the traces of a hard life. But her eyes were a piercing green, almost startling with their beauty, even when she'd been crying.

She gave a tentative nod. "I'm sorry if my Henry's been bothering you. He means well. He just doesn't always read all the signals correctly." She stared at me intently, as though she desperately wanted me to understand something. "He feels things so strongly. He got very upset about your mother. He has a real tender heart for people who are hurting. He even checked two of your mother's novels out of the library."

That scared — no, terrified look came into her eyes again.

"He hasn't been bothering me. He was very kind, concerned. Respectful."

Her expression softened. "Oh, well, good. And thank you for asking about Jase. He pulled through the surgery. We don't know any more. I'm just getting something to eat and then I'm going back in to sit by his bed and talk with him." She chose a chicken and tomato sandwich enclosed in plastic and said, "I'm so sorry about your mother. Any change?"

"She's actually just come out of the coma."

Now her face relaxed, and she smiled. "That's wonderful news. That's amazing. I'm sure you're thankful for that."

"We are."

She paid for the sandwich and then motioned with her hand. "Well, I'm going to go back to my boy."

I wished I could have offered her something. If I were Hannah, I'd promise to pray, and I *would* pray. In fact, Hannah had spent most of her time at the hospital praying — as she sat by Momma's bed or in the little chapel on the third floor. And once a day she updated the CaringBridge site with *how* to pray for Momma and how God was answering those prayers.

But I didn't pray.

So I just said, "Yes, of course. It's nice to meet you, and I hope your boy gets better real soon." I watched her walk away, shoulders slumped forward, arms crossed tightly across her chest, and I felt just about as sorry for her as I did for her husband.

HENRY

I was getting near the printing plant, only gonna be a few minutes late, when my phone rang. I don't like to answer the phone when I'm driving, because I don't have a Bluetooth thing. Don't even have one of those smartphones. Jase one time called mine a dumb phone, and that made Libby and me chuckle a little. But I went on and answered it and then wished I hadn't.

"Hello, Henry."

I felt my mouth go all dry. "Hey."

"You screwed up."

I couldn't think of anything to say.

"You there?"

"Yeah, Nick. Yeah, I'm here."

"Well, what're you doing getting that lady spread all over the news, all over everywhere, and her not dead?"

"She moved right when I pulled the trigger."

"That's not my problem."

I knew he was right, but I didn't want to

admit it.

He was yelling now and cussing up a storm. I was having a hard time concentrating on the road.

"You planning to finish her off?"

"Mighty hard to do that right now." My voice was all choked up, when I needed to sound confident.

"That ain't my problem either. My problem is that I haven't gotten my second half of the payment." He stopped talking for a few seconds, then took this deep breath. Could hear it over the phone. "Well, I tell you what, Henry. You let her live. You do that. But I know about your son and his heart problems, and I know you have a real pretty wife. Hate to see something happen to one of them."

Now my hands were shaking on the steering wheel. I found a gas station where I could pull off. Usually it was the side effects of my meds that made me a little jittery. This time, I guess it was the side effects of fear.

How'd this man know about Libby and Jase? I wished I'd been taking the meds after all, because then I would be thinking clearer.

"Listen to me, Henry." Now his voice was all syrupy sweet. "And listen good. If I don't get my share of the pay in two days, I'll go ahead and give your information to the real person who hired you. I bet she's awful mad right now."

She? Somehow I hadn't pictured whoever wanted Miz Bourdillon dead to be a she.

"She's got a screw loose, that woman. First time I talked to her, she started quoting some song to me. Like it was a twisted kind of prayer to kill someone. She said, 'Take her life and let it be consecrated Lord to Thee! You take Mrs. Bourdillon's life. That's your job. Take her life!' Tellin' you, she was nuts."

Why'd he have to keep yelling at me?

"You better get that money to me one way or another, Henry, or your son won't leave that hospital alive. I promise you that. You want to take that writer lady's life, or you want someone else to take your boy's?" He chuckled like he'd said something real clever. "You decide."

"I'm not supposed to pay you, Nick! That's not how it works!"

"It's how it works now." And his phone went dead.

CHAPTER 10

Thursday

PAIGE

Daddy must have called Aunt Kit with the news as well, because she burst into Momma's room a little after noon. She was wearing a bright pink, tight-fitting exercise shirt and black leggings and tennis shoes; her hair was pulled back in a ponytail and her sunglasses were pushed up on her head. She pecked me on the cheek and said, "Oh, thank God! Thank God! She's opened her eyes. She's back. My JoJo is back."

I wanted to beg Aunt Kit to stop talking so loudly, but Daddy gave an almost imperceptible nod, as if to say, *Let her be. We're all just so thankful Momma's opened her eyes.*

"I rushed here as soon as your father called — right in the middle of my gym class."

"Thanks, Aunt Kit." I glanced at Daddy,

246

who motioned for Hannah and me to follow him out of the room.

"We'll leave you to spend a little time alone with Josephine," he said, but the excitement that had been in his voice all morning had disappeared.

JOSEPHINE

In and out I went, in and out. The light and the dark and the light again. I knew they were around me, the people I loved, or was it the angels? The angels had been there at some point. I felt a strange calm as I pronounced the words in my mind, my very favorite words, "Lord Jesus! Lord Jesus!"

Then darkness.

I woke again to a shrill cry and laughter, rough and deep, and then I felt tears on my face as Kit leaned over and kissed me.

"Oh, JoJo!"

Her face was tanned and pulled taut, her lips painted bright pink, and when she moved her hand near my face, I saw the same shade of pink on her perfectly manicured nails. Dear Kit! My crazy, beautiful Kit!

I smelled her exotic perfume. . . .

2000 . . . "Well, you certainly have it made in the shade, JoJo. Two little girls and another contract for a novel."

Josephine didn't say anything. She wished Kit would celebrate her successes for once instead of acting jealous.

"Wish I could sit back and write books for a living." She took off her sunglasses and lifted her eyebrows. "And this view. Oh my! I could kill for this view!"

They were sitting in rocking chairs on the wraparound porch in the newly built home on Bearmeadow Mountain, sipping ice-cold lemonade and watching the sky fade into a soft lavender, casting shadows of ever-deepening green across the undulating peaks.

"You must be making a small fortune to be able to afford this."

How Josephine longed for the heartfelt conversations of their younger years.

"We're indeed thankful to have found this spot of paradise. You're always welcome to visit."

Kit gave a long cackle. "No longer afraid I'll steal your precious Patrick, I guess."

"Kit!" Josephine surprised herself with her harsh tone. She stared at her sister until at last Kit met her eyes. "Stop it! Stop your ridiculous chatter and talk to me! Talk to me the way you used to. You used to see into my soul. Now all I hear is bitterness and pain."

Kit's face went hard. "Easy to judge when

you've got everything."

"I said stop it!" Josephine's voice rose another decibel as streaks of violet and crimson and amber painted an astonishing scene before them. "You of all people know how hard my life has been! I won't let you sit there and feel sorry for yourself!"

Kit melted a little, set down the glass of lemonade, and turned to look at the sunset. Her profile so perfect, so paint-brushed perfect. "I've ruined my life, JoJo. It's completely run away from me, and I have no idea how to get it back."

"JoJo! Can you hear me, Jo? Thank God, you're awake. I was so afraid, Jo! I thought you were going to die, I really did."

I could feel her clutching my hand, and I tried to squeeze it back, tried to blink my eyes.

She didn't seem to notice, but kept talking in that way she had, nervous energy and high-strung emotion. "They told me not to talk about the past, only happy things, but not everything's old news, JoJo. You know that. All I've been thinking since the assassination attempt was that if you died before I could talk to you, I'd blame myself for so many things!"

I heard her words *assassination attempt,*

blame myself, smelled the perfume, and floated off into blackness again.

PAIGE

In spite of Momma's amazing improvement, I felt an almost literal heaviness descend on my shoulders. Aunt Kit seemed to have that effect on me. I rode the elevator down to the main floor, slipped outside into the nippy October afternoon, and walked around the parking lot, staring out at the mountains surrounding me. Ten minutes later, I was chilled and ready for my afternoon cup of tea.

I had just put the plastic top on my cup of chai and stepped from The Bean Shop into the lobby when Henry's wife came out of the bathroom across the way. She was blowing her nose and crying openly. Had Jase died? I touched her arm and said, "Can I get you anything, Mrs. . . . ?"

She looked up, startled, and brushed her hand across her face. "Libby. My name is Libby." She kept pulling her arms around herself as if she were cold.

"Can I get you anything, Libby? A cup of coffee? A candy bar?"

At first I didn't think she'd heard me. Then she looked me in the eyes and grabbed me in a hug so fierce I almost dropped my cup of tea.

"The doctor just gave me bad news." She was shaking, trembling, as she talked. "Jase has pneumonia, really bad." She gave a little hiccup-like sob. "And he's real weak. I can tell they don't think he's going to pull through." She looked so fragile that her fierce grip took me by surprise. Like she was hanging on to me for life.

"Oh, Libby, I'm so sorry." She finally let go of me, and I said, "Let me get you something to drink."

"I've got some water." She pulled a bottle from her purse and took a slow sip. "Sorry to bother you like that. I'd best get on back to my boy."

We walked to the elevators together, and when the doors opened we stepped in with four or five other people. Libby kept swiping at tears while everyone else had their eyes turned down. I got off with her on the third floor.

Libby asked, "Isn't your mom on the fourth?"

"Yes, but I thought I might sit with you for a few minutes if that's okay."

She looked grateful.

The waiting room for the Pediatric ICU was much like the Neuro Trauma ICU waiting room above. Several healthy and vibrant

251

Ficus trees sat in the corners of the room, and a picture window let in sunshine and a view of the mountains. A small fridge was available for families of the patients to use, as well as a microwave, an electric kettle, and packets of instant coffee and hot chocolate and tea bags. A boisterously colorful flower arrangement sat at the information desk, giving the room a faintly sweet scent of late fall roses.

Libby sank into a chair, buried her head in her hands, and sobbed. Loudly. A middle-aged couple and a teenaged boy looked over at us, sympathy on their faces. Then they looked away.

I surprised myself by setting down my cup of tea, kneeling down in front of the comfortable chair where she sat, and pulling her into a hug. I held her tightly and said, "I'm so sorry, Libby." I didn't know what else to do.

We stayed like that for a few minutes, and when she had calmed down a little, I asked, "Is Henry coming today?"

She shook her head. "No, he's working today and tomorrow. He won't be here till tomorrow night."

"Is there anyone else you could call to come sit with you?"

She fiddled with her hands and said, "I

just got off the phone with my pastor. The whole church is praying, but they can't come — our town's almost three hours away."

Once again I wished I had something to offer her. "Where are you staying?"

"We've got a really nice room at the Rathbun House. I'm so grateful for that." But she said it in between jerky little hiccups of emotion.

Then I had a thought. "Would you like me to ask the chaplain to come visit you?"

She looked startled. "There's a chaplain? I hadn't thought of that."

"Yes, yes. She's very kind." Chelsea, whom I had met on Sunday, was a middle-aged plus-sized woman who radiated goodwill and kindness. Hannah had talked with her often in the past few days. I figured she was mainly on call for families when the patient was dying, but I didn't say that to Libby.

She kept turning her hands over and over in her lap. "I need to get back to my boy," she whispered.

"Yes, go on back. When I find the chaplain, I'll ask her to go to Jase's room."

Libby's eyes filled again. "Would you? Oh, thank you, Paige. I think the Lord sent you here right at this moment so I wouldn't lose hope."

I had nothing to say to that, but I added, "Did you know there's a little chapel on this floor too? It has beautiful stained-glass windows and comfortable chairs where you can sit and pray." This, of course, I knew from Hannah. I had never ventured in.

"Thank you, Paige," she repeated, squeezing my hands in hers and staring at me with those brilliant green eyes. "Thank you."

As she left the waiting room, I determined that I'd bring some of the baked goods that were accumulating at our house down here to share with her. That was at least something. And I'd send her some flowers too.

We stayed with Momma all that day, Hannah and me and Daddy and Aunt Kit. She kept her eyes open for an hour or so and then she closed them, and I'm pretty sure she was sleeping again. The doctors called it sleep cycles. The fact that Momma was waking at some points was a huge improvement. Even Dr. Moore seemed surprised and pleased.

Of course Hannah said, "It's because so many people are praying specifically that she will open her eyes and respond to pain." She glanced at me and smiled. "I've been reading up on brain injuries on the internet too."

With all the excitement of Momma coming out of the coma, I hadn't thought any more about the possibility of a reader who had confided too much in her. She had zipped up the Glasgow Scale, but the fact remained that someone had tried to kill her. It was only then that I recalled Drake's text about TAY, The Awful Year. I shivered, mentally going through the list of possible suspects that Hannah and I had compiled.

Daddy sat next to Momma, whose eyes were still closed. Hannah had already spent a half hour reading her the latest posts on the CaringBridge site. I was just about to start reading her some of the emails from her fans when Detective Blaylock came into Momma's room — without knocking — holding up a letter like he'd struck oil. "Let's go to the waiting room. I have something to show you."

Once we were in the hallway, safely out of earshot of Momma, he held out the letter. "She wrote again!" he said.

"Who?" I asked, but I already knew. The envelope was pink.

"The one who sent those letters last month," he confirmed.

Daddy and I met eyes, and I got goose bumps.

"Officer Hanley went by your house this

morning, and the neighbor lady, Mrs. Samson —"

"Swanson," I corrected.

"Right, Mrs. Swanson had just picked up your mail, a bag with a bunch of letters for your mother. As you can see, this one has the same pink envelope and paper, same block print."

"But what does it say?" I wanted to jerk the paper from his hands, but miraculously refrained.

He read us four short sentences.

" 'I told you so. How many times do I have to warn you? Now look what's happened. You brought it on yourself!' "

Sweat broke out on my brow, and I honestly thought I might throw up. What did *that* mean?

Daddy didn't exactly look surprised or even upset. His inscrutable expression frightened me. Hannah stood beside him, an arm around his shoulder, and Aunt Kit muttered, "Well, that's just plain weird." But she actually seemed a little freaked out.

Did these warnings have something to do with The Awful Year? Drake said he had more things to share with me, tomorrow night. If I could wait that long. If Detective Blaylock didn't ask me any more questions meanwhile. . . .

But all that evening, at the hospital and then back at home with Milton licking my hand and Hannah poring over comments on CaringBridge, all I could think about was how my world had changed completely during The Awful Year.

I lived a charmed childhood until halfway through my ninth year, flitting like a butterfly from our idyllic home on Bearmeadow Mountain to my private girls' school in Asheville and to our church in the suburbs. We spent vacations not at nearby Myrtle Beach but taking a luxurious month at La Grande Motte.

Charmed.

The people who lived on Bearmeadow Mountain were a close-knit community of wealthy young professionals and even wealthier retirees. Of course I didn't register that as a child. I simply enjoyed the cook-outs at the clubhouse, the treasure hunts in the woods, and canoeing on the French Broad River. And I spent lazy afternoons at Drake's house. His parents, Mr. and Mrs. Ellinger, were my godparents. Drake being the youngest of four boys, his parents doted on me as the daughter they didn't have. Often, when Daddy was working late and Momma was holed up writing her books, Mrs. Ellinger would drive me to my after-school activities and to children's choir practice at church.

When the Ellingers separated, and eventually divorced, I was almost as devastated as Drake, although I tried not to show it. At nine years old, this was my first experience with great loss. When I heard adult whispers about infidelity, I looked the word up in the dictionary and got very, very mad.

Bad news, suffering, and evil . . . these things broke Momma's heart. But they made me just plain mad, even as a little girl. Mr. Ellinger tumbled off his pedestal and came crashing to the ground. Every title that had been bestowed on him now mocked him: an elder in our church, a businessman with great integrity (I looked that word up too), a model in the community, and most importantly, my devoted godfather.

For all my nine years of life, I had happily accompanied my parents and Hannah to church. I felt safe and known there. But with Mr. Ellinger's fall, another word sneaked in and wrapped itself around me: hypocrisy. The Awful Year was the year of a new vocabulary I was too young to learn.

Then two months after Drake's parents separated, Momma's mother took an overdose of sleeping pills and never woke up. Everyone called it an accident, but I already knew the word *suicide,* and I wasn't fooled.

When Momma's father passed away on a chilly afternoon later that same year, my vocabulary increased again. Cirrhosis of the liver. My faith, however, decreased and eventually just dried up.

I felt close to my French grandparents, even though I rarely saw them and only spoke a little French. I loved my American grandparents, too, but in a distant sort of way. When we visited them in Atlanta, I was always afraid I might mess something up at their huge, immaculate home. Grandfather was another upstanding figure in society, just like Drake's father. A brilliant business-man, a lifelong member of St. Mark's Episcopal Church, a board member for all kinds of important places. He was also strik-ingly handsome, with his silver hair and deep gray eyes.

Aunt Kit showed up drunk at Grand-father's funeral. *Inebriated.* Another of those words I learned during The Awful Year. And at the reception following the service, she took me aside and listed in graphic detail all of Grandfather's sins. "He'd stay out all night drinking and sleeping with whores and then come home in the wee hours of the morning drunk out of his mind, and slap your grandmom around. Then he'd take a shower, dress in his Louis Vuitton suit, and head to work as if nothing had ever happened. And your grandmom was too pitiful and proud to leave him! She just kept up the charade, year after miserable year, until she finally decided she'd had enough, and she checked out of life altogether. He was a drunk and an adulterer, and I'm glad he's dead." She said other things too, punctuating them with curse words I had also never heard before.

By the time Momma found Aunt Kit and me in the ladies' restroom at St. Mark's, I'd heard way more than I should. I knew the Ten Commandments, and two men I had respected, even adored, had broken them. Mr. Ellinger and Grandfather were both hypocrites! Aunt Kit was many things, but bless her heart, she was not that. She said exactly what she meant, whether sober or drunk.

So The Awful Year kept getting worse and worse. . . .

I continued to attend church until I was eleven or twelve, but by then I had a very robust vocabulary and an attitude. One night I explained to my parents precisely why I refused to go to church from there on out. For a while Hannah, in her youthful zeal, tried to witness to me, tried to explain that we were all sinners in need of a Savior, tried to tell me to hold on to Jesus, not to people who would always disappoint. But eventually she got the message with my silent stares. I just wasn't interested.

HENRY

No way could I go to work with that man threatening my boy and my wife. I felt that boiling rage inside just building and building. I made it back to the trailer, but just barely, getting all jittery and trying to work things out in my head. But then I thought about how upset Libby would be if I lost my job again, so I changed my mind and went on to the print shop about nine and worked all the way till nine that night.

The psychiatrist said when I got all beyond myself with the anger, I had to do something quick. But I couldn't remember what to do, except take the meds. If I took the pills, I'd calm down okay, wouldn't I? So I sat there in my La-z-Boy chair for about an hour, then went ahead and took a handful of pills. Don't know how many. I swallowed four cans of beer real quick and then started pacing around the trailer and didn't once call Libby to check on her and Jase because I couldn't let her know the shape I was in.

I just paced and drank more beer and then

261

I guess I passed out on the floor, because I woke up to the sound of gunshots. I sat up straight and terrified, but it was just my cell phone ringing awful loud.

"Hey, Libs." Light was coming in the trailer windows. I tried to get my mind to cooperate. "How's Jase?"

"Why haven't you answered your phone!" She was almost screaming. "Jase has pneumonia, Henry! They're afraid he isn't going to make it!"

Libby wasn't one to fall to pieces for no reason. She was strong. So I knew things must be really bad, the way her voice was all high-pitched and desperate-like. I was trying to get my eyes open in spite of that blinding headache and feeling like I might puke.

"Slow down, Libs. Tell me again. I'm sorry, Libs."

"I sat with him all night, Henry. They think he's going to die, I just know it." She was crying. "And I kept trying to call you. Where've you been, Henry? Leaving me so afraid and then with Jase getting worse?"

"I'm sorry, Libs. I-I worked twelve hours. Boss was real happy." I couldn't think of what else to say.

"I've been talking to Mrs. Bourdillon's daughter, to Paige. She said she met you."

"Yeah. That's right."

"Henry, maybe you better stay away." She started sobbing again.

"Don't pay no mind to what I said yesterday morning. It's gonna work out. I'll go to work today and then drive to the hospital. I'll be there by eight. You tell my boy to hold on, Libs." Tears were streaming down my face, and I knew she was crying real hard too. "You tell him to hang on. His pa's coming, and everything's gonna be all right."

Friday

PAIGE

"Don't leave us, Daddy! Please don't leave us!" I whimpered.

He took me by the shoulders, looked down into my eyes. "Paige, I have to go. Right now. But I need you to trust me."

Why did his face look so serious? So pale?

The world tumbled around me. I tried to say something, but a big ball of sorrow blocked it in the back of my throat.

"I'm coming back, sweetie. I'm coming back."

I sat up in bed, choking on the fear, my pillow wet, my eyes caked with sleep. I grabbed my pillow to my chest and held it there like a soft and fluffy protective shield.

Who was I kidding? Nothing would protect us. Nothing at all.

When I came downstairs I found Hannah hunched over a cup of coffee, her hair falling in her face. I thought she was looking at stuff on her phone, but then she lifted her head, and her face looked splotchy and red. "About The Awful Year, Paige. I think I can talk about it now."

I stared at her blankly.

"You okay, Paige?"

I heard a ringing in my ears. "Kinda. I just had a dream about it, about Daddy. And now you want to talk about it." I shivered a little, my whole body tense.

"Daddy . . ." She cleared her throat. "Daddy went away, and it was scary for a while because Momma was gone too."

"He went to jail!" I yelled.

Hannah's jaw dropped.

"You know it's true," I accused.

"I know. Of course I know. But why are you yelling at me?"

"Because we're afraid to say it, afraid to say that Daddy kept going away for a few days at a time, and then one time he even went to jail overnight, and Momma was gone for a long time at The Motte, and we felt alone and afraid for Daddy because he was acting so strange and we didn't know why. . . ."

264

Hannah grabbed me around the waist. "Shhh. Shhh. You're yelling, Paige. It's okay. No one has to know about all that stuff. It's got nothing to do with Momma getting shot. No one has to know."

"But they *will* know. I'm sure they've asked Daddy a thousand questions, and he's just protecting us. He feels guilty that he didn't insist that Momma go on to La Grande Motte in September, the way she always does after a novel comes out. And don't you think it's way too weird that the detectives haven't said a word about his being in jail once, even if he was just there overnight?"

Hannah's head was bent again, like she was praying over the cup of coffee, or else spending every bit of energy on not freaking out. "Paige, he went to jail because of a DUI. And it never happened again. I guarantee you, it has nothing at all to do with Momma and some crazy reader."

I shrugged, the image of Daddy leaving us still vivid in my mind. "How do you know that, Hannah? How can you be sure?" I lowered my voice, afraid the walls would hear and accuse me. "All those years ago, Momma was away at The Motte, but Daddy was away in his mind."

When I closed my eyes, I imagined Detective Blaylock and Officer Hanley leading Daddy away to jail. Again.

CHAPTER 11

Friday

JOSEPHINE

Something was smothering me! I flailed my arms and tried to pull it off. And the pain in my head, bone-crushing pain! I was screaming as loudly as I could! They were there, they were around me. Couldn't they hear? If only I could yank this mask off, they could hear!

Patrick's face came close. He stilled my hands. "Precious Feeny, it's all right, sweetie. I know the tubes are uncomfortable, but you need them right now. They're helping you breathe. You can't pull them out."

From far away I heard Hannah crying. "Look! She's in pain. She's crying. We've got to do something."

A voice I didn't know came close. A soft hand on my face. A woman's voice.

267

"Josephine, Josephine. I'm the nurse practitioner, Dr. Lenski. We're going to give you something to help the pain."

A soothing voice. She was still talking, but as if far away.

"This is normal behavior for a patient with a brain injury. She may be disoriented or confused for a while. Every person is different, and every injury is different. She may seem restless or have trouble concentrating or sleeping. Some patients become physically aggressive or agitated — as you just saw, with her pulling at the tubes. And all of that could change depending on the day."

"I can't bear to see her like this," Hannah wailed.

My firstborn cried easily. Not so with Paige.

The calming voice again. "This stage can be very disturbing for the family. Your mother may behave very uncharacteristically, but these are very positive signs. She's making amazing progress. . . ."

Voices kept fading in and out, but Patrick was still holding my hands. Yes, I felt that.

"You must be patient. Inconsistent behavior is also common. Some days will be better than others. She squeezed your hand several times at your prompting, but that may not happen again for a time . . ."

Had anyone told me what was wrong? Patrick said I was at a hospital. Kit said there was an assassination attempt. What on earth did she mean? Why did my head throb so horribly? Why wouldn't they let me move? Why was the blackness coming again . . . ?

2001 . . . Her first novel garnered mixed reviews and modest sales, but the second one! It soared straight onto the *New York Times* bestsellers list. Josephine was not prepared for the attention, the adulation, the demands for interviews, and all the fan mail!

Hannah and Paige didn't like their new nanny. Patrick had more responsibility at the office, staying late almost every night. And Kit! Another relapse, with screaming and cursing and a hospitalization.

Josephine remembered her dark days as a child and adolescent, when she had felt that hole grow bigger, when she was certain she'd fall in. And she was so incredibly tired.

It was no surprise that the cruel letter took her down.

She was sitting at her little writer's desk, looking out on the fall foliage with its magnificent array of colors. The chestnut trees a bright yellow, the dogwoods almost russet, and the maples! Oh, the maples boasted a multicolored palette of brilliant reds and yellows and oranges. She was blithely creating another story when Patrick brought in the mail. She'd received so much fan mail in the past month since the publication of her second novel that she couldn't keep up with it. She always took the letters seriously and used to answer quickly. Impossible now.

She opened a letter in a pink envelope, expecting roses of affirmation.

I wish you would burn in hell. Your story caused my daughter to jump off a bridge to her death. I HATE YOU!

Josephine squealed and dropped the letter as if it were burning her hand. She sank to the floor, buried her face in her hands, and screamed. When Patrick hurried back, he found her with a wild, unbalanced look in her eyes.

How could a piece of paper — pink stationery, no less — precipitate a nervous breakdown? All the years of being perfect and kind and doing the right thing split apart and the hole in her head became an earthquake and she fell in headfirst, begging God to save her somehow. Her saviors that time ended up being therapy, her husband, and, eventually, La Grande Motte.

Josephine looked out over the palm trees to

where the waves of the Mediterranean were licking the fine, dusty sand and the wind was blowing it up into tufts and swirls. She sat on the balcony, bundled in a fleece blanket, a cup of tea beside her. Her place of rest. The doctor had ordered calm and peace and solitude. Time for prayer and meditation and long, long walks. Rest. Wait. Do not write. Not now. Just rest.

She put on her parka and leggings, pulled a scarf around her neck, and went out into the fierce blue of November. The beach was deserted except for a few brave souls zipping far out in the sea on the sailing boards. Windsurfing, they called it. How they did not drown, Josephine could not guess. She walked and prayed and carried the Bible verses on cards with her, whispering the truth into the wind. And she rested. But in the calm, the terrible and beautiful calm, she heard nothing.

The stories were gone.

"I don't think I can keep writing, Patrick. The stories aren't there. It's emptiness."

They were walking along the beach, his big hand tight in hers, the sun starting to cast shadows behind them.

"Shhh, Feeny. Don't think about that now. Remember, now is the time to rest. Rest."

"Yes. I know. But what if they never come back?"

"We'll talk to the publisher. We'll ask for more time."

"You know it's because of the medication. Should I go off the antidepressants?"

He drew her close and said, "One day at a time, my beautiful girl. We'll figure this out one day at a time."

But Josephine knew she could not go off the medication. The stories had gone, but so had the horrible accusing voices and the terrible darkness. She missed the stories, but not those voices! How could she be a wife and mother with the raging darkness?

Patrick said, "You will not answer the mail. You won't even read it, okay? We'll hire someone to keep up with that for you. You just write."

But he didn't understand that the letters made the writing worth it. The words from readers, so sincere and heartfelt, gave her hope in the midst of the numbing pain.

Later she was walking along the empty beach with the sea lapping up and occasionally tickling her toes, really startling her with the icy splash. And it came in a whoosh, like before. A scene. It flickered for a moment and wrote itself in her mind and then she saw it, all of it at once.

A story.

Josephine fell to her knees, the wet sand seeping through her jeans, and wept.

When she returned from La Grande Motte, fresh stories sprang daily. Josephine overflowed with thankfulness. She got out the stack of Bible verses written on file cards, some of them over twenty years old, then took a large piece of plywood, sanded it smooth and stained it a maple color, and glued the file cards one by one onto the wood. It made a beautiful kaleidoscope of truth, the cards green and yellow and pink and white, some written on flowery stationery or just scribbled on a pretty napkin. She découpaged them all to the wood and called the resulting artwork her testimony, her Lucidity Lath.

"It's beautiful, Momma," three-year-old Paige said when Josephine hung the board on the back of her office door. "All those colors and the words make me smile, and your handwriting is so pretty."

When she spoke to women's groups, Josephine never shied away from the truth — her need for antidepressants to regulate her moods, her need for counseling, her need for complete rest, her need for Scripture and people. She told it all in living color, always ending with, "God's Word brought me back from the edge of despair . . . from insanity."

PAIGE

I dreaded my meeting with Detective Blaylock. He wanted to see me last night, but I begged exhaustion. Waiting hadn't helped at all; I'd hardly slept. I felt like I had a noose around my neck, and if I wasn't careful it would end up around someone else's.

He had set the appointment for ten, and I arrived at the hospital early to check on Momma first. I was excited at her progress and yet unglued by her obvious discomfort. No matter the nurse practitioner's assurance that this was normal, no one enjoyed watching a loved one make agonized grimaces while flailing her arms spastically in every direction as she tried without success to grab at the tubes.

I still had fifteen minutes before my appointment, so I headed down to the Pediatric ICU on the third floor in search of Libby. I'd brought her several casseroles from home, a box filled with chocolate treats from the Chocolate Fetish, and one of the many flower arrangements that had been delivered to our home. Another dozen decorated Momma's hospital room. And Mrs. Swanson daily trekked to our church

274

with a car filled with flowers to be delivered to nursing homes and homebound people.

I set the casseroles and desserts in the small fridge and headed for Jase's room. When Libby saw me standing outside the door with an enormous arrangement of white orchids, she burst into tears. Then she motioned for me to come in, took the vase from me, and set it on the windowsill.

Jase was lying in the bed, hooked to at least as many tubes and machines as Momma. He had a mop of chestnut-colored hair almost as thick as mine, but the rest of his body, his face and hands, were as white as the sheets that covered him. I bit my lip hard to keep from crying out at the sight of this little boy, a small human being, being kept alive by so much machinery. At least Momma had lived a very full and fulfilling life for fifty-some years. But this child? A six-year-old with a very slight chance of survival? How was that fair? How was that anything but soul-stopping tragic?

I grabbed Libby's hand, and we stood there staring at her boy, and the tears came cascading down my face as I whispered, "He's beautiful. Your Jase is just beautiful."

Detective Blaylock found a quiet corner of Café 509 where we could talk. I tried to read his expression. Resigned? Hopeful? Annoyed?

"So Paige," he began, tugging at his black beard, "your father and I have talked several times at length, and you'll be happy to know that I've studied your family a bit more, as you suggested."

I got it. He was feeding me my own medicine.

"I believe I have most of the facts, but I need your and your sister's memories."

"Okay." I heard Daddy begging me again. *"Paige, just answer his questions, honey. Please don't be belligerent."*

"Your mother had a history of nervous breakdowns. What do you remember about those?"

"I don't see why you're asking me when you already know."

"Trust me. I have a reason."

"Momma says that writing a novel is like giving birth. You become so heavy with the story, and then it finally sees life. She says she is all done in afterward. It sucks everything out of her. So Daddy sends her away to rest. I wouldn't call that a nervous breakdown. She's exhausted. I think it's pretty wise of them, actually."

"Okay. But several times she received very dark mail from readers, and that upset her. . . ."

"Naturally."

"And your father?"

"Daddy is very protective of my mother. They're super close. I've told you that. So of course he feels her pain."

I knew what was coming and couldn't steer the detective away.

"I'd like to ask you a little bit about the months in 2007 when your mother was in France."

I thought of my dream from the night before. "What about them?"

"Can you tell me what happened with your father?" He noticed my steely stare and silence. Detective Blaylock gave his by-now-familiar frown. "He and I have already talked about it, Paige. He specifically asked me not to mention anything about what you and your sister call 'The Awful Year.' I've respected his wishes for six days, but now, with this third threatening letter as new evidence, I need to get your take on that time. What happened, how you and your sister fared during those months your mother was away and your father was often gone too."

"It was horrible and scary," I blurted. "The year was already a disaster, long before Daddy . . . went away. Both of Momma's parents died — tragically. Her best friend got divorced. My aunt relapsed big time."

"And your father sent your mother away to the beach in France?"

"Yes, like always."

"And about how long was it between when she left and your father started going away?"

I didn't see why he was questioning me when he could have the bare facts. "I don't remember. It all smudges together in my mind."

"Do you know why your father went away?"

Of course I knew. "Because he had a big project at work, and it came at exactly the wrong time. So he had to get other people to care for us." Even as I pronounced the words, they sounded false in my ears.

I took a deep breath and turned my eyes down. *Get the conversation away from Daddy.*

"I've had ideas about who would want my mother dead. I think it could be a reader who revealed too much to Momma and panicked."

"Panicked?"

"Yes, decided to kill Momma before she turned on her."

Detective Blaylock looked unconvinced.

I had a flash. "A long time ago, when I was really little, there was an unstable woman who accused Momma of being responsible for her daughter's suicide. She wrote a threatening letter, I think. Maybe Daddy has told you about it. A crazy woman. Her daughter was the one who read Momma's books. This lady was just really, really torn up and bitter about her daughter's death and needed to blame someone. I never saw the letter, but Daddy would know if it still exists. Maybe it's that woman."

Detective Blaylock was hunched over, scratching his head and then flipping through notes he had scribbled in a small spiral notebook. For a moment he reminded me of Columbo, minus the cigar — I'd loved watching reruns of the rumpled homicide detective with Momma when I was younger. He found the page he was searching for and said, "We're trying to see if anything about The Awful Year could have to do with the assassination attempt. But we're also looking at these three pink letters." He glanced down at his notes again. "You say a deranged woman wrote your mother years ago? It would be a big help if you could find that threatening letter so that we can compare it to these recent ones."

"I can try." Why had Daddy not mentioned that to Detective Blaylock? And would he know if the letter was still somewhere in the house?

"Thanks, Paige."

I thought I'd gotten away with it again, but then he closed his notebook, straightened up, and steered the conversation back to Daddy.

"I'd like to know the events of those last months of The Awful Year, after your mother left. When your father was often away too, and when he ended up in jail." He doubtless saw my face fall, and added, "I'm sure it was all extremely painful." That brief sentence sounded compassionate. "But it'd be very helpful for me to hear what happened from your point of view. I know you were pretty young, but anything you can remember could help. Sometimes even the tiniest detail can shed new light on a case."

I closed my eyes. Anything I could remember? I remembered everything.

"We spent the night at our friend Drake's house. Momma had a book signing that Daddy wanted to attend and then she was leaving the next day for La Grande Motte, as usual. We'd already told her good-bye after school, and she'd cried a little. We never liked her to go away, but we knew she'd be happy at The Motte. And weeks alone with our father were always fun."

Usually they were fun. I cleared my throat and stared at my hands.

"When we got home from school the next day, my father was already there — which was strange. He got us a snack, and when we'd finished it he told us to go into the den, he had something to tell us. But he didn't really explain. When we walked into the den, we found Mrs. Swanson there. Daddy said there'd been an emergency at work, and he had to leave for a few days."

I took a bite of the pumpkin muffin I'd ordered, thankful to have my mouth too full to talk for a moment.

"Now? But Momma just left! Don't go too!" I remembered begging. And I remembered that Daddy had the strangest look on his face, his brow furrowed so tightly, his face so downcast, that for a moment I wasn't sure it was my fun-loving father looking at me. I kept begging and begging my father not to leave. Normally I didn't get too emotional about Momma leaving. That was Hannah's specialty. In truth, I wasn't upset about Momma. It was Daddy's odd composure that unsettled me.

But the detective didn't need to know that.

I finished chewing my bite, looked at Detective Blaylock and continued. "We wanted to know where he was going, why we couldn't go along, but he just said we had to trust him. I remember Hannah asking, 'Is Momma okay?' and he said, 'Yes, of course. She'll be in Paris soon and take the train to Montpellier, like always.'

"So he went away for a few days, and when he came back, he didn't seem like himself. He even forgot to pick us up at school two times, and that had never happened before. He kept leaving every few days, because he had some work project that had to be handled, so we spent a lot of time with sitters and neighbors.

"Usually when Momma went to France we talked with her once or twice a week, but not this time. Daddy was so distracted he'd forget about calling, and when we'd remind him, he'd be mad. One day I got really mad back and told him I wouldn't get in the car unless he promised we could call her after school. . . ."

I was not going to tell the detective every stinking detail, but boy, did it flash through my mind.

Daddy grabbed me by the shoulders and shook me. "No, Paige! Stop your whining. I said it's bad timing for me! And your mother needs her stint away. I don't want to hear another word about this!" Daddy was yelling,

282

his eyes blazing. He looked furious and stormed out of the garage.

"Paige? You okay?"

I felt my cheeks go red, nibbled another bite of muffin and nodded. "Yeah. Our father never raised his voice, but he did that day and it shook us up a little."

"I'm sure it did," Detective Blaylock said, pulling on his beard and frowning at me like he knew very well I was leaving out the juicy parts of the story. I hurried along.

"Anyway, that went on for several months, I think. Momma being gone. Daddy leaving for what seemed like long stretches and us staying with Mrs. Swanson or some church friends for sometimes a week at a time. Everybody treated us royally, but still, we felt upset and kind of abandoned."

And when Daddy was home with us, his odd behavior continued. The outbursts, the anger. It was anything but fun.

"But the scariest night was when I went into the kitchen to get a drink of water before bed, and I found Daddy sitting in the dark with an empty wine bottle beside him. He was crying."

After another bite of muffin, I hoped this last story would satisfy the detective.

"My parents only drink wine occasionally, maybe when they're out to dinner at a nice restaurant. Because there's alcoholism in Momma's family, they don't keep alcohol at home. But that night, I knew my father was drunk — I'd seen Aunt Kit like that. And then a few weeks later he didn't come home at all, and Mrs. Swanson came rushing over to stay with us. The next day I heard her talking on the phone, telling someone else she had to stay with us because our father had gotten a DUI. I didn't know what that meant till I asked Hannah." I shrugged and added, "Anyway, it was just one more awful episode in the whole awful year."

When I'd finished my remembering, I felt worn out and deflated. The feeling that our whole world had fallen apart was as vivid as though it had just happened.

Detective Blaylock gave me a fatherly pat on the back and said, "Thanks for sharing all this, Paige. I know it wasn't easy, but believe me, it's helpful." He pulled at his beard again. "So the first time your father went away was the same day as your mother left for France, is that right?"

I nodded.

I had ratted on my father, and I felt rotten about it, but at least I hadn't shared all the gory details, and I definitely hadn't shared the part that was now worrying me the most. That was the weekend that Aunt Kit had come unexpectedly. When she found us eating dinner with Mrs. Swanson in charge, she asked where Daddy was. I told her he had to go away for work, and she laughed.

"Oh, I'll bet he did," she said. "I know what that's about, honey. My father went off gallivanting a lot too."

Mrs. Swanson had quickly shut Aunt Kit down, but I had heard yet another new word. And when I looked it up I wondered what Aunt Kit meant. Was she saying Daddy wasn't really working? That he was doing something else? What?

At nine I hadn't understood Aunt Kit's insinuations about my father. But now, at seventeen, I thought about her accusation, and I felt sick to my stomach. Ever since the shooting, Daddy had looked so shaken and displaced and . . . and guilty. Yes, my father looked guilty. Just as he had during The Awful Year.

HENRY

I worked all day in a frenzy, my hands shaking like crazy, and the boss kept looking at me sideways.

"My boy's not doing so good," I told him.

"Go on and be with him, Henry. Be careful driving to Asheville now. You don't look so good yourself."

285

"I can finish my work, Mr. Dan. No need to let me go, I swear." I was sweating, feeling dizzy, and Mr. Dan had a real worried look on his face.

"You're okay, Henry. I'm not firing you. Go on and be with your boy."

So I left the printing press in the early afternoon, but I didn't go to Asheville. Not yet. First I went back to the library and turned in that book. Miz Garrison was there, and she looked at me kinda funny.

"You okay, Henry?"

I'd forgotten how bad I must look, having drunk all that beer and taken way too many pills. "Just had a rough night worryin' about my boy. He had his surgery and he's not doing so well."

Her startled expression softened, and she said, "I'm sorry to hear it, Henry." She took the novel from me and put it in one of them little shelves on rollers, then looked back at me with that same expression on her face.

"Don't suppose you got the latest one of Miz Bourdillon's books here, do you?" I was feeling real sick to my stomach, and I bet my face was all pale and greenish.

I shouldn't have asked that. Should have just hurried out of there. But she brightened and said, "You're in luck! Someone just returned one of our audio copies this morning. Do you have a CD player?"

"Yeah, I do."

"Well, if you'd like to listen to the audio version, it's really well done." She fetched it from the cart and checked it out for me.

"Thank you," I said and hurried out of the library and around the corner to my truck, where I threw up all over the parking lot.

PAIGE

I flew into Drake's arms as soon as he rounded the corner in the hospital corridor. "Thank goodness you're here!" I grabbed his jacket in my fists and held on tight, resting my head on his chest, listening to his heart beating just the way it should, with no tubes attached.

After a moment he pulled me away and said, "Hey, hey there. Calm down. Let's go sit."

I mashed my lips together, feeling heavy, a weight, that noose. "Could we get out of here for a little while? My head's about to explode."

"I was going to suggest the same thing, but can I see Momma Jo first?"

"The nurse shooed us out of the room and ordered complete rest for two hours. Then Hannah will sit with her. But we've reserved your place by her bed after dinner."

I looped my arm through his, totally natural, the way we used to walk when I was still a little kid and he was a teenager.

"I thought we'd grab something to eat downtown." He patted my hand. "I know just the place."

Of course he did. He drove us straight down Biltmore until we reached Battery Park Avenue ten minutes later. The familiar red and yellow sign greeted us — *Chai Pani, Indian Street Food* — and my mouth started watering. It had the best chai in town. "Thanks," I whispered, a knot in my throat.

"You need some food that you can actually taste, Bourdy. Hospital fare can get old."

We stepped into the dark interior with its red walls and little white Christmas lights hanging from above. The smells! Spicy, aromatic. My stomach growled loudly, and Drake glanced at me and grinned.

I felt my insides do a little dance.

We ordered green mango chaat and Pani's signature matchstick okra fries for starters. Drake got a beer, and I had well, yes, chai.

We'd never done small talk well, so I wasn't a bit surprised when he immediately said, "I told you I remembered something else about TAY. I've been thinking about the sequence of the events. Remember how for years and years there was a woman who attended every single one of your mother's book signings — all throughout the Southeast? We joked at first about her overly devoted fan. But then when it kept happening, we got a little nervous and called her the stalker?"

I chewed on an okra fry. "Yeah. Hannah and I were just talking about her a few days ago."

"Did anyone ever figure out who she was? Did you ever actually meet her?"

"Oh yeah, we've all met her. Her name is Charity Mordant. We hadn't seen her in years, and then last month she suddenly showed up at one of Momma's signings. She's a little overly enthusiastic, but she's nice. A 'real number' — that's what Momma calls her. She's loud and boisterous and wears gaudy jewelry and way too much makeup, and her clothes are colorful and eccentric." I closed my eyes for a moment and could perfectly picture Charity Mordant rushing over and smothering Momma in a bear hug, like they were the best of friends. "She's strange but not deranged."

"How can you be sure?"

I shrugged. "I don't know. I guess after she freaked us out that first summer by coming to every signing, well, we got used to her. She won us over."

"Exactly."

"What are you talking about?"

"I don't really know. I'm just bringing up things that I've been thinking about." He smiled, his blue-green eyes twinkling a little and his dimples showing, and he looked so absolutely handsome, as well as cute and winsome, that my stomach fluttered in the way it had when I was thirteen.

He didn't notice and started twirling a pen in his left hand and then tossing it from hand to hand. "Okay, here's a completely different scenario. You know I spent half of that year on your couch with your mom listening to my endless tirades. One day she was in tears when I came in. You and Hannah were off somewhere, maybe with your dad. And she was crying and shaking and holding a letter in her hands. She said something like, 'Drake, forgive me. I'm being pursued by an irate woman. Again.' She cried a little more and then she told me about the other times she'd gotten these very upsetting letters from a grieving lady accusing her of putting dark thoughts in her daughter's mind."

"Yes! I was just telling Detective Blaylock about that. Except I didn't know that woman wrote more than once. Wow." I pushed a few fries onto Drake's plate and said, "Eat."

He took a bite and continued. "So my parents were divorcing and Momma Jo's parents had both died, and your mother's novel had just come out. Your father sent her away to France to rest, right? But before she left, she got the letter from an angry reader — the letter I saw. And then your dad was gone a lot. . . ."

Drake had started on the green mango chaat. He groaned with pleasure at our favorite Indian snack food, a mixture of potato pieces and chickpeas, sour Indian chili, coriander, and other tangy spices. "Delish."

"And landed in jail for a DUI," I finished. "And we stayed with a bunch of different people. And Daddy was acting so weird. I told the detective all that." I lifted my eyebrows. "Well, a watered-down version. And I didn't tell him about the time Aunt Kit came and stayed with us for a few days. She kept talking about Daddy as if he were a real jerk and said he was out gallivanting." I made air quotes around the word. "I never thought about it again until now. She meant he was seeing someone else, Drake. Having an affair . . ."

"Impossible!" Drake said.

But we'd thought the same about his father, and we'd been wrong. Drake looked me in the eyes.

"Don't go down that road, Bourdy. Please."

"I won't. I agree, it's impossible." I sounded confident, but there was something I couldn't admit even to Drake. Daddy's explanations of his frequent absences that fall *were* very sketchy. And that didn't sound like innocence to me.

We walked along the French Broad River, the air biting and fresh and the sun starting to dim. I wanted this to be my life. Not the hospital. Not conversations about stalkers and murder and insanity. I just wanted to enjoy this stroll with Drake and let the beauty of the area seep into my soul and forget for an hour the horror of the past week.

I leaned into Drake and again, it was natural and comforting and innocent. He was treating me exactly the way he always had, as my big brother, my protector, my best friend. Certainly not like a boyfriend. My heart was beating a bit unpredictably, and I silently berated Hannah for putting thoughts in my head.

"I know it's all pretty heavy on you, Bourdy. And I know you're trying to be strong for your dad. But you don't have to be strong for me. Let's not talk about this anymore right now." We walked into a little gazebo that jutted out over the river, and he leaned his back against the railing. "Tell me about college choices and SATs."

I rolled my eyes. "No, thanks." He was right. We should change the subject, but I couldn't. I needed to ask the next questions, the ones that strangled me. "Do you ever think about marriage, Drake? I mean, with what happened to your parents? Does that affect you?"

"So, no more talk about murder, just divorce?" But he was smiling down at me.

"I'm sorry. It's just that with that detective's questions, I keep reliving things that scare me. Your parents fell out of love, and I think my parents . . ." I refused to cry. This was not the time for that!

He lifted my chin. "What is it, Bourdy? What do you need to say?"

I had to ask him the one question that I'd never asked anyone. "Drake, do you think a person can love too much?"

He got a pained expression on his face, seemed to wrestle with a thought, but then simply said, "Explain."

"Like I said, I didn't tell Detective Blaylock everything. I couldn't tell him what it is I'm really afraid of. But Momma did have depressive episodes, and sometimes she told Daddy it was too dark. And if she kept getting mean letters, maybe Daddy just lost it. I don't think it was an affair. Surely it wasn't . . ." I covered my face in my hands and let out these huge gut-wrenching sobs.

His arms came around me again. "Shhh. You're not thinking straight, Paige. If there's one thing I know, it's that your dad loves your mom."

After I composed myself a little I said, "I know that. I do. But what if he loves her *too* much? What if he did something that seemed like love to him, but it wasn't?"

"What are you suggesting, Bourdy?"

"Maybe he tried to find the person who was sending those letters so that Momma wouldn't have to deal with someone who kept making her crazy. Would he do that?"

He scrunched up his face. "Are you suggesting that your father deliberately sought out the person who had sent menacing letters to your mother and threatened him or her?"

I grabbed him and held on tightly, desperately, the way Libby had done to me earlier in the day. "Maybe. I don't know. I'd rather it be that than an affair. And I have this memory that just keeps pressing in, but I can't quite recall it. Something important. But I do know that Momma hadn't received any mean letters for the past few years. They stopped coming a long time ago." Still holding on to Drake, I groaned. "And I'm sure Detective Blaylock is going to ask Daddy about them. I mentioned the very first one to him. I thought it was weird that Daddy hadn't said anything yet."

Several couples walked past the gazebo. When we were alone again, Drake whispered, "Look, Bourdy, maybe you could write down everything you remember about the letter from long ago and the ones now. Just put your thoughts on paper and leave your poor dad out of it. Let the detective talk to him."

"You're right. Of course you're right. I'm just a mess at the moment. A complicated mess." *We used to call Momma a complicated mess.* I let go of him, swiped my eyes and nose, and tried to clear my head. Tried to think of something else to talk about. "So you really aren't dating anyone?"

How did that escape?

He smiled. "You and your sister. Always asking the same questions. You'd think you were related." He was staring out at the river and could not see the deep blush on my face, but I felt it. "And the answer is the same as always. Nope. At least not anyone seriously."

I deflated a little. What did *that* mean?

"Bourdy, this year is really demanding. Not a lot of time for a love life." He changed positions, leaning over the railing of the gazebo, and I caught his reflection in the water, dark and deep and smooth.

"Yeah, you engineers have it rough."

"But let's go back to your original question. Do I ever think about marriage? Of course I think about it sometimes."

I was so relieved to be talking about anything, anything at all to get off the subject of Daddy's love for Momma. "Well, let me know when you decide to get married, okay? So I can prepare myself. Remember how jealous I was when you were dating girls in high school and I was, what, about thirteen? How I had that crazy crush on you?"

He nodded. "I remember it well. Sorry to have caused you so much pain." He had a teasing tone in his voice, but something about it sounded serious too. "No, marriage will have to wait for a while."

"Till you finish your degree and get a good job and, of course, find the right girl."

I suddenly didn't want to be talking about this subject either.

"No. Not exactly like that. I mean, of course I plan to finish my degree and get a job. But I've already found the girl. That's why I have to wait. . . ."

"What? That doesn't make sense! A minute ago you said you aren't dating anyone seriously, and now you claim to have already found the girl." I felt tears in my eyes again. Frustrated, I balled my fist, trying to ignore the liquid that trickled down my cheek. "Sorry. I think I'm just too tired to be having any kind of conversation at all."

He wasn't facing me, had his hands still braced on the railing, and he was staring out into the waning day. He was silent for a minute. Then he said, "I'm just waiting for you to grow up, Bourdy." He turned around and looked straight into my startled eyes, took me by the shoulders, and gave the sweetest grin. "Just waiting for you, is all."

CHAPTER 12

Friday

JOSEPHINE

2006 . . . Hannah and Paige were playing in the sand at La Grande Motte, building a castle to imitate the town. Josephine had a big floppy hat covering her head, and she was sitting in a folding chair that kept her close to the ground.

"Can you recite that poem again, Momma?" Paige asked.

Paige had finished reading *A Wrinkle in Time* earlier that week and now she wanted to read anything else by Madeleine L'Engle. Josephine had no access to a library with books in English, but she had access to her memory. "This is a poem by Ms. L'Engle. I think it is very beautiful," she had said the day before and then had begun to quote "Second Lazarus."

Paige had listened to the short poem again

and again, smiling each time Josephine pronounced the last sentence about how pain is sometimes necessary in order to experience true freedom.

Josephine recited it yet again, and Paige looked up from their sand castle and beamed. "It's beautiful, Momma. I like that poem! It's like that verse on your Lucidity Lath. You have to lose your life to find it."

How could an eight-year-old grasp that poem when she herself could barely take it in? But Paige had an astute mind, brimming with imagination and depth. How Josephine longed to protect her creative daughter from all the emotional damage she had experienced in her own childhood. Thank goodness Paige did not spend much time with Josephine's parents and Kit. Like her mother, Paige had a penchant for writing stories. Fortunately, she did not brood and hide in deep places in her mind. When she was mad or upset, she displayed it for all the world to see.

Paige's voice came in and out. She used to love to recite poetry with me. We memorized Shakespeare and Emily Dickinson and Robert Frost and beautiful passages of Scripture. But after The Awful Year, she rarely recited anything at all.

A shadow passed across my mind, and I prayed, "Lord Jesus, care for my Paige. Help her find her way. Help her." I thought I was praying, but I couldn't hear the sound of my words.

The Awful Year — what was that? Was it a poem that Paige wrote? I tried to think of the present. Hannah was here, but she was supposed to be in France. I knew that. But Paige seemed stuck in my mind as a little girl, a little girl who wrote mystery stories and quoted Madeleine L'Engle.

Then she was holding Hannah's hand and saying in that sober, serious way of hers, "This is an Awful Year, Hannie. Nothing but an Awful Year." What did that mean? I had no idea.

HENRY

I drove like a madman toward Asheville, everything messed up in my mind. I had to kill Miz Bourdillon! I didn't even want to anymore, but I knew I had to do it. Both of my guns were ready, but my hands were shaking like crazy, which wasn't any good.

"You gotta do what you gotta do." Pa's words kept on echoing in my mind.

I turned on the radio, and it was still on Lib's favorite station. A preacher was reading from the Bible. Gospel of St. Matthew, but some modern version, sounded like to me. I concentrated real hard on what he was saying.

"Later when Jesus was eating supper at Matthew's house with his close followers, a lot of disreputable characters came and joined them. When the Pharisees saw him keeping this kind of company, they had a fit, and lit into Jesus' followers. 'What kind of example is this from your Teacher, acting cozy with crooks and riffraff?'

"Jesus, overhearing, shot back, 'Who needs a doctor: the healthy or the sick? Go figure out what this Scripture means: "I'm after mercy, not religion." I'm here to invite outsiders, not coddle insiders.' "

It was just a lot of noise in my brain. I needed to talk to Miz Bourdillon, see if she could forgive me, so maybe God wouldn't punish me by letting Jase die.

I didn't want to kill her anymore, but I had to get the money and pay Nick to protect my boy. I tried to think what to do, what to do, but my head felt like it was splitting in half. Finally I pulled off at a rest stop and sat in the car.

Birch! I'd call Birch, and he'd tell me what to do.

But he didn't answer his cell, and I didn't want to leave him a message asking if I should kill Miz Bourdillon. So I sat in the car for a while and drifted off to sleep, which was about the only way I was gonna find any peace from the noise in my head.

PAIGE

The doctor was making his rounds at ten that night, his eyes still bright, still moving with a nervous energy while I could barely stifle a yawn. But I had nervous energy too! Drake's proclamation had come totally out of nowhere. We'd walked back to his car hand in hand, both in shock. I certainly didn't have the mental reserves to process what had just happened, and Drake didn't say anything else.

Now he, Daddy, Hannah, Aunt Kit, and I were gathered in Momma's room.

Dr. Moore stared down at Momma. "Josephine, Josephine, can you see my finger?"

Momma's eyes followed his right hand as he slowly moved it from left to right.

Then, with the same hand, he took hold of Momma's hand and asked, "Can you squeeze my hand?" He chuckled. "That's a good grip, Josephine." He looked over his shoulder, nodding to all of us.

"Can you tell me where you live, Josephine?" He bent down low, his ear almost touching Momma's parched lips. To our shock, those lips moved, and a garbled sound escaped. We all laughed at that.

Hope! It surged up in my heart, making me feel giddy and buzzed. Dr. Moore continued talking to us as he directed us into the hall and away from Momma's hearing.

"Josephine is keeping eye contact briefly. You saw that she followed my finger with her eyes. And she responded to my command by squeezing my hand. These are very good signs. She also seems to distinguish where sounds are coming from, she's showing emotion, and she's trying to vocalize. Be very careful to notice when she is tracking — when she watches you as you move around the room or turns her head toward you when she sees you or hears your voice."

I wanted to hug Dr. Moore, but refrained. Such good news! Daddy shook the doctor's hand and murmured, "Thank you. Thank you."

To which Dr. Moore responded, "You don't need to thank me. Thank Josephine. She's the one doing all the work."

As the doctor left us in the hallway, Daddy's slumped shoulders straightened a little. We were all yawning.

"Go home, Daddy," Hannah said. "With this great news, surely you can rest a little.

Aunt Kit, you too."

Daddy nodded and said, "Hannah, I think you should try to get some sleep too, before you fly out tomorrow. You can still visit Momma in the morning before we need to leave for the airport."

Hannah looked unconvinced, but then she acquiesced. How I didn't want her to leave! I needed to tell her about my walk by the river with Drake. Tell her that she'd been right all along.

"Drake and I will stay here with Momma," I said.

I glanced up at him to be sure, and he nodded and smiled.

JOSEPHINE

2007 . . . Drake, still dressed in his cross-country uniform, lay sprawled on the couch. "Dad had an affair! An affair! And my mom's losing it. They fight all the time. Warren and Alex came home from college last weekend and just about freaked out. Smith and I, well, we just lock ourselves in our rooms till they calm down. And it feels like, even though I'm the youngest, I've got to be in charge of the family now."

Josephine remembered that feeling all too well.

"It feels so heavy. So dark and heavy."

Poor Drake. He had a sensitive side that neither of his parents really understood. Ginnie believed in hard work and few hugs and Bert . . . She sighed. Bert wanted an athlete for a son, not an engineer. A football player, not a runner.

"You have to learn how to carry the burden, Drake, by giving it to the Lord. He carries it. It's too heavy for us."

"How?" he begged, his voice so anguished and angry. "I'm mad at my parents, and I don't tend to pay much attention to God right now. He certainly isn't paying attention to us."

"Oh, but He is."

"How?"

"He's letting you vent to me." She took a deep breath and said, "Drake, I've struggled with depression most of my life. Oh, we didn't call it that back when I was a child and a teenager. But I recognize the signs in you. I tried so hard to carry my family, and I had a faith that sometimes made it all the more complicated. As though it was my Christian duty to figure everything out and make things better. But it didn't work. I just kept slipping further into that hole in my head, and my parents and sister and others were too occupied with their own struggles to see how it affected me. But it did."

"What happened?"

"I begged God for help. And not more than a few days later — after I had been literally weeping on my knees before the Lord — I met a very wise young woman. We were on a ski retreat. She was probably in her early thirties, and I was a sophomore in college, so it scared me to death to say anything. But she was an artist and exuded compassion. And I just felt so strongly in my spirit that God had put me in her path or her in my path, however that works."

"And?"

"She helped me find help. Helped me see how to let the burden go. Helped me redirect my spiraling thoughts."

"Did she help you plug up the hole?"

"She pointed me to the One who could do that."

"And did it work?"

"Our lives are a journey, Drake. A beautiful and excruciating journey filled with different seasons. In that season of my life, thanks to that dear woman and a few others, I got some tools — I call them tools, maybe God's toolbox — to deal with the depression better. It didn't go away exactly, but I could recognize it better, could prepare myself." She struggled to admit the next thing. "And Drake, I had to let my family go. I loved them, I was there for them in many ways. But I couldn't carry them."

"And that worked?"

"Let's just say I learned to set boundaries — to distinguish what was my part and what wasn't. It certainly didn't make everything better. Not nice and neat. But I survived."

She tried to read the expressions on his young face: hope, defiance, perplexity. She so dearly wanted to leave Drake with hope. Hope. She would not tell him that the depression often returned. Nor would she admit the long and painful journey with Kit. Those were true, but so was what she was telling him right now. He could have hope.

HENRY

Woke up feeling real groggy. I had a couple of hours to listen to the CDs of Miz Bourdillon's book as I drove to Asheville. It kept me kinda concentrated and awake and made me forget about Nick's threats.

This book was about a rich society lady back during the Civil War who grew up on a plantation in Georgia. Her father owned lots of slaves, but she herself was against slavery and stood up for the black people. And it was about a slave who'd been treated something awful, like a piece of trash.

And there she went again, Miz Bourdillon, writing a story that reminded me of myself.

All my life I was nothing but a piece of trash. Ma and Pa never meant me to be born. Just two screwed up teenagers screwing around, literally, and here I came. So they went on and got married, and there I was, messing up all their plans.

I don't know if God is real. But if He is, I think He had a real good idea about family. Imagine me saying that with all the horror of my own. What I mean is no matter that Ma didn't want to get pregnant and sure didn't want to marry Pa — once I was born, she just somehow loved me. She wasn't no tender mother or anything, but one time when Pa was at his worst with me, Ma came in and screamed at him, "You stop it right now, Amos! Now!"

And he was just glaring at her and holding my arm like as to break it, and says, "Why?"

And she was crying and then begging, on her knees begging, "Because I love him, Amos. I love my boy." And Pa just let me go, dropped me to the floor. And I don't remember what happened after that.

But most of the time I was just in the way. And even though I liked going to school and I did okay, Pa didn't care one bit about learning. The only books in our house were Ma's romance novels and Pa's girly magazines. I looked at them a lot when I was real young and then wished I hadn't, because afterward I felt all dirty.

Guess most of my life I've felt dirty, like someone left over or a mistake or worse. A sinner, that's what the pastor at Libby's church calls people like me. He says, "A sinner like you," and looks out at the people in the pews, and then he whispers, "A sinner like me." He says we're all the same before God. Sinners in need of God's grace.

Well, I don't know about that.

But listening to this book, boy, did it have me crying. It was just like what I'd heard that radio preacher say, and just like what Jesus was doing in the Gospel he read! Just exactly! You know how funny that is, when you read something and then next thing you know, you're seeing it again somewhere? Libby doesn't believe in coincidence. She says it's God's Spirit speaking, trying to get your attention.

Well, something got my attention, because Miz Bourdillon's heroine was doing that exact same thing. It was after the Civil War, and she was this real good person that everybody liked. I think the lady was head of some Southern women's group for rich white people. Anyway, she had a meal, and she invited the poor men who was all maimed from the war and some of the local prostitutes and their pimps. She didn't call them pimps, but I knew that was what they were. And she invited former slaves who were having a bad time, and she even invited a man from town who was in the KKK. He was a bigwig in the community and boy, was I scared that man was just gonna go on and start hanging the former slaves — she called them freedmen, but didn't sound to me like they were very free.

Anyway, it was clear what she was showing. Like if it had been today, the lady would have been inviting gays and immigrants and refugees and religious people too.

She filled up her house with all those people. And it wasn't because she felt sorry for them.

She was real clever, Miz Bourdillon, the way she wrote it. Everyone that lady invited she'd gotten to know a little bit somewhere in the story. And there were some highfalutin rich folks who were about as mad as Pa got sometimes, yelling at her and saying she was a piece of scum, but then there were about half those rich ladies who went right ahead and helped her with the meal and sat there in between the different "outsiders" — that's what I'm calling them, borrowing it from St. Matthew. Miz Bourdillon didn't give any labels at all. And the thing about how she wrote the book was that you just believed her. And you felt all warm and cozy inside. And I got tears in my eyes, too, because I knew, I just knew, that I'd have been invited, too, if I'd been lucky enough to cross that woman's path.

That wasn't gonna happen, of course, because it was just a story, but I reckoned something even ten times better could happen. I could talk to the author herself. Because there wasn't any way she could write something that pretty and touching if she didn't believe it herself. Leastways I didn't think she could. If she believed it and if it was true, well, maybe she could forgive me and maybe Jesus could forgive me, too, and wash away all the layers of dirt that had been clinging to me just about from the day I was born.

JOSEPHINE

Paige was talking softly. "Momma, something amazing happened tonight. I-I don't even know how to say it."

I opened my eyes and slowly, slowly turned my head so I could see her. She sat huddled in the chair, a fleece around her, her thick chestnut hair falling over her shoulders. She was grasping my hand, and maybe she had dozed off, but after a moment she straightened in the chair. "Momma! Look at you! Your eyes are open again. Oh, Momma! Can you squeeze my hand?"

I tried, and I must have succeeded because she said, "Great! Great!" But then she was blubbering like a baby, and my Paige never cried.

"Drake and I left the hospital earlier and got dinner at Chai Pani — you know, that great little Indian restaurant in town? And we were talking about so many things . . . hard things, but then something amazing happened. He just all of a sudden admitted that he liked me, Momma! I mean, liked me in a romantic way. Isn't that amazing? Hannah had been teasing me about it, but I didn't believe her for a second, and then it came out, and I don't even know what to think. He said he wants to wait for me. As in marriage. I'll be eighteen in two months. Am I crazy, Momma? Did he tell you this?"

I was smiling in my head and heart, but I don't think she could tell. Dear Paige. She had a way of going on and on and on when she got excited. Yes, Drake had told me of his affection for Paige, more than once. I was sure of that. When he told me, I could not remember. But I had read his eyes when

312

he talked about Paige, and it was pure love.

And now he had declared it to my daughter. I was actually chuckling to myself. At least it felt like a low rumble beneath all the tubes. She kept talking, and I wanted to stay awake, but something kept pulling me down and away.

HENRY

I sped on through the night, praying I'd make it before my boy died and asking God why in the world he let my boy have that operation if he was gonna die one way or another. I drove faster and faster and felt the adrenaline and everything pulsing, pulsing.

Had to talk to Miz Bourdillon and explain about everything. I was sure she'd understand, and then Jase would get better, and I wouldn't ever kill anyone again.

Now I knew, way down in my bones, what I had to do. Once I got it figured out, I felt kinda peaceful, like I'd been praying for. Funny how all the sudden it seemed like I could be a better father to my Jase than Pa was to me. I could almost see Jesus standing by my boy's hospital bed and helping me talk all nice and soft and convincing to him. I could be different with my boy. The dirt could be washed away, and I could change.

I was thinking about these things, pretty excited, when I finally pulled into the hospital parking lot. That bright neon sign was flashing the hospital's name, but for me it was like an angel flashing a message, and that message was that Jesus would invite me to eat with Him and so would Miz Bourdillon. And all the sudden I just felt flooded with that thing called *hope*!

I was gonna be different — not dirty, but clean. Even with Jase doing so poorly and Nick threatening and all. If only I could see Miz Bourdillon, I just knew that she was gonna forgive me, and everything was gonna be okay after all.

Or was it? Even if she forgave me, the police weren't about to, were they? And if I didn't kill her, well, then whoever hired me was maybe gonna kill my boy and Libs.

As I parked the truck, I heard my phone ringing in my bag, but I didn't stop to answer. I rushed into that hospital with my head exploding with possibility, Glock in my belt, hidden under my flannel shirt in case I needed it to convince someone I was serious. I hurried on up to the third floor and found Libby in the waiting room. When she saw me, she about fainted.

"Henry! Henry, what's the matter with you? What's the matter?"

Why was she looking at me like that, when I had it all figured out in my mind about peace and hope? I started feeling queasy again with a little panic mixed in. "Gotta see my boy! He still alive, my boy?"

Libby was crying and holding on to me. "Yes, yes, he's still alive, Henry. But you've got to calm down. You have to be calm before we see him." Her hands started trembling as she brushed the hair out of my eyes. "You look like a wild man, babe."

I paced around the waiting room for a while. Good thing we were the only ones there. Every few seconds Libby would say, "Breathe, Henry. Breathe. Get a hold of yourself, now!"

Finally, seemed like an eternity, she judged I was calm enough, and we went into that hospital room. The walls was just plain ole white, and there was this big fancy plant over by the window, and it was white, too, and Jase looked as white as the flowers and the walls and the sheets. But not a healthy white. Yellowish kind of white. I looked at all those machines with their lights flashing green and red in that sterile room and went over to the bed, staring down at my boy with his eyes closed and mouth half-open

315

and a hole in his throat where another tube came out.

"He's dead!" I choked out, and leaned over that bed, about ready to pick him up. But Libby threw her hand out. Tiny thing, but she had a lot of strength too.

"No, no, Henry. The machine is breathing for him, babe. He's alive. Don't scare him."

"They've cut open his chest and now he has a hole in his throat. They're killing my boy!"

"It's called a tracheotomy, Henry. They had to do it to help him breathe. He's got pneumonia. But the trachea will heal. It'll be okay."

I turned to face Libby, thinking about Nick's last words. If having his chest and throat broken open didn't kill him, someone else would do it. Now my hands were shaking real bad, and Libby took them in hers, so small and warm, and said, "Look at me, Henry. Look at me."

I finally got my eyes to obey, and she took my face in her hands now, in that way she had to calm me down. "Jase is having a bad time, and he needs us to be here with him."

"They think he's got a chance?"

"They aren't promising anything, but they say he's doing a little better."

I sat there by Jase's bed for a long time,

watching how his reddish eyelashes just lay so still on his freckled face. Tried to get those threats out of my mind, but it wasn't easy. I finally started thinking about Miz Bourdillon's book and everything I'd figured out on the way to the hospital, but then I was hearing that man's voice, pure hatred, threatening to kill Jase.

"We gotta get the police to protect our boy, I tell you, Libs." I felt real desperate for Jase and so confused. I buried my face in my hands and just started weeping. "I gotta see Miz Bourdillon."

Libby shrank back from me. "What?"

"Gotta see her. Ask her." Everything was real blurry.

"Henry, she can't answer questions. She can't talk at all."

"She has to. And I have to tell her too." Soon as I said it, I knew what to do — just clear as day.

I left Libby in that room with my boy just barely breathing. Raced out into the hall and to the stairway and up the steps to the next floor. Had to wind my way around a little, but I found the Neuro Trauma waiting room. Paige was sitting on one side of the room and a teenaged boy was lying on his stomach across some chairs on the other side, looking at his phone.

I went over to Paige real quiet like and bent down and touched her on the shoulder. "I need to see your mother," I whispered.

She jumped a little, and her eyes got real big when she recognized me.

"I'm sorry, Henry. Only family can see her," she stammered.

"I gotta see her. She's gotta tell me how to save my boy's life."

I looked behind me and that teenager wasn't paying any attention to us, so I pulled out my Glock and grabbed Paige's arm. Hated to scare her like that, but I said real soft, "You gotta take me to see your mother."

PAIGE

Some things in your life seem surreal, and seeing Henry waving a gun and then grabbing me by the arm and ordering me to go into Momma's room, well, it was like an out-of-body experience. I froze, as if looking from afar at this giant blond man who towered over me, his eyes wild, his face a mixture of fear and menace.

Then I shrank back, panic and anger and a need to protect Momma all bubbling to the surface. Someone was yelling at Henry, "Why are you pointing that gun at me?" and then I realized it was *my* voice. "You

318

think I would take anyone who's pointing a gun at me to see my mother who just got shot in the head?"

The giant deflated, his strange eyes apologetic. "I ain't gonna hurt you, Paige. I promise. Ain't gonna hurt your momma either. Just need to ask her a few questions, is all." He lowered the gun and pushed me forward.

The kid who had been lying on some chairs across the room glanced up, took in the scene, and scrambled out of the room.

Then out of the corner of my eye I saw Libby come in; she had a panicked look on her face and kept saying, "Easy, Henry. Listen to me. Jase is going to get better."

I stared at her and mouthed *Get help!* She nodded, her eyes as wide as mine must have been, and backed out of the waiting room and took off down the hall, without Henry noticing. Drake had gone down to Café 509 to get a hamburger from the grill. *Come back, Drake,* I kept saying to myself, maybe even praying it to God.

Henry started crying. "Need to talk to your mother awful bad, Paige. Gotta tell her what's happened. You gotta take me, and I don't want to hurt you. But you gotta take me in."

He shoved me a little with the nose of the

pistol, and that sent cold chills zipping through my body. "There's a policeman in front of Momma's room, Henry."

"Gotta see her, Paige. You can convince him to let me see her. I know you can."

Heart in my throat, gun in my back, and Henry's hand grasping my arm in such a way that it hurt, we walked toward the room. The policeman wasn't there, and I felt another flutter of terror as I opened the door and we stepped inside.

Momma was lying there, eyes closed and motionless. Henry held me by one arm, the gun still pointed in my back, and went to Momma, leaning over the bed.

"I done something real bad, Miz Bourdillon. I'm so sorry I shot you, but I was just doing my job, trying to get money for my boy's surgery. Wasn't nothing personal. Sure am glad you're alive. I heard you've opened your eyes some, so maybe you can hear me.

"You gotta know it wasn't me who wanted you dead. You gotta understand that. I'm gonna protect you, but I gotta protect my boy too. So you just go on and get well. I know lots of people are praying for that, and my Libs . . ." With that, he turned around and noticed she wasn't there. "Where's Libs?"

"She went back to Jase," I managed to

choke out, but that wasn't where she'd gone at all, and surely at any moment the police would be here. My mind was racing, my hands shaking. Henry had just admitted to shooting Momma. *He* was the shooter.

But he *wasn't* the one who wanted Momma dead. That's what it took me a split-second to realize. Someone else had hired him to kill my mother. Henry was still talking.

"I'm so sorry, Miz Bourdillon, but I want to know about forgiveness. Got so many questions."

Momma's eyes were still closed, and something in my brain actually prayed, *Let her be asleep, God, don't let her hear this or see this, please.*

But just then her eyes opened, and her face registered pain and fear. She threw her arm out awkwardly to the side. I took it in my hands, whispered to her, and tried to calm her down.

Henry was sobbing now, one hand holding the gun to my back and the other wiping the tears off his face, over and over. Blubbering. I couldn't tell if he had noticed Momma's opened eyes or not.

"I want to know if the person who shot you can ever be forgiven? Does it work like that?"

Then I heard the trample of boots in the hallway, and the door burst open and voices were yelling at Henry, "Put down your weapon!"

And I panicked, afraid that the moment he put the gun down, poor deranged Henry would be dead.

"Don't shoot!" I yelled. And Henry, eyes all alarmed and scary, let go of me and dropped the pistol. I threw myself in front of him, waving my arms as I faced three policemen with their guns aimed our way, screaming, "Don't shoot him! Please, please. Don't shoot."

CHAPTER 13

JOSEPHINE

The face staring at me was pale and frightening, the eyes a glassy blue, the whitish hair shaggy and unkempt. I wanted to back away, but I couldn't make my body move. I tried to open my mouth to scream, but nothing came out. He was ranting about a shooting, a book, forgiveness. Paige was there, too, and I heard the fear in the way she was breathing, and I felt afraid too. We needed to leave, quickly.

I must have flailed my arm because Paige took my hand and whispered in a voice that barely sounded like hers, "It's all right, Momma. I'm here."

And the man kept ranting and then I saw the door open and policemen rush in. I didn't understand what was happening, only that this man was in trouble and Paige

323

was crying and begging the policemen not to shoot. And I could not move, no matter how hard I tried.

PAIGE

I was still hyperventilating when they put the handcuffs on Henry. A nurse was tending to Momma, who jerked and moaned in a ghastly way. Drake was cradling me in his arms and saying, "Bourdy, Bourdy, are you okay?"

But I could not speak. I had floated away again, hovering over Momma as the nurses, three of them now, tried to calm her spastic movements. She gargled pitiful sounds and her eyes were skewed and terror filled, like a prisoner in a death camp. The nurses must have added a sedative to her cocktail of meds, because a few minutes later she calmed and her eyes closed.

I breathed again, and turned to see Henry leaving the room, the policemen pointing their handguns at his back. And he had the same horror-filled anguish on his face as Momma.

A nurse had me sit down right on the floor in the room, and she knelt in front of me. "Breathe, Paige, breathe. Slow, that's right." She was shining a light in my eyes and saying, "She's in shock," and then, "Paige, are you hurt? Does anything hurt?"

I realized then I was shivering uncontrollably, but I managed to shake my head. "I'm not hurt," I mumbled.

"Let me take you to a place where you can lie down for a while," the nurse was saying.

But I shook my head again, my eyes riveted on Henry being escorted from the room. "That man is the one who shot Momma," I whispered.

From somewhere far away I could hear Libby wailing, "Please don't take Henry, please!"

I crumpled into Drake's arms and everything went black.

HENRY

Libby almost lost her mind when she saw me being led away in handcuffs. She was screaming and crying after those policemen to make sure I took my meds — that they'd help level me out. And the cop kept trying to calm her down, telling her it was gonna be okay. But we all knew nothing was okay.

I had been so sure, just a little while ago. If I had only gotten to ask Miz Bourdillon all my questions. She could hear me, I saw it. She'd opened her eyes and was listening to me. She was. And then those cops came in and ruined everything and hauled me away in their patrol car to the police station.

The interrogation room was small and empty of everything except a table — which was bolted down, I noticed right away — and two chairs. There were little cameras, two of them, up in the corners of the room. So I figured maybe someone else was watching us, but I didn't know for sure. Didn't scare me, though. Pa's interrogations were a lot scarier than this, and I had the scars to prove it.

A man called Detective Blaylock sat on the other side of the table and just stared at me for a long time, not talking. He kept pulling at his thick black beard, like he had something stuck in it, but all that was stuck was me.

"Henry, mind if I call you Henry?"

I shrugged. "Okay."

Just me and that Detective Blaylock sitting alone in the little room. He said, "Before we start, I want to make sure you understand that you have rights, Henry." He paused, like he wasn't sure I could understand him, so I nodded. "Since this is a criminal investigation, you know, the lawyers want us to go over this stuff. You watch TV, you've heard it before."

I'd watched a lot more than TV, but wasn't no use saying anything about Pa.

The detective cleared his throat. He was kinda fidgety, but not mean acting.

"You do have the right to remain silent. Anything you say can be used against you in court. You have the right to have an attorney present with you during questioning, or to consult an attorney prior to questioning. If you don't have an attorney or can't afford one, the state will appoint one to you. And at any time during our questioning, you can choose to stop the interview. Do you understand these rights?"

I nodded, but then I saw he wanted me to say it out loud, so I answered, "Yes. I got you," and he had me sign a waiver.

Then he started asking me a bunch of questions like "What's your name? What's your birthday? What's your wife's name? Your son's? Where are you from? What's your address?"

Went on and on and on, those questions. And I was feeling really tired. Run down. Didn't seem too important, those questions, but after a while that detective seemed okay, like he was almost on my side. He was recording everything I said with a fancy little machine, and then sometimes he'd jot down something in a notebook, but that didn't bother me. I knew what I could tell him and what I couldn't.

"Henry, you admitted that you're guilty of shooting Mrs. Bourdillon. That's attempted first-degree murder." He stared at me with his dark eyes, not exactly threatening. Like he expected me to smile and say, "Yep, that's right." But I said nothing.

"And you're guilty of taking a hostage with a weapon." He waited again, but I wasn't paying attention because all of a sudden I was seeing Paige's eyes all horrified and scared, and I felt real bad about that.

But the detective just kept on talking, real calm like, telling me everything I was guilty of and that I'd have a real long prison sentence. He added, almost kindly, "Henry, you'll be found guilty, and you'll never see your family again."

He waited as if I should agree with him, but I figured I'd better keep my mouth shut. So we sat there in silence for a while.

Then he tried again. "It's clear that you pulled the trigger, but it's also clear that you aren't the one who wanted Mrs. Bourdillon dead. Someone hired you. Who was it that hired you to kill Mrs. Bourdillon?"

I fidgeted for a while with my hands and felt the sweat break out on my brow. "I don't know — it went through my contact."

328

"So you don't know the name of the person who wanted to have Mrs. Bourdillon assassinated?"

"That's right. I don't know."

"And what is your contact's name?"

"Detective, sir, I have a sick boy in the hospital. Real sick. Barely hangin' on. The minute I tell you my contact's name, my boy is as good as dead. My wife too."

"We'll protect them. We've got guards at the hospital twenty-four hours a day."

"If I got into Miz Bourdillon's room with a gun, I expect my contact could get into Jase's room too. I'm not gonna tell you, Detective. I'm not."

He cursed, rubbed his hands over his face, and cursed again. "You'll go to jail for attempted first-degree murder, Henry. You could be in jail for the rest of your life. But if you can give us any information, then I'll talk to the DA about waiving the lesser charges and pleading the attempted first-degree down to an aggravated assault." He started tugging on his beard again.

I could tell he was trying to help me. "And what good would it do me to be out of jail if my wife and son are dead? Sorry, Detective."

He sat silent and stone-faced. I didn't think he was gonna say anything else, but then he said, soft, almost pleading, "Don't you want whoever planned this thing to be behind bars?"

I didn't say anything. I was trying to figure out if Nick would risk coming to the hospital to harm my boy now that it was overrun again with police.

They took me to a cell, and there were some other men in the cells next to mine, just staring at me with angry, prowling eyes. I lay down on a cot and pulled a blanket over my shoulders and tried to picture Jesus in the jail, right here with all us sinners. And it must've worked, because sometime in the night I fell asleep.

PAIGE

No one seemed surprised that the incident went viral. The teenager who was in the waiting room when Henry grabbed me followed the police when they rushed to Momma's room, and he filmed the whole scene on his phone. Before Drake could even get in touch with Daddy and Hannah and Aunt Kit back at home, Hannah had seen a video on Facebook of me screaming and shielding Henry while police stormed the room and Momma lay trancelike in the background.

It freaked Hannah out completely.

When she and Daddy and Aunt Kit arrived at the hospital, the whole place was swarming with police, and an officer brought them in a back entrance while a whole crew of police stood outside the front entrance.

I sat in the waiting room and couldn't stop shivering, even though Drake bundled me in his fleece jacket and a big wool blanket provided by the hospital. The nurse attending me suggested very calmly she take me to a bed in the ICU to lie down, but I begged her to let me stay with Drake and my family in the waiting room. She did persuade me to take a sedative, but I didn't want to sleep.

"How's Momma?" I'd ask every time I blinked awake, and Hannah would run her hands through my hair and say, "She's fine, Paige." But I kept moaning, "I should have refused to take him into her room! It's all my fault."

"Oh, Paige, don't entertain those thoughts, sweetie," Daddy said. "You did a very courageous thing."

Hannah begged me, "Let me take you home, Paige. You've got to sleep, and you can't do it here. Please."

"Bourdy," Drake added, "you're going to help your mother the most by getting rest. The police will have plenty of questions for you tomorrow."

Finally I gave in and let them lead me out of the waiting room, but then I stopped. "Libby," I whispered.

"Who?" Drake asked.

"I've got to find Libby — that man's wife. She must be out of her mind with worry."

Drake looked me in the eyes. "Bourdy, you've had enough excitement for one night." That was the understatement of the year — Momma responding to me, a declaration of love, and then being taken hostage.

"Please, let me check on her, just for a sec."

"Bourdy . . ."

"Please?"

Drake glanced over at Daddy, who frowned and shook his head *no*.

"Please," I begged again. "Her son is dying and now her husband is in jail. She doesn't have any family or anybody at all here with her."

Daddy shrugged. "Just for a minute, sweetie. You've got to get some rest."

Hannah gave me a hug, and then Drake and a policeman escorted me to the elevator, and we rode down one floor. Another policeman stood outside Jase's door. He glanced up at us, looked at the other officer, and nodded. When we stepped into

Jase's room, Libby was sitting in the chair by his bed, hunched over, wringing her hands, a shattered expression on her face. I went to her and grabbed her in a hug.

She stiffened a little and looked scared to death. Then she said, "I'm so sorry, Paige! About everything — what Henry did to your mother and then to you. I'm so sorry."

Then her arms tightened around me, and she cried her heart out.

"They're going to take me downstairs for questioning. I begged them to do it up here in the waiting room. I don't want to be far from my boy. They said I can spend the night in here, but I have to be questioned first." She looked so small and lost. "Look at him now, Paige. So pale and weak. I'm so scared."

I grabbed her again. "Call your pastor, Libby. Tell him what's happened. Tell him you need someone from your church to be here." Then I blurted out, "And I'll stay with Jase until you get back." It took a moment for this to register, so I said it again. "I'll watch over him, Libby. I promise." She melted in my arms and cried.

Drake and I sat there until Libby returned sometime later. I dozed in and out to the sounds of the machines beeping and breathing for Jase. But Drake stayed wide awake. I could not make anything out of Libby's expression when she returned, nothing except the anguish and horror I had read on her face earlier. I hugged her tightly again, and then Drake helped me to the elevator, where my knees immediately buckled, and he picked me up in his arms, following the policeman to his patrol car.

I must have fallen asleep in the car because I woke up once again in Drake's arms. He carried me into the house and tucked me into bed. I remember mumbling, "How is Momma?" and then was out.

Saturday

I woke to light streaming through my bedroom window and a feeling of dread. Then I remembered — Henry shoving me with the gun, Momma's terrified face, the police. . . .

I pulled myself out of bed, stretched, and tried to pry open my eyes, but the effects of the sedative made that nearly impossible. I took a hot shower, and as the water blasted me I let myself sob under its protective stream. Then I wrapped myself in an oversized towel and walked to my window to look out at the mountains beyond. When I glanced down at our driveway, I gasped and backed away. Four police cars were parked there, red lights flashing, and a group of people stood just beyond, cameras poised and waiting for something. I also recognized a few of our neighbors. A policeman was turning away other cars.

I threw on a pair of jeans and a sweat shirt and rushed downstairs. Hannah and Daddy were sitting at the breakfast room table, and when I walked in Daddy rushed over to me and held me tightly. "Paige, sweetie."

I took in my surroundings. "Who's with Momma?"

Daddy said, "Ginnie."

Drake's mother, Momma's closest friend.

"She saw everything on the news and came to the hospital at midnight." This from Hannah. "She persuaded us to go home and sleep. Drake went back to be there with her. And Aunt Kit just left a few minutes ago. She's heading back to the hospital so Ginnie can take a break."

"The nursing staff begged us all to rest. As you can see" — Daddy nodded to the bay window in the kitchen — "we had quite the police escort."

My mind was so fuzzy. "Why are they here?"

Hannah pointed to the news headlines staring back at me from Daddy's laptop: *Josephine Bourdillon's daughter taken hostage,*

335

saves mother and shooter.

The room started spinning, and I collapsed in a chair. "What does it mean?"

"They're calling you a hero, and there are reporters out there waiting to get a glimpse of you." Hannah gave me a wink. "Reporters, and some of Momma's fans."

"Unbelievable," I whispered.

"You should hear what people are saying." Now Hannah led me into the family room. There on the TV screen, a reporter was standing in our front yard — *our yard!* — holding his microphone in front of an older woman who spoke excitedly.

"I've read all of Mrs. Bourdillon's books. I'm one of her biggest fans. Just had to come up here and see where she lives. And her daughter. What a brave young woman!" Then she wrinkled her brow. "Although I can't imagine why she had pity on the assassin. That man deserves to die!"

I had barely assimilated this comment when the reporter turned to a middle-aged woman who was saying, "Mighty thankful that they've caught that scum. I tell you what — he should be hung!"

Running across the bottom of the screen were the words *Author's devoted fans demanding death penalty for hit man.*

The video changed from our yard to a

scene in front of the police station where Henry was being held. A policeman was blocking a small crowd of people from advancing to the entrance. They held up handmade signs that read *What happened to police protection?, Kill the killer!,* and other horrible things.

I collapsed on the leather sofa, thankful that poor Henry had been locked away *inside* the jail.

JOSEPHINE

"JoJo, it's me again, JoJo. It's Kit. Everything just gets crazier and crazier, doesn't it? Do you understand what's happening? Listen, I'm sorry I made such a fuss over the money. And what happened with Patrick. Please, please just forget about that whole nasty business."

Kit's face was so close, her mouth moving frantically, but what exactly was she saying?

2007 . . . Two days after their father's funeral, the family lawyer called Kit and Josephine, and Patrick as well, to his office. After welcoming them and expressing condolences, he said, "Patrick, as you know, Dick named you executor of the will."

Patrick nodded. Josephine's stomach was in knots. This was not a surprise to any of

337

them, but Kit's eyes still blazed anger.

The lawyer continued, "There is quite a bit of cash in Dick's main account, and then the IRA and the two Foundations. The property was appraised at two million. . . ." He kept quoting figures, but Josephine could barely hear him. All she saw was the fury on Kit's face.

"The trust funds have specific instructions . . . sum of money for both Hannah and Paige. The rest of the inheritance is to be split evenly between Kit and Josephine."

Kit looked relieved.

"With one rather significant stipulation. Kit's account is to be managed by Patrick."

Josephine wilted. What had her parents been thinking? Hadn't she discussed this with them countless times? She and Patrick didn't want any more responsibility for Kit. It was a noose.

Kit, mad as a hornet, screamed obscenities, accusing Patrick and Josephine and the lawyer of manipulation. But in the end, the will won out. And the noose tightened again. Truly an Awful Year, just as the girls proclaimed.

HENRY

Had that TV blaring at the police station when they brought me out of the holding cell for processing the next morning, and

338

sure enough, there I was on the screen, holding my gun and pointing it at poor Paige and then dropping it on the floor and Paige jumping in front of me. And I don't know why she did such a thing, because I knew good and well them cops could have shot me dead without endangering Paige or her mother. You could see it clear as the sky on that video they kept replaying.

I must've asked that question out loud, because one of the cops said, "You idiot! She saved your skin so you'd tell her who ordered the hit. But once you do that . . ." He grinned at me and drew his finger across his neck. "You'll be dead meat. You've got thousands of people demanding you confess to who was really behind the shooting before they hang you." He laughed. "You're safer in here with a bunch of thugs than out there with those people who like Miz Bourdillon's books. Ain't that something?"

And he didn't know the half of it. Because I reckoned the people who liked Miz Bourdillon's books were the religious sort, and shouldn't they be the kind of people who'd show forgiveness and compassion instead of pure red-hot hate? Didn't make sense to me. Then I got to thinking again about how Jesus wasn't real kind to the Pharisees — I knew about them from Libby's church.

They were the religious experts.

I wondered how many religious folks nowadays acted like those Pharisees. And then I wondered long and hard how Jesus would feel about them.

But mostly I was worrying about my boy and wondering how poor Libby was doing and hoping she'd come to the jail to see me and tell me about Jase. Had a real bad feeling about all of it when just yesterday I'd thought some things were beginning to make sense.

PAIGE

Daddy was the one to find the letters, four of them, filed away, not in the plastic containers in The Chalet, but somewhere in his office. All in pink envelopes, all the notes on pink stationery, all with the same block print as the most recent ones.

When I'd finally remembered to tell him about Detective Blaylock's request, Daddy had gotten such a look of resignation on his face that I almost said, *Never mind.*

He brought them up to my bedroom, where I was lying on my bed, with Hannah perched on the twin bed across from me. "I kept these, but I certainly didn't want your mother to know I still had them. Each one sent her into a fit."

"Why'd you keep them, Daddy?" I asked.

He got a far-off look in his eyes. "I guess I always knew we'd need them someday."

"I'm pretty sure if Detective Blaylock examines these, he'll find they're from the same person," I said. "Why didn't you show the letters to him right away?"

He sat down on the edge of my bed and said, "It was just way too complicated, girls. That's why."

I wanted him to say more, but he just leaned over and kissed me on the forehead and said, "You rest, my dear. Hannah, you make sure of it, okay? Stay away from the internet and the TV with all the madness. Aunt Kit will be back home in a little while, and then I'm going back to see Momma." Then he added, "Paige, Detective Blaylock would like to talk to you about what happened last night. He wanted to give you a chance to rest, but whenever you feel ready, he said he'd be happy to come by the house."

"He can come this afternoon, Daddy. I think it'd do me good to talk to him."

A few days ago, I couldn't imagine ever saying that.

"I'll let him know. Now rest."

When Daddy left the room, I said, "Hannie, please don't go back to France. Not now. Not with everything going on."

She caught me in her arms. "Shhh. Daddy's already cancelled my flight. I'm here. I'll stay with you."

"Merci."

"Je t'en prie." And we met eyes, both sets tear-filled, both of us slipping back to France for just a few seconds.

I was thankful for Daddy's orders — and the nurse's — which kept us away from the internet and the TV and everything leaking out over Facebook and Twitter. I had never been part of something going viral before. And I was thankful that our home was guarded by a mass of policemen and that Momma's room and Jase's room at the hospital were also under "tight surveillance" — Detective Blaylock's words — and that poor Henry Hughes was safe behind bars.

I said it out loud to Hannah. "Of all the ironies, *safe behind bars* takes on a whole new meaning now, doesn't it?"

Hannah made a face. "His poor wife and kid. Saddest thing in the world. But I can't say I feel very sorry for *him.* He did shoot Momma in the head!" She was fiddling with her hair, carefully pulling it into a French braid, one section over the other. Then she let go, and her thick mane untwisted slowly, almost elegantly. "Were you scared? Do you want to talk about it, you know, having a gun in your back and all?"

I honestly could not begin to describe the emotions coursing through me. Terror, exhaustion, relief, hope for Momma, and that giddiness bubbling up again in the midst of everything else. Drake liked me! When I explained our conversation to Hannah, including Drake's declaration, she gave a sigh worthy of a heroine in a Victorian novel. I half expected her to swoon. "What do I do now, Hannie? I'm so confused."

She tweaked my cheek and laughed. "Drake's already told you what to do, and what he's going to do. Just wait."

Now *I* sighed, a deep-down moan of happiness and frustration, and Hannah and I met each other's eyes and burst into laughter and then we doubled over with it and soon we were both laughing hysterically. When we finally quit, we hugged each other again and then we both fell fast asleep on the twin beds in my room.

I woke up to someone yelling, high pitched, strident, piercing. "I don't give a donkey's hee-haw what any policeman says!" Mrs. Swanson's voice carried up to the third story. "I am going down to that hospital and planting myself by the door, and I am not

343

budging! I have the biggest bladder in the United States, and you won't catch me leaving Josy's room unguarded so that some madman can burst in with precious Paige and threaten to kill them both!"

Hannah and I tiptoed down the stairs, stopping halfway between the second and first floors, hidden from view. But we could see the scene before us — Daddy pulling on his overcoat, Mrs. Swanson already bundled in a ski parka and a bright red scarf covering her starched white hair, and Aunt Kit, dressed in her hot pink exercise outfit, lounging on a barstool at the kitchen island.

"Kit, you're in charge of Milton." Mrs. Swanson calmed a little and continued. "You just stay here and take him out — he's been needing it four times a day. Poor thing, he's gotten real nervous and that plays on his bladder. And the postman will bring all the letters to the front door; he leaves them in a postal bag so don't you dare get confused and throw that away, you hear?" She gave Aunt Kit a withering glance. "Won't come for a little while, but you be sure to stay right by the door. With all the police and the reporters and fans, well, I wouldn't be surprised if they all try to rush in the house. Heaven help us! I hope those policemen have a little more backbone than that dimwit supposedly guarding Josy's room last night!"

"I need to get back to Atlanta," Kit protested. "I have a gym class this afternoon."

"I don't want to hear a word of your belly-aching, woman! Your sister's just woken up from a coma and the assassin tried to kill her again and your niece to boot, *and* now they know there is someone else after Josy, so you just hush up and do what I say. And leave poor Paige and Hannah alone. Let them rest. You're needed right here a lot more than at some sissy gym class." She paused, then added, "All right, Patrick. Let's be off."

Hannah and I tiptoed back up the stairs and our giggling fit started again.

An hour later, Hannah was downstairs with Aunt Kit when I went into Momma's chalet to sit in the quiet. Here I could stare out into the back woods with the mountains peeking in the distance over the tall firs just outside her window. I saw no police cars or reporters or crazy fans from here. I wanted to escape for just a little while longer. Momma always closed her door while she worked, but the door to the office had remained open now for a week. When I pushed it shut from the inside, I was greeted with Momma's Lucidity Lath, hanging on the back of the door. Running my hand over the smooth, clear stain, I got tears in my eyes.

"It's so pretty, Momma. I want to learn those verses too."

And I did. Day after day, I sat in Momma's chalet, a book in my hands, all comfortable on the cushions she'd put in the corner just for Hannah and me. As soon as we learned how to be quiet, we were allowed in The Chalet to read books. And I read her Scripture board. Verses so beautiful, so hope filled, but also verses of anguish and questioning. An abbreviated version of the Bible hanging on the back of her door.

"Just one of the tools I use to keep me focused on the truth," Momma often said.

Tears began falling down my cheeks, tears of remorse and anger and bitterness.

Drake had questioned and believed. I had questioned and grown aloof and angry.

I decided to take the board to the hospital. Now that Momma had her eyes open, I wanted her to see something more hopeful than white walls or a blond stranger begging for forgiveness with a gun.

CHAPTER 14

Saturday

JOSEPHINE

"Please don't be alarmed by this setback. Considering what she went through last night, she is doing amazingly well." That soft voice was talking to someone.

Patrick was holding my hand and then softly kissing my lips. I could feel the hot tears that fell on my cheeks. My Patrick. He was so sensitive. Now he was stroking my arm, and I tried to smile, to tell him thank you for the massage.

I must have mumbled something, all garbled like, because he touched my cheek in the gentle way he had and said, "Oh, Feeny. You're so brave. Don't worry, my love. You're not going to let what happened last night stop your progress. And Paige is fine."

Now Patrick was gripping my hands and

347

whispering. "No more secrets, Feeny. I told the detective everything that happened. It's okay. You're going to be fine, and there will be no more secrets, my love."

What had happened? My head had that crushing pain. I was thirsty. I closed my eyes and saw the man crying and saying he was so sorry he shot me. He shot me?

Or had someone shot me during The Awful Year? Was that our secret, Patrick? Was that why I was here now?

PAIGE

When Detective Blaylock arrived, Aunt Kit left with Milton for a walk, casting confused glances over her shoulder as Milton dragged her out the back door, far away from the crowd out front. Hannah hurried the detective inside before the press could snap any photos.

Now Detective Blaylock sat across from me in the den in an oversized tan leather chair. I was tucked under a blanket on the couch. Hannah had fixed the detective a cup of coffee, and I had my chai. A plateful of pastries sat on the glass-topped coffee table and a fire crackled in the fireplace as if this were merely a cozy visit between friends.

"How are you feeling today, Paige?" he began, reaching for a chocolate-covered macaroon. He took a bite and then a long sip of the coffee. His eyes were red and his uniform crumpled. I wondered if he'd slept at all.

"It's all a bit surreal."

"You're a brave kid." I thought I saw a hint of admiration in his tired eyes. "A face-off with three armed policemen."

I shrugged. "Like I said, it was all a bit surreal. I was trying to protect Momma. I was afraid she could be accidentally shot."

He nodded.

"And," I added, taking a long sip of chai and not meeting his eyes, "I was afraid they'd kill Henry."

"Henry? You're on a first-name basis with him?"

"We met in the ICU waiting room Monday night. I've talked with him a few times. And with his wife, Libby."

"That's right. The officer with you last night told me you stayed with their sick son while Mrs. Hughes was questioned." He stared out the picture window. Then he set down his coffee, hunched over his knees, deep in thought, and shook his head, as if clearing it of a few cobwebs.

I nibbled my lip, managed to glance up at him. "I guess I felt sorry for them. Their situation." Now I let my gaze wander to the blazing fire. If I closed my eyes I was thirteen again and the youth were sandwiched into every spot of this room, singing praise choruses while snowflakes crystallized on the windows. And Drake was sitting next to me.

"Henry admitted he shot Momma, but he said he was hired to do it. So I guess I reacted to that instinctively. I mean, what good would it be to kill him without knowing who hired him?"

"Exactly." Detective Blaylock actually smiled at me. "But just so you know, once Henry put down his gun, my men weren't going to shoot."

I gave a halfhearted grin. "Well, that's reassuring."

The conversation felt lethargic, as if the detective were slowly pulling a rope of information out of me, hand over hand, and I was unwinding, with no strength to resist. Why *would* I resist?

"Paige, can you recall exactly what Henry said to you and then to your mother? It'd be helpful to have your testimony." His digital recorder sat on the coffee table waiting for my answer.

"He confessed. I mean, he literally confessed his guilt to Momma." I couldn't banish the image of Henry in the cafeteria asking me those questions — questions that held the meaning of life — and then the image of him beside Momma's bed, pleading for her to answer the same things. "He's desperate for his son, but he also just seems desperate for life. And he's been reading Momma's books. He told her he's read two of them and is halfway through another." As best I could remember, I related my conversation with Henry in the cafeteria.

Detective Blaylock furrowed his brow, fidgeted as usual, looked like he was trying to decide about something, and finally said, "We've found out more about the guy — Henry Hughes."

"Does he have a record?"

"Not much of one. But his father did. Small-time crook. And he was shot during a convenience-store heist — right in front of his son. Henry's mother had died a few years earlier."

"That's . . . that's horrible."

"Yes, it is. Henry grew up around violence. And he's got a sick son. Needs money. Evidently his son has had a lifetime of heart surgeries."

I was processing this information and placing it alongside the man I'd gotten to know. "So he hired himself out to save his son. But that doesn't help us figure out who hired him."

"He claims he doesn't know. Says his contact is the middleman in this affair."

"Poor Henry!" I whimpered. My head was pounding, and I buried it in my hands.

The detective didn't say anything.

Massaging my temples, I said, "Yeah. I know it seems crazy, but this whole scenario is crazy, Detective Blaylock. I don't really know why I feel protective of poor Henry and Libby and Jase. I just wish I could help them."

"He won't say a word about the person who hired him. Says the guy has threatened his son, and Henry believes he'll follow through. He's terrified." He cleared his voice, cocked his head, tugged on his beard. "Would you be willing to talk to him, Paige? See if he might open up with you?"

I brightened and straightened up. "Sure! I can do that. Sure!"

"You might be able to ask questions in a way that takes him off guard." Detective Blaylock winked at me. "You're real good at that."

I thought the interview was over, but we were only at an intermission. He checked his cell phone and said, "Paige, your father is coming back here, and he'd like to have a conversation with you and Hannah and the young man, Drake, about those months when your mother was away during The Awful Year."

I bristled. "What about it?" When he didn't answer immediately, I said, "Is Daddy a suspect?"

He reached over and took my shoulder. "Paige." His eyes bore into me. A long pause. "Put your mind at rest. Your father is not a suspect."

Not a suspect, but he had kept all those letters and not told the police about them and now he was coming to "have a conversation" with us. What did it all mean?

Detective Blaylock continued to look me in the eyes. "Paige, your father wants to tell you the real story. . . ."

I felt a chill zip up my back. *The real story? What has he been keeping from us?*

"And who will stay with Momma?"

"I believe your Aunt Kit is heading back to the hospital. And your neighbor is there."

I groaned. "You should talk to Aunt Kit. She's the strangest person in the whole family."

"Oh, I have, Paige. You're right. She's a very interesting character." He chuckled, then added, "I'm heading back to the station." He left the den, then reappeared a moment later, reminding me again of Columbo. "One more thing — I'll have an officer pick you up tomorrow afternoon and bring you down to the station to talk with Henry. Will that work for you?"

"That will work," I answered, but the enthusiasm I'd felt about meeting with Henry had evaporated, replaced by dread of what my father was going to tell us now.

When Drake and Hannah and Daddy arrived back home they joined me in the den, me with my cup of chai, the others with mugs of coffee. Daddy looked like an elderly stranger as he began to talk, hunched over his coffee, his eyes turned down. Hannah, Drake, and I huddled together on the couch and listened to his monologue.

"I came home from work early . . . at noon. I planned to surprise your mother with a lunch date before we headed to the airport at two. But when I walked into the house, Milton was whining and pawing at the door. You know how anxious he always gets when he sees your mother packing her bags. I just patted him and called out to let her know I was home, but there was no answer. I started up the stairs to The Chalet, expecting to find her trying to answer one last piece of fan mail, and Milton tried to block my way.

"But she wasn't there, and by now Milton was barking at me. He bounded back down the stairs ahead of me and into our bedroom. I found your mother in bed, and at first I thought she was just taking a nap. Then I saw the way her arm was hanging over the bed, the bottles on the bedside table. . . ."

"Oh, Daddy," I whispered.

"I called 911 in a panic and carried her downstairs to wait for the ambulance. Once I knew she was going to survive, I hurried back from the hospital, determined to clean everything up before you girls got home from school. My worst nightmare had come true, except —" Daddy paused, finally raised his head and looked at us one by one, his eyes all glassy with tears. "She hadn't died. I marveled at the timing. If I hadn't come home early . . . I decided I would make up a story, anything except the truth. Anything except that Feeny had tried to take her own life.

"I hadn't been able to protect her enough *before*. But *now,* now I could protect her from the aftermath. I decided not to tell anyone else, except Mamie and Papy. You girls would think your mother was at The Motte, taking a break as she always did after a novel came out."

Daddy's voice kind of petered out for a moment, and I could see in his eyes that he was reliving the whole horrible incident. He cleared his throat and sat up a little straighter and continued. "She stayed at the hospital in Asheville for a week, until she was stabilized. Then I enrolled her in a mental health facility near Knoxville that offered a three-month treatment program for women suffering from depression or other mental illnesses.

"I was allowed to visit her often. The program encouraged the family to take part in the healing, and I felt torn. Should I bring you girls into it? Perhaps I was wrong to keep it a secret."

In Daddy's eyes I read a desperate plea for us to understand his dilemma. I *did* understand and felt sick to my stomach. But before I could reassure him, he kept going with the story.

"I was trying to protect your mother. I was absent from you girls, and that made everything even worse than it had been during that truly awful year."

He took a long, low breath and let the air out slowly. Then he wiped his hands over his face and sat back in the wing chair. I started to say something, and Hannah rose to go over to him, but he shook his head

356

and said, "Let me finish, kids. I need to tell it all, at last."

I braced myself. Were there worse secrets to be revealed?

"I started drinking. I missed some important deadlines at work. Then I got the DUI. I didn't seek help — from the Lord or from others. I thought keeping the secret was the right thing to do, but it wasn't.

"Your mother needed me to be near her, but so did you girls." Daddy met our eyes again and said, "I'm so sorry. So very sorry about it all."

Daddy wasn't away on business or "gallivanting," as Aunt Kit had accused. He was trying to save Momma.

Because Momma had tried to kill herself.

That was Daddy's secret, the one that made him stop smiling. He was living with the knowledge that his wife had attempted suicide. And he feared that if he didn't protect her from everyone and everything, if he didn't make her well, she might try it again.

My parents rarely argued, and never in front of us, and Daddy had the softest voice. Momma said it always surprised her to see him so competitive and almost ferocious playing soccer, since he was kind and even-tempered off the field. For all my growing-up years, he had played on a local amateur team, just for fun. He'd dreamed of playing on a professional team when he was young. According to Momma, he had the talent but had sacrificed the dream for her because she didn't do well when he was away.

She'd get a little teary whenever she'd tell this, and Daddy would look at her tenderly, with the sweetest smile, and what I read in his eyes was his great love for Momma and how he didn't think of it as a sacrifice at all.

But I thought of that word *sacrifice* a lot.

I grew up seeing my parents sacrifice for each other in lots of little ways and some great big ones. I didn't know as a child if those sacrifices were wise or foolish, but I knew one thing. My parents knew a lot about real, deep-down love. They knew it hurt, they knew it cost something valuable, they knew it was worth keeping.

But now I understood the full extent of Daddy's sacrifice. I had been right. Daddy *had* loved too much.

I didn't realize until he finished telling us the story that I was clutching Drake's hand, fiercely clutching it, and resting my head on Hannah's shoulder. Daddy gave a huge sigh, wiped his face with his hands again, and leaned forward, resting his elbows on his knees. "I'm sorry we never told you before. We thought it was for the best. I'm so sorry, kids. I'm going to tell Aunt Kit tonight. I just . . . I just wanted to share it with you three first."

I read sorrow and relief in those soft brown eyes. As one, Hannah and Drake and I got up and surrounded him. When he stood up, we engulfed one another in a tight and desperate hug.

HENRY

They fed me some lunch and a lady brought me my meds and sat there watching as I popped them into my mouth. One was for my PTSD, I knew, but the others were the same as they'd given me the night before to calm me down. She stuck her finger in my mouth to make sure I swallowed them down. Of course I did. Wasn't any need for me to be holding my Glock anymore.

I wondered about a lawyer. I figured we'd need one real bad, but we sure didn't have money for that. But then I remembered the detective said the state would get me someone if I needed.

They took everything from me — the Glock, of course, and my phone and my keys and my wallet. I wondered if there was any way the police could figure out which phone number was my contact's. Kept thinking about the instructions Nick gave me and the way he shouted at me over the phone the other day. I still thought it was real strange that a woman wanted Miz Bourdillon dead. And saying, *"Take her life and let it be consecrated,"* or whatever. Even when Nick was shouting that at me, I recognized those words. They were from a song they sang at Libby's church. I thought it was pretty strange that whoever hired me knew about that hymn. For sure they did, because no way would someone say those words who hadn't ever heard the song. And why would anybody want Miz Bourdillon dead in the first place?

Ended up surprising myself by praying that somehow, whoever had the idea to kill Miz Bourdillon would step out of the shadows and into the light.

JOSEPHINE

2007 . . . Josephine held the familiar-looking pink envelope, pink like cotton candy or summer roses or a child's barrette. It looked light and delicate and innocent. But she knew what was inside. A voice of wisdom in her head said she shouldn't open it. She ignored it.

You think you've hidden it so well, but you

know you're guilty! It's your fault she died! I've told you to stop writing your stories before someone else hurts themselves! Why don't you just take your life like my daughter did? That would solve all our problems!

The words on the paper blurred as she sank into the leather sofa and listened to deafening silence.

You know you're guilty.

Yes. Yes, she did. Guilty of a thousand lies that swarmed around her like bees. It was too complicated, twisting and turning in her mind.

The tunnel got dark again. She wasn't reasoning well. She wasn't reasoning at all.

What was it she was guilty of? It felt so nebulous and yet so real. Yes, she was guilty. She was guilty of not being good enough for her parents, for Kit, for readers, for Patrick and the girls; she was guilty of not being perfect. The darkness grew, and she couldn't see God's forgiveness or grace. The hole increased.

She looked at the letter. *Why don't you just take your life!*

But that was her mother's legacy. How could she put her family through such grief?

She couldn't do it.

Or could she? Of course she could!

In the darkness, she knew it would be better, so much better for those she loved if she

361

were not alive.

The idea landed so gently in her mind that she thought it was a gift. And once she had the plan in place, the darkness lifted, not toward the light, exactly, but to a neutral gray. A calm in the eye of the storm. She had a plan. She would not torture her family or herself anymore.

Josephine gathered pills, she wrote letters to Patrick and the girls. She slowly removed the beautiful Huguenot cross and put it into an envelope for Paige. And she felt relief, such great relief.

And Jesus, forgive me, but I will soon be with you.

It was a miracle that Patrick found her alive. She had planned it carefully, done her research as a good novelist should. But he found her, he saved her, and he spent his sanity on resurrecting hers. From the hospital ICU to the inpatient treatment center and the therapist and beyond, he was there.

Patrick succumbed to exhaustion and stress. The girls felt the terrible strain in those months alone with him, but they had no idea of the truth. He created a lie, refused to let anyone know what Josephine had done. He feared the publicity from this suicide attempt would send her right back to death's door and beyond. When she was lucid enough to talk to the girls on the phone, she listened to them sob about their daddy being angry and absent and forgetful.

They never told the girls what really happened.

But they lived with a lie that weighed them down.

PAIGE

After Daddy's confession, Hannah left for the hospital, but I just sat numb on the couch in the den, staring at the TV screen. The media's coverage of my family was nonstop, showing video clips of downtown Asheville where the shooting occurred and then of reporters and fans outside the hospital as Momma lay in her coma. And of course, over and over and over, the video of Henry and Momma and me and the police.

Predictably, the American people reacted as they always did with big news stories. Everyone had a right to voice an opinion, and many did so with vitriol. It seemed that the craziness of the past hours had only escalated as people screamed their accusations at Henry Hughes over every possible social media platform. Some even paraded in front of the police station where Henry was being kept, holding up signs demanding the death penalty.

Who *were* these people? Surely not Momma's beloved readers who wrote heartfelt letters about how her books had changed their lives. Thank goodness Momma couldn't see the rage on their faces or read their cruel words! Were people so fickle? Or was this a mass of humanity who simply needed a fight, any fight, and who used the public arena to air their private anguish? I didn't know, but something was brewing in my mind.

Now a photo of Momma flashed on the screen, followed by one of me — both taken at The Motte the year before. We both looked pretty and polished.

Next came a mug shot of Henry, looking like a blond version of Frankenstein.

I gave a shriek, and Drake came from wherever he had been and sat beside me.

"Bourdy, this isn't helping you at all," he said, and he clicked the power button on the remote. "Or this," he added, as he picked up my cell phone from where it sat beside me and put it in his jeans pocket. "You go see Momma Jo for a little while. I'll stay here. Milton and I will take care of Aunt Kit when she returns." He gave me a wink.

I shrugged and stood up, letting Drake

enfold me in a hug — warm, sturdy, secure.

An officer took me out the back of the house and through a wooded path to another part of the subdivision where his patrol car was waiting. I had a baseball cap pulled low on my head and was wearing sunglasses. If this was what being a celebrity felt like, it stunk. Looking back, I saw that cars were still snaking up the mountain road to our home.

When I got to Momma's room, I felt deeply grateful that she was sleeping peacefully.

Hannah met me at the door, eyes shining. "She's been calmer!" she whispered excitedly. "She's understanding everything I say. She doesn't seem as agitated, thank the Lord."

"That's great news," I said, and I meant it, but my voice lacked enthusiasm.

"Mrs. Swanson and Aunt Kit left a little while ago," Hannah said, and we grinned.

"Between Mrs. Swanson and Drake and Milton, I think Aunt Kit will be in good hands."

"But what about Daddy?"

"He's finally resting at home. Poor Daddy. I think his confession wore him out."

Hannah and I spent the next hour with Momma, who remained asleep. I had put the Lucidity Lath on the windowsill in between a flourish of bouquets. Now I plucked one of the flower arrangements from the sill and asked Hannah, "Do you mind if I go down to the Pediatric ICU to check on Jase?" I cleared my throat. "And Libby?"

"You don't need to ask my permission, Paige. Of course, go. Momma would want you to offer comfort to them too."

I bent down and kissed Momma's cheek. "I love you, Momma." Holding the flower vase in one hand, I gathered up her laptop in the other and just shrugged when Hannah looked at me quizzically.

The policeman sitting in front of Jase's room gave me a sympathetic smile and motioned for me to go in. Libby was lying on a long bench that had been transformed into a bed. She had a blanket pulled haphazardly around her, and her strawberry-blond hair fell to the side and brushed the floor. She looked almost as vulnerable as Jase. I set the bouquet of yellow roses beside the orchids and tiptoed over to his bed. When I looked down at him my stomach cramped, seeing his immobile form. But the machines were beeping their proclamation of life.

I plopped down in the chair by his bed and tried to process the last week, from the terror of the assassination attempt to the dread that had invaded my heart when I thought about Daddy and The Awful Year, to Drake's declaration that he was waiting on me and then Henry taking me hostage. I thought of my father's confession this afternoon and of the thousands of emails and Facebook posts and tweets and snail mail letters declaring their love and prayers for Momma, and I thought of the Caring-Bridge site, which had garnered not only hundreds of personal comments but quite a few donations. I wondered why someone had harassed Momma for so many years with those pink letters and why Momma and Daddy never reported it to the police before or *after* The Awful Year. And I wondered how hard it would be to find the letter writer now.

I tried to understand the way my heart had gone out to Henry and Libby and this frail little boy lying so still in front of me. And what were we to make of the crowds watching our life on the news and over social media as if we were the newest series on Netflix?

It all felt incredibly heavy.

I sat beside Jase's bed while Libby slept, and I whispered almost like a prayer, "Open your eyes, little boy. Please wake up and get well. Please." Then I repeated the gesture I had made with Momma — I brushed Jase's hair from his forehead and kissed him there.

As I listened to the silence, I opened Momma's laptop and let the thoughts that had been brewing seep onto the computer screen. If Hannah had been there she'd have given me a look that said, *Do you have any idea what you're doing? Would the police approve?* But I didn't need anyone's approval. This was pure instinct.

First I set up a GoFundMe account for Jase. Then I went to Momma's Facebook page and posted: *Good news! Momma is stable again after the horror of last night. And we've also learned more about her would-be assassin. We understand now why he did what he did. He hired himself out to raise money for his six-year-old son, Jase, who needed open-heart surgery. That doesn't make what he did right, but we don't want Jase to be the victim of this. Even now, the little boy is fighting for his life. If you want to help the Bourdillon family, please leave the would-be assassin alone. Help us find the person who ordered the assassination attempt. If you know of anyone who has expressed anger at Momma, get in touch with the authorities in your hometown. Don't post any names here. And if you want to make Jo-*

sephine Bourdillon smile, donate money for Jase's medical expenses here.

I inserted the link to the GoFundMe account, and attached the photo of Momma with Milton, and pressed Publish. Then I went to her Twitter account and tweeted an abbreviated message with the same information and the same photo and the hashtags #JosephineBourdillon and #SaveJases-Heart.

I left Jase's room and went back upstairs to see Momma. Hannah was crouched over her, holding her hand, praying and whispering hope. Momma's eyes were still closed.

In a flurry of words, I explained my Facebook and Twitter messages to Hannah.

"You're a modern-day Robin Hood," she said.

"Except I'm not stealing anything."

"You're not stealing money," Hannah clarified. "But you're stealing the attention away from Henry and raising money for his son. That sounds Robin Hood-ish to me. Only you would think of something like that." She smiled. "It's a good plan, Paige. We'll just have to wait and see if it works."

Sunday
Sure enough, as we slept, my Facebook and Twitter posts went viral. Drake, who had

spent the night on the pullout couch in the den, knocked on my bedroom door early Sunday morning to announce the news. Hannah and I threw on sweat shirts over our pajamas and hurried down to the kitchen where Daddy, just back from the hospital, was making bacon and eggs. On the TV in the den, the reporter Lucy Brant was explaining to the world about my Facebook and Twitter posts and the Go-FundMe account for Jase.

The comments on social media were totally polarized, from those proclaiming that Henry still deserved the death penalty to others who tweeted and posted on Facebook, *Give him some grace!* And little by little, money started coming in for Jase.

It felt like we could breathe again.

I couldn't wait to get to the hospital and tell Libby.

When I reached Jase's room I found her curled up in a chair. "I brought you a piece of quiche and a blueberry muffin and some juice."

I watched her beautiful green eyes fill with tears, and she said, "Thank you, Paige. Thank you so much. For everything — the food and flowers and just coming to check on Jase. It means a lot." She glanced down at her phone. "I just got a text from my pastor. He and his wife are driving over right after church."

"I'm so glad."

She nibbled at the food, and I hovered nearby. I almost told her what was happening out there in cyberspace, but for some reason I refrained.

Henry sat in the interrogation room, all forlorn and washed-out, a pale, ghostlike giant. He nodded when I came in, accompanied by a policeman.

"Hey, Paige. Right nice of you to come see me." Then his face sagged. "Awful sorry I scared you like that the other night. I'm awful sorry about everything."

I nodded and couldn't think of a reply. Finally I said, "Hey, Henry. I brought you something." I handed him a copy of Momma's most recent book and then sat down in the only other chair in the room. The policeman stood off in the corner.

That made him smile. "How'd you know I was reading this one?"

"Detective Blaylock told me you'd asked for it."

"Did he? Well, that was right nice of him. I don't have anything else to do, so I figured I could finish reading it." He had his cuffed hands resting on the little table between us.

"I saw Jase and Libby a little while ago," I offered. "Jase is hanging in there. The doctors say his pneumonia is clearing up. Lots of people are praying for your boy, and the pastor and his wife are there with Libby. They're staying at the Rathbun House too."

He nodded. "Thank you, Paige. I'm hoping they'll let me see Libby soon."

"Yeah, that would be great, wouldn't it?"

I took a breath, rehearsing Detective Blaylock's suggestions. *"You might be able to ask questions in a way that takes him off guard."* Unfortunately, so far I'd been lousy at following the detective's advice.

I didn't mean to be so blunt, but it came out. "Do you know why they let me come see you, Henry?"

He narrowed his eyes and then shrugged.

"They want me to try to get information out of you. To see if you'll tell me the name of the person who hired you."

That didn't seem to worry him. He shrugged again, his big shoulders hunched up. "I told that detective the truth — I have no idea who's really behind it. Just the man who talked to me, Nick."

Then his eyes got wide, and he looked scared, like he was afraid he'd said too much. But I just placed my hand over his and said, "Can you tell me what this man said to you, Henry?"

"He called me on the phone with the instructions. Can't say anything else about him." He turned his eyes down. "But the thing is, he's just a middleman. He's not the one who pays the money or pulls the trigger."

I tried to hide my disappointment. "Is there anything else, Henry, any other information that you could give us?"

He shook his head too quickly, then looked down at his cuffed wrists. "Naw."

After an awkward pause, he turned his pale eyes on me and completely changed the subject. "Paige, what do you make of all those people on the TV and the internet wanting me dead? I mean, of course they're right. I tried to kill someone. I deserve to die." Tears came into his eyes, shocking me. "But what's been bothering me is that your momma's books have all those religious themes, and lots of the people who read them call themselves Christians.

"And those same Christians are some of the ones wanting me dead. Your momma, in her books she talks about grace. I thought that was the point of Jesus coming. I thought Christians were supposed to be different." He reached his burly hand up and wiped his eyes.

He grabbed my heart with that statement. I knew just what he was talking about.

"Well, I used to go to church," I told him, "until two of the people I respected the most turned out to be horrible hypocrites. And even though my sister always says that I shouldn't judge Jesus by His people, I can't help it. The Bible says we should be able to tell people are Christians by their love. I feel the same way as you, Henry. I want to see love, not hate. I want to understand what grace is."

"Yeah. Well, I sure hope they ain't all hypocrites. Least your momma isn't. And I just bet there are other good people out there too."

He looked pitiful to me, like a gentle, remorseful, defeated giant.

"Anyway, thank you for the book."

"You're welcome." I stood up to leave and said, "If you want to talk any more, Henry, I'll come again. I'm happy to come again." Then I added, "But you need to get yourself a lawyer. Promise me you'll do that, Henry."

The look he gave me said he understood.

As soon as I was out of the room, I called Detective Blaylock on my cell. "He said the middleman's name is Nick. That's the only thing I got from him."

As soon as I said it, a little voice sneaked

up behind me and whispered, *Way to go, Paige. Now you've ratted on Henry too.*

HENRY

I sat on the little cot in my cell and thumbed through Miz Bourdillon's latest novel, the one I'd started listening to on CD, till I found the place where I'd left off. I kept on reading and was surprised by all the ways that rich lady in the story was showing love, real love, like I wanted and like Paige wanted.

Then all the sudden I could hardly breathe, and my pulse throbbed in my head.

I'd gotten to a part about the slave girl — except now she was a freedwoman. Well, she'd had so many really awful things happen in her life that I couldn't quite wrap my mind around it. And now they were gonna take her boy away from her, and that was just the last straw. And she'd been real strong and brave before, when they took her son away, she fell to the ground and wouldn't talk to anyone but the Lord Almighty. And she was singing that same hymn, the very same one that that person who hired me had quoted. *Take my life and let it be consecrated, Lord, to Thee.*

Then, with her heart breaking in two, she stopped singing that ole hymn and just kept saying, over and over, "Lord, take my life! Take my life! I don't want to live anymore. Please, Lord, take my life."

As soon as I read that I closed my eyes, trying to pull those exact words out of my memory. What had Nick said? Sat still for a long time until I finally got it. *"She started quoting some song to me. Like it was a twisted kind of prayer to kill someone. She said, 'Take her life and let it be consecrated Lord to Thee! Take Mrs. Bourdillon's life. That's your job. Take her life!'"*

This time, I didn't just *think* it was kinda strange to quote words from a hymn with directions about how to kill somebody. This time I *knew* it was strange, and suddenly I knew *why.* I knew just as sure as I had shot Miz Bourdillon who had hired me to shoot her. And it wasn't any crazy reader.

It was Miz Bourdillon herself, telling me plain as she put it for that freedwoman in her story. *Take my life.*

■ ■ ■ ■

Part Three:
The End of
Myself

■ ■ ■ ■

CHAPTER 15

Three Weeks Later

PAIGE

The leaves turned brown and found their way to the ground, the trees stood naked and embarrassed-looking in the November wind, and the sky threatened snow but none came. I went back to school, Hannah returned to Aix-en-Provence and Drake to his university, and Momma was transferred to a rehabilitation center not far from the Mission Hospital campus. Henry was assigned a lawyer who had him plead not guilty at his arraignment. Evidently, even though everyone knew Henry *was* guilty, this was typical procedure — a five-minute formality where the judge accepted the plea and set the trial for some time within the next year. No bail was posted, and Henry was taken to a maximum-security prison about an hour from Asheville to await his trial.

But Jase stayed on the third floor of Mission Hospital, fighting for his life.

I'd gotten into a routine; I'd go by the rehab center every day after school to visit Momma. I winced at all the ways the physical therapist was torturing her, but her stiff, immobile limbs were gradually starting to move in ways that showed Momma had some control. She kept making incredible progress, considering that she needed to relearn how to do life — everything from talking and moving her limbs to thinking. She communicated through eye blinks and hand squeezes and, occasionally, with short spoken sentences, and she understood what we said to her perfectly well. She didn't remember anything about the shooting, but when Daddy talked to her in private about the thing during The Awful Year — the suicide attempt — she evidently remembered that perfectly well.

With the secret off his chest and Momma making steady progress, Daddy acted more like the playful father I'd always known. He brought Milton to all my soccer games, and he rarely refrained from letting the referee know if he'd made a bad call.

Aunt Kit visited Momma on weekends and stayed at the house with us and actually helped out a little with meals, which surprised both Daddy and me.

Hannah kept up the CaringBridge site from France, and I posted photos of Momma and Jase on Facebook and kept reminding people to contribute to Jase's GoFundMe account.

Detective Blaylock found several sets of fingerprints from the pink letters that weren't mine or Hannah's or Momma's or Daddy's, and the police were looking to see if any of those could lead them to whoever sent the letters. If they did, I didn't hear about it, no matter how often I badgered Detective Blaylock for more details.

And the police had another lead. They'd found a number on Henry's cell phone that was also on Momma's. We found that quite surprising, and frankly, had no idea what to make of it.

But Henry sat in his cell and kept his mouth clamped shut.

Drake and I texted numerous times throughout each day. I didn't particularly like long-distance dating but thankfully, we knew each other so well that when we miscommunicated (which happened often), we'd give each other the benefit of the doubt. He came back home on the week-ends, and he and I would visit Momma at rehab and then venture into Asheville's art district on Saturday afternoons, peeking into the industrial-buildings-turned-art-galleries.

Sometimes he held my hand, but he never kissed me, not once. Finally I confronted him about it. "I hope you didn't take one of those vows where you can't even kiss a girl until after you're married," I blurted, and he laughed so loud and long that I felt my face turn beet red.

"My, aren't you a judgmental little snob, Miss Bourdy," he teased. He saw my eyes flash anger, and he laughed again. "Please just hurry and grow up. This phase you're in now is maddening."

I wanted to pummel him with my fists, but in the end we both laughed hysterically.

I visited Henry another time and listened to his soul-felt questions, except they weren't quite as soul-felt as before. He didn't rave about Momma's books as much, and he didn't beg to see her. He said, "I still have questions for your momma, Paige. Sure do. But I don't think I'll ever be able to ask them. Not now."

And though I pried and pried, he wouldn't explain what he meant.

His eyes weren't quite so frightening now, but that wasn't exactly reassuring to me, because in those eyes I could see that Henry knew something that he wasn't saying. I wanted so badly to shake it out of him, and I actually did say, "Henry! Please, won't you tell us what you know? It will help everybody. The police will be able to find the person responsible and that will mean safety for Momma and for Libby and Jase and you. Think of it, Henry. They could even lessen your sentence!"

But he wasn't swayed.

When I asked Detective Blaylock if there was any way Henry could get his sentence shortened if the real perpetrator of the crime was found, he said, "That depends on the jurisdiction, the judge, whether or not it goes federal, and whether or not the hired killer cooperates with the investigation. Think of it like a chess game — the real target isn't the queen, it's the king. If you have to let the queen go to get checkmate, then you'll do what you have to do. DAs and investigators understand that."

How I longed to find the king, and the American public seemed to agree with me.

We'd been choosing our "American idols" for years now, and once we did it, they were catapulted into stardom. But this was the first time I'd thought about how America also chooses her criminals, deciding who gets condemned and who goes free. Some days I could not bear to look at Momma's Facebook and Twitter accounts because of the hatred and ugliness some people expressed. I didn't know what the authorities would decide for poor Henry, but four weeks after the shooting, three weeks after I'd started up the GoFundMe account for Jase's medical expenses, public opinion began to shift.

Thanksgiving was just around the corner, and America decided to practice generosity, and more and more people felt sorry for Henry. Yes, he was guilty of a terrible crime, the sentiment went, but wasn't someone else even guiltier? Of course, they simply transferred their hatred of Henry to the real culprit, but that was okay with me since I figured that person deserved it, whoever he or she was.

Twice a week after school, having visited Momma in rehab, I'd drive to the Memorial Campus of Mission Hospital and go up to the Pediatric ICU and sit with Jase for an hour or so. Sometimes I read to him from the books Libby had brought from the library, and other times I made up stories in which a little boy named Jase was always the hero.

But he never opened his eyes. Every time the doctors tried to take him out of the induced coma, Jase had a life-threatening setback. The pneumonia had cleared up, but his little body remained incredibly weak.

Libby alternated her days between her job three hours to the southwest, nights at the hospital with Jase, and trips to the jail to visit Henry. I honestly had no idea how she kept going, such a tiny woman with such incredible stamina and drive. I brought her food that our friends kept us abundantly supplied with and left it in the ICU fridge so that she didn't have to worry about cooking or spending money eating out.

One day she'd just arrived at the hospital from her job as I was getting ready to leave. While she peeked in on Jase, I heated up a casserole for her in the microwave in the waiting room. I fetched her out of Jase's room, sat her in a chair, and placed a plate in front of her. "Eat, Libby."

She wilted a little, gave a sigh, and whispered, "Thanks, Paige. Thank you." Then she bowed her head and closed her eyes briefly, asking the blessing, I guessed.

When she opened them again and took a bite of the casserole, I couldn't stop myself from asking, "How do you do it, Libby? I think you're the strongest person I've ever known. How do you keep going?"

She looked shocked at my question and

blushed. "Me, strong? No. I don't really know how I keep going. I think it's just the Lord carrying me. There are verses in the Bible that talk about God keeping us in perfect peace if we trust Him. I don't always feel peaceful, but somehow God keeps letting me put one foot in front of the other."

She took another bite, chewed for a minute, and then turned her green eyes on me. "A lot of people are praying for us, and I talk to my parents almost every day. They're really good about encouraging me. And the church is too. You've met a few of the people who have come to see Jase. And my mother, bless her heart, she's gotten a leave of absence from her job to come stay here with Jase."

Her eyes misted. "And all that money coming in, Paige. Why, it's amazing." She reached over and touched my hand. "Thank you. Thank you for everything you're doing."

"I'm really glad I can help in a small way."

She took another bite, and we sat in silence. Then she said, "Henry never cared much for church. He's seen too much of the evil side of man. But then with your mother, oh, it's so odd, the way things work. After she survived his shooting, Henry began to read her books. And now he reads the Bible too. He asked me to bring him one! He keeps talking about forgiveness and grace."

She blushed again. "Of course it's awful, everything that's happened to your mother, and Henry's part in it, but I'm thankful for your mother and her books." She gave a timid smile. "They've got them on audio at our library, and I've already listened to three of them as I drive back and forth from home to Asheville and then up to see Henry. I don't mean to sound insensitive, but your mother's books are part of the way the Lord is carrying me and giving me hope."

I chewed on Libby's comments for a while, just like she was chewing on the food that I kept piling on her plate.

Over the course of several weeks, Detective Blaylock questioned Libby about Henry's past, his PTSD diagnosis and his medications, and what he'd been doing before the three other surgeries for Jase. She told him the truth — that she had no idea — and she confided to me that she didn't think Henry had hired himself out before those surgeries because they certainly had never received large amounts of cash back then.

Once, she shared with me about how she'd met Henry at a bar when she was about my age, and she'd felt sorry for him. That was how she put it. She could tell he was real messed up. "But there was a kindness about him, at his core, in spite of what was on the outside and his awful background. He was bright and good. He just needed some help to keep him steady." She whispered it to me with tears in her eyes. "And I knew he loved me, really loved me." They married when she got pregnant with Jase, and when she told me that, she got a sad look on her face and said, "We repeated his parents' mistakes, one by one."

Fortunately, Libby wasn't raised by criminals, but wise, caring parents, and she started taking Henry to church, hoping to create a healthier family dynamic for the three of them.

But after Jase's second heart surgery, Henry refused to go anymore.

Every incremental step forward with Jase seemed to be followed by a huge step backward. Once when I was there reading a book to him, all kinds of alarms started going off, and a troupe of nurses and doctors rushed into the room and hurried me out. I heard "Cardiac arrest" and "I can't find a pulse" and "Try again! Try again!"

I didn't know what to do with myself. I texted Drake and Hannah to pray, and then

I actually ran down the hall to the little chapel. I stood alone in the room, staring at the stained-glass depictions of the Blue Ridge Mountains in every season. A table and chairs sat in the middle of the room, and there were two kneelers in front of the windows. The whole space exuded peace, and without knowing exactly why I was doing it, I sank onto a kneeler and whispered, "God, if you're out there, *do* something! It's so unfair! Momma's making progress. Can't you spend a little sympathy on Jase? Please don't let him die!"

The doctors got his heart beating again, and I often thought about my plea. What it said about God, but more than that, what it said about me and what was going on in my heart.

JOSEPHINE

Most days in rehab, I felt enormously thankful that I was alive, but often it came after an excruciating fight with my body and mind, neither of which functioned in obedience to my commands. At times in the past when I could not remember something, Patrick would tease me and say, "Feeny, are you off wandering in your mind again? Who knows where that will take you!"

Now I wandered off in my mind throughout each day, but Patrick did not tease me. He urged me on, as did Paige and Ginnie and Drake and Kit and Mrs. Swanson and Hannah and my church friends and so many others, from near and far, each applauding my newest achievement. I learned the yes and no system through eye movement and head nods or shakes. When I began swallowing, really swallowing, Paige celebrated with contraband — my favorite ice cream, smuggled in from a popular ice cream parlor in Asheville called The Hop. Medications and therapy helped me stay awake and alert for longer periods of time, and gradually my limbs behaved more normally, conquering the spasticity that caused my joints to be so painful and tight. Progress was slow, but I had every hope I would speak coherently and walk again.

But would I write again? That I did not dwell on.

My memory flitted in and out, like the red-breasted woodpecker who hovered over the birdfeeder at home, then flew away, only to return a few seconds later and settle on a ledge. I had no recollection at all of the days before the shooting, but bits and pieces of the past months occasionally landed in my conscious mind. I gradually recognized words again and began reading like a first grader. My speech was impaired, but occasionally I was able to communicate in very short sentences. At other times, the words would not make it out of my mouth, and I was reduced again to blinking and nodding.

Detective Blaylock came to see me several times. He would recount some bit of information — maybe three or four sentences' worth. Then I would nod or blink or show in some way that I agreed or disagreed with this information. But every time he came to the following question, I went blank.

"Josephine, we found a phone number on your cell that was also on Henry's. Did you receive a strange, upsetting, or threatening phone call recently?"

This did not compute in any part of my brain, and I read the detective's frustration in his posture, the way he tugged at his beard and sat forward in his chair, a little more with each visit as if he was trying with all his might to extract some valuable clue by pulling it out of my mind.

I remembered Kit's laments during my first days of awaking from the coma. I remembered her declaring that she was to blame for something, and something about money. When she sat with me now, her strident voice frayed my nerves. I read behind her eyes that, like the detective, she too desperately wanted me to remember something else. But whatever it was had flown out of my memory during the coma.

The Lucidity Lath sat on a desk in my little room, right by my bed so that I could read it. Except that I could not read. My cursive on the cards looked like the lovely loops and squiggles the girls had made with their Spirograph as children.

But gradually I caught the fragments of my life before this accident, and tried to make sense of them.

Although I might have preferred The Awful Year to have been completely erased from my mind, it hung there, brilliant and huge and startlingly clear, like a harvest moon in October. The fact that the girls knew the truth about my attempt to take my life brought me a deep sense of relief, a lifting of the lies, a wholeness before my family and my God. As for Patrick, he came back to all of us in a deeper and happier way, almost as if he had receded into the sexy young soccer player from decades ago.

For all those years, Patrick and I had kept up the story — the lie — that I was simply away for three months and Patrick had been so stressed that he started drinking and wound up with a DUI and an overnight jail stint. But the truth that I had tried to take my life left remnants of fear in me, in spite of the treatment program and medications, and that fear had buried itself deep in my soul. Wouldn't it be safer for me if other loved ones knew the truth? And what about all those threatening letters? I'd received four by then. I was afraid of myself and afraid of some unnamed person who wished me dead.

But I played the charade of peace. For Patrick. He had sacrificed so much. Living with the lie had obviously drawn us closer in a distorted type of way. And though I had confessed my sorrow at this deception to the Lord hundreds of times, I never felt the nudging of the Spirit to come clean. Or perhaps I had squelched it quickly whenever it inched up my back into my head. I lived with the guilt of allowing Patrick to choose the lie. It complicated our love, our faith, our family.

2008 . . . During her stay at the mental institution, Josephine read the works from the Lost Generation. She had studied them all, T. S. Eliot and James Joyce and Ernest Hemingway and F. Scott Fitzgerald and many others, in high school and college, and had found herself strangely drawn to their lives as they tragically navigated genius. Unbalanced, one even raving mad, they wrote dark beauty. She was no genius by her own estimation, but she obviously had a penchant for the darkness. When it threatened strongly she almost became a very minor actor in a similar play, where creativity won over sanity and brought self-destruction.

Many nights, after she'd cried for Patrick and the girls and herself, Josephine cried for the Lost Generation, for their desperate grasping at life through liquor and liaisons.

Her faith proclaimed hope. That was what she wanted to write. Hope.

She also wanted to choose health and love for Patrick and Hannah and Paige over writing, over the looming insanity.

But during those terrible, anxious months with therapy and medication and begging Patrick to let her tell the true story, she didn't see hope.

God, why are you punishing us, punishing all of us, for the hole in my head that caused me to write stories that drew wrath from readers and plummeted me toward destruction?

Josephine didn't write while she was at the facility; she just sat and listened to nature and watched for God in the mountains and waited with feverish anticipation to be released, for life to resume, for a simple stroll on the beach at The Motte.

Then at last they said she could go home.

Patrick's arms around her felt like safety and security and protection and love. His lips on hers tasted so sweet and tart, like the first raspberry in late spring.

"Now the whole horrible lie can be put to rest. We won't talk of it again, Feeny."

But he soon saw the flaw in his logic. She had escaped the media attention of a suicide attempt, but her mind had not fully recovered.

He lay close to her in bed, his body eager and needy. Josephine went to him, eagerly too, but afterward, the darkness encroached. A hint of hope and light and love and then, the darkness.

"Patrick, I think I should stop writing."

"No, Feeny. That was never the intent of all this."

"I know. But my writing makes me afraid and infuriates others."

"It blesses others."

"That letter writer wanted me dead."

"Someone who was unstable."

"Someone whose wrath influenced me to do something unthinkable."

"But you're stronger, now, Feeny. You've healed."

"But how can we be sure I won't receive other hate mail?"

They couldn't, of course, and the fear made the hole grow wider again.

She tried to hide her deepest reflections from Patrick, but they inevitably leaked out. "Patrick, you know how the apostle Paul says, 'To me, to live is Christ and to die is gain.' That's how I often feel."

"I'm not surprised you feel that way, Feeny. You love Him so." But he knew that was not what she meant.

"I twisted that verse, sweetie. I used it as fuel for my dark thoughts, and they got darker than ever before, Patrick. And I began to wonder if it would be better if I weren't alive. I told myself that my life had hurt your life and the girls and others."

"I know, Feeny. But hasn't therapy helped? You've worked so hard to be healthier."

"Yes," she whispered. "Yes, it has helped."

But Patrick saw then that this lie would never be put to rest, and he took the blame on himself.

He found her on the porch later that evening, watching the sunset. He settled into the rocking chair beside her, and they breathed in the sweet scent of the first roses that climbed the latticework and peeked over the porch railing. He reached across the space between them and grasped her hand. Squeezed it. She continued to stare ahead.

"Feeny, look at me."

She shifted in the rocker, drew her knees under her and faced him.

"Feeny, are you telling me that you might try to harm yourself again?"

She couldn't bear to hear the pain in his soft and gentle voice.

He stood up, lifted her from the chair, his arms wrapped around her with a loving strength that might never let her go.

"I hope not. I promise I will do everything they suggested in the program." Everything except to tell the truth to her children and her closest loved ones.

She saw a counselor once a week, and she continued taking medication. Patrick watched her carefully and called her often from work. The medication had helped the darkest thoughts go away, but it didn't rid her of the guilt she felt that Patrick's sacrifice caused him to lose his joy, and they both knew that the lie was hurting their marriage and the family.

But in some ways, time does heal, even a lie. They loved again, they laughed, they spent their month at The Motte, and they watched Hannah blossom into a sparkling young woman, full of faith and kindness and good sense. Paige suffered different consequences from The Awful Year. When she announced to them much later that she refused to go to church with a bunch of hypocrites, Josephine knew she was talking about her grandfather and Drake's father, but in her heart she felt accused and said to herself, *I'm the biggest hypocrite of all.*

CHAPTER 16

November

HENRY

Life in prison was hard, even dangerous, like what I'd seen sometimes on TV. Had to keep my head down, be real wary of others. But some of the inmates felt kinda sorry for me when they found out I had a sick boy. I was thankful for how they watched out for me a little. I knew I could get myself killed in prison.

I got assigned a lawyer, a real nice young man named Zeke with lots of know-how. I thought it was pretty crazy of him to have me plead not guilty before the judge, but Zeke assured me it was just how things had to be done. Finally I went along with it, even though I sure was guilty, and he knew it.

Detective Blaylock came to see me often, always itching to get more information about who hired me. Zeke didn't like it one bit when I agreed to see him, and he always made sure he was there. But I wasn't afraid of saying too much. I hadn't told Zeke the truth about Miz Bourdillon, but he was smart, and he knew I was hiding something.

One day Detective Blaylock scared me a bit when he said, "We've found a suspect, Henry. Someone we're sure is linked to this case. A man by the name of Nick Lupton. Do you have anything to tell us about this man?"

I started sweating big-time. How'd they find out about Nick? Sure, I had his number on my phone, but I didn't see how that proved anything. At least I hoped it didn't.

Didn't say anything to the detective, but he wasn't dumb either. He saw my reaction. I wished I could've told him about Nick, but what if they questioned him and let him go and then he did what he'd threatened to Jase? My poor boy was still struggling for life, and I wasn't about to let Nick make things more complicated.

I sure wished Miz Bourdillon could talk. I needed to ask those questions, questions that were burning themselves into my mind, again and again and again.

I felt sorry for Detective Blaylock, because of course he made sense to himself. Sure we'd want "the guilty party" off the street. Except the guilty party was Miz Bourdillon herself, and I couldn't tell him that. I didn't figure he'd believe me anyway.

And I felt sorry for Miz Bourdillon too. Maybe she had as many questions about life as I did, and maybe those questions got all twisted in her mind like they did in mine. Mainly, I didn't figure Jesus would go pointing His finger. Seemed like He was always telling us to look at our own hearts first. And I knew mine was pretty black.

But I thought about it a lot, and here's what I decided. I would ask to talk to Miz Bourdillon. And if she could forgive me for shooting her, well, then I was gonna try real hard to forgive her for setting the whole thing up in the first place.

Maybe that was grace.

Thank goodness, they let Libby come to see me in the prison twice a week. We had to talk through a little hole in the plexiglass and couldn't touch each other, but at least I could see her beautiful face.

A couple times I almost told her about Miz Bourdillon being the one who really hired me, but I couldn't put that burden on her tiny shoulders when she was already carrying so much.

She tried to sound upbeat on her visits, saying things like, "Paige brings me food and flowers, and she fixed something so as people are sending in money for Jase's medical expenses," and "I don't know why she's treated us this way, babe. But I'm thankful."

The first time I heard about that fund to help with Jase, I got a little angry, because it seemed like a lot of pity from people we didn't even know. I don't like to take handouts. But after I thought on it for a while I knew it was a good thing . . . because there wasn't any way I'd be providing for my family any time soon.

The next time Libby visited I told her, "Funny how Paige is the one who says she's not all religious, and yet she's acting like Jesus would be acting toward us."

Libby didn't have anything to say to that, but she smiled a little. She liked it when I put Jesus into our conversations.

One day Libby came in with her eyes all sparkling and said, "Jase is getting better! They took him out of that induced coma, and he opened his eyes. Our boy opened his eyes, hon! And he saw me — he knew who I was, and he's gonna be getting stronger now. Doctor said he finally made it over that big hump that was holding him back. His lungs are all clear, and his heart is beating just like it should. They regulated the medicine, and he's tolerating it okay. He can swallow now, and they've got him drinking some powerful liquid that will give him the nutrients he needs."

We reached toward the plexiglass and made like we were holding each other's hands when really they were just mashed up against the glass. I tried to hold back my tears, but they just went on falling down my cheeks like that trickling water in the creek near the trailer, gurgling up something like hope.

Libby brought me all kinds of books to read that she checked out of the library. She brought me a Bible, too, like I'd asked her. I wanted to read them Gospels and see if Jesus was like the radio preacher said and like the characters in Miz Bourdillon's books. Had plenty of time to read in prison. Went through all of them pretty fast, Matthew and Mark and Luke and John. Read them all straight through in about a week.

I'd never read any of them at all, much less all four of them straight through at once. But here's what I saw.

Just like I'd been thinking, Jesus was always, always hanging around with sinners.

Eating meals with them and helping them out and being real tender with the worst of them — some lady yanked out of her lover's bed, and a bunch of prostitutes and people like me — the rejected people in that society. And He wasn't too nice to the religious folks, which made them awful mad.

And it got me to thinking a lot about Miz Bourdillon's books and all the stuff that had been running through my head for weeks and weeks.

If Jesus came to earth today, I wondered if He'd be in the big fancy churches. Well, maybe He'd go in there and preach a sermon in His jeans, but then I just bet He'd ask some of the gang members to have lunch with Him. And He'd invite those poor trafficked gals and probably a bunch of those gay people who didn't seem to be welcomed at churches, and maybe even, maybe He'd invite me to lunch too. Now wouldn't that be something to see?

Liked that story in Mark, too, about the thief on the cross, and how Jesus told him he was going to get to be in paradise with Him that very day. And that was confusing, because no way was that man gonna have any time to do good works or say he was sorry to whoever he'd hurt. He was fixing to die. But Jesus invited him on in to paradise.

When I told Libs about all those thoughts, her face that was so often all tight and worried-looking got real soft, and she smiled at me, a big smile, the kind that made her bright green eyes light up. She said, "It's grace, babe. That's what it's called. Grace. You're forgiven, and you don't have to pay anything back to God."

I had never heard much about grace. The few times my mother drug me to church, they talked about judgment. Knowing how my parents made their living, I figured they had a one-way ticket to hell and I probably would be riding on their coattails. I never actually read the Bible or had anything to do with any kind of religion except the one that said God helps those who help themselves. And so far, I had never given God one bit of credit for us getting out of our messes. He seemed completely nonexistent.

Still, after reading Miz Bourdillon's books and the Gospels, I thought maybe there was grace.

But if there was grace, why did Miz Bourdillon hire me to kill her? The most twisted logic in the world, and I had to find out why. Because if she didn't believe what she wrote, then I sure as heck didn't want to buy into it either.

JOSEPHINE

Kit visited me at the rehab center on weekends. One day she rushed in, impeccably dressed. "You look good, Kit," I slurred, but she understood me.

"Oh, JoJo! You're the one who is doing unbelievably well. Patrick told me you can go home in a few weeks!"

I nodded. My smile was lopsided, but it still communicated pleasure.

"Well, that's a relief." Her eyes clouded. "And do you remember anything more? You know, about the weeks before the accident?"

I shook my head slowly, contemplating my beautiful, broken sister. She did look better, much better, but I could not remember why. I could only remember before.

2010 . . . To Josephine's great relief, a new lawyer rescinded the order for Patrick to manage Kit's money. Her resentment that Josephine was, as she put it, "her big sister's keeper" had poisoned their already fragile relationship. They couldn't be responsible for Kit's life, but they knew with this new freedom she would do as she pleased. She left for Europe with a man fifteen years her junior, and for two years, the only communication she had with Josephine came through post-cards sent from Tuscany and Zurich and Munich and somewhere on the Romantic Road and then into Prague and Dubrovnik and Athens and Crete and Istanbul and Tunis and Algiers. She ran around Europe and North Africa, but they never could be sure if she was traveling alone or with someone.

Then one day she appeared at the house, tanned and emaciated. "Hey, JoJo." Her eyes were hollow.

"Kit! Kit!" Josephine grabbed her in a hug and was shocked by how thin her sister had become. She was dressed in silk and high heels and had a line of bright pink luggage behind her. She waved the taxi away.

"I'm sorry I didn't give any notice. Plans changed." She tried to keep up the masquerade, but a tear slipped down her cheek.

"Oh, Kit. Come in."

"Can I stay for a while?"

"Yes, yes, of course."

Kit had spent most of her inheritance, and although she entertained Hannah and Paige around the dinner table with embellished stories of her exotic adventures, Josephine was concerned.

"I've got a contract with a perfume company. It starts in a month. Can I stay here until then?" she asked.

"Of course," Josephine said, but once again, she dreaded it.

Kit hardly ate anything at all. She wasn't drinking alcohol, and they never found drugs, but she seemed in worse shape than ever before.

Josephine finally asked her, "Kit, what happened to you?"

"I got mixed up with the wrong people, JoJo." Her blue eyes shadowed. "I know that doesn't sound like anything new, but these people hold long grudges. And they make you pay."

Which Kit could not do.

She left for the photo shoots with the perfume company. That lasted six months. The next time she showed up at the house, she was hiding a black eye under her fashionable sunglasses.

Patrick and Josephine paid her debts, and Patrick managed her stocks. Thank goodness, he had kept control of them. They figured she could live comfortably off these if she could settle down. But Kit had never settled down in her life. She had run headlong into destruction from the time she was thirteen years old.

She moved to Atlanta and lived in the townhouse they had purchased for rental after selling their parents' home in 2007. Kit got some modeling jobs. She reconnected with a few good friends from high school.

Josephine held her breath and prayed.

PAIGE

Jase had a face full of freckles and two dimples that showed up when he smiled. Since he had opened his eyes and was able to eat, he gained strength each day, and he started looking forward to my visits.

"My momma says you've been comin' to see me some. And reading to me. Thanks." He had a smile that warmed my heart. "She said your momma was at the same hospital as me."

"That's right."

"Was her heart sick like mine?"

"No, she had an accident, and it was her brain that was sick."

"And it's better now?"

"She's a lot like you — getting better every day."

He grinned and said, "Well, that's corn-puddin' good!"

Libby's mother had come from south Georgia and was staying at the Rathbun House so she could help care for Jase while Libby was at work. She planned to move into the trailer with Libby and Jase when he was released.

On that day, the whole nursing staff celebrated with balloons and ice cream. I was there when Libby wheeled him outside for the first time. He stood up slowly and laughed when he saw a bird fly overhead. Then he sank to his knees, giggling as he crunched a few dried leaves in his hands. "Mommy, did you see the bluebird? Did you see it?"

HENRY

I'd been in prison for over a month when they finally agreed to let me see Miz Bourdillon. I rode in a police car to the rehabilitation center with my lawyer and Detective Blaylock. They led me into her room, me shuffling along with my feet and hands in cuffs. I was glad to see Paige there with her mother.

I felt a little awkward just standing there staring down at Miz Bourdillon in her wheelchair, so I said, "Hello, Miz Bourdillon."

"Hello, Henry." It came out real garbled like and then Paige whispered to me, "I'll help you if you can't understand her."

I nodded. "You have a real nice room here." Looked like a fancy hotel room to me, not like something you'd find at a hospital, except for the bed.

410

She gave a little nod, and Paige said, "Yeah. We're glad we could get Momma in this facility. It's the best for recovering from head trauma."

She was sitting up all straight and awkward in a wheelchair, and she had on a sweat shirt — a real pretty bright blue one with *Duke* written across the front in cursive — and had an afghan over her lap. I could tell her head had been shaved, but she had on a bright blue beret so that only the sides of her stubby hair showed.

I remembered when I'd followed her, how her hair was all thick and a pretty shade of brown. Now it was all gone.

"Have a seat, Henry," Paige said, motioning to a nice cushioned chair. I shuffled to the armchair and sat down as light as possible. I kept trying to see if I was scaring Miz Bourdillon, me in my prison clothes and my hands and feet cuffed and that detective beside me with a handgun in his belt, but Miz Bourdillon didn't show any signs of fear.

I fumbled with the handcuffs and tried to find my voice.

"Would you like something to drink, Henry?" Sure was glad Paige was there to interpret the conversation, because it didn't seem like Miz Bourdillon was gonna be able

411

to say much. I'd been prepared for that.

"A glass of water would be real nice. Thank you."

Paige left the room and then came back with a tall clear glass. "Need anything, Momma?" she asked, after setting the glass on a pretty round table beside me. I wondered if they'd moved their own furniture into the rehab place.

Miz Bourdillon shook her head, just barely, but I saw it.

"You can go on and ask your questions, Henry. I've told Momma a little bit about them too." Paige sat down again beside her mother.

"I just, well, your books stirred up so many questions in my mind. I wanted to ask you about them." I looked over at Detective Blaylock, and he handed me my copy of *These Mountains around Us*. "This is the only one I got here with me, but I've read four of them now." And I held it out for her to see.

"It's your latest novel, Momma," Paige said, but looked to me like Miz Bourdillon recognized it herself.

I tried to make sense with my questions. "It's all about what you call grace. Seems like in every story there's a lot of grace. People who are real religious or not religious at all, but they're in some pretty awful situations, and they don't think they can ever be forgiven because of all the horrible things they've done or that have been done to them. And I wondered, do you really believe that they could? I like the way you write about grace and forgiveness. It sounds so good. Do you really believe it works that way?"

Miz Bourdillon's hand quivered slightly. It didn't look like she had much control over it. Paige scooted her chair over even closer to her mother and took her mother's hand real gently in hers. Miz Bourdillon looked worried, like she was trying to remember something, and then she mumbled something real deep and guttural that I didn't understand.

"In your new novel, it's in that part where the poor freedwoman has forgiven the awful man who abused her and took her son away, and then she asked God to forgive her for her wanting Him to take her own life." I looked over at Miz Bourdillon, but she was just listening, like she had been. "And finally she's up in those mountains and just starts feeling that grace and forgiveness. Like God's creation has been there forever and reminds her that He has too, and how big He is, and how much He loves her. And it settles on her so she really accepts it." I think my face was all red by now. "Least that's how it sounded to me."

I thumbed through the novel, my hands shaking a bit. I wasn't any good at reading out loud, didn't like to do it. But I needed to ask her, so I brushed the sweat from my eyes, found the page I'd marked, and began to read.

" 'The mountains hold my imagination, and I feel a call to their beauty. Then they fade out of view as the mist floats above and around them, like puffs of smoke. I hover in the mist; I feel the calling of the dawn. I see the first ray of light piercing through the mist and I know. I am forgiven.' Do you believe that anyone can be forgiven?"

Miz Bourdillon rubbed her hands awkwardly together and seemed real tired all of a sudden. But then she looked at me with her pretty brown eyes, really looked at me, like she could see me, and was concentrating real hard. She lifted a hand and said, "Yes. I believe it."

Paige answered for her again. "Momma believes we can be forgiven, even for the worst acts. The Bible is filled with stories of very ordinary people who get into all kinds of trouble, and yet they are forgiven. The secret is what Momma's characters have. A repentant heart. One who wants forgiveness. And an acceptance of God's grace. Nothing earned. Just grace."

Paige said it real sweet, like she believed what she was saying, when she'd told me before that she didn't. But I could tell Miz Bourdillon did.

I felt sweaty and almost light-headed, because I knew what I needed to say next. But how would she answer? "Well, can you forgive *me*, Miz Bourdillon? I'm sorry for what I did to you. I wish I could take it back, but I can't and I'm so sorry. You said God could forgive me, but I'm wondering if you can too. After the awful thing I did to you, can you forgive me?"

She took her time, lifting her head a little so as she was looking me in the eyes. Hers were real soft and sad. She started talking, real slow-like, slurring her words. But I understood her. Maybe she'd practiced it a hundred times before I got there. "I for . . . give . . . you . . . Hen-ry."

She said it so sincerely that I knew she didn't remember nothing about hiring me. Had no idea of it. And watching her struggle to communicate, to move her hands, to hold her head up, I felt washed over with pity. But I forgave her too, just like I'd planned to do. I didn't say it out loud, of course, but inside, in what Libby calls my heart, I forgave her.

She looked out the big ole window for a long time. Maybe she was studying the clouds — they were all fluffy and soft looking. But her eyes were shining, and I saw a single tear roll down her cheek. She moved her hands like she wanted to brush it away, but I don't think she could. She shifted a little in the wheelchair and looked at me. Then she nodded to Paige.

"Momma wanted me to read this to you, Henry. She thought it might be helpful. This comes from a speech she gave for the launch of this novel." Paige scrolled down on her phone and began to read, " 'Sometimes it's quite hard to receive that grace. I know. Believe me, I know. Sometimes you get so low, you feel you've messed up so badly that God cannot possibly forgive you.' "

Miz Bourdillon went back to looking out the window. The clouds were moving by, still all fluffy, but the sky had gotten a little bit darker.

Paige continued, " 'Sometimes we think of harming ourselves because of how bad we've been or how hard our lives have been — like the woman in the book. She can't forgive herself. And she doesn't want to go on living.' " Paige hesitated and gave this sad, sad smile. " 'But it's just that forgiveness has to be accepted, first. It's God's grace. Hard to accept it. Horribly hard. But it is offered.' "

Paige put down her phone and patted her momma's shoulder real gentle-like, and Miz Bourdillon turned her head a little bit so as she was facing me. Tears were running down her cheeks now, but her eyes was so kind, so gentle, so broken.

When she looked at me like that, like she was peering into my soul, I knew.

She was just like me, all messed up and needing a whole lot of care. Jesus would have pity on her, no matter what she'd done. He'd forgive her. And I knew something else. I wasn't ever gonna tell the police the truth about Miz Bourdillon. Even if I rotted in prison for the rest of my life.

PAIGE

At first I was thrilled with the conversation between Momma and Henry. Momma had forgiven him, as amazing as that seemed. She had *chosen* to forgive, just like she'd done so many times in the past. And Henry had visibly relaxed — I'd seen a type of hope on his face — as he received her forgiveness. Still, I felt a little disappointed

417

that we didn't get any new information from him, although that had been a bit of a wild shot.

But soon after he left, Momma became agitated and looked completely worn-out. I worried that it had been a mistake to let Henry visit. We'd recorded the whole thing so that Detective Blaylock and Daddy and I could go over it later, but had the meeting taken too much of a toll on my mother?

"You okay, Momma?" I gave her a cup of water, which she sipped through a straw. "I'll call the nurse to get you into bed."

She shook her head no, her face pale and her hands tight, gripping the arms of the wheelchair.

"What is it, Momma?"

She tried to speak, but nothing came out, and I read immense frustration on her face. I hadn't seen her so out of sorts since she had first come out of the coma. "Let me get the nurse."

She blinked her eyes twice. *No.* She motioned downward with her hand in pitiful jerks until I knelt before the wheelchair. "What is it, Momma?"

"File cab-i-net. Rain-bow folder." She repeated the words over and over in her garbled, confused way.

But when I asked, "Did you say a *rainbow*

418

folder, Momma?" she gave me a blank stare, as if I'd spoken to her in Chinese. I had grown used to those blank stares, but I hated them, reminding me of all that bullet had stolen from her.

I called the nurse then and watched as she lifted Momma out of the wheelchair and into the hospital bed, dragging her like a rag doll. This was normal, but it made my stomach roil. Once she was settled, I kissed Momma and said, "Don't worry about anything, Momma. You're doing great."

I drove back home, feeling exhausted myself. I had an AP French exam to study for and a paper to write for English. But Momma had been adamant about a rainbow folder, so I thought I'd try to track that down for her first.

I slipped into The Chalet and went to the filing cabinet. Momma kept most of her work on her laptop, but occasionally she'd print out things and store them in folders in the file drawers. The top one held folders filled with research for her novels, and the middle one contained all her business information — royalty statements, contracts, written correspondence. The bottom one held everything else. In fact, Momma had inserted a bright little file card into the small metal window on the front of that drawer that read *Family Stuff.* I was pretty sure she was referring to this drawer.

I shuffled through folders in alphabetical order, marked *Books to Read, Bible Studies, Cooking . . . Girls' Activities, Gardening, Home Improvement . . . Photography, Recipes . . .* All these I had seen before. But there was nothing marked *Rainbow,* nor did I see any folder that was particularly colorful. What did Momma mean?

And then I remembered. I had seen a folder with a rainbow on it lying on my father's desk.

I hurried down to his office, flicked on the light, and stood before his desk. Several neat piles of folders and loose papers sat on it, but the folder with the photo of a rainbow, which I'd seen soon after the shooting, was not there. But it had to be somewhere, and Momma had been so insistent that I find it.

I shuffled through Daddy's desk papers again, and then I opened the big drawer on the left side of the desk, which I knew held miscellaneous family things. In the back of the drawer I saw the edges of a colorful folder sticking up, as if my father had tried to put it back in a hurry. I pulled it out. Sure enough, the photo of a real rainbow shining through a waterfall greeted me. I opened the folder and saw that in the upper left-hand corner on the inside of the folder, Momma had placed a sticker on which she'd written *If I Should Die.*

I felt chills course through me. How morbid.

But then I smiled. I remembered learning that bedtime prayer as a young child.

Now I lay me down to sleep.
I pray the Lord my soul to keep.
If I should die before I wake,
I pray the Lord my soul to take.

Momma thought the prayer terribly inappropriate for a child and had changed the words to the version that she had found on some cross-stitched tapestry:

Now I lay me down to sleep.
I pray the Lord my soul to keep.
Guard me, Jesus, through the night
And wake me with the morning light.

I much preferred this rendering myself.

I placed the opened folder on my father's desk, intrigued. Why would Momma have an entire folder dedicated to a children's prayer she disliked?

She didn't.

When I flipped through the contents, I

421

found three elegant ecru envelopes inside, the kind that went with Momma's monogrammed stationery. She'd written a name on each envelope: *Patrick, Hannah, Paige.* The envelopes weren't sealed; the flaps were just tucked in. Hands trembling, I opened mine and took out three sheets of stationery filled with Momma's lovely cursive. And there was something else in the envelope. I reached in and lifted out a gold chain. Hanging from it was Momma's Huguenot cross.

I held up the chain, and as the cross rotated slowly, I watched the dove hanging so innocently below it.

"My little stinker. I tell you what — I'll give you this cross when you're old enough to understand the significance of that little dove. It'll be yours."

I blinked and swallowed, set down the cross, and picked up the letter.

Dearest Paige, my up-and-coming author with the biggest imagination (bigger than my own) and the loveliest soul. Dear daughter, I'm sorry I'm not here to see you soar into the place the Lord has for you. But I want you to remember how very proud I am of you and how I believe in you. Believe in yourself and let your out-of-the-box thinking guide you, but under the care of the Holy Spirit. . . .

I dropped the pieces of stationery, my heart pounding.

Momma, why did you write that?

Had she had a premonition of the shooting? There was no date on the letter. I sank down on the floor and stared at those pages, afraid to pick them up.

Had Momma been so afraid of this stalker that she had written us letters?

The thought broke my heart, and I shook it away. Me and my big imagination, right? Right? *Right??*

And just as quickly as that thought went away, I was hearing Daddy's explanation of what Momma had done during The Awful Year. *Attempted suicide.* Then I was hearing myself reading to Henry Hughes the responses Momma had given at the book launch about forgiveness and grace. *"Sometimes we think of harming ourselves because of how bad we've been . . . like the character in the book. She can't forgive herself."*

Then Detective Blaylock was telling me, *"We've found a phone number on both Henry's and your mother's phones."*

Sometimes we think of harming our-

selves. . . . She can't forgive herself. . . .
Oh, Momma. Oh no. Not that.

CHAPTER 17

November

HENRY

That evening, after I talked with Miz Bourdillon and Paige, they took me to a private room at the prison to meet with Detective Blaylock. Like always, my lawyer was with me. The detective didn't say anything about my visit with Miz Bourdillon. He leaned over in his chair, elbows on his knees, and looked me right in the eyes.

"Henry, we've located Nick Lupton, and we're bringing him in for questioning. Is there anything you want to tell us first?"

I started sweating real bad. What should I do? What if they couldn't get enough evidence to put him away? He'd think I'd ratted on him, and then turn on Jase and Libby. And now with Jase out of the hospital and home!

I was gonna have to tell that detective

what I knew about him. My lawyer, Zeke, had begged me to do at least that much. "Any information you provide will give us a much better chance for a plea bargain," he'd said over and over. It wouldn't help them track down Miz Bourdillon, because I reckoned Nick didn't know anything about her. But maybe that detective would dig down and find out more dirt on Nick and that'd land him in jail.

"Detective, I've already told you — if you pick up Nick and then let him go, I swear he'll kill —"

He interrupted me. "Henry, we've got a policeman with your boy twenty-four hours a day, seven days a week. And we're watching out for Libby too."

I let that sink in. "Well, I hope so. Like I've told you, Nick's just the middleman. He connects the employer with the employee, if I can put it that way." I fidgeted with the handcuffs. "Don't know if it always works that way. Told you before, I've never done nothing like that before. I did it for my boy."

Detective Blaylock was still leaning forward, listening. "Tell me about the instructions you received," he said.

"Nick told me it all over the phone."

"And what were these instructions?" His

dark brown eyes were peering at me, like he was trying to pull something out of my mind.

"Told me where to find that lady and stuff."

He sat up straight and pulled at his beard. "Can you remember anything else at all?"

"Nothing else."

Then the detective surprised me by changing the subject. "Henry, do you have any idea why Mrs. Bourdillon would have a phone number on her phone that is also on yours?"

I sure did, but I wasn't gonna say it. "No, sir, I don't."

He squinted his eyes, stood up, and leaned his arms on the table. "Think about it, Henry."

But I wasn't gonna tell. "No, sir. No idea."

JOSEPHINE

Agitated. That was how I felt after Henry Hughes left my room at the rehab facility. No, not just agitated. Tormented. I had probably alarmed poor Paige with my actions, but something had seemed so important to communicate.

I struggled in my mind to remember.

2015 . . . "I need the money now! Now, JoJo!

Look at me. They're threatening me. I promise if you give me the money this time, it'll be the last time."

"I don't believe you, Kit."

"You are so selfish!" Kit let out a string of curse words. "All you care about is your precious Patrick and those girls! Well, I'm family too! Don't forget it."

Josephine closed her eyes and sighed. At almost sixty, Kit acted more like a teenager or a two-year-old throwing a tantrum. "I will not enable you, Kit. This pattern has repeated itself on and on for your whole life. We will not give you any more money. We will not lend it to you either. This is your problem to solve. I won't have my family sucked into your drama."

Kit, furious, eyes blazing, screamed threats and obscenities. "You cannot send me away! You cannot refuse me."

"I can and I am."

"Fine! But just know that if anything happens to me, it will be all your fault!" Then she added, "And don't you think your Patrick is squeaky clean, JoJo! He's no saint! He's no better than me. No saint at all!"

Kit stormed out of the room and then the house, slamming the front door, and Josephine heard Patrick running after her.

What was I looking for? A folder, yes, a

rainbow folder. Looking in my drawer for that stationery, my monogrammed stationery. So pretty. The girls liked that stationery. I would write the notes on this paper.

But I already wrote the notes! I gave Paige the cross.

What was I going to write in their letters? Oh yes. *Take my life. Take my life and let it be consecrated, Lord, to Thee.* Such a beautiful hymn. But someone was twisting the words. Take my life! Take my life!

Was I saying that or was she?

She was lifting her ebony arms to the sky and entreating the Almighty to take her life! I remembered now. She would not take her own life, but she begged God to take it. She was tired of living.

Oh, that poor, poor woman. Life had been so hard.

Had life been hard for me?

My head was aching. I saw in my mind's eye the rainbow folder and the letters to Patrick and the girls and I heard the woman, Angel, screaming it. "Take my life!"

But Angel was my protagonist. I made her up. Didn't I? What happened at the end of that story? Did she die? What happened to me?

I should ask Patrick. But I couldn't. I had to ask him something else. About something

Kit had said.

"And don't you think your Patrick is squeaky clean, JoJo! He's no saint! He's no better than me. No saint at all!"

Another lie. Surely it was a lie.

What did she mean, Patrick? Patrick!

For all of our marriage, I had never once doubted him. Now I was afraid.

Had Patrick given up on me? Had he given in to Kit?

Was our love a lie? No! Of course not. Right?

I needed to ask Patrick.

It was too complicated, twisting and turning in my mind.

And if Patrick . . .

"Take my life!" She said it! Did I say it? Did I pray it, dear Lord?

The woman in my story sang those words, sang the whole hymn. But then she had used them against herself. She kept saying, "Take my life, take my life!"

Had I said that too? The pounding in my head grew louder, and the rainbow swirled into a dark cloud and then the thunder was crashing through the windows, the lightning blinding me. Surely not! Not darkness again.

I sat up straighter in the wheelchair. I tried to cry out. Had I signed my death warrant?

Was I remembering it now? Was I the person who had hired Henry Hughes?

PAIGE

Daddy had protected Momma the first time, but should I do it now? I had no idea. I paced and cried and all but beat my head against the wall in Daddy's office. What in the world should I do? I stuck the letters and the Huguenot cross back in the folder for the time being. I could not even bring myself to read the rest of Momma's letter to me. I felt so confused, but right under that confusion lay a bubbling mass of anger.

My mother had hired a hit man to kill herself!

And I knew why.

She wanted us to think it was perpetrated by someone else. We had discussed the issue of suicide before. My grandmother's . . . the guilt, the horror for the family. And I distinctly remember Momma saying, "I understand the effects of depression, how off-balance it can make someone, but I cannot imagine doing that to my family."

Except she *had* attempted it during The Awful Year.

And now, she had imagined something else!

How *dare* she?

She was out of her mind, and I hated her for it.

Thank goodness Drake was on his way home for the weekend. I texted him, *Please come to the house ASAP. Bad news.*

As I waited for him, I closed my eyes and thought back to what I'd told Drake and Hannah that first night we'd been together after the shooting. That Momma seemed normal; that Momma and Daddy were fine.

But in truth, I had been so preoccupied with my life during those weeks before the shooting that I had no idea how they were doing. I was starting my junior year, preparing for and taking the SAT, playing first-string on the girls' soccer team, and we had a good chance to win the regionals this year. I wasn't home. At all. And I certainly hadn't been taking my job as Momma's assistant as seriously as I should have. I should have never shown her those two threatening letters. My one responsibility was to protect her, and I'd failed.

If I'd been paying more attention, I'd have seen that Momma wasn't fine or normal.

I closed my eyes and knew it, knew it so clearly.

In those recent weeks, Daddy had been afraid Momma was going to try to take her life again. *Like the other time.* I could barely admit that thought.

So why, why, why did I show her those letters? How could I have been so naïve, so caught up in my life?

At that moment, I felt such crushing guilt — and I wasn't one to feel guilty. Anger and resentment I had aplenty. But guilt? No way.

I pushed the guilt away, shoved it to the back corner of my mind and let the rage brew so that, by the time Drake arrived, I was so angry I couldn't see straight. He read wrath on my face and said, "Let's take a walk, Bourdy. You look like you need to get outside."

As we began our climb to the highest point on Bearmeadow, I spit out my story. "My mom is the biggest hypocrite of all! Why do the people I think model living as Christians the best do incomprehensible things? Momma tries to kill herself, and Daddy lies about it and gets so stressed out that he gets a DUI and goes to jail. And then she actually hires someone to kill her! What do I do with all this?"

We'd reached the top and stared out at the vista of mountains, void of color, just endless variegated browns that looked stripped of life. I was heaving, out of breath from the climb.

To his credit, Drake said nothing for a

long, long time. He stood behind me, his arms wrapped around me as if he could harness the anger. I kept staring out at the mountains and thinking about Momma sitting in the wheelchair and mumbling those words that led me to the truth.

Then my mind drifted to the character in Momma's most recent novel, the freedwoman who'd wanted to kill herself. A hundred years earlier, she had stood where I was standing, at least in Momma's imagination. And she'd begged God to take her life.

He hadn't. That would've been a real downer for one of Momma's novels, which generally have somewhat satisfying endings.

And God hadn't taken Momma's life either, in spite of her twisted plans. I felt the anger build again. How *could* she?

"Why did she do it?" I said, breaking free from Drake's hold. He remained silent again, until I said, "Drake, I'm really asking a question. Tell me something to make sense of this! Please!"

He took my hand, and we began to trace our way along our favorite mountain path. "Bourdy, you don't really know depression. You know anger." He stopped me and brushed his hand on my cheek. "But depression can take you places that are incomprehensible to those around you. Remember The Awful Year for me?"

I nodded, seeing in my mind's eye a teen-aged Drake, miserable and agitated and so needy. The anguish on his face had scared me.

"During The Awful Year, I sank into a deep depression. Sure, it was caused by my parents' separation and eventual divorce. But sometimes depression is just part of a person's makeup. And that's your mother. I think she lives with low-level depression, and at times of great stress, that has morphed into nervous breakdowns. Or what psychiatrists call clinical depression, complete with suicidal thoughts and actions." He stopped and looked me in the eyes, peering into my soul. "Faith and mental instability aren't mutually exclusive, Bourdy."

I chewed on that for a moment. *Faith and mental instability aren't mutually exclusive.*

Poor Momma.

Drake tiptoed up to what he said next. "I think she chose this convoluted plan out of love for you and Hannah and your dad. Yes, it was twisted and crazy, but that was all her mind could invent."

She hired someone to kill her because she didn't want us to think she was committing suicide. Yes, that had been my conclusion,

435

too, although I had not seen any love in it.

"And what do I do now, Drake?"

We were still facing each other. I looked into his blue-green eyes, intense and filled with love. He reached forward with both hands and firmly held my shoulders. We kept each other's gaze for a solid minute or more without saying a word. Finally he said, "You know what to do."

I thought of my family's lies, how Daddy had protected Momma too much, had loved her too much. I thought of the years we lived with secrets, and I thought of the newfound freedom Daddy had gained — really, we all had gained — when the real story was finally told.

"I'll tell the truth."

We hiked the mountains for three solid hours, sometimes in silence, and sometimes I'd come to a full halt and let loose with another string of angry accusations. I even confessed how guilty I felt for not doing my job well those weeks before the shooting.

"So many things drove her to it, I guess. Living with the lie from The Awful Year, the stress of the books, Aunt Kit's crazy antics, the threatening letters." My poor mother. "Will she be arrested?"

"I don't think that's a worry."

"Daddy will want to keep it secret."

"He might surprise you."

I wanted to tell the truth, but I thought of all the vitriol on social media that was already spinning out of control as people hypothesized about the real culprit. If the world found out that it was Momma, what would happen?

We'd tell the truth to Detective Blaylock, I decided, and to those closest to us, but not to the world. I imagined it would eventually become public knowledge, but not from me.

We came to a little stone chapel on the crest of the mountain. Momma had told me its history — it was over one hundred-fifty years old — when she was researching for *These Mountains around Us.* Ivy climbed along the outside walls, giving it an almost European look. Drake knew how much I loved to sit on a wooden bench inside with the stones from yesteryear around me. I'd dream up stories and type them into my phone. On this day, I shivered. I'd perspired on our hike, from physical and emotional exertion, and now I felt chilled.

He came and sat beside me, put his arm around me, and took both my hands in his other one. "Someday I'm going to marry you in this place."

Of all the things that could have come out of his mouth, this one had never crossed my mind. I felt my stomach drop. Then the anger came. "Are you *serious*? This better not be your proposal because it absolutely stinks! I haven't got on any makeup and you've never even kissed me, and I'm not even eighteen. . . ."

He gave that deep, annoying belly laugh of his and gathered me in his arms, and then he kissed me, really kissed me so that everything in my whole body started tingling.

He let me go way too quickly, his eyes dancing. "Satisfied, Bourdy? And no, it wasn't the proposal. I was just letting you in on my thinking." Then he kissed me again and said, "Now please, hurry and grow up!"

Much later, hand in hand, nearing my house, I asked him, "Why do you put up with me, Drake? I'm a hot mess."

He shrugged. "I figure once all the anger leaks out — and hear me, Bourdy, some of it is perfectly legitimate — the real Paige will shine even brighter."

"I'm not so sure the anger will ever be gone," I countered.

He scrunched up his nose and acted like he was in deep thought. "Trust me. It'll be okay."

I wasn't convinced. "What do you think about me not attending church?"

"I'm a lot more concerned about your heart than your church attendance."

"Henry thinks Jesus wouldn't be hanging out with the church folks. He thinks he'd be eating with the sinners."

"Sounds rather biblical to me," he said.

I stuck out my tongue at him. "I really appreciate Henry's way of looking at faith. And his real questions, honest with no hypocrisy. He asked Momma if she believed in forgiveness and grace. The ultimate hypocrisy is that Henry sees it in Momma's books, but she doesn't believe it for herself."

"It's irony, Bourdy. Not hypocrisy. The whole thing is ironic. But she *does* believe it. You know good and well she believes it. She just went on a rabbit trail in her mind, and she didn't *receive* it for a while. Almost every Christian I know has done that at some point in his or her journey."

He nodded my way, and I almost retaliated in anger. But instead I whispered, "What if I never come back around to faith? What if I just stay on this rabbit trail forever?"

"It's a journey, Bourdy. You'll come back."

When he said it so simply, with assurance, I *wanted* to come back. I felt a stirring way down in my soul.

We'd reached the house, but before we went inside, Drake said, "I have no doubt about it. Jesus is a gentleman, and He won't force His way in, but once He's there, He woos us back, one way or another. With you, it might be a little rough. I personally wouldn't challenge the God of the universe to a wrestling match, Bourdy, but if you must, you must. He always meets us where we're at."

CHAPTER 18

November

JOSEPHINE

I am alive. I am supposed to be dead, but I am alive.

The words echoed through my brain for weeks, when I was in the coma and after I came out. For most of that time, I could not put anything else to those words. But after Henry's visit, I added, "I am alive. I am supposed to be dead. *I tried to be dead.* At least I think I did."

Sometimes I felt great confusion about this. My memories continued to blur together.

But one truth resonated loud and clear: I was alive!

The wonder of this truth permeated every inch of my body. I literally felt it in all of my limbs, even when I could not move them. I was overcome with thankfulness.

441

Instead of the expected condemnation from my overactive imagination, all I heard was *You are loved, you are worth it, this gift is for you. Take it, like a bouquet of flowers, like a view of the sun setting over the mountains, like your first glimpse of the Mediterranean after so many months. You are alive, and I love you.*

My Savior's voice. Soft, gentle, persistent. Drowning out the accusations.

I should be dead. At the very least, I should be deeply brain damaged and unresponsive. But I was alive and on my way to a new type of health.

I felt great sorrow at what I had done, but the shame, the self-deprecation, and the guilt did not land in my soul.

This was my first hint of the larger concept of grace. And the verses came back to me. Those verses had not left. They were embedded in my memory. *For by grace you have been saved through faith; and that not of yourselves, it is the gift of God.*

The gift of God, the gift of God. A gift. A gift.

Healing from a gunshot wound to the head, from any traumatic brain injury, takes one thing above all else. Time. Although I had coherent thoughts, I could not always express them in a coherent way. My reactions were at best unpredictable, at worst frightening. I had lost my autonomy, my independence, at least for the foreseeable future. Often this realization causes a head-trauma patient to succumb to depression. But I had already been there.

And I had tasted grace in a new way.

I knew I could not let this grace be only for me. I had to tell the world the truth about the hole in my head — not the real one from a bullet, but the one whose name was depression.

Paige and Hannah and Patrick had explained, delicately, about how the news of my shooting had gone viral on Facebook and Twitter and other social media platforms. They shared how the video of Henry and Paige and me in the hospital had aroused great wrath at Henry and how Paige's explanation of the reason for Henry's actions had placated some. But Kit, always the truth-teller, no matter how bluntly, was the one who said it best. "Well, the jerk who shot you was not the one behind the whole scheme. I still want him to be electrocuted, but now everyone is calling for the blood of the perpetrator. In my humble opinion, both deserve to die."

Both deserve to die.

Yes, that was true.

But with my new revelation of grace, I did

not feel fear. I had woven many intricate themes into my novels, themes of God being able to bring good out of evil, themes of forgiveness and grace, themes of the least likely person telling the truth and that changing the course of history.

Now it was time for me to live it out.

I would tell the truth. To my family first, to my inner circle next, and then, to the whole world. Let the vitriol come. If I had survived, I knew beyond a shadow of a doubt it was because God was going to bring greater good out of what I had meant for harm.

I thought of Joseph in the Bible, before his brothers, the ones who had sold him into slavery. When he revealed himself to them years later, as the second-in-command in Egypt, they were terrified. What would their powerful brother do to exact revenge on them? And instead he said, "Do not be afraid, for am I in God's place? As for you, you meant evil against me, but God meant it for good in order to bring about this present result, to preserve many people alive."

Joseph's proclamation had saved the nation of Israel from obliteration. Somehow, I felt that my experience could save many lives in another way. Depression was a silent killer. I was ready to fight it now. Not only for myself, but to save many lives. I would tell the truth, and God would do what He willed.

Later in the evening, I asked Patrick and Paige and Drake to come to see me. Patrick picked me up out of the bed and set me gently in the wheelchair. I had to tell them the truth, but how?

Paige sat next to Drake, holding his hand so tightly that her fist looked taut. I read anger in her eyes and fatigue in Patrick's. Drake's eyes exuded warmth.

I had not planned how I would communicate this truth. I sent a prayer heavenward for them to understand and I said, "I did it."

I thought they would question me, but no one said a thing for a few moments, as if my words were too garbled for them to understand.

Then Paige said, "I already know, Momma."

Patrick's hand came over mine, protective and strong, as Paige told what she had discovered in the rainbow folder. At first she wouldn't look at me, and her tone was accusatory. But gradually she relaxed a little.

Patrick listened to Paige with tears in his eyes that gradually turned to confusion and then surprise.

"Paige. You looked in that folder with the letters to you and me and Hannah?"

"Yes. Momma told me to. After Henry left she was so agitated. I guess reading that part in the novel reminded her of what she'd done." Paige said more softly, "What *you'd* done, Momma. You said over and over, 'Filing cabinet. Rainbow folder.' Like you had remembered something. I guess after you planned the whole thing, you wrote those letters for us to find. But they weren't in the filing cabinet." Now Paige turned back to Patrick. "You'd already found them, hadn't you, Daddy?"

"No, no, that isn't right at all," Patrick said.

"You didn't find them?"

"I did, Paige. Yes, I did. But that was years ago." He took my hand again. "Feeny, you wrote those during The Awful Year. I found them that day. . . ." Patrick cleared his throat and turned away. "That day when you took an overdose of pills."

I nodded, trying to keep track of what was being said.

Paige cocked her head. "What do you mean, Daddy?"

"Back in 2007, I found the letters you had written to each of us, Feeny, and read them

446

all. I read them while you were in the hospital recovering. I read them, thanking God that you were alive. You had put the Huguenot cross into the envelope with Paige's letter.

"I didn't show them to anyone, of course. I should have burned them, I suppose, but I couldn't. I think I wanted them to remind me of what a close call we'd had. And maybe it was a way to punish myself for not having paid close enough attention to the warning signs, Feeny. I should have recognized them."

No, my dear Patrick, no, nothing was your fault. Nothing.

"I hid the folder with the letters, but I took out the Huguenot cross and gave it back to you, Feeny. Do you remember that?"

Yes, I nodded. *Yes, I remembered. I was at the treatment center and Patrick came and knelt beside me. "I think you've been missing something that you certainly need." He fastened the chain around my neck. We met eyes. I knew he'd found the letters, but when I tried to say something, he put his finger to my lips and said, "Shhh, Feeny. It's over. It's done."*

"But I know I saw that folder on your desk right after the shooting," Paige insisted. "I went into your office because I was looking for the photo of Momma and Milton on the beach, the one where the cross shows up so well. And the folder was there. I noticed it because it seemed so odd that you'd have that kind of folder sitting on your desk, Daddy. But I didn't think anything else about it. I stared at that photo of Momma and Milton, and then I went to look for the cross. I wanted you to have it at the hospital, Momma. But I couldn't find it anywhere."

I could see my daughter struggling to put her thoughts together. "I had no idea that the cross was actually in the rainbow folder." That hint of accusation filled her voice as she looked at Patrick. "Did you bring out the folder from wherever you'd been keeping it, Daddy?"

Patrick gave a heartfelt sigh. "Yes. Yes, I did."

"But why? And why would you put Momma's cross back with my letter?"

"I'm sorry, Paige. After the shooting I panicked. I was so afraid, Feeny, that you had hired the shooter. I knew the plot of the newest novel. I remembered the freedwoman's twisted plea for God to take her life. I was so afraid. . . ."

Patrick was fighting back tears.

"I thought maybe you had taken those letters out to use again, Feeny. But I found

448

them right where I'd kept them all these years. And the cross wasn't inside the envelope for Paige. I cannot tell you how relieved I was to find it where you always kept it, Feeny, in the jewelry box by our bed. I put it back in Paige's letter for safekeeping. Or maybe just to punish myself again. . . ."

"So all along you thought Momma hired Henry!" My daughter sounded so belligerent, so angry.

At that moment, Drake took her hand, much like Patrick was holding mine. He must have given her hand a squeeze, because she turned to him, saw the expression on his face, and her face relaxed the slightest bit.

"I did. Yes. How in the world could I say that to the police?"

"Oh, Daddy! You were protecting Momma, just as I thought. And now I know why — protecting her from the past and from the present."

I thought I saw Paige wipe a tear out of the corner of her eye.

"You're right again, Paige. Right about everything. Except that when I found the letters and the cross where they should have been, well, I felt a sliver of doubt. And now, I don't know. I just don't know." Patrick came and knelt beside my wheelchair. "Sweetie, I think that you're confusing what happened a month ago with what happened years ago, during The Awful Year." I detected a strain of hope in his voice.

I was too tired to argue so I whispered in my garbled way, "Maybe. I don't know." Did I write those letters? Did Angel cry out *Take my life*? Or did I? Did we both? Perhaps we would never know. And what about Patrick and Kit? That I could know, but I was much too afraid to ask.

"I don't understand at all!" Paige said. "This is weird. And very confusing."

Patrick nodded. "I agree. I'm so sorry, Paige. We'll discuss it more soon, I promise. But right now, I think your mother needs to rest."

The expression on my daughter's face showed anger and confusion and resignation. Drake had his arms around her as they left the room. Again, I read kindness and understanding in his eyes. Patrick stayed with me for another hour, holding me close and patting my hands, a low sob escaping every now and then.

Right before he left the room I said, "Truth."

"Yes, Feeny. This time we're going to tell

the truth. We will figure out what is the truth and then we'll tell it. No matter what."

I slept from eight that evening till noon the next day, and when I awoke, Kit was sitting by my bed with the same questions in her eyes. Now I understood.

I gathered my strength and forced my voice to pronounce the words. "You and Patrick."

She wilted. "I was furious and jealous. You were turning me away. I was desperate. You have always been right. I was jealous of all you had. I wanted to make you suffer, JoJo. I wanted to drive you crazy with worry."

"It worked." I had so much else I wanted to tell her, to explain. But those two words were all I could pronounce, and when I did, her face fell with a grief that no plastic surgeon could lift.

"Oh, JoJo! I pushed you over the edge! I wanted you to feel as much pain as I was feeling. I was so selfish. I *am* so selfish." She began to cry in her theatrical way.

I did nothing but stare at her.

She wiped her perfectly manicured finger under her eye and sat up straight. When she spoke again, her voice was calm. "But it wasn't true. Patrick has only and always had eyes for you."

I repeated those words in my mind, like a favorite hymn. *Patrick has only and always had eyes for you.*

Kit whispered, "I'm so sorry, JoJo! I'm so sorry." She reached for my hand and when she looked at me, I saw the Kit of my childhood, her eyes bright and pure and loving. "This whole thing has been a wake-up call for me. Finally. I've realized a little more about the depth of what you had been struggling with for so many years. Can you ever forgive me, JoJo?"

I sat for a long time without even trying to pronounce a word, just soaking in the depths of those bewitching eyes, so hurt, so confused, and now so filled with remorse and love.

"Yes," I whispered.

One word was all that I managed, but perhaps it lifted a lifetime of guilt from Kit's shoulders. I don't know.

Two days later, I had finished my physical therapy session for the morning, and Patrick had bundled me up in my wheelchair under a mound of blankets and pushed me out into the rehab center's beautiful greenhouse. The air was chilly but so refreshing. My favorite place to sit was in the section of the greenhouse overflowing with every imaginable type of orchid. We'd invited Detective Blaylock to join us there, intent on sharing what was sure to be a shocking revelation to him. Patrick had scooted the chair right up beside a flower I was admiring and placed my hand on a delicate petal. I felt the velvety, almost silky texture and mumbled, "Perfect."

The detective found us in the greenhouse, and by the look on his face I knew he had something to share with us too.

We followed him back into my room. Patrick got me settled and comfortable and fixed the detective and himself a cup of coffee. We had grown to respect and even care for Detective Blaylock. He never shared much about his private life, but over the course of the weeks we'd known him, it became clear that he lived for his work. On this day, his dark eyes were red with fatigue, but his excitement was tangible.

"I wanted to talk to you both about all those threatening letters. We've got a match on some of the fingerprints. Finally." He took a sip of coffee and brushed his hand through his beard. "It took quite some digging, but we've got a name. Minnie Shorer."

Patrick shrugged. "That doesn't ring a bell for me." He was sitting right next to my wheelchair, and he took my hand and asked,

"Feeny, do you know someone named Minnie Shorer? A reader?"

I blinked *No,* but Detective Blaylock was not finished. "I don't imagine that name means much. But we found another name that she goes by. Charity Mordant. Do you know anyone by that name?"

I could not make quick movements, but I felt my heartbeat quicken. I nodded slowly.

"She's one of Jo's biggest fans," Patrick confirmed. "Comes to many, many of her signings. Or at least she used to." He glanced at me. "And she was at one in Atlanta recently, too, I believe."

Detective Blaylock flipped through his little notebook. "She was arrested in 2008 for child abuse — evidently she physically attacked her ten-year-old grandson. She's been in and out of psychiatric hospitals the last five years. She was most recently re-leased last July. And Charity, or actually Minnie, lost a daughter to suicide about fifteen years ago."

Oh no.

"Her fingerprints were found on the threatening letters you've received over the years, and on these last three. And it was her phone number that we found on both Henry's and your cells. We're going to bring her in for questioning."

The detective and Patrick kept talking, but I was seeing Charity again and again and again. Coming to my signings in three different states, bringing me gifts, calling me now and then on the phone and even showing up at our house — which had been a little unsettling at the time.

"Do you hear that, Feeny?" Patrick's voice was jubilant. "Feeny, do you understand what this means?"

Detective Blaylock furrowed his brow, glanced from Patrick to me with a question in his eyes, but Patrick was laughing, laughing, and shaking the detective's hand, pumping it up and down, up and down, and saying, "Thank you! How can we thank you enough for all your work? This is amazing news! Wonderful news."

"Of course it's wonderful news," Detective Blaylock said, seemingly bewildered that Patrick would need to state the obvious.

Patrick let go of the detective's hand and said, "I'll explain it to you, sir. This changes everything. Everything!"

When he left the room with Detective Blaylock, I had completely floated away from the conversation and regressed into someone who could not make a sound come out of my mouth while a concoction of confusion and hope settled into my soul.

I hadn't slept much since Momma's talk with Henry and the whole crazy incident about the rainbow folder. All kinds of emotions paraded through my mind: that deep anger, even hate, that had surfaced, the guilt at my part in the whole affair, the acceptance of what Momma had done, and then the possibility that she hadn't done anything at all. I lay awake at night and wondered how in the world my mother's life had suddenly become a riveting whodunit, complete with totally unexpected plot twists.

But Daddy was giddy — that word perfectly described his mood.

Still Charity Mordant had not admitted to anything, so while Daddy celebrated, I figuratively held my breath and spent several nights tossing and turning.

When Detective Blaylock brought Charity in for questioning at the police station, he videotaped the whole interrogation and asked Daddy and me to watch it the next day.

I recognized her immediately, not only as the woman I saw on several occasions when I was a girl, but also from her appearance at one of Momma's speaking events during the past summer. She was a hefty woman, dressed in a brightly colored floral pantsuit with plenty of gaudy accessories. She plopped down in the chair, her face flushed, and began to fan herself with her hand.

After a few minutes of basic questions, Detective Blaylock pulled out a stack of pink stationery. "We know that you wrote these letters. Your fingerprints are all over them."

She looked defiant. "And since when is it against the law to write letters to an author?"

"Not against the law, ma'am, but you have to admit, when the letters coincide with the timing of an assassination attempt, well, that brings questions."

"Assassination attempt! I had nothing to do with that!" Her eyes were wide and afraid.

Detective Blaylock ignored that, and said, "Until recently, Josephine Bourdillon hadn't heard from you since 2007. Why exactly did you write these three letters?"

Charity was sweating profusely, pushing her permed hair off her forehead. "Josephine just kept writing, and she didn't pay any attention to me, and I knew someone would get hurt. I knew it! I was just trying to warn her, that's all! And you see? I was right!"

"I believe the first letter you wrote to Mrs. Bourdillon claimed that one of her novels put suicidal thoughts in your daughter's head. We got a search warrant for your house, Mrs. Mordant, and we found several of Mrs. Bourdillon's novels there. All of them signed by the author. We found the novel you were referring to and passages had been underlined with notations — threatening notations — on the side. In your handwriting. This is pretty convincing evidence of some type of involvement."

Charity stood up, shaking her head from side to side. "No, no, no!"

"What did you tell Nick Lupton, Charity?"

She sat back down, clutched her hands together and leaned over the table. "I don't know a Nick Lupton! I swear it!"

"What about Henry Hughes? You tried to call him on the day he was taken to jail."

She looked surprised, then recovered. "I have no idea what you're talking about."

"I think you do."

Charity's confused and slightly jovial appearance changed drastically with the detective's last statement. Her face grew hard, and she stood up and said, "I want to speak to my lawyer."

In that moment she looked and sounded different, like someone who could be dangerous.

When Daddy and I finished watching that video, I was sweating as profusely as Charity, but Daddy began pacing around the room. It took him several minutes to compose himself. "Don't you see, Paige? It really was this woman. She hired Nick Lupton, who hired Henry. It wasn't your mother. Feeny didn't do it. She didn't do it."

And even though she had yet to admit to the crime, I agreed that the evidence pointed strongly to Charity Mordant.

It was the twist in our story that I hadn't expected. When I'd found supposed proof of Momma's guilt, I'd been devastated, and I could not have imagined the wonder I now felt at her innocence. Momma had often commented when writing one of her stories, "Truth is stranger than fiction, you know, Paige."

Indeed.

HENRY

Two months after I went to prison, Libby and Jase moved out of the trailer. Libby found herself a good job about twenty minutes away from the prison and a nice apartment not too far from her work. She even found a new church that she and Jase like real well. That church's got something called a prison ministry, and some of those folks come and see me pretty often. I like their visits.

I enjoy lots of things about life now. Isn't that something to say in prison? But I take my meds, and I have a routine, and I'm even studying to get my high school degree. They've got courses you can take right from prison. Study the Bible, too, with the chaplain and a lot of other men like me, the ones who are sorry and repentant.

My lawyer is hopeful about the judge lessening my sentence when my case goes to trial since I gave information about Nick. I guess we can always hope.

Jase goes back to Mission Hospital about every month to get a checkup and so far his heart just keeps on doing what it's supposed to. He's still a little bit scrawny, but that doesn't matter, because Libs says he eats enough to feed a horse. So I know he'll be putting on weight eventually. Sometimes he comes with Libs for a visit. I've started talking real soft-like to my boy, and when he looks at me I don't see fear in his eyes. He doesn't look ashamed either. Just corn-puddin' happy to see me.

I was dang-blasted surprised with what they found out about Miz Bourdillon and that woman who hired Nick. Sure glad I never said nothing about what I suspected. But one time when Paige came for a visit, she told me that she'd thought it was her mom, too, and so did her dad, and Miz Bourdillon even thought it herself. Paige told me about the letters her mother wrote and the first attempt. I was real sorry about that.

And she told me about the woman, Charity Mordant, and how she tried to drive Miz Bourdillon crazy with her threats, but in the end she decided she'd hire someone to kill her. Nick's the one who told it to the police. Had all the proof the police needed to arrest her. I sure was glad Nick knew how to keep all that information. When Paige explained it to me, I told her how Charity was right clever, how she'd used the words in Miz Bourdillon's own novel against her as part of the instructions she gave to Nick.

So Charity and Nick and me, we're all in jail, awaiting our trials.

I don't know how it'll turn out for me, but I'm really glad it wasn't Miz Bourdillon after all. Felt some kind of huge relief when I learned all that.

Libby likes Paige a lot. So does Jase. He doesn't get to see her real often, but he talks about her. He even remembers her reading to him in the hospital when he wasn't out of that coma.

Libby got a check from Miz Bourdillon to cover all of Jase's past and present medical expenses. When she told me about it, well, I couldn't quite take it in. Now Miz Bourdillon was being like Jesus to us, and I had the hardest time wrapping my mind around the twisted way it all came about. Didn't really have any way to say thank you.

When Jase found out about what she'd done, he said, "This is like what you mean, Papa, about good coming out of evil, isn't it?"

We'd told Jase about what I did. We decided it was the right thing to do.

"The way you got to know her was for a bad reason, but now she's our friend and she is helping us."

Libby says he's precocious. She says it means he's got soul smarts. He sees deep.

462

Well, maybe so. He's been through enough to have earned that, I guess.

PAIGE

Hannah came back home for Christmas break. I sat in between Drake and her on the couch, in front of a roaring fire. A huge fir stood regally decorated in one corner of the family room. Snow fell outside the picture windows, and we watched the mountains change clothes from drab brown to wedding-dress white. Our stockings hung on the hearth: *Momma, Daddy, Hannah, Paige, Milton, Drake, Kit.*

Daddy wheeled Momma into the family room, right beside the fireplace. He pulled the leather armchair beside her and sat down in it, taking her hand. Milton padded in from the kitchen and plopped down right in front of Daddy. Aunt Kit was in the kitchen preparing what she called "a wonderfully festive, nonalcoholic drink."

She served us as Daddy turned on the TV so that we could watch the evening news together. We knew what was coming.

Lucy Brant was dressed in a dark burgundy designer suit. She was reviewing what had happened in the past two months — the shooting in October, Momma's week in a coma, Henry taking me hostage at gunpoint, his arrest, the continuing search for the person who had hired Henry, Momma's gradual but remarkable recovery, and then Charity Mordant's arrest in late November when Nick Lupton provided evidence of her involvement, along with the evidence the police already had.

"Now, Josephine Bourdillon, the beloved author, has released a statement to the public." The camera switched from Lucy to footage of Daddy and Momma, sitting on the couch in our family room. The news channel had filmed it the day before.

With Momma looking on, Daddy read a statement that I had written from Momma's point of view. Creating it was slow work, as I would craft a sentence or two and read it back to Momma to make sure I'd expressed her thoughts correctly. It had taken the better part of a week. The shooting had thrust her into the public eye, and she wanted to take advantage of this opportunity to talk about depression and its effects.

"Although Josephine has no memory of the shooting, she does remember what happened in the months and years prior to the incident," Daddy was saying on the screen. "Josephine, with the help of our daughter, Paige, has written a statement that she would like me to read to the public on her behalf." He cleared his throat and began.

" 'I am overwhelmed with thankfulness for all your many expressions of kindness to me and my family in these past two months. Your prayers and notes and actions have been a great source of strength for me and my family and encouraged me on this long road toward recovery.

" 'Now I would like to share a little bit more of my personal story, my journey, with the prayer and desire that it may be of help to some of you.

" 'I have struggled with depression ever since I was a small child. Circumstances and family dynamics contributed to this, but the fact is, I was born with what I have called 'a hole in my head.' I know this may sound ironic or even disrespectful, since I also have a literal hole in my head from the gunshot wound, but please hear me out.

" 'For decades before this shooting, I lived with this dark hole called depression. As an adult, I have had three nervous breakdowns and wrestled with suicidal thoughts. There are certain demons that we creatives face. For me, producing each novel was like giving birth, and afterward I always felt completely depleted. When this was combined with other difficult life circumstances, it became a perfect storm.' "

At this, I glanced over at Momma, who was sitting in her wheelchair. She was grasping Daddy's hand, sitting erect in the chair and nodding slowly as the footage of Daddy continued to play.

" 'Back in 2007, I tried to take my life. Despite having a wonderful, loving family and community and a deep faith in Jesus as my Lord and Savior, I had slipped into a terrible spiral of hopelessness. By God's grace, my attempt failed. My road back to mental and physical health came from my support group as well as mental health professionals and medication.

" 'Perhaps you have a loved one who is struggling. You may not understand this person's suffering, but please don't shame your loved one. I beg you instead to seek help.

" 'And if you are the one who is struggling, if you have thoughts of harming yourself, please hear me. Depression is a real and often silent killer, but help is available. It is not weakness to ask for help. It is self-awareness. Seek professional advice and take medication if needed.

" 'Please don't believe the lie that the world would be a better place without you. You have something important to contribute to society. You are loved, you are important, and grace is freely bestowed to you by a loving God who values every human life. It's why we celebrate Christmas. A Savior came to save us from ourselves.

" 'I am unable to communicate the depth of my gratitude at being alive. If God has allowed me to survive death twice, I believe He has work left for me. I do not know if I will be able to write another novel, but I can tell my story, and I am committed to working with organizations to raise awareness so that every individual has access to the assistance and services available to combat depression and prevent suicide.' "

On the screen Daddy was clearing his throat, and you could see tears in Momma's eyes. Scrolling at the bottom of the screen all during this time was the number of the suicide hotline.

" 'God bless you all, and may this Christmas season be filled with wonder and grace.' "

When the report was over, Daddy turned off the TV. We all wiped a few tears and then sat in silence, embracing a holy moment, with the snow falling outside, clean and pure and new.

Daddy wheeled Momma into the dining room with the rest of us following. The cherrywood table was decorated just as Momma liked, with her fine bone china and silver flatware and crystal glasses. Because sometimes, she liked to say, occasions need beautiful things to help us celebrate.

Momma didn't have any preconceived notions of what her honest avowal would do. None of us did.

In the next few days after the TV report, Twitter and Facebook and Instagram and the rest of the internet were filled with polarized responses. Many people posted comments saying *I understand her, I've been there.* But there were also those who disagreed about medication or felt Momma had no business "airing her dirty laundry" to the world.

Pinterest blossomed with all the cover photos of Momma's novels and then beautifully decorated pins of quotes from the books.

Several big chain bookstores kept selling out of Momma's books as people clamored for them. *The perfect Christmas gift,* the bookstores and online sellers proclaimed. *Josephine Bourdillon's novels speak of the grace she believes in and shares in her testimony with the world!*

I visited Henry a few days after she made

that public statement on TV. He got a good laugh when I said, "With all Momma's truth telling, she's probably going to lose some readers."

His wide shoulders just started heaving up and down, and he laughed so hard he got tears in his eyes. "She may lose some Pharisees," he said, "but I guarantee she'll gain a lot of them real sinners."

I thought Aunt Kit would throw one of her famous temper tantrums, calling Momma a hypocrite. But if she did, I never saw it. Instead, she visited often, always sober, and seemed to have a new love or awareness or caring or *something* for Momma.

Mrs. Swanson said, "Poor Josy. I always knew she was fragile. I should have watched her more carefully back then. I often wondered what the real story was."

Most of our neighbors and friends showed compassion for Momma, many calling her brave to be so vulnerable, but there was also the inevitable whispered criticism from those who thought she was too outspoken or disagreed with her take on depression.

"Hypocrites," I brooded.

"Humans acting like humans" was Drake's answer.

JOSEPHINE

We're here at The Motte, all of us — Patrick, Hannah, Paige, Milton, Drake, and me. There is an excellent rehab center and I also have my private physical therapist, Suzy, who comes each day.

I use a cane now — I don't need a wheelchair anymore. I take off my sandals with Patrick's help, and we walk onto the beach. I cry at the feel of the sand beneath my feet.

Hannah and Paige are absolute bathing beauties in their bikinis, their long hair whipping in the mistral, their bodies tanned. They kidded me that they were going topless at The Motte this year, like all the French girls, but it was just to get my reaction. Sometimes I laugh now when what I mean is to look shocked.

The girls love it. So does Drake.

I hope and pray that Drake will have patience to wait on Paige. She is a hot mess, as she says, but I believe he can handle her.

Sometimes I worry about her. She has the gift. The imagination as big as the world, the drive, the naïveté, too, that thinks she just might do something special. But she has something I don't. She has grit. And I think, well, I pray that will protect her from the voices, the depression, the bad endings.

I take this time at The Motte with my family as a miraculous gift.

I breathe in God's forgiveness each day and breathe out His grace.

So much grace.

Some people ask me what it's like to be forgiven, to feel grace. It's like walking on a long stretch of beach with nothing in sight but sky and waves and sand. With the sun piercing its brightness, the water tickling my toes, the roaring of the sea singing omniscience and power and yet, a deep peace, the waters changing from sandy brown to light green to a heavy blue, the waves cresting with the white peaks and then rushing to find my toes.

It is my Father's love, as endless as the Mediterranean Sea when I stare out at it from where Patrick and Hannah and Paige and Drake and Milton are crowded around my chair.

I awoke from my coma, and that was the first miracle, considering the wound. But the second and bigger miracle occurred when I awoke to how much I was loved by God. It washed over me like a wave in the Mediterranean and drew me into blissful moments of hope and joy.

I had to get to the end of myself before I

could figure out how to live again. I thought quite literally and horribly and morbidly that the end of myself was dying. Depression does that, and don't let anyone tell you differently. We sensitive souls feel everything so deeply. Everything matters, and I could not differentiate between the really big deals and the big deals in my head that tormented me time and time and time again.

People have different reactions to suicide. Some get mad. *How could that person be so selfish?* Some get holier than thou. *Well, he's gone to hell — don't you know it's the biggest sin in the world to kill yourself?* Some nod and say nothing because deep down inside they've had the same thoughts and that terrifies them.

But Henry, he had a different approach. He said that we humans are all real messed up and needing God's forgiveness and grace. And in his words, I understood in a deeper way the gift of forgiveness that I gave to others but had such a hard time bestowing on myself or receiving from God.

Of course, Henry says it's my stories that helped him find these things too.

I marvel that, when I finally came to the end of myself, what I found was a whole lot of grace.

EPILOGUE

June 2018

PAIGE

Some people say Momma will never write again, but I know they're wrong. She says I'm the one with grit, but she has it, too, in a soft and gentle Momma kind of way. She has a strong desire to tell the world more about her struggle with depression and her discovery of a deeper kind of grace.

I think it will happen.

After an initial drop in readership, the sales of her novels picked up again. Momma, true to her word, started a fund to provide money for people struggling with mental illness who could otherwise not afford help.

Henry passed his GED last month and has been accepted to college. He and Libby will both be attending the same online university. Jase's face crinkles into this great mass of dimples when he explains that his parents are going to college from jail and from an apartment.

Charity Mordant got life in prison. She pleaded insanity, but the jury figured she had plenty of wits about her to torment Momma with letters for fifteen years and push her toward suicide and then plan the murder. And I think Detective Blaylock discovered a lot of other pretty horrible things she had done.

Nick Lupton had several aliases. When Detective Blaylock finally tracked down his different identities, he had a list of crimes long enough to keep him in jail for thirty years. But since he was the one to confirm Charity's hiring him and his hiring Henry, plus giving the detective the names of other people he'd worked for, he got a plea bargain down to twenty years.

At Henry's trial, nine months after his arrest, his young lawyer did a fine job of arguing his case and got his sentence moved from life in prison to twenty years, for which Henry and Libby were extremely grateful. In the meantime, Henry studies in his cell and leads a "Jesus study for sinners." Every time he says that, I smile.

A person's brain works differently after a traumatic head wound. Day by day we see incremental progress, but Momma will never be the same. "That's a gift," she says, and then she smiles a lopsided grin, but I read deep-down gratitude in her eyes. Sometimes Daddy will swoop her up and onto his back, and she closes her eyes and stretches out her arms, like she's trying to capture the whole Mediterranean Sea in her grasp, and she laughs. Long and hard.

The doctors say it's the brain injury that's changed Momma. Her mind is just as sharp on the inside, but she expresses herself differently on the outside. We let the doctors think what they will. The nurse practitioner, the one who whispered hope to Momma on the hardest days and told me to keep my mouth shut and listen to Dr. Moore, well, she knows as much as I do — as we do (Hannah most of all, with her faith that never faltered) — that it's not just the brain injury.

It's grace.

We all look at life differently now. Henry taught us that. He was never afraid to ask the questions that no one else dared to ask, about hypocrisy and judgment and especially how Momma could write books of transformation and grace without really receiving those things for herself.

She receives them now. After all the years

of struggle, of the dark hole in her head, as she puts it, she embraces life in a new way. As a gift. She will spend every ounce of energy helping others who are locked in depression, who have dark, even suicidal, thoughts, find hope.

I receive things differently now too. I came back from my rabbit trail about a year ago. Drake never pushed me, neither did Hannah or my parents. I just walked into it gradually as I watched Momma and Henry and others I love navigate their faith journeys.

Mostly, I guess Drake was right. Jesus wooed me back.

You listen to Momma's story, and it's sad and even tragic, but there is a silver lining of hope that enshrouds it like clouds hovering over the deep and varying shades of dark in the mountains. "Spiral up to hope," Momma says in a voice filled with awe. "Spiral up to love. Spiral up to grace."

I'm in college, majoring in English lit with a minor in creative writing. I'm doing college in three years. I'm in a hurry, I guess. I have a wedding to plan. Yes, I'm twenty, but in some ways I'm much older. And poor Drake, he's been waiting for me for a long, long time.

Next year Drake and I will say "I do" in

the tiny little chapel on Bearmeadow Mountain with our families around us, even Aunt Kit. Drake will be dressed in a tuxedo with tails and I will be in white with my hair piled high on my head and Momma's Huguenot cross around my neck. Daddy will walk me down the aisle, teasing me and then pecking me on the cheek, and I'll read a thousand expressions of love on his face. Hannah will stand beside me with a cascade of roses. And Momma will be sitting in the front row, petting Milton and wiping her tears and dreaming up another story as only dear Momma can do.

ACKNOWLEDGMENTS

Ever since I was very young, I have struggled with low-level depression. I was the creative child with a hole in her head that no one could see. I often thought if only someone would come and plug up this hole I would be normal, like my friends. But if it got any bigger I would plunge toward mental illness, like other dear people I knew.

Many people have walked with me through the path of depression into freedom and hope. Some of them are in this book. To Fred O. Pitts, my friend and youth leader who said, "Elizabeth, blessed are the pure in heart. You're seeking Jesus — He will be there for you"; to Marcia Smartt, who lovingly embraced me on a college ski trip and walked me through the valleys as dark thoughts whirled; and to many, many others I say, "Thank you. Thank you for being there, for speaking truth to me, for offering hope, for reminding me of my identity in Christ."

I don't have a Lucidity Lath like Josephine's, but I have a collection of file cards from forty years ago up until the one I wrote today, filled with the truth of Scripture. I take daily walks and recite truth. Medication and other treatments have also been extremely helpful to me. I am deeply grateful for psychiatrists, counselors, and others who understand mental illness and offer a professional lifeline to those who suffer.

And so I say to any precious reader who is struggling with depression and dark thoughts: Please get help, in whatever form that may come. Help is available.

Watching my dear mother go through two open-heart surgeries and a massive stroke, I became all too familiar with hospitals and ICU units. I am forever indebted to the nurses and doctors, the chaplains and the staff who served us when we were in the midst of great shock and grief.

My family also experienced overwhelming love and support through the CaringBridge site, as well as through cards and letters and Facebook.

To Ike Barnett, thank you for helping me get into Detective Blaylock's skin.

To my nephew and niece, Austin and Meggin Musser, *merci* for walking me through the process Henry faced as soon as he was arrested.

A huge *merci* to Georges and Susi Kohler, who opened their beautiful apartment at La Grande Motte to me for a sabbatical month. The Motte is where I began writing this novel.

To my agent and friend, Chip MacGregor: You have believed in me and my stories through all the ups and downs of my writing journey. Thank you for your wisdom, perseverance, and good humor. And always remember, *Passez-moi les pommes de terre! Merci!*

To Dave Horton, VP at Bethany House Publishers, what a delight to be once again working together on a novel. Thank you for believing in and championing this story. *Je suis très reconnaissante.*

To the wonderful team at Bethany House Publishers, I am thrilled to be working with you again. A big shout-out to Lucy Bixby, Noelle Chew, Kate Deppe, Elizabeth Frazier, Amy Green, Brittany Higdon, and Brooke Vikla. *Merci* for all you do behind the scenes. Your expertise is invaluable and reassuring.

To my editor *par excellence* and dear

friend, LB Norton, you are brilliant, and you make my stories shine more clearly (and yes, more succinctly). It is a privilege and joy to work together. You must never retire.

To Nichole Parks, my gifted marketing guru, your savvy and expertise have expanded my horizons. Plus you are a delightful young woman, and it is a joy to work with you.

To my Transformational Fiction prayer partners: Lynn Austin, Sharon Garlough Brown, Robin Grant, Susan Meissner, and Deb Raney, our monthly prayer times have indeed been a safe place for my soul. Thank you for praying me through a very rocky season in my writing life and for being dear friends.

To Jere W. Goldsmith IV, my precious and over-the-top generous daddy, and Doris Ann Musser, my energetic and lovely mother-in-law, and to all the others in the Goldsmith and Musser families, thank you for your support throughout all our years on the mission field and my years in writing: Jere and Mary Goldsmith, Glenn and Kim Goldsmith, Alan and Jay Goldsmith, Elise Goldsmith, H. A. and Rhonda Musser, Janet Granski, Scot and Carol Musser, Bill and Beth Wren, and all my nieces and nephews.

So many friends on both sides of the Atlantic pray for the work of my hands. I can't begin to name them all, but here are a few: Valerie Andrews, Odette Beauregard, Cathy Stott, Dominique Cottet, Margaret DeBorde, Marlyse Francais, Kim Huhman, Letha Kerl, Deb Lugar, Laura McDaniel, Karen Moulton, Heather Myers, Trudy Owens, Michele Philit, Marie-Helène Rodet, Thom Shelton, Marcia Smartt, Cheryl Stauffer, Lori Varak, and Ashlee Winters.

To my family at One Collective, thank you for receiving what Paul and I have to offer with grace and for allowing me to pen my stories too.

To my sons, Andrew and Chris, I am in awe of the young men you have become. Your passion, kindness, professional acuity, and humor as well as your love and care for your little momma are blessings not taken for granted. To Lacy, I am so thankful to have you as a daughter-in-love. Thank you for being an amazing wife and mother. I admire you greatly, even if I never drink kombucha!

To Jesse, Nadja'Lyn, and Quinn, your Mamie loves you and likes you over and over and over again!

To Paul, always to you, you are indeed all that is good in Patrick. My soccer player does have the sexiest legs! Thank you for loving me so much and so well. *Je t'aime tant.*

And dear readers, just so you know, I have never received hate mail! Thank you for your patience as I get to know you through social media and beyond. Your heartfelt emails and comments make my calling as a storyteller worth it.

As we are bombarded with the world's truth . . . as life goes viral and everyone knows everything about everyone else . . . as many post their wrath on social media . . . I pray that the world will know that we are Christians by our love.

Because if dear Henry could find that love and redemption, so can others.

May it be.

And finally, to Jesus, my Savior and Lord, the Lover of my soul, the Giver of extravagant grace, and my Faithful Friend, I owe everything to you — my life, my love, my all.

FIND SUPPORT

If you or someone you know is struggling, you are not alone. There are many supports, services, and treatment options that may help. A change in behavior or mood may be the early warning signs of a mental health condition and should never be ignored. There are many different types of mental illness, and it isn't easy to simplify the range of challenges people face.

Here are some things to consider when reaching out:

- If it's an emergency in which you or someone you know is suicidal, you should immediately call the **National Suicide Prevention Lifeline** at **1-800-273-8255**, call 9-1-1, or go to a hospital emergency room. If you can wait a few days, make an appointment with your primary health-care provider if you think your condition is mild to moderate.

- If your symptoms are moderate to severe, make an appointment with a specialized doctor such as a psychiatrist. You may need to contact your community mental health center or primary health-care provider for a referral.
- If you or your child is in school or at college, contact the school and ask about their support services.
- Seek out support groups in your community and educate yourself about your symptoms and diagnosis. Social support and knowledge can be valuable tools for coping. https://suicide preventionlifeline.org/talk-to-someone-now/

DISCUSSION QUESTIONS FOR
WHEN I CLOSE MY EYES

1. Is Henry Hughes sympathetic character in your eyes? Why or why not?

2. Have you ever been in a situation that felt so desperate that you chose to do something that you would ordinarily never consider? If so, what happened?

3. Have you or someone you are close to ever felt like Josephine, with a "hole in her head"? Have you been able to talk about this with others, to find help for yourself or the person concerned?

4. In Chapter 17, Drake says to Paige, "Faith and mental instability aren't mutually exclusive, Bourdy."

Christians often disagree about treatment for mental health issues. Has reading this story changed your thoughts on depression and suicide? How or how not?

5. Paige asks Drake if you can love someone too much. Discuss Patrick's love for Josephine and his decision to keep her suicide attempt secret. Have you ever kept a secret out of love for someone? Can a person love another person "too much"?

6. Which of the characters in the story can you most relate to and why? Whose faith journey can you most relate to and why?

Josephine	Patrick
Henry	Hannah
Paige	Kit
Libby	
Jase	

7. Have you ever had an Awful Year? Discuss the issue of family secrets and their effect on individuals.

8. Why does Paige protect her father? What is she afraid of?

9. Discuss Josephine's Lucidity Lath. What

are some different tools you use to hear truth instead of lies?

10. Near the end of the novel Drake says, "It's irony, Bourdy. Not hypocrisy. The whole thing is ironic. But she *does* believe it. You know good and well she believes it. She just went on a rabbit trail in her mind, and she didn't *receive* it for a while. Almost every Christian I know has done that at some point in his or her journey." Do you agree or disagree? Discuss why.

11. Henry's faith journey is greatly influenced by his reading several of Josephine's novels. Have you ever had a novel touch you deeply and help you as you considered spiritual questions?

12. After reading the Gospels as well as Josephine's novels, Henry comes to this conclusion: "Just like I'd been thinking, Jesus was always, always hanging around with sinners. . . . If Jesus came to earth today, I wondered if He'd be in the big fancy churches. Well, maybe He'd go in there and preach a sermon in His jeans, but then I just bet He'd ask some of the gang members to have lunch with Him. And He'd invite those poor trafficked gals

and probably a bunch of those gay people who didn't seem to be welcomed at churches, and maybe even, maybe He'd invite me to lunch too. Now wouldn't that be something to see?"

What do you think about Henry's line of reasoning?

13. Both Paige and Henry are disturbed by hypocrisy they see in Christians. Paige says, "The Bible says we should be able to tell people are Christians by their love. I feel the same way as you, Henry. I want to see love, not hate." Discuss the effects that hypocrisy has had on you and those you care about.

14. Discuss appropriate ways to agree and disagree over social media.

15. One of the main themes of the novel is how to accept grace. Near the end of the novel, Josephine says, "But Henry, he had a different approach. He said that we humans are all real messed up and needing God's forgiveness and grace. . . . I understood in a deeper way the gift of forgiveness that I gave to others but had

such a hard time bestowing on myself or receiving from God. . . . I marvel that, when I finally came to the end of myself, what I found was a whole lot of grace."

How would you explain God's grace? Do you have a hard time receiving and extending grace? Why or why not?

ABOUT THE AUTHOR

Elizabeth Musser writes "entertainment with a soul" from her writing chalet — tool shed — outside Lyon, France. Elizabeth's highly acclaimed, bestselling novel, *The Swan House,* was named one of Amazon's Top Christian Books of the Year in 2001 and one of Georgia's Top Ten Novels of the Past 100 Years. All of Elizabeth's novels have been translated into multiple languages and have been international bestsellers. For over thirty years, Elizabeth and her husband, Paul, have been involved in missions work in Europe with One Collective, formerly International Teams. The Mussers have two sons, a daughter-in-law, and three grandchildren. Find out more about Elizabeth and her novels at www.elizabethmusser.com.

The employees of Thorndike Press hope you have enjoyed this Large Print book. All our Thorndike, Wheeler, and Kennebec Large Print titles are designed for easy reading, and all our books are made to last. Other Thorndike Press Large Print books are available at your library, through selected bookstores, or directly from us.

For information about titles, please call:
  (800) 223-1244

or visit our website at:
  gale.com/thorndike

To share your comments, please write:
  Publisher
  Thorndike Press
  10 Water St., Suite 310
  Waterville, ME 04901